Bryan Litton

Appalachian Mist

Robert's Story

by

Bryan Litton

Appalachian Mist

Robert's Story

by

Bryan Litton

Prologue

I loved my brother Calvin as long as I can remember. That's not entirely true, I suppose. I worshiped my brother Calvin as long as I can remember . . . and hated him sometimes as well.

You see, Calvin's my momma's oldest son, and I didn't come around until three years later. I got to see how well Calvin did at Little League baseball, Midget League football, Babe Ruth baseball, Junior High football, Junior High basketball, and High School football, basketball, and baseball. He could play just about any sport there ever was—and not only play it, but also play it better than most.

I wasn't ever very good at those kinds of sports—the only one I ever got much recognition for was boxing in the Golden Gloves. I figure the only reason Calvin didn't clobber me there was because he would have been out of my weight class. But he was the one that taught me the basics of boxing . . . everything from the quick double jab with that deceptively heavy left hand to the in-close uppercut that takes most pugs by surprise. The Chief and I built on what he taught me, it's true. But he was the one that showed me the primer.

It's my story, I guess, but it's pretty hard to tell my story without telling Cal's too. He was the main one that shaped my early life. Probably sounds pretty dramatic, but it's the way things were. Momma stayed busy around the house, and didn't have a whole lot of time for "foolin' with young 'uns". (Her house was always spic-and-span, meals were always so on time that a clock could be set by them, and there wasn't any "heat and eat" or "prebought" food around my Momma's house. If anything was canned, you can believe it was because she canned it.) Daddy died when I was just five. He didn't have a whole lot to do with us kids . . . just had neither the time nor inclination to relate to children until they were old enough to walk, talk, and help around the farm.

So my story and Cal's story are pretty well intertwined. He was bigger, stronger, older, and more handsome, by the opinion of most of the girls we went to school with. Of course, they might have just found him more attractive because he was bigger, stronger and older, too.

I'm a fair-sized man, I guess. Six feet, give or take an inch, and about a hundred eighty pounds. Long and lean, and I have been all my life—never needed to diet or do any exercising. Farm work's plenty of exercise for anybody, at any rate. I inherited my mother's "Black Irish" looks, with the dark hair and light blue eyes. I've got bigger hands than my body would merit, and smaller feet in the bargain. Cal used to tell me, "Rob, old boy, if you ever grow into them hands, you'll be a helluva big man!"

Cal was fair-haired, blue-eyed with barn-beam shoulders and a barrel chest. He went about six-three in high school, and tipped the scales at about two forty. He had a jutting jaw, and was pretty vain about his good looks. Next to him, I always looked pretty skinny, and even short.

Calvin was probably every bit as smart as I was, but he didn't care anything about school. Not the classwork part of it, anyhow. He wouldn't have gone if he could have played sports for the school without it. So that got to be what I was known for—I was the kid who always knew what the vocabulary words meant (and how to spell them) without having to look 'em up. I was the smart one, and Cal was the good-looking, athletic popular one. I doubted then that God offered me the choice between the two before we were born . . . But since then I've wondered.

Chapter One

I had my algebra book tucked carefully under my left arm as I waited for the school bus. Calvin didn't have any books at all, but that didn't mean he didn't have any homework, just that he didn't intend to do it. Most subjects came fairly easily to me, but math I had to work at, at least a little bit. I'd been getting straight A's since third grade, and for some reason, it was still important to me. So I did extra problems in Algebra. It would help me when I took geometry in tenth grade, Algebra II in eleventh, and trigonometry in twelfth. I didn't have any idea what trigonometry might be, but that was the highest math class they offered at McClellan County High School.

McClellan County was a typical central West Virginia county. That's to say, poor, poorly educated, poorly paved, and ignored even by the state government, never mind the federals. Forty percent of the county was employed by the Black Gold Coal Mine, ten percent worked for the government at some level, and ten percent were timber men for an out-of-state logging concern, and forty percent had no discernible means of support other than what was still called "the dole". Of course, there were moonshiners, and later in my life, those that were the descendants of moonshiners became farmers . . . of a sort. Their crop had leaves of five, and earned five-to-ten at Moundsville when someone could be troubled to look for it.

McClellan County was named for General McClellan, the top graduate of West Point Military Academy, Class of 1861. He was supposed to be a big hero and rout the Southern forces on the peninsula, take Richmond, and scoot the moon over just a little in the sky in his spare time. His fame and expectations were never actualized, and he was pretty much a ten-minute wonder, but still thought of well enough to get one of the new state's counties named after him.

Perversely, the county seat of McClellan, Jefferson, was not named for Thomas Jefferson. Rather, for Jefferson Davis, President of the Confederacy. Even more than most places, West Virginia was divided on the Civil War, or the War of Northern Aggression. The real gripe with the citizenry of the region was with the state government of Virginia, not with the federal government, or even the confederate government. There's a joke that runs around that the only reason West Virginia went with the North in the war was because Virginia got to pick first, and we just wanted to shoot Virginians. There's more than a speck of truth to it, too. Nearly the entire state is below the Mason-Dixon Line, and the state's rights issues of the Confederacy spoke loudly to our hillbilly pride and independence. Slavery wasn't a question that even needed answering. There were few people in the hills with enough money to even think about owning one. Most of West Virginians even to this day lived and died without ever seeing a colored person.

Calvin was a junior that year. He had already covered himself in glory as the quarterback of the McClellan County Cavaliers. The only quarterback that passed for a hundred yards per game and had as many rushing yards every game in county history. They didn't go undefeated this season . . . but there were high hopes for next year. Calvin would be a senior, as well as most of the offensive line and one of the other two running backs. The third running back would be a junior next year, and had high promise. The defense was also led by Calvin—he averaged two and a half sacks a game as "the most aggressive nose tackle the coach had ever seen"—this in a position not exactly known for passive behavior. But football season was over for the year, and basketball was the next course on Calvin's scholastic "menu".

He said, "So what's the algebra stuff for? Iffen ya didn't take all them sissy classes like algebra and chemistry in junior high, ya wouldn't have to do any work at all. Yer too clever for that homework. Shouldn't have to take books home to get straight A's, smart as you are. Makes people think you're weird."

I knew that it might make people uncomfortable to have a ninth grader working on a higher math than most of the high school kids ever aspired to. But the fact of the matter was that it made Calvin uncomfortable. He couldn't understand why I wasn't leading the junior high squad in football, basketball, and all their other sports as he had done. It was because I hated team sports. And I despised any game that required a ball. I knew well that my ticket to fame and fortune wasn't going to be physical. My brain was going to have to get me out of McClellan County. An academic scholarship to a college, any college, would be my way to avoid the slow starvation of the soul that seemed to pervade my home turf. Strange ideas were to be avoided here. And anybody could be elected to any office, as long as he was a Democrat that arranged the money to keep flowing to the right hands. Different was bad. And the local library wouldn't even carry "Gone With The Wind" because of the "racy stuff". I knew that I couldn't live my life here. I was meant for better things.

"I think it's interesting, Cal. The different ways of figuring stuff up that they show you. And some of it might be useful when we build stuff later on."

"Them damn books ain't gonna help do any damned thing. When we build stuff 'round the farm, we don't need any damned book. We use hammer and nails, and a saw. Them books don't hammer any nails or cut any lumber, so for all the good they'll do, ya could stick 'em up yer ass." Calvin sneered.

There was no point in arguing with him. No point in explaining how if we needed a haying shed for x number of square feet how the book could save us time and effort. Now, we built by what we always heard of as "guesstimate". If that was big enough, then good. If not, then we built additional footage. I always viewed it as slipshod work, but I wasn't in charge of things. Calvin was.

In 1954, seven years ago, there was a boy named Billy James Mackey. He was supposed to be the greatest West Virginian basketball star since Jerry West. He was McClellan County High's leading scorer to this very day, with an average of forty points a game. He was going to play for the Boston Celtics and drive a Cadillac convertible—just ask him. Unfortunately, being an incredible high school ballplayer is an awful like being a big fish in a small pond. Being the best basketball player in our part of West Virginia didn't translate to being all that remarkable a ballplayer on the national level. Now he pumped gas, changed oil, and wiped windshields down at Amoco. Where was the valedictorian of MCHS,

1954? Don't know. He left town on an academic scholarship to WVU, and hadn't been back. Everyone in town remembered B. J. Mackey . . . but besides his family, and me I'll bet no one remembered Joey Williamson.

It was pretty clear to me that athletic stars didn't escape Folsom Hollow. Valedictorians did. So that's what I was going to be. No matter what Calvin thought about it.

The bus showed up, and Cal bounded up the stairs, two at a time. He yelled to his friends in the back of the bus and took great galumphing strides, bumping other kids as he jounced the old bus on its springs. I sighed, and sat next to one of the kids he had hip-checked in the jaw. His name was Jack Thompson, and he looked at me unhappily. He knew it wasn't my fault, but it couldn't help but breed resentment. Jack was in ninth grade too, and we had a few classes together. Even though he lived on the same road, just a few miles up the holler, we didn't play together. Kids my age didn't want to be around Cal. He wasn't very nice to them. So that made Calvin my best friend, mainly by default.

Twenty minutes later, the high school students filed off the bus in a mad rush, beating against everyone in front of them, some on accident, some on purpose. We went on to the junior high school, and the elementary school was just around the block. I didn't mind school very much—but I was a lot like a young lad named Sam Clemens. I was pretty determined not to let my schooling get in the way of my education.

First period was Algebra. About an hour of drudgery. Second period was gym—games with some ball or another. Hated it. Third period was English, which I liked fairly well. We were writing essays about Steinbeck's "Of Mice and Men". I didn't think much of Steinbeck. Fourth period was Biology, at last!

Biology was my favorite. Well, I liked the subject matter too, but what I really liked was Donna Duquesne.

Donna was a black-haired beauty, with light grey eyes. Her hair feathered down around her perfect pale-skinned face, fell to her waist, and looked so soft and fine. It looked like it would just be magical to touch it. Her waist was slim, and she had a beautiful hourglass figure. Her cheeks were naturally rosy: she didn't need rouge. Her lashes were long and so dark it was plain to see that mascara would have been a travesty. Her high cheekbones had her pale smooth complexion skin taut and perfect. She was gorgeous.

"Hi, Robert!" She was coming over first thing again today. "How's Calvin?"

I basked in her attention. I didn't care that I was merely Calvin's surrogate. If his presence isolated me from the boys that might have been my friends, it also let me talk to this angel who otherwise would have ignored my existence.

"He's doing fine, Donna. How are you liking being the head cheerleader?" Nominations and election for the spot had just been a week ago. She'd been the first one nominated, then no one else even bothered, even though she was just a freshman. It would have been a landslide. She was the prettiest, and could also do the best tumbling of any of them. She finished her routines with a backflip that she didn't even tuck her legs in on, just laid out flat in the air with her legs straight out. Then she landed and jumped back up in a sideways split and touched her toes.

She'd had to go to a gymnastic camp over the summer to learn all that stuff. But her parents didn't mind. They had plenty of money, since Mr. Montgomery was the town's only lawyer. Not to mention the editor of the paper, as well.

She tossed her head dismissively. "S'okay, I s'pose. Calvin's playin' basketball this year, ain't he?"

She knew he was. "I think so, Donna. I'll ask him for you, if you want."

Her eyes were glistening and she smiled. I soaked up every bit of it. "Let him know I'll be watchin' him at the basketball games, too!" With that, she went back to her desk, just beating the bell. I sat down and just felt like I could float away, wafted straight into the air by being close to her.

The bell rang, and it was time for lunch. Then fifth period, I had American History. Talking about the Hessian mercenaries in the Revolutionary War. I didn't care much about the Hessians. I was thinking of Donna. Sixth period was Shop. We were making magazine racks. And I didn't care about magazine racks, either. Seventh period was study hall. I studied my memories of Donna.

Chapter Two

I didn't bother trying to talk to Cal on the bus. He was with his high school buddies, and I didn't want to shame him by making him acknowledge a junior high kid as human, instead of an object of scorn.

When we got home, Mom had our snack ready—banana bread and milk from our cows. She was watching her "stories" about people that didn't act like any we ever knew.

"Donna asked about you today, Cal." I offered, seeing if he was in the mood to really talk, or just to hold forth. There was never any telling with him.

"Did, huh? What'd she ask, Bobby-boy? Ask how big my shlong was?" He sneered. Clearly a day for holding forth.

But he wouldn't let it drop. "What did ya tell her?"

"Told her you were playing basketball. She said she'd be watching those games, too." I said, knowing that a refusal to answer would just provoke more snide comments.

"I like that. Keepin' one like that around's a good idea, kid. I think she might just ripen into one worth tastin', when I'm in the mood."

I knuckled my fingernails deep into my palms. Hearing this kind of crude talk about women was something I was used to from Cal, but this wasn't just women, it was Donna. I knew there was no point in trying to argue with him about anything, but I just couldn't help myself.

"She's not like that, Cal. She just likes you, that's all. I'll bet if she knew how you talked about her, she wouldn't give you the time of day, never mind give you a taste!"

"Try tellin' her and see, Bobby-boy. See if she don't think it's just you tryin' ta steal big brother's light. Prime stuff like that wouldn't even be talkin' to ya if you wasn't my kid brother, and ya know it. Doncha?" he sneered. "Doncha?"

These weren't questions; they were demands. "Yeah, Cal. I know." But can't you see how much it means to me? I wanted to ask. Don't you care?

"Ya want her for yerself, doncha? Wanna get yer fingers wet? Wanna hear her moanin' in your ear?"

More demands. But I was through playing. I got up to leave. He grabbed me by the shoulder and spun me around.

All of a sudden, it was as if I turned into someone else. The quick double jab scored twice on his All-American nose, and knowing it was too late to stop now, (no matter how bad I wanted to) I went ahead and threw the right cross to finish the combo. It landed right in his eye, right like I wanted it to.

Unfortunately, fire of righteous indignation coursing through my veins or not, I was still a fourteen year old teeing off on a seventeen year old. A much bigger and stronger seventeen-year-old football/basketball/baseball player. One that had taught me how to box.

His jabs were too slow for me, but he grabbed my hair with his left hand and smashed his right into my gut. I wondered why he didn't hit my face the way I had hit his, but then realized . . . if I can't breathe, I can't scream. If I don't scream, Mom wouldn't be able to hear all the way across the house.

He held me close to him with one arm, and began short punishing shots against my ribs. Painful stuff, that. I wanted to beg him to stop, but I could tell by the look on his face he had no intention of it. He was smiling at me, his nose dripping blood across his teeth. He looked like some kind of feral nightmare.

He then backed up a little, and started hitting me in the head, above the hairline so Mom wouldn't see, I guess. Every time he connected with that left, the world went black for a brief moment. Ernest Hemingway was right when he said that thing about pain not knocking you out. I sure wished it had.

When he was done hitting my head, he drew back a little further. He grinned maniacally at me. "I reckon I know what got ya into this mess, li'l brother. I'll fix that for you right now. Ya started thinkin' with yer balls, kid. Ya let your achin' balls talk ya into bitin' off more'n ya should've."

Now his voice got soft, friendly. "Yer way too smart to let yer balls do yer thinkin' fer ya, Bobby-boy. Let's don't make that mistake again, huh?" With that, he hit me with a variation on that in-close uppercut. It struck me squarely in the groin.

When I woke up later in our room, it occurred to me that Ernest Hemingway was pretty full of shit after all.

*   *   *

*

I was able to stand up after a struggle. I pulled off my shirt and looked at my ribs. Technicolor rainbow. I don't think any of them were broken, but they were definitely worked over beautifully. I felt my scalp, and I knew I would be a phrenologist's dream. I had lumps on my lumps. I leaned over the dresser and looked at my eyes as carefully as I could. One pupil seemed a little larger than the other. I knew that might mean a concussion, but then, it could just be the difficulty of looking at your own pupils in a mirror. Then I took a look at the area that I was dreading looking at.I couldn't believe how swollen my scrotum was. It was the size of a softball, and the skin was stretched so taut I had a fleeting thought that it might actually burst like an over inflated balloon. The muscles all around it were bruised and looked worse than my ribs. The whole area of my anatomy was so sore it seemed like it hurt to look at it.

I walked over to the window. More like hobbled, I guess. I took the screen out, because I had to see how bad it was. I held it very gingerly, and tried to pee out the window to the yard below, like Cal and I often did in the middle of the night. As soon as the muscles in my inner works tried to do their motions, I screamed and fell to the floor. Then, the process started, I pissed all over myself, but it brought no relief, just continuous agony until the stream finally stopped. I looked down at my chest, and saw the pink stain from my urine.

That's when I knew it was pretty bad after all.

Chapter Three

I was still lying there when Calvin walked in later. Might have been a few minutes, or it could have been hours. He looked at me, and a look of intense pain came over his face. He knelt by me, ignored the urine all over me, and lifted me in his arms as easily as if I had still been a newborn. He carried me out to the barn, ignoring my angry protests.

"Look, Bobby, I'm sorry. I lost my temper pretty damned bad. It ain't no excuse, kid, but it's all I can say. When you popped them jabs into my shnoz, I jest saw red." I could see that he was telling the truth. "I shouldn't never've hit you in the stones thataway. Let's see if we cain't get ya cleaned up and patched up."

My fury was cooling rapidly. It was pretty understandable to lose your temper when you're being hit in the face. It looked like I scored some pretty good ones on him from the look of his eye. I hadn't broken his nose, but he did have the beginnings of a slight shiner around the left eye . . . and I was getting an apology for it, too. My rage was finished, but the pain didn't end with it. I still felt like someone was twisting a fork in my guts, and they were really torquing on it when I tried to straighten up.

My big brother undressed me like a gentle little girl taking care of her dolly. He put me in the washtub and added cool water, then added the hot water off the old coal-burning Franklin stove that we had in the barn for the livestock. The warm water hurt some, but it seemed to soothe the deep-seated muscular pain. Cal handed me the soap and a sponge.

"Wash off, Bobby-boy. I'll go fetch your clothes, kid." With that, he headed back into the house.

I took the opportunity to look over my works again. The swelling had receded a good bit, down to the size of a baseball now. I decided to go ahead and live. So I started sponging off, cleaning myself from the dirt of the day and the urine of the past few minutes.

Calvin came back with a suit of pajamas for me. His pajamas. He saw my look, and explained, "I reckoned ya might be a mite more comfortable in somethin' that fit a little baggier."

He was sure right. I couldn't believe how much better I felt with the tight briefs and dungarees off of me. Still hurt like one of the levels of hell, but it was several levels up from the one I was on. He helped me up out of the cooling water, and started to lift me up to carry me back in.

"Let's see if I can walk some, Cal." I needed to know if I was broken up too bad to cover it up from Mom. I took a few halting steps, and knew that she'd probably notice for sure unless I stayed out of sight for at least tomorrow.

"Maybe go camping in the woods this weekend, Cal? You'll have to carry everything, but it will let me get better." I knew suggestions worked better than orders with Calvin.

"That ain't a half-bad idear, kid. Maybe grab some franks out of the smokehouse and head over by the river. I bet Jeannie Riley could come see me tonight, too." Cal was sorry he'd hurt me, but that didn't mean that he wouldn't be turning this situation to benefit him. "I'll go tell Ma."

Cal carried both our rucksacks while I hobbled along behind him. He'd packed the pup tent and had taken a big handful of the Ohio Blue Tip kitchen matches for lighting the fire. We had a bunch of smoked sausages from the smokehouse, and three loaves of Mom's homemade bread. Cal had tried to sneak a jar of ketchup out, but Mom was too sharp for him. She said she'd never get her Mason jar back.

Cal gathered all the firewood we'd need all weekend and stacked it by our fire-ring. We'd camped here before, and had things pretty well set up. He said, "You get the fire started, and I'll pitch the tent."

I shambled around and gathered dried leaves to use as tinder, and snapped some small twigs off to be my kindling. I got the twigs going, and then slowly fed in larger sticks until I had a respectable fire going. Meanwhile, Cal had set up the pup tent, and dug a tarp out of his pack as well. I looked at him surreptitiously while pretending to tend the fire.

He was setting up a makeshift tent with the tarp, some twine, and handy trees. I didn't know why he was doing it, but I figured I'd find out eventually. It was insignificant next to the way I was feeling. I hurt too much to be curious.

He finished with the tarp, turned to me and grinned. "This way, iffen I can get Jeannie out here, you'll not be stuck out in the cold, boy. A roof over yer head and it'll be on the leeward side of the pup tent, too!"

I smiled weakly and nodded. I had hoped for the better accommodations, but I was glad that Cal had thought to bring it . . . this time. Last time, I had ended up shivering in the rain while Cal and his girl (couldn't remember which one, but it wasn't Jeannie) entertained each other. The tarp was a significant gesture on Cal's part. I appreciated it.

Cal grabbed the food sack and brought it over to me. "Since ya cain't move so good, I'll be the fetcher and toter, and you can be camp cook. You'll be needin' a weenie roastin' stick, too." He brought a forked stick over, and said, "Don't be burnin' my franks, kid."

I roasted the sausages over the fire, and Cal cut the bread with his hunting knife. He snatched the first two off the stick, and wolfed them down on the bread. He cut me some more of the bread, and stood up, brushing off his lap.

"Reckon I'll be back after while, kid. I figure Jeannie oughtta be comin' back with me but you never can tell about women. Iffen ya go ta sleep afore I get back, sleep under the tarp, okay? Thataway ya won't have to move for us." Cal patted me gently on the shoulder. "Cook yerself some 'a them weenies. Ya got mine just right."

I smiled at him. "Just right" for Calvin meant evenly roasted all around. My version of "just right" was a lot easier. Charred black and crunchy on the outside. Probably because I knew what we used for sausage casing. "Good luck, Cal. Thanks for bringing the tarp for me."

"A fella's gotta look after his li'l brother, don't he?" With that, Calvin was off, crunching through the underbrush.

Chapter Four

I finished off four of the franks on bread, using Cal's knife to saw off more slabs of bread to eat them on. I examined the blade carefully. It was a carbon steel Schrade, with an ersatz bone handle. Cal should have sharpened it a long time back. I rummaged through his pack and found the stone. I was feeling at least well enough to sharpen a knife.

I could feel my headache leaving. My ribs didn't bother me too much as long as I didn't take too deep a breath. But I could tell it was going to be a while before I walked at an undignified pace. I sighed, and laid my blankets out under the improvised tent. It wouldn't be as warm in the late October night, but it was better than nothing. I used Cal's knife to lop off a few pine boughs to use as a sort of insulating door. I mused over the irony—I would have been able to sleep warmer in the snow. Snow's a great heat-trap. A few decent-sized snowballs and a little shaping with loose snow, and I'd have had a snug little pseudo-igloo.

I thought about cleaning Cal's knife off in the river, but I just didn't feel up to the bank with my groin feeling like it did. I stabbed the hard-tamped soil by the fire three or four times, and let the cleaning go at that. He'd have had time to get to Jeannie's by now. Her dad was a 'shiner, and Friday night would see him out by the still, drinking what he wasn't able to sell. He sold four-year old white lightning, aged in his cellar. Calvin would be able to get to Jeannie's window without worrying about being shot at.

I liked Jeannie well enough. She had a soft voice, and she was slim and petite. She had brown hair and brown eyes, and she'd have been pretty, I think, if she didn't have bad teeth. They were crooked and one looked like it had been broken off, right in front. Everyone knew that her daddy was free with his fists when he was in his cups. And everyone knew that he pretty much stayed in his cups.

Jeannie was always pretty nice to me, too. Some of the girls that Cal brought around treated me like a leper because I was a few years younger. And smarter, probably. Smart kids weren't figured to be real good company for some reason. I never understood why. They would have figured out that it sure wasn't catching, if they weren't so stupid.

I tucked into my blankets, still dressed in Cal's pajamas. They were flannel, and fairly warm. I buttoned up my jacket, and made a pillow out of my rucksack. I figured I'd have a good bit to wait before Cal got back. He'd be back sooner if Jeannie came with him, I knew.

It wasn't nearly as long as I thought. I heard footsteps at least fifty yards out. I didn't comprehend how anyone could move so noisily. The sound of my own footfalls was annoying to me, so I'd worked on walking quietly.

I heard Calvin's voice come through the trees. It was a little slurred and almost mushy-sounding, like his tongue was swollen. "I got 'em good, y'hear? They was three of 'em, but them city boys ain't no match for McClellan County hillbilly muscles."

Jeannie was with him. "Reckon not, Calvin." She wasn't a big talker. She mostly just agreed with whatever Calvin said, and let him carry the conversations. She didn't move anywhere near as loud as Calvin. Of course, her voice wasn't slurred, either. It sounded like Jeannie had gotten into her dad's stash of moonshine for Calvin.

They finally staggered into camp, Cal's arm over Jeannie's shoulders. She seemed to be supporting him more than expressing affection. He grinned at her with a lecherous expression, and grabbed her around the waist. She looked up at him with a smile of her own. It occurred to me that it was a sad sort of smile for some reason. It didn't seem to reach all the way to her eyes. He pulled her to him, kissed her roughly, and let his hands roam over the seat of her blue jeans. She kissed him back, although she had to be uncomfortable stretching up like that. She was a good ten inches shorter than he was, even though her boots had high heels and Calvin was in sneakers.

Calvin said, "I knows what ya really want, girl. It's right yonder in that tent. C'mon." He clumsily fell to his hands and knees and went inside. She looked over her shoulder at my little shelter and smiled. I didn't think she could see me in the dying firelight, but I waved and smiled back. She didn't react to the wave, so I think she was just smiling at the funny little lodge Cal and I had built. She stooped down and duck-walked into the tent with Cal.

There was a little giggling, and her sweater flew back out the doorflap, followed shortly by her jeans. The sweater had almost flown into my little tent. There were sounds of loud kissing, and a little bit later, her bra flew out. I heard the sounds coming from the tent, and it at least sounded like Jeannie was having a decent time. Of course, I wasn't sure, but at the time, my education was pretty lacking in that area.

A few minutes later, and I heard the vacuum seal break on a Mason jar. Since I knew that Mom hadn't let Calvin take a jar from the house, which pretty well meant that it was another jar of Riley's finest. I just hoped that it was the aged stuff instead of raw liquor. Before he cut it down with creek water, Mr. Riley's moonshine was well over "proof". Proof liquor would catch fire from a match, and needed to be at least 50% alcohol. I knew the percentages from science classes, but the hill folk knew how to tell if they were getting stuff even without knowing the formulae. Uneducated is a far cry from stupid, a fact that I remembered all my life.

The noises started up again, and then there was a little snicker. "Ye drank so much you're too knackered to go twicet. Guess them city boys took a bit outta ya after all."

Jeannie's voice changed tone. "Where'd ya put m' clothes, ya big galoot? Ain't got not but painties here. Ya layin' on 'em, ya sot?"

I wondered whether I should tell her or not. It was just Calvin's speed to toss her clothes out into the camp, knowing she'd have to go get them naked in the chilly night air. Knowing that she'd be exposed to little brother's eyes, or at least feel like she might be. Would it be more embarrassing for me to tell her that I knew she was naked in the tent with my brother, or for me to let her go on looking for her clothes?

"Cal, ya rascal! Ye didn't have time to hide 'em anywheres, and th'ain't nowheres in the tent to put 'em! Prob'ly thowed 'em out the tent." With that, I saw her head peek through the doorflaps, looking oddly like a turtle. "Thar!" Her conversation with the unconscious Calvin over, she emerged from the tent.

I know that a gentleman should have looked away, but I could no more have averted my eyes than I could have jumped over the moon. She stood up, and for one moment in her life, Jeannie Riley was beautiful. The dying firelight lit up her front, and the cool October night tightened her nipples up instantly. Her eyes were alive and almost feral-looking as she hunted the clearing around the campfire for her clothes. She was wearing nothing but her panties as she started gathering up her clothes. (I couldn't help but notice that Calvin's last shot hadn't unmanned me, at least.) She looked sad and a little pathetic, but I still couldn't turn away. As she came over to get her sweater, right at the flapless door, she looked in, and her eyes met mine. Curiously, she still made no effort to get dressed, or to cover her breasts with the clothes she had in her hand.

"Hi, Robert. Mind a li'l comp'ny?" She smiled at me, still not covering her body. I really did try to look at her eyes.

Chapter Five

I was stunned. I couldn't believe what was happening. If I'd known the word yet, I'd have thought "surreal". I just scooted back from the doorway in the only invitation I felt capable of at the moment. She dropped down and crawled into the little tent, the motion doing fiercely erotic things to her breasts.

"Thanks, Robert. 'Twas cold out there." She smiled at me, and put her clothes down at the other end of the tent. "Mind iffen I share yer covers?"

"Of course, Jeannie! I'm sorry, I should have offered sooner." I lifted the corner of the blanket and scooted way over so she'd be in the warm spot I'd been occupying. I didn't know what to say to her at all. I wanted to tell her she'd been beautiful, standing there in the clearing, and when she'd been silhouetted by the firelight. But I wasn't sure it was the right thing to say, since she hadn't been doing it on purpose.

"Didja like lookin' at me, Robert?" she asked, and propped herself up on her elbows, looking over at me.

I was so shocked that the truth just shot right out of my mouth. "Yes, Jeannie. You're beautiful."

She just smiled that sad smile again, the one that I'd seen when Calvin had grabbed her. I wondered why she looked so sad when she smiled. I thought maybe it was because she tried so hard to not open her mouth enough that you could see her broken-off tooth.

"Think so, Robert? Or is it just ya'd never seen a nekkid girl 'fore?" She still had that woeful expression masquerading as a smile.

"No, Jeannie. I never had seen one. But that isn't it. You just looked so . . . alive and fierce there. I'd never seen you look like that before." I looked at her, wondering how this might have been happening. I had a nearly naked girl in my tent, in my bed! And she was talking to me like it was the most natural thing in the world!

She got a wary look in her eyes and asked, "Y'ain't just saying that, then? Ya mean it? Ya ain't got to, ya know. I'm here already."

I didn't understand what she meant, really. I thought that maybe she . . . but that was ridiculous. "I do mean it, Jeannie. All I know is that you sure looked beautiful there in the clearing."

"Beautiful. Th' onliest man ever said that to me was my pa. 'N' that was right after he . . . Well, it was when he was explainin' why he . . . Never mind. Jes' stupid talkin' about it to anyone." She looked so sad that I put my hand on her shoulder.

"Jeannie, you can talk to me. I won't laugh or think it's stupid to talk about." I didn't know whether to rub her shoulder, pull my hand back, or leave it alone. So lacking any other idea what to do, I decided that letting it stay there was safest.

She looked at me with tears in her eyes, and said, "Ya really don't hafta play like it matters to ya. I'm already here, y'know."

I didn't really know what to do, so I pulled her over so she'd be laying her head on my chest, and hugged her. "I know you're here, and I'm glad you're here. But I don't understand why you think I'm lying to you. If it didn't matter to me, then why would I pretend it did?"

She started crying a little, quietly. There was no trace of tears in her voice, but I could feel them soaking through Cal's pajama top. "Ya really aren't playin', are ya? Yer not tryin' to trick ol' Jeannie. Ya don't even know why ya ought ta be lyin' to me, do ya?"

"I'm not trying to trick you, Jeannie. And I don't know what kind of lies you think I should be telling." I really didn't.

"Ya should be tryin' to be pullin' my painties down and puttin' yer fingers in me, and tellin' me how beautiful and wonderful I am. Ya should be tellin' me how you love me and how much I matter to ya. That's what all the boys does." And she started crying harder, the sobs audible now.

"Jeannie, honey . . . " I didn't have any idea what to say after that. So I just decided to hug her and not say anything.

She sat up all of a sudden. "Have you ever kissed a girl, Robert?" The tears were gone from her eyes.

"Yes. No. Well, I have, but not a real kiss, I guess. Not really." The only time I'd kissed a girl, well, she'd pretty much kissed me. A little smack right on the lips. But that had been in the seventh grade, in the hallway at school. I found out later that it was part of a game of truth-or-dare that they were playing.

"Wouldja like to kiss me, Robert? I think I'd rather be kissed by you than anybody right now. Because ya don't lie and play games with ol' Jeannie's heart." She moved until she was right over me, lips parted slightly.

"Yes. No. I mean . . ." I didn't know what I meant. "I would like to kiss you, Jeannie, but I don't think it would be right. I'm not in love with you, and I don't want to trick you like you say the other guys do."

"I know that, Robert. But iffen it cain't be love, sometimes having it be loving is enough. Will ya be tender with me? Treat me gentle?" She had a pleading look in her eyes, and I didn't know what to say to her. So I kissed her like that girl had kissed me.

She looked surprised, and even taken aback. "Robert, will ya let me show ya somethin'?"

I didn't know what to say at all. So I just nodded.

"Jes' sit easy, Robert. I'll show ya how to kiss a woman the way she likes it. That way, when there is someone ya love, you can kiss her right."

She covered my mouth very tenderly with hers, and flicked her tongue gently against my lips and teeth. I lay there like a stone, just amazed that any of this was happening. She laughed a little. Not a mean laugh. It seemed more astounded than anything else. "Now you do that to me while I do it ta you."

She bent over me again, and we kissed for what seemed like forever.

She started making slight sounds that I thought might have been enjoyment. Then she kissed my neck. Rivers of fire ran up and down my bruised ribs, and I didn't know if I could get any harder without something bursting.

"Kiss my neck like that, Robert. Ya liked it, dincha?" I nodded. "I'll like it, too."

So I clumsily laid her back on my pillow and propped myself up on one elbow beside her. It twinged my ribs something terrible, but I didn't mind at all. I kissed her mouth again, and she moved her body against mine in a slow undulating motion that seemed like the sexiest thing I'd ever known. She made those light gaspy sounds, and then I started kissing her neck like she'd kissed mine.

She gave a low moan, and I stopped, unsure if I'd hurt her. She just smiled a smile that wasn't sad at all, and pulled my head down to her neck again. I kept kissing her neck, and looked down at her breasts while I did. Should I? Or would that be too much, too far? Would she be angry or hurt?

She just whispered softly, "Go ahead. I want you to." And she pushed gently on the top of my head. So I did. I resolved that if what I was doing on her neck felt good, then it would feel good there, too.

She gasped, and moved against me a little harder. I loved it, but it hurt like the dickens. She grabbed my hand, and held it against her panties. They were damp, and she rolled her hips up into my hand. She held my hand there firmly, and started rocking against it. Her breath started coming out in those gasps full-time now.

"Don't stop what you're doing with your mouth, Rob. Just keep doing that." I had gotten very daring, and taken her nipple between my lips and started flicking it with my tongue. I tried to mimic the motion with my hand on her other breast. All at once, her eyes rolled up into her head, and she gave a low cry. She shuddered all over for a bit, and then lay very still.

Her eyes opened up, and she said, "Yer gentle, Rob. A woman loves that. And ya don't paw and grab. Ya don't act like a woman's boobies are knobs on a radio, or a steerin' wheel of a truck. Ya make a woman feel good. Now let's make you feel good." She slid her hand from my neck to my chest, applying light but persistent pressure. She looked confused when I winced.

"What's wrong, Rob? Did I hurtcha?" She pulled her hand back and pushed me back onto the pillow.

"No, it's nothing, Jeannie." I wasn't going to stop her from touching me even if it killed me. It felt too good at the same time.

She unbuttoned the top button, and slowly kissed her way down my neck to my chest. She put a little of her weight on me, and I just barely was able to support it without wincing. She unbuttoned the next button, and kept kissing my breastbone. Then her hand slipped down to the elastic waistband of my pajamas, and inside.

I couldn't help it. I yelped like she'd set it on fire. She pulled back, and looked very scared and hurt.

"What's wrong, Robert? Doncha want me to touch ya?"

"It's not that, Jeannie. It's just . . . " I didn't know how to explain it. I didn't know if she'd laugh or make fun.

"Take yer shirt off, Rob." She was looking at me with narrowed eyes. She came across like a teacher at school, all of a sudden.

"What for, Jeannie?" I was uneasy. I didn't think she wanted my shirt off for showing me anything like she had already shown me tonight.

"Pertend I feel lonesome with my shirt off without ya take yers off too. Ya don't want me to put my sweater back on, do ya?"

I didn't. So I slowly unbuttoned my shirt. She reached down with a quick movement and tossed both sides of the shirttail away from my center. She nodded slowly.

"Bruised up yer sides purdy good. Now, shuck them pants off." She raised her eyebrows at me when I opened my mouth. "I din't say talk about it, Rob. I said shuck off them drawers." So I did.

She looked sadly at me. She looked carefully at my works, and said, "That's bruised up purdy good too. 'S a wonder 'tworks 'tall right now. But it wouldn't stand for bein' touched a bit, I don't reckon. Worked ya over purdy good, din't he?"

"Who?" I asked.

"Calvin did it. I ain't stupid, no matter what the boys says about me. Iffen there'd been three city boys hit him hard enough to swell his nose and put that bruise on side 'a his eye thataway, the other two would have beaten 'im silly. 'N then I come in here and see you all bunged up . . . A girl'd have to be plumb ignert to not put two and two together. An' I'm clean 'round the corner from ignert." She looked very shrewd and wise . . . which were two things I'd have never thought to call her before tonight. Of course, beautiful and sensual were another two new ideas for me to be applying to her, too.

"Yes, Jeannie. Calvin did it." I didn't see what harm it would do to tell her, since she figured it all out anyway.

"Hitcha on the head too, din't he? Where yer har kivers it up real good, right?" She looked balefully at me, and ran her fingers through my hair very lightly. She nodded.

"I figured. It's what they do." She almost whispered. It didn't seem like she was talking to me at all.

"What who does, Jeannie? Does Cal hurt you, too?" I couldn't believe that my brother would do such a thing. Mom had raised us both up to never, ever hit a woman.

"Not yet, Robert. Cal's never hit me yet." She gnawed her bottom lip and considered. "My pa."

I didn't know what to say to this at all. I wanted to ask why, but I knew why, or at least thought I did. Mr. Riley stayed drunk, and got violent with his liquor. But since I didn't know what else to say, I asked her anyway.

"Why would he do that, Jeannie?"

"He does it for makin' him . . . it don't really matter why, does it?" She started to cry again. This time I knew that holding her was a good idea. So I did.

Chapter Six

She sobbed like a child cradled in the hollow of my arm. I didn't have any words of comfort to offer her. What do you say to someone who was broken up just by talking to you? About her own father? I thought over what she had said, and found one part of it I could maybe offer solace on.

"Jeannie, honey, it's not your fault, you know. You didn't make him do anything. How could you?" She shook her head, denying my words.

"He said . . . he said . . . " she couldn't continue, but even at my young age, I knew better.

"What he said was a weak excuse, Jeannie. If you look hard enough, you can make anything someone else's fault. I don't know what all's going on, honey, but I'll bet you didn't do anything wrong at all. And if he didn't know it, he wouldn't feel guilty enough to try and put it off on you that way." I wasn't sure what the words for it were, but I'd read about it in some of the psychology books at the school library.

"Do ya really think, Rob?" She stopped sobbing, but the tears still ran down her face as she looked up at me. "Do ya not think it's because I'm bad? Not because I'm a slut?"

"I don't think you're that at all, Jeannie. Not at all." I was having trouble forming my thoughts into coherent sentences from my rage. "If a guy was . . . as active as you are, they'd wink and nod and slap him on the back. Doesn't seem quite right that it's just the other way around for girls. After all, who are the guys supposed to be sleeping with?"

She looked dazed. "I never thought 'bout it like that afore. But do you know the worst part? I don't even like it with most of them guys. But it's better than bein' alone. If that's what they want me for, then I don't mind payin' that price too much as long as I don't have to be by myself."

"What's so bad about being by yourself, Jeannie? You're smart, and attractive. You don't need those guys. You deserve a boyfriend that would treat you like a lady." I ignored the fact that until I got to know her this very night, I had the same thoughts about her that she said everyone did.

"People won't letcha change, Rob. You maybe ain't old enough yet ta know it. But oncet they get an idear about ya, it don't matter if y'ain't like that no more. I'll always be that white trash Jack Riley's slut-whore daughter to everyone in Folsom Hollow. Except maybe you." Her eyes looked at me speculatively.

"So what d'you think about me, Rob Taylor? D'ya think I'm a dirty woman?"

"I know better, Jeannie. I know why you've done the things you've done. I know that you're a good-hearted girl who's been done wrong by everyone you ever knew. I just want you to know I don't think that about you. Not anymore. You've shown me different." I had to be honest with her, even if it hurt.

"So the stuff I done with you tonight don't make you think I'm just easy?" Her eyes narrowed again.

"Jeannie, you came to me and offered yourself because I'd at least been kind to you. Because I didn't lie to you and try and trick you. To me that isn't a bad thing about you, but it does tell me how badly everyone else must treat you. If being treated with courtesy and respect is so rare as to engender that kind of response in you . . . to me, it's a pretty damning statement about Folsom Hollow." I hadn't caught myself in time, using vocabulary that I should have known better than to use around people that weren't teachers.

But she never blinked. "So ya think that I'm good, but people treat me so bad that when someone treats me good that I don't know how to act? And that the way they treat me says more about them than it does me?"

"Right, Jeannie. That's exactly what I was saying." I guess that the confused look on my face was a pretty bad telltale.

She laughed. "Din't think that I'd know them words, didja? I toldja I was clean around the corner from ignert. I read a lot. And when I write, I write English just as good as you talk it. Jest when I talk, it still comes out all hillbilly. S'all I ever heard 'round the house, an' iffen I tried talkin' right, I'd get whupped fer puttin' on airs."

It had honestly never occurred to me that Jeannie Riley read anything. I was starting to feel ashamed of how badly I had misjudged this girl.

"Jeannie, would you mind being my friend? I never knew how smart you were, or how pretty you were until tonight. I didn't ever know what a wonderful soul you had, or anything about you, really. I was stupid, and I thought what other people thought about you. I'm sorry for that. I didn't know any better. But I do know better now. I hope you can forgive me for that." I didn't know where my words came from right then. My mother would always wink when I said that . . . she said if your brain didn't know, then they probably came from the heart.

"Yer friend?" She looked at me suspiciously. "Don't have any of them. Not really."

"Me neither, Jeannie. Calvin's the closest thing I've got." I said.

I didn't miss the hurt look on her face as the words struck home for her. "Me too." she whispered. "Iffen ya mean it, I'd really like that."

"Get your clothes on, Jeannie. You'll be warmer. And you can share my blanket for tonight."

"Don't reckon I'd better stick around here of a mornin'. Cal'll be up, and wonderin' where I got off to. Iffen he found me in your tent, he might pound ya again."

"I don't care, Jeannie. I'd like to think you spent a night safe and warm, not worried about who might be hurting you in the night."

"I'll stay, then. I'll just be gone early of the mornin'. Ya don't mind?" She looked suspicious and worried at the same time.

"Of course not, Jeannie. I'm your friend too, I hope."

"I hope so too," she whispered, almost too low for me to hear. She did get dressed, and I held her close and warm throughout the night.

Chapter Seven

When the morning came, I woke up alone. My blankets were still warm where Jeannie had vacated, so I thought that she had probably planted the seeds of my waking with her departure. I wondered how long she had been gone.

I stretched, and noticed that my ribs felt better already. I had always been a fast healer, but I think that Jeannie had worked a little magic last night. I let a nervous hand check to test soreness in the area I was most worried about, and found that it was not quite as sore as yesterday.

I crawled out of the tent, shakily, it's true. The morning chill soon convinced me I ought to try and see if I could wear regular clothes again yet. The shirt Cal had packed was loose, and he had thought to find my very loosest fitting dungarees. There was less discomfort than I had anticipated getting my clothes on and no pain at all. That being done, I gathered some of the wood out of the pile, and began making the fire back over the dying embers. It wasn't too long before I had a decent breakfast-sized fire going. I went over to the pup tent to check on Cal.

He was lying under the blankets, all covered to his chin. He was probably cold, since he hadn't been awake to tie down his doorflaps last night . . . and hadn't had someone else's body heat to warm his blankets.

Overall, I didn't feel too sympathetic. If he had treated Jeannie like a human being instead of some sort of convenience gadget . . .

I gathered up the fishing gear, and headed over to the river. It was early enough that I should be able to catch a few before Cal woke up from his stupor. I liked fishing by myself in the early morning. It was peaceful, and gave plenty of time for thinking.

And I had plenty to think about, I mused. In one fell swoop, I had made a friend, kissed a girl, and . . . started learning about women, and their bodies. It was a good feeling. I replayed last night's events over in my mind, and was smiling to myself when I heard Calvin beside me.

He was looking at me with a bit of curiosity on his face. "What the hell's gotcha grinnin' so damned early of a mornin'?"

He grabbed up the two small catfish I'd caught and pulled his knife out to skin and filet them. "Well? What's so damned good 'bout this mornin'? I've got a poundin' headache and my gut's jest a'roilin'. Iffen yer havin' a good day, maybe ya can share the good with yer hungover brother."

"I just like the morning, Cal. Good fishing, good crisp air, good scenery. You should have seen the sunrise." I carefully avoided looking at him, just in case he had gotten out of his mood of atonement.

He started frying up the fish, and didn't talk much. I looked back at him every now and then, and could tell he wasn't feeling too good. I caught two more small cats and headed back to the fire.

He grunted and took them from me, and looked up. "How're ya

feelin' this mornin', Bobby-boy?"

"Not too bad, Cal. I'm a little sore, but I guess that's to be expected. I'll be all right soon enough. How about you? Want some willow-bark tea?" Cal hadn't believed that I'd found something in my books that would help his headaches. Until I had made him some, that is.

"Tastes fair nasty, boy, but it does the trick. Yeah, go ahead an' stew some up. I'll drink it." Calvin didn't always feel like the anesthetic properties were worth the foul taste. This morning, I had thought that he would opt for the tea.

We ate in silence, since talking hurt Cal's head, and listening hurt it worse. After we finished up the fish, he said, "I'm gonna stretch back out for a spell. Maybe ya could hitch ta town and fetch us back some .22 shells. Maybe see yer Donna while yer there."

I hadn't thought of what we'd do on Saturday. I hadn't even thought of what we'd eat on Saturday, past breakfast-time. We always had fish for breakfast, when we could catch them. For dinner sometimes, Calvin shot squirrels, rabbits, or snapping turtle. Sometimes he'd pop a duck, but I always hated that. I didn't mind the meat, but plucking birds is an awful lot of work.

"I'll need money for the shells, Cal." He knew I didn't have any.

"Why woncha just swipe 'em? It'd save us four bits a box. And four bits ain't all that easy to come by for us, y'know?" He looked vexed, but we'd had this conversation before. I knew that we didn't have much cash money. Most of what Mom earned for cash came from the sewing and alterations that she did for people in town. The rest was from an annual stipend paid from Cal's father's insurance. Fortunately, we didn't need much cash. The house was paid for and we didn't have electricity or natural gas bills. We didn't have an automobile. Instead of buying clothes, Mom bought cloth and sewed them. Most of our food came from the farm. What little didn't come from the farm came from hunting or fishing. We'd trade eggs from our chickens for corn with the neighbors. We'd swap a ham for a turkey and a wheelbarrow full of potatoes. We'd get our neighbor with his mule and plow to break ground for our garden for all the tomatoes he could eat during the summer. .

"Here. Jest about taps me, y'know. Iffen ya wasn't such a sissy . . . " Calvin grudgingly handed over the five dimes. I didn't want to know where they came from. He might have bullied them a dime at a time from one of the high school kids. He might have stolen them from Mom. Or he might actually have done some chores for one of the town folks to earn them. Sometimes he'd surprise me. But I still didn't want to ask.

"I'll be back with the shells. Maybe I could try and get us some squirrels this time?" Sometimes Calvin would let me do the shooting. He was a better shot, and he never let me forget it. Of course, he wasn't better by much. I never let him forget that.

"Depends on how m'head feels later on. I won't be wantin' to shoot iffen it don't feel a whale of a lot better. Besides, I reckon ya earned it. Ya made me the tea, an' ya caught the cats fer breakfast, an' yer goin' ta town ta fetch the shells . . . an' I don't feel like it nohow. Yeah, ya can go ahead, Bobby-boy." I wondered how much the fact that he didn't want to weighed in on the equation.

I only walked for about half a mile before a farm truck passed me headed for town. It was a neighbor from up the holler. We swapped our pork for their beef about every fall. Mr. Horswood didn't mind lifting us kids to town when we passed. He was a talker, and liked the company. Rumor had it he talked so much in public because he couldn't get a word in edgewise around the house. His wife and her mother weren't just talkers—they could talk the hind legs off of a mule.

Mr. Horswood pulled over and opened the door to his truck for me. I hopped in with as much agility as I could manage without making it obvious that I wasn't in top form.

"Morning, Mr. Horswood! What takes you to town so early?" I greeted him cheerfully.

"I'm just pickin' up some things fer the critters. Salt licks, feed corn, an' balin' wire. Ya wouldn't mind helpin' an old man load up, wouldja?"

"I'd be happy to, Mr. Horswood. It's a pleasure to help a neighbor, Mama says. And you've saved me quite a walk this morning, too. If I can save you some trouble in return, then I'm glad to do it." I meant it, too. Mr. Horswood was a neighbor that I admired a lot. He had been Staff Sergeant Horswood during World War II, and had stormed the beach at Normandy.

He'd gotten the Purple Heart, the Bronze Star, and the Silver Star. As much as he liked to talk, he never talked about the war. All he'd say was that time made liars out of all old soldiers, and there were liars enough without his help.

Mr. Horswood asked how school was going, and what classes I was taking. When I told him about algebra, he laughed. "That's great, son. I always liked 'rithmetic myself. There ain't but one right answer, and iffen it's done right, everyone comes up with it. No tricksy stuff in math, y'ken?"

I laughed. I didn't bother to tell him I didn't like math all that well, since I thought it might have been rude. "That's true, sir. I do like the way that algebra helps figure out a lost variable, too. That way, if you're building something, you can measure what you need ahead of time, by plugging the missing variable into your formulae." That much I could be honest about. Math was useful, but hardly a passion.

"Formulae! I ain't heard that word since I was in school! Yer a corker, Bobby Taylor! Formulae! Even most a' my teachers said formulas. Reckon you'll be guvner one of these days, good as ya talk! Formulae!" He laughed delightedly.

I smiled. I was glad I'd made Mr. Horswood so happy, even if I didn't really understand what was so great about the word.

"So what takes you to town, Bobby? Don't imagine yer fetchin' back salt licks!" He laughed again.

"I'm supposed to pick up some shells for Cal to get squirrels with, Mr.

Horswood." I knew what was coming next.

"A gun is a good thing in good hands, Bobby. But they're a dangerous tool. Ya know never to assume a gun is unloaded, right?" When I nodded, he continued, "An' never point it at nothin' that ya don't want dead. Because a gun kills, Bobby. It's what they do."

"Yes, sir." I said, which was all the reply he needed.

"I know I'm jest an ol' man what probably sticks his nose in young 'uns beeswax too much, but I hope ya know I ain't tryin' to be nosy. I'm jest tryin' to look out fer ya. Don't mind, do ya?" He looked concerned that maybe he'd overstepped his bounds.

"I don't mind at all, sir. Firearm safety is the first thing that anyone needs to know about guns. If you can't use them safely, then you shouldn't be using them. That's what Mom taught Calvin and me. She made us learn all the rules. There's no such thing as an unloaded gun. Never point a gun at anything you don't want to shoot. Never rely on the safety latch. Never open a gun to check on a hangfire. And remember they're tools, not toys." I recited the list just as Mom had laid out for us.

"Exactly right, Bobby! I should've known a young feller smart as y'are'd know all that stuff! Yer a corker, Bobby-boy! A regular corker!" He laughed again, and the mood in the truck lightened.

"So how's yer Ma doin'? She gonna win the pies again this year? Ain't never seen flakier piecrust! Ol' Mrs. LuAnn Sanders don't like not bein' able to out-bake her, no sirree! Ya should've seen 'er last spring when

she got the red ribbon again! Ya could see that vein in 'er forehead stickin'
out and her face was redder'n the ribbon!"

I liked Mr. Horswood. He talked about Mom and her pies, Calvin and
his sports, and tested me on state capitals all the way into town.

Chapter Eight

When we pulled into the feed store, I told Mr. Horswood that I'd be right back to help him load up. I needed to run across the street to the True Value. He grinned and told me, "Th'ain't no rush, boy. Reckon I may run inta a feller or two I know." He winked and laughed. I guess he knew what people said about how he talked.

I trotted over to the hardware store and went inside. I waved to the checkout girl and walked past the toys and plumbing supplies. I went up to the loft with the gun cases and the ammunition.

I had always liked to look over these firearms. Like most boys, I wanted a good shotgun, and a deer rifle. And a .22, and a pistol or two, like The Lone Ranger. Maybe even a tommygun like Elliot Ness . . . or maybe Al Capone.

But I was here to pick up some .22 shells for getting small game. Winchesters were the best, I thought. CCIs were the most expensive. But the ones I wanted were the thirty-five cent lead nose .22 Long Rifle shells with the yellow box and black writing.

I picked up the box and turned around. Mr. Granble grabbed my wrist. "Caught ya, ya little thief! I've had it with ya Taylor bastards runnin' around and thievin' from my store!"

"I'm not stealing, Mr. Granble." I struggled to keep my voice calm. He was digging his fingers into my wrist and I was afraid of what might happen if I lost my temper.

"You goddam Taylors ain't got any goddam money! I know yer thievin'! I don't wanna see ya in my goddam store any goddam more!" He started dragging me down the steps to the main floor.

"Mr. Granble, you're hurting my wrist." I was calm—icy calm.

"Goddam lucky I ain't hurtin' more'n yer goddam wrist! Ought ta call the law in and lock ya up in the goddam hoosegow!" He was red in the face, spluttering and spraying his foul tobacco-tainted saliva all over.

I snapped my wrist straight out in a twisting motion, against the thumb side of his grip, just the way that Calvin showed me. It hurt my ribs to do it, but I was too angry to care. Mr. Granble was a tall man, but not very big. Not nearly strong enough to keep his grip if I didn't want to let him.

"You don't want to put your hands on me again. I'll leave, Mr. Granble. Here are your shells." I held out the box to him.

"You goddamn kid! I'll put my hands around yer thievin' neck!" He reached his hands out to try doing that very thing. But I wasn't there anymore.

I had started the footwork that Calvin had started teaching me and Chief had finished. Light flickering steps that carried my slightly crouched and aching body everywhere but in reach. Not trying to get away from the man, just to keep his hands from landing on me.

"Stop dancin' around, ya li'l bastard!" He lunged and grabbed, but the slippery weaves that Chief had shown me made me impossible to touch.

"Mr. Granble, you lost your temper today. You're about to lose your reputation as an honest businessman. I've got the money to pay for these shells." I was on the verge of losing my temper, and wanted to get control of the situation before I hit the man.

He stopped trying to grab me. "Why? Think ya might get caught? That why ya brunged money wif ya, ya li'l shitass?" He looked dumbfounded in addition to just looking dumb. His shirt was all untucked from trying to wrestle someone a third his age, and he was sweaty and out of breath.

I spoke in a very low tone for his ears only. "Take a look around you, Mr. Granble. Look at Mrs. McCall over in housewares. She's going to her bridge group tonight full of stories about your foul mouth. She's going to point out that everyone knows that Bobby Taylor would starve to death before he stole a mouthful of bread. She's going to laugh at how stupid you look with your shirt untucked, your spit running down your chin, and your hair all wild from thrashing around. And her bridge group? They'll be sure and tell their quilting circles. And they'll be full of information for the Eastern Star meeting. Who we both know will tell their husbands, who will be talking at the feed store and the Grille. Do you want to apologize to me, shake hands like a man, and sell me these shells? Or do you want the story going around that you're too stupid to own up to your mistakes?"

He looked around. Mrs. McCall was looking very determinedly at the same china patterns that had been there last week, but if her ears could swivel like a deer's, they would have. His breath didn't get any less wheezy, but he looked abashedly at his shoes and started tucking in his shirt. "Let's see your money, boy."

"I said apologize, shake hands, and we'll conduct our business like reasonable men." I hadn't lost my temper, but when he had insulted my mother, it had been a near thing indeed. "You should be ashamed of what you said about my mother. I wonder what she would think of it."

If possible, he looked even more hangdog than he already did. "Now, Bobby, I did lose m' temper a bit, I reckon. Maybe we could jest shake hands and call it good? I don't mind givin' ya them shells as a . . . " I could tell he just couldn't come up with the phrase 'gesture of goodwill', and I wasn't about to help him. Let him crawl a bit for his prideful, spiteful, prejudiced tantrum. "special promoter. That's it, a special promoter."

"I don't want you to give me these shells, Mr. Granble. That would indicate that all was right between us. Things are not right yet. You haven't apologized. The apology is worth more to me than the forty-five cents or so." I was keeping my voice down to frustrate Mrs. McCall's spying ears. I knew I could make him crawl, but not in front of a witness.

He looked over at Mrs. McCall, who was studying the same plate furiously, but starting to edge over to examine the plumber's snakes that were just one aisle over. "I shou'n't a' said them things 'boutcha, Bobby.

An' I know better'n ta've said 'bout yer Mama. I'd 'preciate it iffen ya'd let me gi' ya them shells . . . special promoter."

"I accept your apology, Mr. Granble. I would appreciate it if you'd ring these up at the front register." And I handed him the shells.

The humiliated expression on his face was almost enough to make me wish I hadn't scorned his 'special promoter'. Almost. I didn't give a damn about his apology to me, but the one to my mother was something that wasn't about to go unsaid. He rang the shells up, and said in a low voice, "That's forty-eight cents, Bobby."

"Thank you, Mr. Granble." I handed him the dimes and waited for my two cents. He handed me a pair of quarters instead. The expression on his face pleaded with me to take his peace offering. He knew he'd acted like a bullying child instead of a man, much less a businessman. He felt dirty and ashamed inside, and I knew it.

But his need to offer atonement did not oblige me to accept it. "I'm afraid you've miscounted my change, Mr. Granble."

His shoulders slumped. His face fell. "I reckon I must've. Thank you, Robert." He swapped the quarters for pennies, put the shells in a small paper sack, and stapled the receipt across the folded top. He straightened and looked me in the eye. "Thank you for your trade, Robert."

I nodded gravely, and opened the door to go back and help Mr. Horswood load up his stuff from the feed store.

Miraculously, he was pulling the truck around to the loading dock out back. I crossed the street and walked up the stairs to start loading. I had figured that he'd have talked the ears off of the crowd of farmers that seemed to have time for shooting the bull in the feedshop before he left.

"Ready to load up, Mr. Horswood?" I tried to grin, but he saw the grim expression underneath my little show.

"In a minute, Bobby. What's wrong, boy? Y'ain't the same pup that went bouncin' up yonder steps."

"Just a little problem with Mr. Granble. We got it all straightened out, sir." I knew that he probably wouldn't buy that story, and would want to know all the gory details.

"What kinda problem? He ain't never give me no problems . . . " Mr. Horswood scratched his head and looked puzzled. "Cou'n't 'e fin' the shells ya wanted?"

I could tell it wouldn't do any good to try to dissemble and dissuade. "He could find them. So could I. But when I picked them up to go pay for them, he grabbed me and accused me of trying to steal them."

"That ol' scoundrel! I oughtta go over there 'n' give 'im a sock in the nose!" I could tell that Mr. Horswood meant it, too. This sure wasn't the trip to town that I meant to take.

"No sir. I took care of it. He apologized for the incident. And what's worse, Mrs. McCall saw the whole thing." I grinned, a real grin this time.

"Mrs. McCall?" He grinned and laughed. "That's the onliest person in these parts that talks more'n I do! I may hafta ask her what all she heard, just fer fun, one o' these days. If yer sure ya got it under control, reckon I'll keep m' old nose outta yer beeswax. Ready to load up, son?"

"Yes sir!" And I did. My ribs didn't bother me much at all.

Chapter Nine

I finished up loading the salt licks for Mr. Horswood, and he grinned and shook my hand. "Mind ya don't put them shells in yer pants pocket, son. Rimfire shells're liable to go off, iffen ya mush 'em against one another." He laughed again, and finished, "Not that a sharp lad like you'd be needin' advice s'old as that!"

"I appreciate it, Mr. Horswood. I hadn't heard that they were dangerous to carry like that." I hadn't, really. But it made sense. The primer for this type wasn't centered in the back like most ammunition. A compression on the shell casing could set it off. I made a show of tucking the box into my shirt pocket, just to show I was paying attention.

"'Course, it's the casin' what flies then, bein' so much lighter than the bullet. But it flies fast, and while 'twon't kill ya . . . havin' 'em in yer front pants pocket might make ya wish it had." He nodded gravely, then gave me a wink and a grin. "'Nough listenin' to old men for ya today. Ya ridin' back with me, or findin' yer own road home?"

"I thought I might stay in town for a bit, since I'm here. A few people I might like to see. I appreciate the offer, Mr. Horswood." And I did.

I headed over to the Folsom Hollow Chronicle offices to see if Donna might be in town today. I tried to think of some casual reason for me to stop by, but came up blank. "Audace, audace, toujours audace!" I counseled myself. It was all the French I knew, and that via Patton quoting Napoleon. But it sure seemed like good advice.

I entered, and there she was, sitting in the receptionist's chair out front. She seemed to be reading a book. Donna just looked radiant—her hair fell around her shoulders like a veil. Her dress was blue with a white lacey collar, and she was wearing stockings. I smiled, and she hopped up like she'd been expecting me. "Hi there, Bobby Taylor! I was just hopin' ya'd be around sometime today!"

That took me off guard. Not that I didn't want to be wanted, but I didn't come into town very often except for school. "Well, it's good to be hoped for, and a better feeling still to have delivered!" I grinned. Not too bad for having just shot from the hip like that.

She didn't seem like the words had wowed her the way I had hoped, just like they were an impediment to the idea she was trying to get across. "I's sittin' here, just a puzzlin' an' puzzlin' over this here 'rithmetic. Papa says iffen I don't get a good grade in it, won't get ta go ta alla th' games like I want. Can ya help me, Bobby? You're the best at math I know. Iffen ya cain't help me, then th'ain't no help for me." She leveled those sad-looking grey eyes at me and I wasn't just hooked, I skipped straight to landed, scaled and filleted.

"What are you having trouble with, Donna? If I can help, then I'd be delighted to be of service, my lady." What I knew of manners came from books about knights and kings, and it sure seemed like a suave and debonair thing to say.

Again, she didn't seem to notice. "Them fractious ratios is jest stupid! Th'ain't no sense to 'em a' tall!" She pouted, pursing those lips just ripe for kissing into a Cupid's bow.

"Ratios? I can help with that, no problem! They're not that hard, Donna. Here, let's take a look at what you're working on." I tugged a chair from over by the waiting area to the desk she'd been sitting beside. "Where are you stuck, anyway?"

She came right over and pulled her chair close to mine. "It's not jest ratios, it's fractious ratios! The ones what're jest like the fractions I almost failed last year! They wanna know the denominators and the common 'uns, and then the least 'uns. They wanna know their multiples and the least 'un o' that!"

I decided telling her that fractions were easy might seem condescending. We'd been working on fractions since elementary school, and looking back on it, Donna had always had a hard time with them.

"Fractions are just like parts of numbers, right? Maybe if you think of oranges and slicing them up"

"Th'ain't no good. Ain't nobody never cut no durned orange into sixty-four parts. Wouldn't be nothin' t'eat of it. Jest rind and runned out juice from cuttin' it so stupid much." She looked sad and hopeless.

So I just grinned. "That's the truth. But let's start with smaller parts, then. Once you learn the beginnings, then you just have to work the new numbers into the formulae."

That word had gotten me some applause earlier, maybe . . . ?

No. "Iffen ya say so, Bobby Taylor. Just don't you go askin' me to chop no oranges into no thousand pieces and make no sense of it!" Here her eyes flashed and she looked fierce. Suddenly I was thinking of Jeannie, and how fierce she looked last night. But I pushed that thought away.

Just then, the office door to the editor/barrister's inner office swung open. "Thought I heard some voices out here. Y'ain't talkin' to yerself, air ya?" Mr. Duquesne backed out of the office, carrying a typewriter. As he turned, he saw me.

"Bobby Taylor? How are ya, son? You here 'bout a paper route? I'm sorry, Bobby, but we ain't got the circulation we oughtta. I'd like to get you on my payroll, but there jest ain't room fer two paperboys right now." He looked genuinely sorry. I was genuinely sorry too. Sorry I hadn't come up with this plausible reason for visiting on a Sunday afternoon.

"No, Papa, Bobby's here t'help me!" Donna looked angelic as she shook her head at him. "He's gonna show me 'bout them fractious ratios! An' take me to the ballgames when I get good grades!"

This was the first I heard of that, but my heart soared within me. "Yes sir, I'm going to try and tutor her in arithmetic. And if you're willing, I'd like to escort her to the games."

Mr. Duquesne puffed his cheeks out like he was trying not to laugh.

He tucked his hands behind his back, and rocked on his heels a bit. "Askin' permission to court her, are ya?"

"Yes sir. I'd like to export; I mean escort her to the games. I'd take good care of her, sir, and not bring her home late, either." Export. Great. If I hadn't been trying to come up with a synonym for escort, I probably wouldn't have tripped over my own tongue. Now that I didn't need one, I had plenty. Accompany. That one would have been perfect. Too late.

"I'll tell you what, Bobby. She ain't gotten a decent homework grade in mathematics all year. If you can help her do that—Now mind, I don't mean you do her homework; I may be just a small-town lawyer and half-ass editor, but I'm smart enough ta see through that—then I'd prob'ly be amenable. From all I hear of ya, yer a good enough boy, and I like the way you've worked on talkin' proper. Shows respect, and maybe a determination to better yourself. Prob'ly already got big plans fer the future, eh, boy?" I just nodded. "Good fer you, Bobby. Aim high; too high, even. Then even if ya miss, you're still higher than if ya'd aimed low and hit." He grinned, patted me on the shoulder, and headed back into his office.

"That was perfect, Bobby!" Donna whispered in a tiny voice. Had I finally done something to impress her? "He fell for that one hook, line and sinker! You're some crackerjack, Bobby!"

I responded in the same tiny whisper. "What are you talking about, Donna? Fell for what?"

"The part 'bout ya courtin' me! That's perfect! Ya can walk me ta the games, and ya can watch me cheer and Cal play, then I can see Cal after!"

I got a sinking feeling in the pit of my stomach, and still she pressed on. "An' iffen Papa'll gimme permission to see you, then you can get me an' take me to Cal, other times too! Yer an angel, Bobby Taylor!"

I paused and thought rapidly. I'd get to spend time with her, as much as I could convince her she needed to learn these 'fractious ratios', and get to watch her at the games with her express permission, and talk with her. To hear her tell it, I was going to be permitted to court her at her house, too. It was the greatest opportunity I could imagine. Right now, she wanted Cal, but that would just make the moment when her heart was finally mine all the sweeter.

"A guy's got to do his best, doesn't he? Glad to help you, Donna. You know, I've always liked you. And you're the prettiest girl in school, too. I think you got robbed from being the ninth grade representative in the Homecoming Queen's court."

* * * *

*

It's hard enough to write about all this stuff without delving a whole lot deeper into how sappy I was over Donna Duquesne. How I thought that she'd love me after she got to know me. How I knew that once she knew Calvin, an angel like her would want nothing to do with him. So if it's all the same to you, I'll just leave it to the imagination.

(Several pages ripped out)

* * * * *

So as I was hitching back in the early afternoon, I decided to stop by the Chief's homestead. He was one of the more interesting people in all of Folsom Hollow. He was also the closest thing I'd had to a friend except for Calvin, and now Jeannie. Donna? She was much more than a friend.

The Chief was Chief Machinist's Mate Michael Xavier Carmichel, twenty-five year veteran of the Pacific fleet, All-Navy Boxing Team middleweight champion, survivor of Pearl Harbor, the Battle of Midway, and the Battle of Leyte Gulf, and the proud recipient of the Purple Heart, The Navy Commendation Medal (With Combat V), The Navy Achievement Medal (With Combat V), and so many other decorations I lost track. He swore like a sailor, drank like a fish, danced the hornpipe whenever he pleased, and made trips into Charleston three or four times a year to procure the services of prostitutes. He was disreputable and contrary, and as apt to spit in an unannounced visitor's face as to shake his hand.

It's not known outside most naval circles, but a machinist's mate is pretty much a jack-of-all-trades for metalworking and mechanical work. They do the work of a plumber, the work of a machinist, and all the work associated with mechanical systems as well. He enjoyed metalsmithing as much as he did boxing, and the only thing that could pull him away from one was the other.

I loved the man. He knew I was interested in boxing, and had taken over my coaching from Calvin when he saw the two of us sparring in the street one day after reading the Golden Gloves poster. He stopped us right there, and told me that "ya gots talent, goddammit. Little peckerhead's got talent, and he's wastin' it practicin' with that damned brawler. He cain't box. He's a slow oaf. A goddamned puncher. Th'ain't no fuckin' skill to bein' a puncher, boy. Just strength and endurance. You let the other son-of-a-bitch wear hisself out punching your head while you wear yourself out punchin' at his, and then y'ain't got a boxing match worth watchin'. No goddamned strategy, no fuckin' skill. Skill's more important than power, boy. Come wif me, you little shit. I'll show you boxin'. Real boxin'." So I had. And he had.

We'd worked on hand speed, the speedbag, the heavy bag, the dodge-bag. He'd worked me on climbing a rope with my arms alone, and then made me jump rope with weights around my wrists. He had shown me his footwork, how to keep circling away from a puncher's strong side. He had shown me his traps, and how to escape from them—he had been known for stepping on an opponent's foot to drive the in-close uppercut home to an anchored target. He had tried to teach me his double-left-hook combination, but I was clumsy with it, and telegraphed it too much. It was well known that particular combination was slow and ineffective. Except when he did it.

I wouldn't have believed it if I hadn't seen it myself. Quick as I was, when he snapped that double hook into the heavy canvas seabag filled with sand, Chief's hand just seemed to disappear, turning into a quick drumbeat. I never realized what a difference there could be between pretty good native talent and a fiery desire that had been trained and cultivated until that day.

I was here, at the Chief's homestead. Incorrect to call it a farm, I knew. He wouldn't operate his land like a farm, and refused to grow even a vegetable patch. The income from his Navy pension and the natural gas wells he had on his land were sufficient for his needs, and he chose to buy the heat-and-eat foods mom scorned. He didn't want to take a wife, either.

"Women's got their uses, boy, but they ain't worth the goddamned trouble. Wantin' this and wantin' that, talkin' a man's ear off and naggin' him to be doin' some goddamned thing he don't wanna be doin'. Ya take up with women, and nex' thing 'round, they're wantin' ya ta be somebody different. They ain't got no goddamned, sense, ya see. Iffen they wanted somebody that'd do all them goddamned things they's after a body ta do, they shoulda looked for the son-of-a-bitch ta begin with. Women's a helluva lot cheaper the way I do it, runnin' down ta Charleston when I needs ta. Easier on a man's soul, too."

I couldn't help but grin thinking of the misogynistic old recluse. He was different from everyone else in Folsom Hollow to be sure. I walked up the middle of his driveway, making sure that the cantankerous old man I knew was behind the curtains knew that I wasn't someone sneaking onto his property. The dogs had begun to bawl as soon as my foot hit the driveway, but they weren't attack dogs. I always figured the only reason that attack dogs didn't appeal to the contrary old man was that he wanted to reserve the pleasure for himself.

I went up to the porch and knocked. The Chief came out immediately, already dressed in his Navy-issue warm-ups. "To the gym, boy."

We both knew that it was just the barn that had been there when it really had been a farm, but he never referred to it as anything but 'the gym'. He had taken great pains to clean out any trace of livestock, and to keep the hard-packed dirt swept much cleaner than any room in his old two-bedroom house. The speedbag, the heavy bag, and all the equipment was kept there. In retrospect, I'd have had to say that the gym was more home to him than the house was.

He put me through my paces, calisthenics, speedbag, heavy bag. We talked while I sweated and ached. He gestured to the bruises on my ribs, "Lucky yer goddamned brother didn't bust one fer ya. Be good fer ya to work out some 'a the sore. Bareknuckle champs used to go fitty roun's an' go back ta work t' nex' day. Good trainin' fer the nex' un." He looked a little sad, though. "'Twon't be too goddamned long before all that shit stops fer good, boy. Yer a better boxer, boy. Ya just are givin' up too much goddamned weight, fer now. A li'l size on ya an' that shit'll come to a screechin' halt."

We talked a little about Donna, and a bit about Mr. Granble. The Chief figured the one for a whore, and the other for a rotten son-of-a-bitch that he ought to set right. I knew that there wasn't any real point in telling him about Donna, but I felt like I just had to share with someone. The only thing I didn't want to share with my peculiar friend was Jeannie. That I was keeping for myself. After my workout, he shooed me off.

"Get healed up, boy. An' go get fed, put some weight on ya, damn yer hide. The onliest thing keepin' ya from bein' able to whup him when he gets ya is size, an' ain't nothin' but time an' eatin' right gonna put that right." With that, he shut the door in my face.

By the sun, I knew it was about four o'clock. High time to get back to the river camp and see about getting Calvin and me some dinner.

Chapter Ten

Two weeks later, my bruises were all gone, the soreness everywhere was all gone, and the slow dignified walk was done with, too. I'd had an active social life, especially compared to the wasteland it had been before that weekend.

I'd seen Jeannie four times, and on two of those occasions, she'd continued my . . . lessons. All of the times we'd talked, and gotten closer through that simple medium as well. I had respect for her that I couldn't have fathomed before. She wasn't at all what I had perceived her to be. We had an odd relationship, I know. We kissed and caressed, but our rapport was that of friends. Sometimes the most complicated things are best understood by the simplest of us. Like a fourteen year old freshman with aspirations ahead and a sixteen year old junior with terror behind.

I had also seen Donna six times. I had tutored her after school for her ratios Mondays, Wednesdays, and Fridays. She'd gotten it after the first Wednesday, but she kept me around to help with the 'funny book' algebra that even the general math classes did, and to talk to about Calvin. The more I got to know her, the better I liked her. She was actually very intelligent, but had no real interest in learning the things that comprised a high school education. She worked hard at the things that she liked, like the gymnastic routines for cheerleading. She had fire, drive, and intelligence in addition to the beauty that had drawn me to her initially.

I'd even gone to see the Chief twice. The first time, he worked me out again, and the second time, after the workout, he started teaching me his other hobby. The Chief made the most beautiful knives I'd ever seen. He had cases and cases of the steel plates he called blanks. He had four or five different grades of stainless blanks, and four different types of high-carbon blanks. The 'mill', as he referred to the little outbuilding, was a smokehouse. He had me working on the grinders, trying to show me how to shape the blank into an aesthetically pleasing as well as functional blade. He whacked me above the ear a few times, complaining that I was much better boxer than knifesmith. But I liked it, and I could tell that I was learning. I knew that the Chief didn't suffer fools, gladly or otherwise, so if he was bothering to correct me, then I must be progressing.

Calvin's repentant attitude had faded before my bruises did, but he was still better to be around than before. He came home tired from basketball practice, and didn't mind sometimes playing checkers or cards with me before bed. Once or twice, we even got Mom to let us deal her in for a game of three-handed rummy. I generally beat Calvin at card games, and he beat me at checkers consistently. But if Mom ever deigned to play with us, either game, she clobbered us.

Mom acted a little put out for the first few days we were back after camping all weekend. She growled at us a little bit for her two strapping young boys to take off all weekend long leaving her with all the chores around the farmstead. But there wasn't any bite behind that particular growl, and I knew it. Her real growl didn't have any complaining to it whatsoever. It was really quiet and short, and barely preceded the teeth. I had worn the switch-welts to prove it. I got the feeling that she knew that something had precipitated the sudden camping trip, but she never asked about it.

We'd gotten grade cards, and I had gotten A's in everything again. Calvin hadn't. He'd gotten an A, two B's, three C's, and a D. The A was in gym. The B's were in home economics and shop. His math, general science, and English courses were the C's. His D was in history. He hated the class. Swore he couldn't understand why 'a bunch of old dead guys in Europe' would be of any interest to an American. Mom just shook her head, and didn't argue with him. She switched him, instead. She never was one to waste words when her actions could talk for her.

All in all, I knew my life was coming together very well. I had a friend in Jeannie, a prospective girlfriend in Donna, a mentor in the Chief, and Calvin and I were getting along better than we had in some time. And I knew that I had the best Momma that any boy had ever had. She was the same as she always was. She cooked, she cleaned, and she took care of our house. She did more with less to work with than anyone I knew.

Mom and I had put up the apple squeezings to make vinegar with. The only cleaning supply that she ever bought was bleach. I figured that was just because nobody had ever told her how to make it. I didn't know yet, but next year I'd take chemistry.

Calvin and I had gone hunting for deer, and we'd gotten one apiece. Calvin's buck was a seven pointer, and would have been eight if he hadn't broken a tine on something. Mine was a three pointer, but thicker through the chest and a bigger deer. I had a shot at the one Calvin got, but I never thought that the antlers were a big deal. I knew you couldn't eat them.

Mom had bragged on both of her hunters. She'd made each of us our favorite venison dishes. Calvin liked slow-roasted tenderloin with Mom's special baste. I liked the garlic-butter fried steaks.

So all was wonderful in my world then in late October, 1963.

Chapter Eleven

Jeannie and I had decided to meet in the barn outside as a 'safe' rendezvous point. It was out of sight and reach of her father, a man I despised more as each day passed. It was also out of sight (and hopefully out of mind) of my brother. For some reason, both of us felt the need to avoid Calvin's notice. It's not that Jeannie had any delusions that she might have been cheating on him. She knew well that it was impossible for someone that was viewed as a convenience item to be unfaithful. I also had no delusions that Calvin would think I'd 'stolen his girl'. Jeannie wasn't his girlfriend, or even his lover. That would imply some love or at least some token possessive feeling. Calvin had no feelings for Jeannie other than enjoyment of what she could give him.

And she had decided to withdraw that from him and the others who had used her in the past. Despite her protestation that the opinion of the town wouldn't change, she had learned that her opinion of herself could. Instead of viewing public opinion as holy writ, she began to believe in what I believed about her. Then, taking it a step further, she began to value herself for what she saw in herself.

"That's the key, Jeannie. What they say doesn't matter. Even what I say shouldn't matter. It's what you think of you, honey." We were laying back on a haybale under a blanket, my arm holding her cuddled against my chest. "But I can tell you what I think and maybe that will help you see the good things about you."

She snuggled in closer and put her arm across my chest. "I've started, Rob. I don't do the stuff wif alla the boys like I used ta. I jus' do them wif ya 'cause I wanna. I'd rather be alone than wif people that make me feel bad."

"Good, Jeannie. If it doesn't make you feel good to kiss me and . . . stuff, then—"

"No, Rob! That ain't what I'm sayin' a'tall! Yer good ta me. Ya don't treat ol' Jeannie like she ain't no more 'count than a hound dog, ta call ta heel when it please ya." She propped up on her elbow and looked in my eyes with a distressed expression.

"I'm glad Jeannie. I'd be lying if I said that wasn't a hard thing to say. I like kissing you and . . . the other stuff. And I like talking to you. I like being able to tell you things that I'm doing without being made fun of. I like hearing about what you're doing. You just finished that book, didn't you?" She'd been reading The Fountainhead, by Ayn Rand.

"Yep. I liked it. Everyone said that the guy was crazy and stupid. But he was just differnt. Had differnt ideas and differnt ways o' doin' stuff." She was not a fast reader, but she was a thorough one. Jeannie read to understand, not just to pass time. We had already talked about what we liked and disliked about Grapes of Wrath and The Great Gatsby. "But that Ayn lady was stupid about that thing he done ta Dominique at the quarry."

I knew what she was talking about. The hero had either raped her or the next thing to it. And because she had been dominated by the man, Dominique fell in love with him. It was uncomfortable for me to talk about with this poor girl who knew more about the subject than I ever could. "I don't think that she really meant it to come across like that, Jeannie. She was trying to make it out like she didn't want to, but she really did. And Roark knew it. So it didn't seem bad to Ayn Rand, I guess."

"But it ain't like that a'tall. It don't make ya love the one doin' it. An' it don't tie yer souls together. It's like they's takin' somethin' good, and usin' it ta hurtcha. Like iffen somebody give ya a purdy dress, but they's ta take an' use it ta choke ya." She couldn't meet my eyes when she talked about it.

"I doubt she really knew what she was talking about, Jeannie." And I hoped I was right.

We talked about the book, and she told me she was starting on Les Miserables. I hadn't read that one yet. I told her about the Chief and how he was teaching me about the knives.

"Will ya make one fer me? A purdy li'l knife?" She looked so childlike and eager, I couldn't help but laugh.

"A pretty one may be beyond my reach just yet, Jeannie. But I'll see if the Chief would let me try." I smiled at her.

"That Chief o' yers . . . I don't know 'bout him. He talks tough an' mean, but sometimes he looks so sad." She looked very speculative.

"He talks tough and mean because he is tough and mean, make no mistake. He's living the way he wants to. He doesn't owe anybody anything. And he's got all the company he wants, which isn't much. Just me, most times." I didn't see why anyone would think the Chief was sad. He was doing just what he wanted to do.

"Maybe. What d' ya talk about?" she asked.

That was a tough one. Did I want to tell her what the Chief said? Would it make her sad to know what he thought about her? Or all women, for that matter? "What do you mean, Jeannie?" I asked back, stalling for time to think.

"Does 'e ever talk about why he ain't got no wife?" Without an outright lie, I couldn't see a way out of it.

"Sometimes, Jeannie. He doesn't want women around to boss him. When he wants to . . . well, he visits Charleston a few times a year for his companionship." I may have started my 'education' as far as women go, but I still blushed a little to talk bluntly in mixed company.

"He goes clean to Charleston ta buy his women? Why? They's plenty 'round here'll give it away." She frowned, puzzling over this.

"He doesn't like to get involved with them, see? He says it's cleaner and more honest that way."

"Reckon a girl hurt 'im pretty bad, don't you?" She looked at me quizzically.

It had never crossed my mind to wonder why the Chief didn't want a wife. I had taken all his statements at face value. Now that Jeannie had mentioned it, I guessed that she was probably right. She still surprised me with her insights. Her point of view was so different, I often hadn't ever thought of looking at an issue from her angle. "Maybe so, Jeannie. That would explain a lot about how he feels about relationships."

"What's 'e think 'bout you an' me bein' friends?" She grinned.

"Doesn't like it much, to tell the truth. Says that women are always trying to get a guy to change. Thinks that you and Donna are nothing but trouble for me." Asked point-blank like that, I didn't have much choice.

"Might be half-right." she said softly, almost too soft for even my ears to hear. I wondered if she meant herself or Donna. "So how's the studyin' goin' with 'er, anyhow?"

"She's doing pretty well in Math now. And her dad's letting her be on the cheerleader squad. Did you know that she's only the third ninth-grader ever to make the squad?" I started bubbling over with information that I didn't want to share with Calvin.

"I reckon you've mentioned that oncet or twicet." she said, a little wryly. "Ya still sneakin' her out ta see Calvin after the games?"

I was. I only had done it twice, though. He had other plans after the other games. They'd gone walking around the river camp once. The other time, Donna had hopped into the back of the truck with Calvin and they'd roared off to a party somewhere. "Just a couple of times, Jeannie. When I see her next, she's glowing. She's just happy to have his attention."

"Best watch it, Rob. Be more'n his 'tention she'll be havin' iffen she ain't lookin' sharp. How'll ya feel 'bout that, iffen it was ta happen?" She wasn't asking to hurt me, wasn't asking to be mean. She was asking out of genuine concern.

"I don't think she'll do that, Jeannie. She's just enjoying being squired around by Calvin Taylor, the athletic high-school hero." I hoped, anyway.

"He won't be payin' much 'tention to her iffen he don't start gettin' what 'e's after, ya know. How'll she feel 'bout that, iffen 'e don't wanna spend no more time 'thout gettin' it?"

"I don't know, Jeannie." I hadn't really thought about all that was going on. It was enough to be near Donna a few times a week. And to have Calvin happy to see her, and not running her down to me.

"Best figure it out, Rob. One way or t'other. 'Cause ol' Jeannie don't think ya got too long to puzzle on it." She looked sad. But then she looked at me, and smiled.

"Maybe you'd like ta not think 'bout it now. Maybe iffen ya had yer druthers, ya'd kiss ol' Jeannie instead." She leaned back down and reclined against the bale of hay with her arm over her head.

I reckon she was right. Kissing her was lots more pleasant than thinking on the things she'd brought up.

Chapter Twelve

Calvin was on his way to breaking the scoring record for McClellan County High's basketball. Eleven years ago, James Jackson scored 1431 points over his four-year career. Midway through his third year, Calvin had 976, and was going strong. He hadn't fouled out all year, was over 85% from the foul line, and wasn't a ball hog, either. He led the team in assists and points scored. He also was second in rebounds, third in blocked shots, and second in stolen balls. He was having a terrific season, and everyone knew it.

Especially Donna. She and I continued to work on her mathematics, and I showed up dutifully to walk her to the games. I carried her duffel bag with her cheerleader outfit and pom-poms for her, and basked in her presence. Tonight was another game, and she was looking forward to visiting the river camp with Calvin afterward. Calvin and I would be staying the night at the camp, and we'd packed our kits to entertain. Calvin brought his guitar, and I had my harmonica. We had marshmallows, graham crackers, and Hershey bars for making s'mores.

I showed up at Donna's right on time, hair combed carefully and shirt tucked in. Her father responded to my knock.

"C'mon in, Bobby! Lookin' sharp, young fella. That girl ain't ready yet. She's gonna change clothes soon as she gets there, but she's gotta look good for her walk to school, I reckon. Typical woman, ain't it? But we wouldn't have 'em any other way, eh?"

"No sir. I sure wouldn't, anyway." I grinned my best young-lad-come-a-courting grin.

"Good enough! Let's have us a little jaw while we wait for her hair to get perfect, Bobby." He suddenly looked serious. "Donna says there's a group of you 'uns gonna go campin' by riverside."

"Yes, sir. That's our plan, anyhow." But why would Donna be telling her father about the river camp?

"I don't know that I'll be lettin' Donna stay out all night thataway. She ain't but fifteen, son. I know yer a smidge younger yet, but fifteen's old enough to get in a helluva spot o' trouble, Bobby." He was speaking gently, yet firmly. "I sure would hate fer her t' end up in any trouble, boy." He kept accenting the word trouble, like he meant something altogether different.

"That's the last thing I'd want for her either, sir." It was. I had no idea where he was going with this.

"Bobby, will you gimme yer word on something?" He looked hard at me. "Somethin' damned important."

"Sir, I don't know if I will or not. I'll listen to what you'll ask, but I don't care to offer promises about things I haven't heard yet." I frowned. This was awfully serious.

"Fair enough, boy. In fact, I think I like yer answer a helluva lot better than an unqualified 'yes.' Bobby, are your intentions with my daughter honorable?"

"Yes sir! Honorable and nothing but!" I was shocked.

He looked at me a long time, just drawing on his cigarette. "I dunno why, boy, but I believe you. I do think you'll keep your word."

He stood and paced around, carefully looking where he was going, hands clasped behind his back. The cigarette perched on his lip blew smoke over his shoulder like a train's exhaust. "Bobby, I'm puttin' a lot of faith in yer reputation an' yer word."

He was? For what? I didn't understand any of this conversation whatsoever.

All of a sudden, his demeanor changed. His soft hillbilly accent disappeared like it had never been. I instantly knew that this was the way he spoke in business, not friendly conversation. He had on his 'lawyer's face'. "Donna asked me to let her go camping with your group after the game. I was firmly opposed to it. I've given a lot of thought to this, young man. I still don't like it. But I also feel that sometimes a leap of faith is required. I will permit this, despite my reservations. Understand, Bobby, I'm putting my trust in your word."

I felt as though a vise were being cranked shut on my chest. "Yes sir. I understand." I knew that I had promised that my intentions were honorable. And they were. I also knew just as well that Calvin's were as far from honorable as it was possible to get.

The courtroom demeanor vanished in a trice. "Alrighty, then, Bobby. Do believe yer gonna be okay. Di'n't mean ta come down all hard on ya." He clapped my shoulder with a big grin. Just then, Donna came down the stairs.

She was radiant. Her hair was up in a French braid, and her cheeks were rosy with excitement. Her full lips looked just ripe for kissing. She was wearing a navy blue skirt that came just past her knees, and a white cardigan sweater over a light blue button-up blouse. The sweater clung delightfully to all the curves of her delectable body. She was smiling, and that perfected the picture. I love her smile.

"Bobby! How're you doin? Did Daddy tell ya? I can come campin' wif yer party!" I noticed that there was a second duffel beside the customary one that I carried to all the games. "Ya gotta have me back of a mornin' 'fore ten, though!" She winked and smiled.

I couldn't help but smile back, though the deception was burning in my stomach like I'd gargled with battery acid instead of Listerine. Her smile is infectious, and contagious. Contagious because it makes you smile back, no matter how you feel. Infectious because once the bug's bitten you, there's not any recovery.

"Ya ready ta go, Bobby?" She thrust her arm out for me to take, and I scooped the handles of the duffels with my right hand. "Ain't he a gentleman, Poppa?"

"I hope so, girl. You two have ya a good time, and be careful now, y'hear?" He looked so serious and worried that I wished I could reassure him more . . . but that wouldn't be fair, either. He had good enough reason to be edgy.

Donna and I walked arm in arm up the street to the high school gym. She and I talked lightly of the upcoming game, and how her math scores had improved. I ushered her to the locker room and handed her the duffel with her cheerleader paraphernalia. She took it with a smile, and leaned over and kissed my cheek right in front of the other girls.

I blushed, not with embarrassment, but pride. I carried the other duffel over to the bleachers to watch my brother warm up.

Calvin was shooting shots above the key, keeping three balls in rotation, one in the air towards the basket, one being bounced to him, one being retrieved by the benchwarmer freshmen. He hit about four out of five, even at this pace. He looked utterly at ease, ensconced in his element. A natural athlete, he made it look effortless. And for him, it was. He practiced just because he enjoyed it, not because he needed to work at it. He saw me, and paused long enough to wave and grin.

I waved back, and smiled. I found a seat fairly near the front, where I could watch Calvin and Donna excel in their chosen areas. I spotted Jack Thompson, the boy Calvin generally managed to bump into on the bus, sitting a few rows up. I waved at him, and he gave a half-hearted wave back. I wished I could see Jeannie, but we both knew that if Cal saw us sitting together at the games, he'd give us both a hard time. She also cast some doubts as to whether Donna would like it. I knew that Jeannie was just a friend, and that Donna would understand. Jeannie wasn't convinced, and persuaded me to not let the subject come up.

The cheerleaders came bounding out of the locker room, cartwheeling and tumbling as they came. The other five girl's gymnastics seemed abbreviated after Donna started. Handsprings, cartwheels, back handsprings and finishing up with that back flip, fully extended. She was poetry in motion. She landed, and leapt up immediately into a split in the air, touching her toes and landing again. She clapped and cheered, and the rest of the girls with her.

Calvin tipped her a jaunty salute, and she grinned like he'd just sent her a thousand long-stemmed roses. She waved back at him, and he smiled a little too. Then he turned back to the team. Donna gave me a wave and shook her pompoms at me. I laughed.

And so the game went. Calvin scored thirty-eight points, had eleven rebounds, four steals, and a record seven blocked shots. I hated playing team sports, but I sure liked watching my big brother do it. He was something to see. Donna flipped, cheered, and was the top member of the pyramid that the cheerleaders did at halftime. I believe we might have won the game, too.

Chapter Thirteen

The showers were over, and Calvin came piling out of the locker room, evidently still full of energy, since he was horsing around with the other players. Most of the fans had already left, and there were only a few of us waiting, mostly parents and friends of the team. Donna had finished up in the girl's locker room about ten minutes ago. She sat next to me on the bleachers, quiet and full of anticipation. I liked watching her, excited as a kid on Christmas.

I wondered idly how many people Donna had told her father were going to be at our little camping party. I wondered if Jeannie would show up, too. I had deliberately placed a great deal of room between Calvin's tent and the tarp that I used. The pine boughs I used for a screen at the back were woven tightly, and I'd even gathered all the remaining snow for a windbreak . . . and a way to break up sight line between the shelters. If Jeannie did come to the campsite, she'd be able to slip in and out without attracting Calvin's notice. Or Donna's either, for that matter.

When Calvin came over, he threw his arm over Donna's shoulder familiarly, and said, "Y'un's ready ta go?" He waggled his eyebrows at Donna like he had really made a witty double-entendre.

Donna just smiled and nodded, standing up. I sighed, and did the same. I enjoyed Calvin's company, even when he was being mean. Likewise, I loved spending time with Donna, and just absolutely rolled around in her attention, but I hated spending time with her and Calvin together. She became a different person, almost. She was a dynamic and enthusiastic conversationalist when she talked to me. Donna was confident, warm, and independent. She was a wonderful person, infatuation aside. Even if she hadn't been gorgeous, I would have been smitten.

But when she got around Calvin, it was as though another personality emerged from storage. She was meek and quiet, doting and subservient. Her smile was even different. I knew what I felt, despite not having the words then to express the sentiment: Donna was charmed, not in the sense of the social atmosphere, but in the manner a malignant sorcerer might have desired.

As we walked together, me leading the way by about twenty yards, I pondered not only what I thought, but what Jeannie had said. How was I feeling? My introspection deflated me a bit, because I discovered that I was depressed about how well Calvin and Donna got on. Of course, I wasn't surprised to realize that I really did love Donna. It may sound like an adolescent crush, but even in later years, I knew that I loved her even then. So what of the rest of what Jeannie had said? What would I feel if Calvin hurt her, as I knew he was bound to? What if I was wrong and he didn't hurt her, but they went on, happy together? What was I hoping for?

I was disgusted with myself for one of the scenarios that popped into my traitorous head. What if she fell into my comforting arms after Calvin broke her heart? I could make her whole again with the strength of my love. Sure, I liked the end result. But how willing was I for her to have to bear pain in order for me to achieve my ends? Not very, I discovered. I might fantasize about the results, but the path that needed to be traveled to get to the destination was too unpalatable for even my traitor imagination to enjoy.

I found to my surprise that I was still the one carrying Donna's duffels. Upon further reflection, I wondered if that was intentional on Calvin's part. With me to fetch and carry, it freed up his hands. With his hands free and me walking ahead like a medieval footman, he could be exploring Donna's lovely curves and caressing her body the entire time we were walking to the camp. I gritted my teeth and went on walking.

On the other hand, when she saw my brother, she absolutely glowed. She was as in love with him as I was with her. So what did that make me, for resenting it? I needed to grow up, I chided myself. If being with Calvin made her feel like being with her made me feel . . . I needed to accept that. Loving her as much as I did, it wasn't too much of a stretch for me to not only accept it, but to relish her joy in him. Seeing her so happy was worth the pain to me that it wasn't me that elated her so.

Having thought all the things that Jeannie had asked me about through, I wished I had her to talk to about them. She hadn't been at the game at all. Not unusual, really. Since she'd started to get her self-respect back, she hadn't been nearly as 'popular' as she had been before. Her offers of 'dates' had dried up, and there weren't new swells in the ranks, since her reputation among those who hadn't ascertained the new Jeannie was still that of the old Jeannie. Unfair, I thought, but about standard for human interaction. People pretend to be civilized, but their social behavior is as cannibalistic as the most primitive tribes. Civilization is just a veneer, and a spotty and thin one at that.

I arrived at the camp and heard Donna and Calvin still behind me about thirty yards or so. I started lighting the fire that I had laid out earlier in the afternoon. When the tinder caught well, I started plundering through the sack to accumulate the construction materials for our camp treats.

To start with, we needed to toast the giant marshmallows. I had also laid out the sticks for toasting them in the afternoon, so it was the work of a few seconds to spear the confections and sit to wait for the fire to get ready for me. Donna and Calvin were moving very slowly, but still moving toward the camp. They were lots less noisy than a drunken Cal and supporting Jeannie, but they still made enough noise for me to track their progress fairly well. I wondered why they were moving to the camp so slow.

The fire was going fairly well, and I had the first three s'mores assembled with precision before they arrived. Toasted to perfection for s'mores is a matter of personal preference, like most camp cooking. For Cal, the marshmallow is to be lightly browned all around, without a trace of blackening at all. For me, I preferred them to resemble lumps of coal, just about dripping off of the stick.

I'd made Calvin's s'more exactly and perfectly—graham cracker topped with four squares of the Hershey bar, undivided. Then the lightly browned marshmallow, topped with the graham cracker, mashed evenly but not to the point of forcing marshmallow over the edge of the bottom cracker. Mine was a little rough—dripping marshmallow protruded, but that was to be expected with a charred marshmallow.

Not knowing how Donna liked hers, I went ahead and made hers like Cal's. I went ahead and started to toast the next batch. S'mores were a rare treat for Calvin and me, mainly because the ingredients were all store-bought. We always had plenty to eat, and a roof over our heads, but we were cash-poor. To eat as well as we ate would have been an expensive proposition if all the food had come from a grocery, but familiarity had bred contempt. To eat store-bought was a special occasion.

They were giggling and playing as they collapsed together in a heap, directly across the fire from me. Donna's face was flushed, and her hair and clothes were mussed already. I quashed the feelings of resentment and concentrated on enjoying her enjoyment. Calvin produced a pint Mason jar that seemed to be half-empty already. I had a sinking feeling that it was more of Riley's finest. I wondered why there was only a pint, instead of the usual quart that Calvin bought. But I decided that was probably for the best, after all. With just a pint, Calvin wouldn't get so hung over the next morning. He wouldn't get so mischievous and capricious as he had the night he'd slung Jeannie's clothes out of the tent.

But I soon saw that I'd misjudged the circumstances rather badly.

Calvin wasn't drinking any of the moonshine.

Chapter Fourteen

Donna's voice got louder as the night went on. Calvin was meting the white lightning out to her at a carefully measured pace, evidently dosing for optimum effect without unconsciousness. She was weaving and smiling, laughing and cuddling closer to Calvin. I waited until she got up giggling to sneak off and do the necessary.

"Calvin, what are you doing?"

"What's it look like, li'l brother? Jest consider it lubrication, kid. Ain't hurtin' her any, an' ya can see I ain't perzackly pourin' it down 'er throat."

I knew he was right. Donna was taking the jar from him anytime he'd let her. It was just . . . unsporting, I guess. I didn't feel like he was playing fair with her. The deck was already stacked against her, with him being two years older and a sports hero. Not to mention all the experience Calvin had 'wooing' women. She wasn't experienced enough to understand that he didn't really care about her, and wouldn't thank me for telling her either. "Maybe not, Calvin, but how about not giving her any more of it? Because I asked, if for no other reason."

"Jest fer you, li'l brother!" Calvin tipped me a wink, and tipped the jar back, finishing the last inch in the bottom. I didn't feel like he'd conceded much of his ill-gotten advantage.

"Thanks, Calvin." I was itching to ask him not to take advantage of Donna. But I knew already from the way she was leaning into him and kissing him deeply that he'd be able to argue that point. If she wanted him, what kind of fool would turn her down? I wished I could talk him out of it.

"No problem, Bobby-boy. Ya wanna go fer a walk when she gets back? Maybe a couple of hours. I'll take good care of 'er, boy. Doncha worry 'bout nothin'." Calvin leered knowingly.

I couldn't stand it. I knew what was going to happen if I left. The only thing that let me leave anyway was knowing it would happen if I stayed too. I decided to talk to Jeannie if I could get to her house.

I knew it was only a couple of miles away, and that Mr. Riley would be out at his still whooping it up. I started out through the woods, picking up a stick for a staff. Well, okay, to whop on all the greenery, taking out my anger at Calvin on the foliage.

It didn't take very long before I saw Jeannie's house in the clearing. Her room was the one at the far end. I began working my way quietly towards her window.

I gathered up a handful of stones and tossed them against her shutters. She opened them almost immediately. "Robert?" she asked.

"Yes. I'm here." I moved closer, since she wouldn't have made a sound if her father had been in the house.

"Help me out, Robert." She held her arms out and I lifted her out as smoothly as I could. She was already dressed in a heavy sweater and a sheepskin jacket, wool-lined.

"I've got the camp set up, Jeannie. The tents are far apart, and there's a snow windbreak in front of it. Do you want to get out of the house tonight?" I figured that she did. Mr. Riley drank heavily throughout the week, but Friday night he really outdid himself.

"I guess so, Robert. It's not as though I got anywheres else ta go." She smiled wryly. "An' I reckon ya know I's ready an' waitin' fer ya ta come. Don't gotta pertend that I wasn't wantin' ta see ya."

"I wanted to see you too, Jeannie. And I guess I needed to see you too. Cal's getting Donna drunk, Jeannie." I desperately wanted her to say something that would make everything all better.

"Reckon he needs ta do that?" She looked skeptical. "From what I've seen, Robert, that brother of yours might as well be importin' coal. She's his fer the askin' already."

I turned away, grief-stricken. I knew it, and she knew I did. But I wanted to hear something different. I didn't know what I was wanting from her, but I knew what it wasn't.

"Robert," her voice was quiet and gentle. Her hand touched my shoulder and gently turned me to face her. "Robert, ya knew she might, right? That she really loves 'im?"

"But he doesn't love her, Jeannie!" I protested.

"She don't know that, does she? An' there ain't no tellin' her anyhow.

An' if yer tryin' to stop Calvin from bein' with 'er, reckon he's had time already to get what he wants, doncha?" She hugged me close. "I'm sorry, Robert. I know t'ain't whatcha would have wanted. But ain't no cure fer it, neither. You'll be there fer her, though. You'll be there long after Cal's cast 'er off, woncha? You'll have me fer a friend ta lean on, too." She hugged me down to her shoulder. That should have made me feel ridiculous, since I was so much taller than she was. It was comforting, though. I wrapped my arms around her waist and squeezed.

"C'mon, boy. Take me to yer tent and we'll talk. I wanna be gone when Daddy gets back from the still." She led me by the hand like a child.

"Jeannie, I don't know what to say or do, but just being around you makes me feel better." I still felt crushed, but not like the world was ending.

"I know, Robert. Sometimes the onliest' thing in the world that helps is havin' somebody ta be miserable with." She squeezed my hand. We walked back to the camp quietly.

Cal's tent was dark and quiet, and I stacked a few pieces of wood on the embers so that the fire would be good and hot in the morning. Jeannie went straight to the tent, and I knew she had to have noticed the little secret I'd learned.

When I went over to our shelter, she was grinning. "Where'd ya trick ta that?"

I grinned back. "Mr. Horswood told me to try it. Said he'd learned it in the army." I decided to leave the candle burning. It's amazing how much heat just a simple candle gives off. Enough that we couldn't see our breath in the tent, anyway. Jeannie snuggled close to me.

"Lay yer head on m' shoulder, Robert. I know I cain't be her. I ain't the same thing ta ya as she is. An' I ain't sure that I'd wanna be. You're a good boy, Rob. An' I reckon you'll get to be a good man. I'm glad of ya bein' my friend. An' I'm proud ta be yourn. I want ya ta have what ya want. An' iffen that's Donna, I'm hopin' you'll have her. But I'd want ya ta think on it hard, Rob. She ain't never gonna feel about ya like you do fer her." A lone tear trickled down her cheek.

"I hope ya can live with that, Robert. Iffen I had the sight, I'd say fer sure. But I can jest give ya a guess. You'll end up with her oncet Calvin's done. She'll love you, one of these days. But you ain't Calvin, and she's got her heart set on him. Don't matter that you're better'n him. Not to her. She's not a bad person, Robert. But she loves him the same way you're lovin' her. An' love like that ain't somethin' that turns off fer nothin' nor nobody."

I didn't know what to say to her speech. I did know that she wanted me to hold her. And I knew that I wanted to be held. Sometimes, it's best just to stick to the things you're sure of. So we held each other.

Chapter Fifteen

The morning came, and as the sun crept up, Jeannie kissed me gently. We hadn't talked much, but we'd communicated silently. "I'd better go, Rob. Don't let Calvin see it hurts ya ta see 'em like that. He cain't help himself. He'll rub it in." She kissed me again, and slipped out of the tent and through the woods quietly as a nymph.

I stoked the fire up, and looked through our packs to see what I wanted to make for breakfast. I decided that French toast was fancy enough camp cooking for anybody. Even Donna. First, I put the frying pan over the fire to heat up, and then I cracked the eggs into a bowl, whipped them with a fork, and set the bread and bowl in my tent to heat up a little. I thought that the bread was too close to frozen to take the batter well. I plundered out our hunk of bacon and started slicing it into strips. The rich odor of frying bacon should bring my brother and Donna out of the tent.

I fried the bacon carefully, liking the pieces flat and uniformly cooked. This was one of the main reasons I took over the job of camp-cook. Calvin threw the slices of bacon in hurly-burly and slopped them around with a fork. This invariably led to the tails of the bacon being underdone to my taste, and too dark in the middle. Not to mention the fact that it was a mess to serve and eat when the bacon was a ball of strips that way.

I was right. The tent flap opened and Calvin came out in a fine mood. He was smiling, even. I didn't realize what was different about this morning at first, and kept feeling uncomfortable, like my fly was unbuttoned. Then I grasped that it was Calvin's smile. Normally he was too hung over to even consider a grin when we'd spent the night at our camp. Evidently, he'd only had the one swallow of moonshine last night.

"Mornin' li'l Bobby! Bacon smells damned good, kid. What else'r ya puttin' together for chow?" He was definitely in a fine mood.

"I planned on French toast instead of eggs and toast. Don't have any sorghum or honey, but it should go down pretty well anyway." I ached to ask if Donna was still in the tent, and if she was all right. "Donna didn't get sick last night on all that moonshine, did she?"

"Nary a bit of it, Bobby-boy. Jest a li'l bit friendlier." He laughed. "She's a fine 'un, boy. Hot-blooded an' eager ta please. I'm glad ya put me on 'er trail." He clapped me on the shoulder, and moved to warm his hands at the fire.

I hoped he couldn't see the tension in my shoulders as I struggled to restrain myself. I had the urge to find out if he could still land those slow but heavy haymakers since the Chief had been working with me on footwork and slipping punches. I was amazed at the ferocity of my internal thoughts. I hadn't imagined how badly the situation would enrage me. I finally swallowed my fury and was able to look at Calvin again.

"I didn't do it for you, Calvin. She really cares about you, you know.

I wanted her to get what she wanted," I said, rather coldly.

"She did, young buck. She got jest what she wanted." Calvin tipped a wink with his pronouncement. Luckily, (though to this day I still don't know which of us the lucky one was) he rose to walk to the woodline and urinate.

I pondered while I made more bacon. I decided that I needed to see how Donna was reacting before I went off half-cocked. Just because I felt that she'd been tricked, seduced, lied to, and taken advantage of, didn't mean that she wasn't happy with it. Maybe she even went into this thing with her eyes open. It wasn't for me to judge. I calmed down and decided to reserve judgment.

Just then, Donna opened the tent flap, and came out, bouncy as if she was still cheering. She was wearing one of Calvin's heavy sweaters, and looked much better in it than he ever did. Her hair was disheveled, and her eyes were a little puffy from sleep and alcohol. She looked beautiful.

"Mornin', Bobby! Yer bacon smells delicious! Where's Calvin?" She graced me with that smile, and I melted. I just pointed to where Calvin stood, back to us, finishing up his morning necessary.

She giggled. "T'ain't very polite, is it? Betcha wouldn't go doin' that in front of a girl thataway, would ya?"

I sensed a bit of condescension in her voice, like I was being accused of Puritanism. "I don't guess I would, Donna. Seems pretty low-rent to me." Of course, when Calvin had started, she hadn't come out of the tent.

"Bobby, I wanna thank ya. Without yer help, me 'n' Cal couldn't never've gotten together. My daddy don't like him. He likes you though. An' it's all because a' you that Calvin can court me." She looked at me so touched and sentimental. She honestly thought that Calvin was courting her. I couldn't tell her that she was wrong. And I didn't even want to think about what the proper name for what Calvin was doing to her was. I just smiled and nodded, not trusting myself to speak. There was no telling what truths might slither past my lips if they weren't guarded carefully.

Calvin slowly returned to the campfire, smiling the entire time. I thought that perhaps I was misjudging him, that maybe Donna was special to him. It wasn't inconceivable that he just didn't know how to express it, especially to his little brother. It didn't fit in with the tough guy image to care about women, or their feelings. He sat down beside her and threw his arm over her shoulders casually.

"Donna, ya ain't et 'til you've et one a' Bobby's camp breakfasts. 'E makes French toast good as Ma does." I exulted in the compliment. Calvin didn't say things like that, usually.

"I'm lookin' forward ta tryin' it. The bacon smells better'n any I ever smelt." She was pointing one of her dangerous smiles at me.

"Me 'n' Bobby butchered that there bacon out ourselfs. Weren't the best we ever done, but we got a pretty good renderin' out'n that hog." Calvin enjoyed the fall slaughter, and was proud of dressing out our own meat.

"Ya mean you two kilt that pig with yer own hands?" Donna looked aghast.

"'Course we did, girl." Calvin looked amused.

"That's jest awful! How couldja kill an animal that ya fed and petted and took keer of thataway?" She was truly appalled.

"Don't be stupid, girl. 'S a damned pig. So what? Where'd ya think all that meat inna grocery come from?" Calvin was starting to get vexed.

"But ta kill it thataway . . . don't seem right." Her grey eyes brimmed with tears. "An' to jest sit here an' cook it like it ain't nothin'. I don't want no bacon, Bobby."

"Donna, yer actin' like a half-wit! Ain't she, Bobby?" Calvin was feeling truculent about her rejection of the meat he'd valiantly butchered.

"Doesn't matter to me, Calvin. If she doesn't want to eat the bacon, then there'll be plenty of French toast." I really tried to make things smooth again.

"Well, girl? Er is that bad fer killin' the chicken that might 'a' growed out of the goddam egg?" Calvin sneered.

"I ain't tryin' ta make nobody mad, I jest don't wanna eat bacon. French toast sounds real good, Bobby." She was looking at me for help, despair in her eyes for provoking my brother.

"Calvin, it's all right. Don't worry about it." I tried, but I guess my armor wasn't shiny enough to dazzle Calvin.

"Bullshit, girl. And bullshit ta you, too, Bobby Taylor. Ain't no sense in stickin' up fer someone wif a bunch 'a' stupid idears like not killin' pigs to get meat." Calvin grabbed a handful of bacon strips and crunched into them noisily, daring her to say something.

And I had to admit, despite how nastily he was putting it, Calvin did have a point. But he wasn't taking into account how tenderhearted Donna was. She was a gentle soul, and didn't like the idea of killing the pig. So? I knew the only reason that it was a problem all of a sudden was that Calvin had forced her to acknowledge where the food she ate came from. She was a town girl, and sufficiently divorced from the food chain to be able to think of meat as something that originated in a grocery. Far from angering me, I thought it was endearing. Tenderhearted little Donna.

Donna's eyes began to tear over, and I couldn't help it. "Calvin, leave her alone. She doesn't have to eat the damned bacon if she doesn't want. And nobody's asking you to not eat it. Let her be," I said.

Calvin laughed. "You sissy. Tryin' ta defend 'er from me. Wantin' ta be her hero." He was right. That's exactly what I was doing. And exactly what I was wanting. "Watch this, Bobby. Hey Donna?"

She lifted her reddened eyes to look at him.

"Donna, iffen ya don't eat that goddam bacon an' thank me for killin' that pig, an' then thank Bobby fer cookin' it, I ain't gonna let you come out with me no more. I'll quit seein' ya, an' what we done last night'll be the last o' that ya get from me." He looked at me, cruel and hard. I didn't know if he was doing this to hurt me or her, but I wasn't having any of it.

I leaped to my feet, ready to go another round with him. For the girl I was in love with, again. But Donna cried out and jumped in between us.

"Bobby, no! Calvin, I'm sorry. I'll eat the bacon. Gimme a piece, please?" Her voice had a pleading tone that was so at odds with what I knew of her character! "Thank ya fer killin' the pig, Calvin. An' Bobby, I 'preciate yer cookin' it. Told ya how good it smelt. Thank ya, boys." She grabbed the piece of bacon out of Calvin's gloating hand like a drowning woman clutching a rope.

As she ate the bacon hurriedly, I noticed her stifling gags. I had to turn away from it. I knew just how she felt.

Chapter Sixteen

Later that morning, after the disastrous breakfast was finally over, Donna and I started back towards town. I had promised her father to have her back before ten. We should be making that deadline with at least an hour to spare. We were walking, and I didn't intend to hitchhike at all, to savor every moment of her company.

Calvin had kissed her thoroughly and deeply before relinquishing her to my company. He looked at me afterward with a look of smug satisfaction on his face. I still didn't know why he'd perpetuated the entire incident over the bacon. Granted, he'd always been proud of his role in providing for the family, but the episode had to go much deeper than that—his reaction was wholly and irrationally out of proportion.

"Donna, are you okay?" I didn't know how to start.

"I'm fine, Bobby. I jest didn't wanna eat that bacon after I heard y'all had killed the pig yerself. I know it's funny—I eat bacon alla time an' never thought nothin' of it. Somethin' about that bacon comin' from a pig ya'd knowed and fed and raised yerself . . . don't make no sense a'tall." She seemed apologetic for her squeamishness.

"Donna, honey, there's no reason to be sorry. You shouldn't feel bad for not wanting to eat something like a silly piece of bacon. I'm the one that's sorry. I shouldn't have made you feel like you had to eat it." I really couldn't understand why she'd jumped up and grabbed the slice from Calvin.

"I dunno why . . . but all of a sudden, 'twas like I didn't have no choice. I didn't want Calvin angry at me. An' I didn't want you and him gettin' into a fight about some dumb ol' bacon. I was afeard 'e might hurt ya, Bobby. I know he'd be sorry later, but he'd do it in the here-an'-now an' never be able ta stop hisself." She reached out and took my hand as we were walking. "I didn't want ya hurt, neither, Bobby. Yer a fine fella, an' the sweetest boy I know."

"Thanks, Donna. I would've whipped him or died trying if it would have stopped you from having to eat that stuff. I could tell that the idea of it was making you sick." As I watched, she slowly dropped my hand, and turned to the ditch running behind the road. Her hands dropped to her knees, and she vomited violently. Not knowing whether to comfort her or to pretend I didn't notice, I opted to comfort her. I didn't feel that pretending oblivion was a very credible reaction. I put my hand on her shoulder, and said, "It's okay, Donna. Let it out, honey."

She did. I couldn't believe that such a petite girl could have eaten enough to expel that much. She seemed to bring up everything that she'd eaten in the past week. I pondered whether the throwing up had more to do with the liquor purging from her system or the eating of the bacon. I offered her a handkerchief to wipe her mouth with when she was done. I wished I had something to offer her to get the taste out of her mouth.

"Thank ya, Bobby. Yer awful good ta me. Ya wanna stick 'a' gum?" Miraculously, she offered a stick of Wrigley's out of her sweater pocket. I checked carefully to see that she had at least two before I accepted it. Gum was a rare treat indeed! I wondered idly where she'd gotten it.

"Cal give it to me last night. Said I'd be wantin' it fer gettin' the mornin' taste outta my mouth. Shore need it now! The stick I ate up afore breakfus' ain't doin' a bit 'a good now." She fingered the empty packet, and carefully folded it and stowed it back in her pocket.

Calvin giving her the gum was an odd commentary on him, to my way of thinking. Getting her drunk and probably taking advantage of her was deplorable. Yet he gave her a fairly thoughtful and valued gift. Calvin had always had a sweet tooth, and giving her the gum was an astonishingly noble gesture on his part. Calvin had always had a sweet tooth, so it wasn't that he didn't want the gum. I imagined that he probably stole it, but the action of giving it to her was no less gracious for that.

"Donna, did Calvin hurt you or anything?" It was the closest I could come to asking if he'd taken advantage of her. I wanted to know, and I wanted to help, if there was anything I could do. At the same time, I didn't want to know, and would have done anything to stay ignorant.

However, it didn't look like it was anything that Donna was ashamed of. Or even that Calvin had taken advantage of her, despite his evident intentions. "Hurt me? Jest a little bit, but they all say it does the first time." Her eyes were wide and innocent looking. "He was as gentle wif me as could be."

Curiously, her face registered pride, as though she'd achieved something remarkable.

I had no idea what to say, and spluttered and stammered. She laughed and looked very cosmopolitan and sophisticated. Such a direct turnaround from the naiveté of a few moments before! "He didn't use the liquor ta make me, Bobby. I wanted to. I love 'im, and I wanna marry 'im. I know I'm young yet, but in a few years, I reckon we can."

I couldn't believe what I was hearing. She had gone into this aware of what he'd wanted . . . it was as if I found that the world was suddenly flat. "Donna, you want to marry Calvin?" It was the only thing that she had said that I felt capable of responding to.

"Sure do. But I'm real fond 'a you too, Bobby. Yer the best friend a gal ever had. I couldn't've ever gotten to be with Calvin if it weren't fer ya. You'll be the best brother-in-law!" She looked like she was absolutely floating, living a dream.

"Does Calvin know this?" I couldn't imagine Calvin married to anyone, never mind this angel.

"I tole 'im last night. He smiled an' laughed and said he loved it. Said I'd make a fine wife, an' was the purdiest gal in Folsom Hollow." She puffed a bit with pride.

Smiled and laughed. Said he loved it. I'll bet he did. But she was the prettiest girl in Folsom Hollow. "Donna, I sure hope things work out the way you want them to."

"They will, Bobby. Now that me'n Cal are together things cain't help but be perfect!" She threw her arms around my neck and hugged me tight. She laughed.

didn't have much else to say to that. We walked along the road, hand in hand. She felt very friendly and loving towards me. Not exactly what I wanted, but I guess it was as good a start as any. She knew I was there to defend her, even if we both thought it would cost me a beating. Did she know how I felt about her? Should I tell her? I only knew one person that I could talk to about it and get an honest answer. Calvin would laugh at me and mock me. The Chief would scorn me for taking women seriously enough to have a real relationship with them. Mom was . . . my mother. A boy just can't talk about women and his feelings and things like that with his mother.

Jeannie was the only person in the entire world that I could talk to about it.

Chapter Seventeen

After I dropped Donna off at her house and waved cheerfully at her father, I headed back up towards the Riley place. I hoped that Mr. Riley was occupied with his hangover this morning and not out and active with his old double barrel. Feeling much more exposed in the daylight than when I'd made this very trip last night, I hung closer to the treeline. I scooped the pebbles again, and launched them against Jeannie's refastened shutters. They didn't fly open this time, though, so I needed to scout further around the cabin.

The kitchen window was unshuttered to let light in, and I saw Jeannie at the sink, washing dishes. A shrill whistle made her look up and display her crooked grin. She waved me in, thereby letting me know that her father must be out on an errand or at least conducting his disreputable mischief elsewhere. I stuck my head in the door. "Hey, Jeannie!" I whispered.

"It's okay, Rob. Dad's gone inta town ta get more yeast." She seemed very happy to see me, and I wondered if she'd been okay since she'd left camp early that morning.

"How are you doing, Jeannie? It's good to see you. I missed you even though it's only been a few hours." It was addicting, having a friend. Until I had one, I never realized how much I needed one.

Her eyes looked misty and soft there for a minute. "I missed you too, Rob," she almost whispered. "How'd things go arfter I left?" she asked, in a little louder voice.

"Not so good. Calvin made a scene because Donna didn't want to eat the bacon."

"Why didn't she wanna eat it? Yer a fine cook. Not like Calvin—iffen he'd a' made it, I'd understand completely. Raw ends and burnt middle. Don't give a body a good feelin' when ya know alla them diseases ya can get from undercooked pork." Jeannie looked inquisitive.

"Something about the fact that Cal and I had killed and butchered the hog made her queasy about eating it." That was the only way I could think of to explain it.

Jeannie's nose wrinkled like a curious rabbit. "So? Somebody's gotta kill 'em iffen they're gonna get eat."

"I don't understand why, but at least I understood what. Calvin got nasty with her and made her feel like she had to eat it." I didn't want to tell Jeannie that I almost got into another fight with Calvin after she'd left.

"Sounds silly ta me. Don't matter, though. He shouldn't 'a made her do it." She finished up her last dish and set it in the strainer to dry. "What say we go fer a walk an' get outta here 'afore Daddy gets back? We can talk out there."

Jeannie and I walked through the woods to the barn, and nestled into the hayloft, sharing our body heat under a blanket. It felt good to be with someone who I could trust and talk to . . . not to mention the cuddling and 'lessons' that she was giving me.

"I think Cal might like her some, really. She told me that Calvin gave her a pack of gum to get the morning-after taste out of her mouth," I said.

She raised a suspicious eyebrow, and looked like she might have been stifling a laugh about something. "He did, did 'e? 'Taint much like 'im, is it? Calvin ain't much on givin' what he ain't gotta give ta get what 'e wants. Maybe he really do like 'er then. Then what, Rob? Where's that leave ya?"

"She also told me that she and Calvin . . . " I didn't know quite how to finish, but fortunately Jeannie was used to my shyness.

"They did? Cain't say it s'prises me none. She wanted 'im; time'll tell iffen she's happy wif what she got. How're ya feelin' 'bout it?" She leaned back a little to be able to see my face clearly. She could tell a lot from looking at me while I talked. Sometimes more than I liked.

"I thought that he was taking advantage of her with the liquor, but she said that he didn't. Said that it was what she wanted. I didn't know what to think of that. And I also didn't know how to react to the fact that she said that she wanted to marry Calvin. I don't think Calvin's planning on any such thing, Jeannie." I hoped I kept my tone neutral and my face straight.

She eyed my face speculatively. "Yer still hopin' that she's gonna fall fer ya, ain't ya? I dunno iffen that's gonna happen, Rob. She's pretty daffy fer Calvin. Maybe even daffier fer 'im than you are fer her." All of a sudden, she looked a little sad, and bit her bottom lip with her crooked teeth.

"What's wrong, Jeannie?" I pulled her head over to rest in the crook of my shoulder.

"Nothin', Rob. Nothin' important." She snuggled in tight. "What if she don't never come 'round, and stays hooked on Calvin? What're ya gonna do then, Rob?"

I loved the way that she called me Rob, instead of Bobby, or even Bob. It seemed more manly and special somehow. I wondered how it might sound coming out of Donna's mouth. "I don't know, Jeannie. What could I do? She's the only girl I've ever wanted, ever since second grade. Back when you were still in third grade, wearing gingham and sporting pigtails."

She nipped her bottom lip a little tighter, then released it to talk. "They's other girls out there, Rob. Not maybe as beautiful on the outside, but they'd prob'ly appreciate ya more. Girls that didn't think that Cal walked on water because he can thow a ball. Ya might do better ta look at some 'a them iffen what ya wanted was ta be loved back the way ya can love."

"Being loved back isn't nearly as important as loving, Jeannie. As near as I can tell, the giving of love is more for the sake of the giver than for the recipient. It makes me feel good to love her, Jeannie. I'd feel even better if she loved me back that way, but just to love her is enough. Ayn Rand was wrong about that part, you know. She acted like love was about fair trade too. Love isn't about a trade; it's about a gift. If it's a conditional gift, dependent on getting a gift of like kind in return, then it can't be true love.

Love's only real if it's given freely, and for the sake of the giver, I think."

"I know that's right." she whispered, almost too soft for me to hear. "Loving's definitely more for the giver. You cain't help it, can ya, Rob? You cain't help loving who ya love. An' it don't matter iffen they don't love ya back, I guess. Lovin' 'em means that ya love 'em even iffen they don't love ya, sometimes, right?" She looked at me with wide eyes, and I just nodded.

"Sometimes yer a wise ol' soul, Robert Taylor. And sometimes ya jest don't understand what ya don't understand. Yer too right 'bout that thing about lovin'." She sighed, then snuggled into my shoulder again, and wouldn't say any more about it.

We cuddled and kissed and played gently and lovingly with each other all afternoon. Sometimes I tried to talk some more about what she meant, but she would have none of it.

"Time enough ta talk a' that later. Fer now, I just wanna feel ya close ta me and bein' lovin' towards ol' Jeannie. Iffen it cain't be love, sometimes bein' lovin' is enough, remember?"

Those are simple words, and a simple sentiment, but it was the greatest truth of Jeannie's life. It was some years before I understood what that statement meant to her in all its particulars.

Chapter Eighteen

Time passed, as time tends to do. Basketball season ended, and Christmas came.

I made Jeannie's little knife for her, though its "purdiness" was debatable. A small skinner, it had a short triangular blade of high-carbon steel, and the hilt was a simple piece of lightly curved rosewood, without cross guard. Simple work, the Chief had told me, but nothing to be ashamed of. My next project was to be a bit more challenging. He wanted me to make a hunting knife that was a tough grind indeed.

I'd made Calvin a gun rack so he could hang up the rifle and shotgun in our room. For Mom, I'd made a spice rack in shop class. For the Chief, Jeannie had pinched me a quart jar of Riley's finest. For Donna, I'd managed to save up money to buy her a small bottle of the fancy perfume in the drugstore. My heart triphammered when I gave her my carefully wrapped package.

She'd laughed delightedly and kissed my cheek, flinging her arms around my neck. She had gotten me a book about mountain men and the ways they had lived. I was tickled. Of course, she had probably picked out the book with a ruler, knowing how much I loved reading. There was no doubt, it was the thickest book I'd seen, besides dictionaries or encyclopedias at school.

Calvin gave me a speedbag he'd made from pigskin he'd tanned himself. I was amazed. This was several hours of painstaking labor. Calvin was occasionally so thoughtful and insightful, especially around the holidays.

Mom had made us three new shirts apiece, and two pairs of pants. She'd even sewed a new jacket for me, and an oilcloth Macintosh for Calvin. It was hard to tell how long she'd been stitching on them, between embroidery jobs and cross-stitch samplers that people had commissioned from her.

Jeannie had given me the very best gift of all. She'd quilted us a new blanket for the loft, and had hand-stitched a pillow for us that was soft and wonderful against the skin. They were treasures, not only because of what they were, but because they had plainly been made with care and tenderness. She had thought of what I could use and what I would like . . . and had the insight to make the right call.

Winter slowly passed, and as Jeannie and I spent our time in the loft, we lay on top of the blanket to cuddle and kiss instead of under it. Baseball season started, with Calvin at centerfield, covering it like a blanket. Donna was still cheering him on, still doing the best gymnastics of all of the girls. Ninth grade slowly grated past, and I still led the class in GPA, edging out Jimmy McFarlane by the grace of his mononucleosis three weeks ahead of the biology final.

Summer came, and I won my weight class in Golden Gloves. The Chief had actually grudgingly complimented the way I had used his footwork to slip punches and the weaving head movements we'd worked on so many countless hours. I had also spent weeks grinding the blade of the hunting knife with the odd alloy he insisted on. The Chief threw my first attempt at the knife he wanted me to make into the river. He said he was disgusted and acted furious, but I thought he was secretly proud of my progress.

Calvin and Donna spent a good bit of time together, and Calvin was curiously quiet about it. Usually he was not just graphic, but actually pornographic in his descriptions of his conquests, but he never talked to me about her. Perhaps he really cared about her. Or maybe he just didn't want to spark a fight again. I saw him watching me shadowbox in our room, and if the flicker in his eyes wasn't fear, it was at least respect.

Mom watched everything going on. She had to have noticed Jeannie and me. And I was pretty sure that she had noticed Donna and me. Calvin and Donna would have been impossible for her to ignore. But she kept her silence. She never mentioned noticing any of us or our groupings. If I didn't know better, I'd have guessed that she didn't know.

And so the summer passed . . . if I didn't have everything that I wanted, I was satisfied with what I did have. In the intervening years, I have often thought wistfully about that summer, when I didn't know enough to be contented with being content.

Chapter Nineteen

Sophomore in high school. It's not such a bad spot in life. Calvin was a senior, and still the golden boy of the sports teams. Jeannie was a senior too, and she often waved to me in the hallways. To greet me more familiarly would have made problems for both of us. My classes were a little more difficult. I had English/Composition, Chemistry, Geometry, World History, Gym/Health, French, and Metal Shop.

At least I had one class with Donna. That way, I could help her with her French. I thought that was very romantic, French being the 'language of love'. I looked forward to being able to converse with her in that amorous tongue, like our own secret code. She was enamored of the language too, and actually worked on her accent to make herself sound like Miss Millefleur. I thought it was neat that she had a French last name, and told her so. She told me that her family was descended from veterans from Lafayette's troops that came to aid in the Revolutionary War. Some of them decided to stay and settle in this new land.

I was still officially dating Donna . . . at least as far as Mr. Duquesne was concerned. I enjoyed our talks, as long as we kept clear of the subject of Calvin. She was more and more willing to do that as time went by. She could see that it made me uncomfortable. I tried not to let her know how much she meant to me, but I'm pretty sure that she did. Fortunately, she cared enough about me to never force the issue, to not make me talk to her about it. She loved me . . . but as a friend. I thought last fall that was a good place to start. It was. Regrettably, it seemed like Donna thought it was a good place to finish, too.

Mom started teaching me how to cook that fall. She said it was important for a boy to be able to do 'woman's work' for himself. When I asked her why, she said it would keep him from being fettered to a woman just so she'd be taking care of him. She growled in her deep, gravelly voice that she hoped I'd be able to do for myself until I found a woman good enough to marry. No sense in getting in a rush, she said. When I asked about Calvin, she just shook her head angrily. "That boy don't listen. Th'ain't no point in tryin' ta show a mule how ta dance. It don't work, an' it annoys the mule."

The Chief and I had kept up working on the boxing, although he told me that he'd taught me all he could teach me about boxing. He looked like he wanted to say something else, but seemed to be holding it in abeyance. My knife was coming along slowly. He was making me grind the majority of the blank with fine grit, in order to be able to stop me in case I started to make a mistake. The blade was slowly shaping, and he wouldn't tell me what he had in mind for the rest of the knife.

Jeannie and I became even closer. We talked about our dreams and aspirations. We spoke of the things we disliked about Folsom Hollow. She taught me how to talk with and please a woman. I encouraged her to talk proper English, even though she lapsed often. She and I weren't inseparable, but it was a near thing. She and I still spent a lot of time up in the loft of the barn under or over the quilt she'd made me.

"Rob, what are ya gonna do after high school? You've got less than two years left." Jeannie cuddled against me, her bare breasts against my bare ribs.

"I don't know, Jeannie. I want to go to college, but I'd need a scholarship for that. I couldn't put enough money together to go to school without one. Not without working for a semester, and working part time through the semester I attended. That'd take forever! Even with summer school, it'd take at least six years. I'd be almost twenty-four before I got my diploma!" I couldn't imagine being that old. It's amazing how old twenty-four looks when you're only fifteen.

"Ya oughtta get one a' them scholarships, Rob. Yer gonna be valedictorian, ya know. Nobody's even close to ya in yer class. An' yer takin' tougher classes than that Jimmy McFarlane, too. Don't valedictorians always get scholarships?" Jeannie wasn't teasing. She really didn't know. And I guess I didn't, either. But I knew that sometimes they did, because B.J. Mackey had never come back home from WVU.

"I hope so, Jeannie. I don't think I could take spacing my classes out while I was working. That'd be way too slow. But what are you going to do?" I really hadn't ever thought about what she was going to do. She was a part of my life, and I just assumed that she'd be there in Folsom Hollow. Doing what, I'd never even contemplated.

"I like readin', but I really don't like school. An' I doubt that I can get a scholarship, nohow. My grades're good, but they ain't like yers. I think I'd like to sit back and think 'bout it a while, maybe. Kind of call 'time-out' for a bit. See what happens." She leaned back onto her elbow, making her breasts jiggle fetchingly.

I kissed her lips gently, and slowly moved down her neck. She gasped when I got to her breasts. I wasn't real sure what was I was going to do after high school. But I sure knew what I was going to do right then.

Chapter Twenty

"Bobby, what's wine taste like?," Donna asked.

"Grapes, I guess, Donna. Why?" I couldn't fathom why she'd be interested in wine. I knew that some folks around town made wine. Dandelion, elderberry, strawberry, and blackberry were the usual flavors.

"'Cause they's always drinkin' wine in France. 'Specially Paris, I think. All them movies about France and Frenchies show 'em drinkin' wine an' eatin' them fancy cheeses. An' Miss. Millefleur says that French wine 'n champagne is the best. I dunno where we'd get some wine ta taste it, though. An' them cheeses, they don't sell 'em down ta Johnson's. I ast Mr. Johnson 'bout 'em, an' 'e didn't know what I was talkin' 'bout."

I was amused in a mean kind of way. Her French diction was so much better than her English that if one only spoke briefly with her in French, one would definitely make the wrong guess about her native tongue. "Well, I don't know about the cheeses, Donna. But I'd bet that the Chief would fetch me a bottle of wine from Charleston, if I gave him the money for it. Maybe he'd look for the cheeses, too. He's planning on heading there in the next few weeks. I'll ask him."

"Wouldja, Bobby? That'd be great!" Her eyes sparkled, and she smiled and laughed merrily. When she was pleased with me, I felt like I'd be willing to do anything for her.

When I talked to the Chief about it, he laughed. "Silly fuckin' kid. She ain't gonna like the stuff, anyhow. Tell ya what, Bobby: I'll fetch a bottle a' the French stuff and a bottle of the cheap wino-wine. My treat, kid. Just to show ya what goddam fools women are. An' I'll look fer yer silly-ass pansy cheeses, too. Might find some of 'em in Charleston. An' I'll bring ya back some Wisconsin Colby, too. Jest so's ya can see. Women's damn fools, boy. An' the people who tell ya 'bout these 'delicacies' are the ones sellin' 'em. Don't taste worth a shit, boy. But I'll show ya, not jest tell ya."

"Thanks, Chief. I really appreciate you picking up the tab." I hadn't expected that from him. It really didn't seem in character, from what I knew.

"When I'm in Charleston, I'm out on a tear anyhow. Iffen I didn't spend the money on somethin' worthwhile, I'd be spendin' it on drinks fer whores or somethin'." He grinned and clapped me on the shoulder with an iron-hard hand. "Yer a good boy, Bobby. I don't mind spendin' a smidgen on ya iffen it'll help ya wif yer gal. Ain't sayin' yer way's any damn good, boy. My way's better by half. But you'll learn that on yer own, I reckon." He tousled my hair with his hand, and shook his head. "Get on outta here, Bobby. Go chase both yer women, and hope they don't catch ya at it."

I considered walking back into town to tell Donna the good news, but thought the better of it. After all, I didn't know when the Chief was going, anyway. Never mind that her father might be a little tired of having Bobby

Taylor around his house. Giving permission to court his daughter was a big step, but I was pretty aware of the fact that no father ever wants to see his daughter grow up. He's terrified that she might meet a boy just like him when he was her age.

I contemplated going to see Jeannie, but remembered that Mr. Riley was going to be in the house today. Jeannie had mentioned he was down with the flu bug that was going around. That told me that going to see if Jeannie was able to talk wouldn't be a good idea. I'd just have to see if she would come out to the farm later tonight. She generally came out right around dusk, if she could get free.

I decided to go home. I'd already seen Donna and the Chief today, and Jeannie was unavailable. Maybe Calvin would feel like a game of one-on-one, or checkers, or cards, or something. Or Mom might have something for me to do either for her or with her. If nothing came of either Cal or Mom, I figured I could finish up "The Scarlet Letter" before dinner.

Calvin was cleaning out the gutters when I got home. He saw me, and hollered, "Get on up here, Bobby-boy!" He grinned and waved me up the ladder.

Glad to see him in such high spirits, I clambered up beside him on the roof. "Hey, Cal! How much do you have left to do?"

"I've got two sides done, so we've just got halfway yet ta go. Wanna help, Bobby-boy?" He threw a handful of yucky wet leaves at me playfully.

Sure!" I grabbed a handful of the decomposing muck out of the gutter and threw it over the side. Here in a bit, I was willing to bet I could catch him napping and toss a handful down the back of his neck.

We worked and played with each other until we had the entire gutter clear. We were both filthy with the slop, but laughing and joking the entire time. Calvin and I had good times together, as well as fighting like . . . well, like brothers, I guess.

We climbed down, and ran to wash off. Mom would kill us if we'd shown up for dinner without cleaning up first. She always told us that we knew when dinner was, and if we couldn't at least show up on time and ready for the table, her compost pile for the garden would get our meal. And she meant it, too. Calvin had gone without a few times testing her. He'd come in from football practice without a shower, and she'd snatch his plate away like he'd been a leper. I always knew better. Mom was no one to trifle with.

Dinner was my favorite: meatloaf, mashed potatoes, gravy, green beans, and corn. I liked fresh beans and corn best, but the way Mom canned them, she didn't lose much. We talked lightly over dinner, me telling Mom about French class, my grades, and how the metal shop teacher didn't know half what The Chief had already shown me. Calvin didn't react like usual, either. Usually, he cuffed me for bragging when I talked about school, or even The Chief. Tonight, he just seemed amused, and went so far as to tell us about some of the new plays they were going to try in football. This was a big switch, because you'd have thought the football plays of McClellan

County High were even secrets from God, the way he guarded them.

Mom seemed in a happy mood too. She always liked it when Calvin and I came to the table hungry and in high spirits. It pleased her to have us do chores around the house, like cleaning the gutters. I think it was more important to her to be teaching us to be productive and useful than to get the labor out of us, though. She wanted us to be ready for the world when we were old enough, and having us accustomed to hard work was one of her goals.

Mom had made blackberry pie for dessert, and had some cream whipped to put on top of it. We always ate dessert from saucers, for some reason. Mom claimed that was all they were good for. She didn't drink her coffee or tea with a saucer unless the preacher was company. She thought they were stupid. "Iffen ya cain't keep yer drink in yer cup, wipe the mess up with a rag, why doncha?"

She told us about her sewing, and how she thought that the dress pattern that Sue Ellen Sweeney chose for her bridesmaid's dresses was too revealing by half. "Ya can see the whole tops of their bosoms in 'em. An' there ain't hardly no back to 'em a' tall. Skirt's too short fer decent folks. Make 'em look like girly-dancers, 'stead 'a bridesmaids. I'd like ta see the maid of honor could look honorable in them can-can dresses. Can-can. Ha. Will-will, more like." She looked disapproving, but laughing with us at the same time.

Calvin asked Mom if he could have a cup of coffee with his pie. I waited to see what would happen. She looked at him with her gimlet eye silently. It was tough to tell what was going on in her head when she wore that expression. "Reckon yer old enough ta drink coffee, boy. Yer still a boy yet, Calvin Taylor. Lots is a man by the time they's your age. Yer close, I 'spect. Be ya careful, son. Don't go thinkin' yer smarter 'n y'are."

Calvin got his cup quietly, and looked at me with pride in his eyes. Not gleeful one-upmanship, just pleasure in Mom's words. Granted, she hadn't told him he was a man, but for her, that was a loving speech. She didn't shower us with affection and compliments the way a lot of mothers did. Her way was a harder way, but not without love. She showed her love by teaching what she could, by providing us with the very best she could, and by encouraging us quietly. She was a coach, not a cheerleader.

I looked at my family while we ate pie quietly. I loved them both so much. They were both such wonderful people. I didn't mind not having a daddy around like the other kids. I knew my life couldn't be any richer if we'd had a dozen people in our family.

Chapter Twenty-One

About six weeks later, in mid-November, the Chief returned to Folsom Hollow. He'd brought four bottles of wine, five different kinds of cheeses, and a small can of caviar. He said, "It's s'posed ta go on some special little hard bread they got, but I figger saltines ain't much differnt."

"I sure appreciate it, Chief. This is just the kind of stuff we're reading about and talking about in French class. Donna will go crazy over the fancy cheeses and wines. I know if you didn't bring it back with you, we'd never have gotten to taste this kind of stuff in Folsom Hollow." This was by no means an exaggeration. In that time, there was no mail-order industry willing to ship you anything imaginable to any location. And even if there had been, I didn't have any money for luxuries. In fact, if we couldn't make it or trade for it, there wasn't much money for necessities.

The Chief brushed aside my thanks. "It ain't no big deal, Bobby. Glad enough ta show ya some things that the world's got out there. By the time I was yer age, I'd done traveled clean ta California. Ran off young, aye? Didn't wanna stay 'round an' be no miner like my ol' man. Now, wanna lay me a wager, boy?"

I didn't know what he had in mind, but I decided to humor him. "Wager about what, Chief?"

"Betcha that silly gal o' yourn ain't gonna like the real wine. Betcha she likes this stuff." He waved a bottle of Thunderbird and a bottle of Wild Irish Rose. "An' I'll betcha she likes this here cheese more'n the foreign stuff she thinks she wants." He pointed at a block of Wisconsin Medium Colby.

I decided to hedge and stall. I'd learned better than to think I knew better than the Chief when he'd offered a bet. "Why do you think that, Chief?"

"'Cause this wine's a goddam acquired taste, boy. An' this slop," he waved the cheap wine again, "tastes a lot like hopped-up Kool-Aid. This cheese here," he pointed at the brie, edam, gouda, feta, and bleu cheeses, "is fancy stuff. Again, ya gotta learn ta 'preciate it. This," he picked up the Colby and threw it at me, "just tastes good, an' any goddam fool can tell it."

I knew he was almost certainly right. The closest Donna and I had ever come to French wine and cheese was reading about them, and hearing Miss Millefleur rave about them. "What might you be interested in wagering, Chief?" I didn't think he was wrong, but if I could let him win this, maybe it would be a way of showing him I appreciated it.

"Let's bet . . . " He thought for a second, and finished, "dinner at yer house, with yer mama cookin', mind, against . . . why don't you pick?" He grinned. He knew I admired his old All-Navy boxing gloves, and loved looking at his Navy .45. He laughed and waited. He wanted to see if I'd have the audacity to suggest either one.

I didn't imagine he'd let either one of them go, but I knew he wouldn't want to let me have the pistol. So just to tweak his nose and see if he'd back down, I said, "The All-Navy boxing gloves. Are you that sure of yourself, Chief?" and laughed.

He laughed uproariously. "Ya goddam punk! Why, ya ain't fit to lace them gloves, boy! But I'll tell ya what, I got something here y'ain't never seen. Look here, Bob." He stood and reached over the refrigerator and pulled out a wooden box. It was about twice the size of a cigar box, and had odd ideograms either carved or burned into the lid.

"This here's something I been keepin' for almost twenty year, boy. Dunno why I kept it. An' I don't need it nor want it. But that don't make it worthless. A young feller like you . . . what wif likin' ta squire women 'round an' all, he might jest have him a use fer this." He unlocked the box, and pushed it across the table to me.

I looked at the box carefully. It was a thing of beauty. The wood was highly polished, and shone like burnished copper. The ideograms in the top were burned into the wood, which was familiarly fragrant. Cedar, I thought. I asked, "What does the writing mean?"

"It means 'love' dammit. And 'beauty'. But that's just the goddam box! Open it, Bobby, fer Chrissakes!" The Chief growled, but I could tell he was excited to be showing this to me. Or maybe just to be showing it to anyone.

I opened the lid, and gasped. Inside, lay a flash of almost electric blue cloth with watermarks. Silk. Real silk.

"Get it out, boy! I ain't opened the box in over a decade, an' I wanna see if it's ruint or still worth bettin'!" I could tell he was really just excited, not angry, but I reached into the box and unfolded the cloth.

It was a gorgeous silk robe, with an embroidered circle on the back. The hand-made patch was of a tree unlike any I'd ever seen. It was croggled and bent, but somehow was still a thing of beauty. The watermarks on the silk dappled throughout the cloth, and there was further embroidery on the sleeves, near the cuffs. It looked like vines or something. The vivid colors were almost enough to take my breath.

"Well, boy? Ya wanna bet fer that ol' robe? I'll throw in the box, too. Iffen ya win our wager." It was plain that there was a story behind this . . . garment. It was entirely too lovely to be called a robe, or housecoat.

"Where'd it come from, Chief? It looks Oriental. Did you get it in the South Pacific?" I knew he must have. It looked too barbarous, too exotic, to be from anywhere I'd ever been.

"Got it a long time ago, Bobby. Got it when I was still a punk fireman on my first cruise. Handmade in Hong Kong. They called it a kimono, but it ain't but a robe. An' it's one of a kind, too. They even made the cloth special fer me." The Chief looked strangely sad for an instant. "The box says 'love', an' I got it when I still was young an' foolish 'nough ta buy that line 'a shit. I thought maybe that ol' robe might do ya some good, you still bein' young an' dumb, an' I don't need it, like I said."

"It's beautiful, Chief. Are you sure you want to gamble with something so precious?"

"I tole ya, I don't need it." He looked away.

"Chief, this is too small for you. It's even too small for me. And I don't think either one of us would look very good in it. Why'd you get it, anyhow?" We both knew I was just teasing him. I knew it had to be for a girl. I just couldn't figure out why the Chief would ever get something so thoughtful, so exquisite, for a woman. He plainly didn't care much for any part of them . . . other than the part that he rented. I just couldn't understand.

"I got it fer a girl, a long time ago. Like I said, I was a young an' dumb fireman on my first cruise. I was gonna get married when I got back." He looked like he was done.

I hadn't heard any of this story before, though, so I thought I'd find out as much about it as he'd tell me. But getting information from the Chief about things that weren't boxing or metalwork was like trying to push a rope. It took patience and persistence. "I never knew you got married, Chief."

"I didn't, Bobby. 'Cause women ain't no damn good, an' they sure as fuck ain't for trustin'. I didn't know that then, though. Just like you don't know it now." His face hardened up again, and I knew I'd taken the wrong tack.

"What was she like, Chief? This girl that you didn't marry?" Maybe this was the door in.

"Well, Bobby, I was sparkin' this beautiful girl. Face like an angel,

Bobby. She had hair the color of ripe wheat, an' eyes like cornflowers. She had the purdiest smile, an' she had an hourglass figger. With some extry minutes thowed in all the right places. She was a hashslinger at a diner right off base, an' we was in love. Ha! That's what I thought. When I got back off my six month cruise ta go see my girl, she's four months pregnant. I ain't no Einstein, but I can do that kinda math alright." The Chief's eyes were far away, looking through time as well as space as he told me this story.

"Anyhow, I don't need it no more. An' I thought you might like givin' it ta one a' yer damned girlfriends. Dunno which one you'll give it to, even if ya win it. If ya even bet! What's it gonna be, boy?" He snapped back to the present, looking as if he'd never said a word about his waitress. I decided I'd pushed the man enough.

Noah's son was punished for uncovering his father's nakedness. How unforgivable is revealing a man's heartsickness? Especially considering the depth of pain that it obviously had caused. The man had never forgiven women in general for what this one had done. Jeannie had said that she thought that must have been what happened, but I never dreamed that she'd have been so right. This iron man, this hardened soul, had spent his life scarred from an experience when he'd been little older than I was right now. I was rocked by the candid way he'd told me, and decided to comment on it would be a clear-cut case of adding insult to injury. Better by half to redirect the conversation to the wager he'd suggested.

"I guess I'll have to take the bet, Chief. That kimono's too pretty to leave in a cabinet. I don't know if I'll win. In fact, I don't think I will. But it's worth a shot. The chance of winning that from you is worth explaining to Mom that she's got to cook for you." I tried teasing him to lighten his spirits. I hadn't meant to bring down his mood. And I really did want to have that robe.

I imagined how it would look on Donna. My mind's eye painted a beautiful picture, with her smiling alluringly over one shoulder. Her hair was over her other shoulder, and with the sash of the kimono snugged, she was a vision. The swell of her hips, offset by her slim waist, wasn't exactly exposed, but hinted at strongly by the cut of the garment.

I wanted to see Donna wearing that kimono, I knew. And then I had to ponder this question: Did I want my brother to see her wearing it? I shook my head. That wasn't for Calvin. Strictly pearls before swine.

I resolved that if I wouldn't ever see my vision in reality, I'd deprive the world of it. If not for my eyes, then for no man's. But I hadn't given up hoping for my dream.

Chapter Twenty-Two

I had everything set up carefully in our barn. I'd packed ice from the Chief's freezer to chill the bottle of wine he said should be cold. I'd gathered the saltines and caviar. I'd laid the cheeses that the Chief said should be cold on top of the ice bucket. Mom's crystal glasses weren't a set, but individual items she'd gathered over the years. They were pretty wineglasses, and Mom probably would have switched me good if she'd known I pinched them. She wouldn't notice the dried flowers I'd put in her blue glass vase, though.

This was the first time I'd been able to entice Donna out on a 'date' with me that she didn't end up with Calvin. She was still besotted with him, and while I was able to invite her out and escort her to where my brother awaited, I hadn't ever been able to have her to myself except while I tutored. Both of us acknowledged that if I took her out of her house, away from her father's watchful eye, to help her with math, she'd never get anything accomplished. Not as far as schoolwork went, anyway.

I'd walked into town to pick her up, dressed in my best. Mom had sewn me a white button-down shirt, and I had a tie that the Chief had given me. My pants were the only pair I owned that weren't denim, a pair of black slacks that were dressy enough for a 'country gentleman.' My belt was the good one Calvin had given me for my birthday. He'd made the belt and buckle himself. My shoes were shined. I couldn't wait to see what Donna would wear to our 'French party'.

I knocked on the door, and Mr. Duquesne opened right up. "Hello there, Bobby! Come on in and have ya a seat! How's that chemistry comin'? I know yer a regular Jean-Paul Belmondo in that there Frenchy stuff!"

"Hello, Mr. Duquesne. I'm learning a good bit about chemistry so far, sir. Now we're dealing with exactly what ph measurement means, and how the different substances react in various buffers. It's as interesting as such things go, I suppose." I still hadn't ever figured out why my school seemed so much more interesting to this man than his daughter's. He had never cared much for her grades, nor for any of the classes she was taking.

"Say somethin' in French, Bobby. Tell me somethin' 'bout Donna in that there language o' love!" He laughed like he'd said something absolutely hilarious.

I thought for a moment. "Donna est tres jolie. Elle a mon coeur, monsieur. Je trouve votre fille formidable, mais malheureusement, elle aime ma frere, pas moi." Donna is very pretty. She has my heart, sir. I think she's terrific, but unfortunately, she loves my brother, not me.

He slapped his knee and just about roared with laughter. "Yer a fine 'un, Bobby. Ya speak that stuff jest like in the movies! What'd ya say, anyhow?"

I smiled. "I just said that she was very pretty, and a terrific girl, sir."

"She is that, son. I hope yer takin' good care of 'er. What're y'all doin' tonight, anyhow?" He turned his eyes upon me, and the incisive look was at direct odds with his laughing demeanor. He was friendly, but hardly a fool, despite his act.

"We're going to have a French party, sir. We've got some imported cheeses, and a small tin of caviar for sampling. I'll take good care of her, sir. You don't need to worry about me at all." The one question I had always been afraid he'd ask was, "How many of you are going on this camping trip/French party/hiking trip/exploration of the caves/canoe excursion?" I think even now though, he'd never have asked that. He didn't want to know.

Finally, Donna came down the steps. She was wearing a powder-blue angora sweater, with a navy skirt. Her hair was up in a white ribbon that matched her hose. She was also wearing a navy beret, evidently in keeping with the French motif. She looked beautiful.

"Bonjour, madmoiselle!" I couldn't help calling to her as she smiled.

"Bonjour, monsieur! Comment va-tu, aujourd hui?" She greeted me, asking how I was doing today.

"That's enough 'a that stuff! Dunno iffen yer talkin' sappy love-talk in front a' yer ol' man!" Mr. Duquesne laughed, but I noticed that the laugh didn't reach all the way to his eyes.

"You're right, sir. It's rude to exclude you from our conversation, and I apologize." I nodded.

"Don't be such a grump, Daddy! Yer makin' Bobby feel bad! We's just sayin' hi!" Donna pretended to be piqued, and stomped one delicate foot.

He laughed again, and this time it looked like he meant it. "Y'all have a good time. Bobby, you have my girl back here 'fore midnight, y'hear?"

"Yes sir. I'll make sure of it." And I would, too.

Donna and I left, walking the few miles to our house arm-in-arm. She was animated and excited, and for the first time, it wasn't over the fact that she'd be spending time with Calvin. I was delighted in her company at any time, but to see her so thrilled over doing something with me was absolute ecstasy. I told her about the treats I had in store for her, and that the Chief had even brought back a tin of caviar. She laughed and clapped her hands, threw her arms around my neck and kissed me. Cloud nine, I'm telling you. When we got to the barn, I handed her a blindfold. I wanted to see her expression of surprise when she saw the actual layout of our little 'wine and cheese' party.

She looked skeptical, but put the blindfold on without argument. I led her to the small 'table' I'd set up, a piece of an old Dutch door on a hay bale. I'd actually gotten chairs for us, and used flour sacks stuffed with hay for cushions. I seated her, as any gentleman would, and moved to my side of the table. I asked her, "Would madame care to start with a taste of white wine, or the red?"

She giggled, and took off the blindfold. When she saw the cheeses and crackers, her eyes grew wide, and her mouth trembled a little. When she saw the wines, she gasped. And when I withdrew the piece de resistance, the caviar, from behind me, she actually cried a little.

"Oh, Bobby! This is the best surprise anyone ever done for me! I cain't believe we're gonna eat caviar! We's just like the rich folks in the movies! An' them Frenchies in our book ta school! Yer the best friend a gal ever had!" She wiped her tears away, and said, "What wine ya wanna try first?"

I grinned. The romantic surprise was working its magic. She'd been so touched she actually cried! "I would recommend the white to open with, madmoiselle. It shouldn't stain the palate as the red might." I said in a snooty voice, pretending to be a maitre d'. The Chief had actually mentioned that would be a good idea, if I wanted to get the actual flavor of the wines.

"Sounds good," she said, uncertainly. She didn't know what to expect, and to be honest, I didn't either.

I worked the corkscrew into the bottle of white, and slowly pulled it out. I'd asked the Chief about letting it breathe like in the movies. He'd snorted and said, "You damn kids'll never tell the fuckin' difference." I decided to believe him.

I poured her a small amount into her glass, and did the same for me. "You're supposed to sip it and swish it around in your mouth, then spit it out."

"I ain't!" She looked indignant. "Ain't gonna spit, Bobby Taylor! An' you best not spit in front 'a me, neither. Don't care what they say, that's jest rude!"

I thought about mentioning that Calvin spit in front of her on a regular basis, but decided to let it pass. We had a shot of getting through our date without mentioning him. And since that was generally our common ground for discussion, I didn't want to include him tonight. So I laughed, instead.

"Okay, Donna. We won't spit it out. But then we should cleanse our palates-" I stopped. She was looking confused. "Get the taste out of our mouth," I explained. "Before we try the other kind of wine. Otherwise, we won't be able to appreciate the difference."

"Okay, Bobby. If you say so." She looked dubious, but wasn't ready to argue that point. She sipped a bit of the wine in her glass. "Ugh! This is horrible!"

I was astounded. The Chief had warned me that she wouldn't like it. He was sure enough of it to offer a wager. But I had just known that Donna and I were frustrated natural-born sophisticates, and were going to love the wine. So I tried it.

"Good God! That can't be right!" It wasn't at all like I'd imagined. If this was 'good' wine, why in the world would anyone want it? A very peculiar flavor, and one that I couldn't say I appreciated at all.

"T'ain't at all what I thought it'd be, Bobby." Donna looked so crestfallen. "Maybe ya jest have to get used ta it?"

"I don't think so, Donna. I think it just tastes like that. Want to try some of the red, instead?" I hoped to salvage the evening with the other bottle of 'good' wine.

"Sure. Cain't be worse'n that stuff." She dumped her glass out rather than finish it.

I suggested, "Maybe try a piece of the cheese with a cracker while I get this bottle open?" She nodded.

"Which one do ya think I oughtta try? First, I mean." She looked hopefully at the cheeses. Surely they wouldn't disappoint her.

"Try the brie, Donna. Put a little on a cracker. Tell me what you think of it." I hadn't tried any of this stuff. I expected good things from these cheeses.

I poured the red wine out into our glasses, after dumping my white just like Donna had. I recorked the white bottle as best I could. I hoped that The Chief liked the stuff, or else it would just go to waste. Yuck.

"This cheese cuts funny, Bobby." I looked, and the middle of the little wheel was gluey and soft. The outside was hard and seemed dry.

"Maybe just dip some of the soft stuff onto a cracker. I think that's what we're supposed to do, anyhow." She did, and a funny look came over her face.

"Ain't too bad, really." She dipped another cracker, and held it out to me, smiling. I wondered if I dared to . . .

Instead of extending my hand for the cracker, I dipped my head, never giving up eye contact. I took the cracker on my tongue slowly, and flicked the tip of it against the outside of her finger. She gasped a little, looking away hurriedly, and I thought maybe I'd pushed things a little too far. I straightened back up and paid attention to my brie and cracker.

It didn't taste bad, but it sure wasn't all that good, either. I wouldn't have walked a mile for it, anyhow. I tried a sip of the red wine in my glass. "This is a little better, Donna. Try it."

She did, and agreed, "It ain't as bad as the white stuff, Bobby, but I cain't see how them Frenchies drink this stuff all 'a the time. Ain't very tasty a'tall." She dipped another cracker and said, "This cheesy stuff's purdy good, though."

I said, "Well, let's try some of the other cheese, too. Want to try the edam? Or the gouda?"

"I'd like ta try some 'a that there blue stuff. Why's it blue, anyhow?"

I knew, but I wasn't about to tell her. Something about eating mold just wasn't stimulating to the appetite. "I don't know, Donna. Maybe we'll ask Miss Millefleur on Monday." I cut a small wedge of the cheese and put it on a cracker, then extended it to her. What would she do, offered the same opportunity she'd given me?

Instead of playing the same game, she smiled a little and took the cracker in her small hand. "Thank ya, Bobby." She took a small bite, and said, "I like this one better. It's kinda funny-tastin' but it's good!"

I smiled, inwardly deflated a bit. I'd hoped . . . oh, well. "Would you like to try this other wine that the Chief thought we'd like better?"

"Sure! I done finished this stuff. But I don't think I want no more 'a it." She held her glass out as I unscrewed the lid of the Thunderbird. She took a small sip and said, "This is sweet! I like this lots better!" She smiled and laughed.

I grinned, and thought about how it looked like the Chief was right. I poured myself a small libation, and tried it myself. "You're right, it is sweet." Taking another sip, I said, "A little too sweet, really. Wonder how come?"

She laughed and said, "Prob'ly jest 'cause it ain't as fancy. Fancy folk don't hardly drink no sugar in their tea, neither."

I wasn't sure that argument held much water, but I didn't care. She was interacting with me, about something we both were interested in, and that was good enough. We sipped the wines, and ate all the fancy cheeses. Some we liked better than others, but we ended up liking all of them.

"Ready to try the caviar, ma cherie?" I wondered if she'd let me get by with that.

"Reckon so, Bobby." She wouldn't look me in the eye, and I wondered if I'd embarrassed her.

Caviar tastes like salty fish slime, and we both hated it. We drank a good bit of the Thunderbird washing the taste out of our mouths.

"The Chief said we'd like this cheese better than those, Donna. Want to try it?" I sliced a few pieces of the Colby off the block.

"Why not?" She laughed. "Iffen I like it better'n I do them other cheeses, that'll be goin' some." I let her serve herself, not wanting to press the issue. She ate a piece or two, and said, "I like it fine, Bobby. But I think I like that brie stuff the best."

I held out the cracker with the brie on it, and this time she bent her mouth to it. Summoning up my courage, I waited until she swallowed, and moved my head slowly down to kiss her. She looked astonished at first, and then a sad, scared look darted across her face. She turned her head quickly so that I ended up kissing her cheek, instead. She blushed a little bit, and didn't say anything. I felt like an idiot.

Coughing in an attempt to kill the silence, I poured myself another glass of wine. I decided to sample the Wild Irish Rose, and offered Donna a glass. She smiled, a little sadly I thought, and nodded. Neither one of us liked the cheap red wine, so I saved that for Calvin. He wasn't picky about his drinking.

We did finish off the bottle of Thunderbird, and being unused to alcohol, I got a little tipsy. We sat and talked about stuff in France, and laughed. I didn't go over and put my arm around her like I'd planned on, since I'd pushed too hard already. But we had a good time. And as I walked her home, I noticed that not even once had Calvin's name come up.

Chapter Twenty-Three

I'd taken the bottles of 'good' wine back to the Chief yesterday. He'd laughed and said, "I tole ya so!" when I told him of our reaction to it. "When's dinner, Bobby?" he laughed.

"Not so fast, there, Chief! She did like the brie better than the Colby!" I laughed right back. "So how do you want to do this? Call it a push? Or both pay up?"

He laughed some more. "I know you want the robe, boy. An' ta be honest, I'd like a home-cooked meal. I'm a good cook, mind, but I'm too goddam lazy to do it. Takes all the flavor outta a meal to cook it yerself anyhow."

I pondered telling him about how the date had gone, but thought the better of it. I didn't want to hear another 'tole ya so!'. I asked what he'd like Mom to cook for dinner instead.

"Don't much care, son. Fried chicken's always a winner, but I ain't married to the notion. I don't care much fer bird 'less it's fried, though. Navy broke me 'a that. Damn if they din't love feedin' a man bird! I'm right fond 'a taters, any way ya cooks 'em. An' iffen it's beef, I like mine blood-rare. Don't like all the juices cooked outta my meat. Other'n that, I'm about as easy as a Subik Bay whore." He grinned. "I'll try an' keep my tongue fitten ta be 'round a lady, boy. Ain't used ta it, though. Ain't been in the presence of a lady in so fuckin' long, I'll hafta be on my toes."

I sighed in relief. It was going to be a lot to ask Mom to cook for the Chief. She didn't approve of his language, of his lifestyle, or even of the Navy. If he'd come in to her kitchen and cussed, she'd have flat out come unglued. I didn't want to try telling him what to do, but his voluntary participation sure made me feel a lot better.

"So'd any 'a that shit help a'tall? Or is ol' Donna still stuck on yer rotten-ass brother?" Chief looked at me like he already knew the answer.

"I think I made some headway, Chief, but I might have pushed a little too hard," I said. "But I do think she's pretty hung up on Calvin. Wants to marry him, even."

That dumbass broad. Calvin ain't the marryin' type, 'specially iffen she's shakin' her tail his way 'thout it." The Chief was pretty disparaging towards all women, but he held Donna in especial contempt. I'd often wondered if it was because she preferred Calvin to me.

I told the Chief I'd talk to Mom about when, and get back with him. He grinned and said, "Yer prob'ly the onliest person I can think of I'd trust to pay up his debt 'thout any security, but ya can go ahead an' take that there box wif ya." He winked, and said, "Now get on outta my house."

I went home to talk to Mom about it on the double-time. "Hey, Mom?"

"What, Bobby-boy?" Her voice sometimes still surprised me with its almost unnatural timbre. It was as deep as most men's, and a little raspy sometimes, too.

"I need a favor, Mom. Could you invite the Chief over for dinner sometime in the next couple of weeks?" I knew she wouldn't like it, and she might ask me why.

"I reckon I could, Bobby. Why'd I go an' do that fer, though? Why'd I want that man in my home?" She looked at me speculatively. "Y'ain't playin' matchmaker again, are ya, Bobby?"

She was reminding me of the time I tried to get her and the mailman together. I liked the mailman, and he had that funny car with the steering wheel on the wrong side. He was pretty dumfounded when I told him I thought Mama liked him, and he should ask her to marry him. When Mom heard about it, she switched me good.

"No, Mom. I don't think you and the Chief would make a good pair. You're both too strong, too dominant. And you don't approve of him very much. Not that he approves of you very much, either."

"Whaddaya mean, he don't approve o' me?" Her eyes flashed and I knew I'd better explain myself in a hurry.

"Not of you personally, Mama, just of women in general. He doesn't think most women are trustworthy." I hoped I wasn't making things worse.

"He's right. 'Course, most men ain't either. That includes him. Ha. What'd your Chief say ta that?" Her grin was back.

"He'd laugh, Mom. And he'd probably agree with you." I could see that as his reaction easier than anything else.

"I reckon it'd be okay, Bobby. But why come? I know he's yer friend, an' he's the one taught ya boxin' an' knifemakin'. But he ain't never come out here 'fore. You's all time headed out ta his place, not here. I ain't 'shamed a nothin' here, but y'ain't never had no comp'ny over 'fore." She eyed me curiously, and I felt a lot like a criminal under the lights.

"No, Mama. I'm not ashamed of our house, or anyone in it. I just thought that the Chief might like a good home-cooked meal. And I don't know any better cook alive." A little flattery couldn't hurt anything.

She gave a grunt in reply. She knew I was buttering her up in a way, but she also knew she was an outstanding cook. And she knew that I knew it, too. "Good enough, then, Bobby. Maybe this Friday? An' I reckon he'd like 'bout anythin' I make? Or do ya have somethin' special in mind?"

"Well, Mom, as long as it isn't chicken, the Chief'll love it. He says he 'et too much bird in Uncle Sam's Yacht Club."

"That ain't too picky fer me. Reckon I'll mix up somethin' right nice. Do ya proud, Bobby-boy. Jus' so y'know t'ain't fer him, son. I'm cookin' special fer you. An' I'll be nice an' polite, but I ain't gonna pertend I approve of 'im," she warned. But she winked, and I knew that she was half-playing.

"Thank you, Mama. I don't expect you to approve of everything about him, but he has some good points. I think you'll like him, despite yourself." I grinned. I thought that this was going to be interesting, to say the least.

I went to tell Calvin the news, but he wasn't in our bedroom. I checked the barn, and he wasn't there, either. I sighed. He'd probably gone into town, either to steal something, or to sneak a visit with Donna. I didn't know how she got free from her father when I wasn't the conduit for her, but somehow she found a way. Whenever Calvin went into town to see her, he invariably did.

Then I figured I could tell Jeannie about it, at least. I never could tell how she was going to take things, or how she was going to react to news. Some things that seemed like the best news in the world to me, she would wall up and get quiet about. And some things that seemed depressing to me, made her open up and comfort me about it, without seeming very upset about it herself. So I decided I'd head over to her place and see if she was available.

When I knocked on the door, Jeannie answered. She had a fresh bruise on the side of her cheek. "Hey, Rob! Let's head out of here a while, hey?"

I couldn't begrudge her time away from that place, even if I had wanted to. I hated what was going on in that house, but I didn't know what I could do to stop it. I let her lead me out to the river camp, which had become a semi-permanent sort of thing on the very edge of our property. My impromptu shelter had become a shack, if not an actual cabin. No window, it's true, and the door was just a weighted sash of the tarpaulin that had once served as my roof. But it did have a hand-laid stone fireplace, chimney and hearth, mortared with creek-mud. And it did have the benefit of privacy, and an old oil lamp.

How bad, Jeannie?" I wasn't going to let it slide this time. Too many times had I allowed her to put me off, to not talk about it. I had a guilty feeling that the main reason that I let her divert the conversation was that I didn't want to have to think about it.

"Oh, Rob, it's nothing to worry 'bout. He just gets thataway when he's been drinkin', ya know. So what's been going on with ya? Ain't seen ya in a few days." She grinned her sad version of a smile. The one that tried be a smile that didn't show her teeth.

"No, Jeannie. We'll get to that in a bit. How bad?"

"Not as bad as sometimes, Rob. He just clouted me with a stovelength a little bit. But I didn't have to . . . well, ya know. I didn't, not this time, Rob." She looked at me shamefacedly. She always looked to me for reassurance, and approval, after he'd been at her. And God help me, I still didn't know how I could get it stopped.

"That's good, at least, Jeannie. Come over here, girl, and lean up against me." I held my arm out to cradle her to me. She always needed to be cuddled and touched . . . but sometimes she really didn't want to be touched. At least not in any way that she took as sexual.

"Thanks, Rob. I don't know what I'd do iffen it weren't for you." She leaned into my arm, and laid her head on my shoulder. She snuggled in close, looking to share my body heat.

"Jeannie, honey, if there's anything I can do to help . . ., " I decided to let the offer just stand right there. I knew she wouldn't take me up on it, but there wasn't much I could really do.

"Just bein' here, Rob. That's the biggest thing I need from you right now. So what's been goin' on with you, anyhow?"

It seemed puerile and irrelevant now, but I dutifully told her about the 'French Party', and that the Chief was coming over for dinner. She laughed her contagious laugh, and squeezed me to her tightly. The idea of my crusty old boxing coach coming to dinner with my family did seem rather funny, now that I thought about it.

But I still had no idea how to help my only real friend in the world.

Chapter Twenty-Four

The Chief came over right on time, which was a plus in Mom's eyes. But he came driving in his Lincoln, which was not. She didn't approve of flashy cars, and the Chief's Lincoln was flashier than most. If he'd driven his old pickup, it would have made a better impression, but I guess he wouldn't have known that.

He was wearing a button-down oxford underneath a sweater, and a pair of khaki slacks. He was dressed in Sunday clothes, like this was a date or something. I was glad he'd dressed up, though. Mom seemed to like the fact that he'd dressed as though it was an occasion of some significance, anyhow. His shoes were polished to a high gloss, too. Mom was forever telling me that a man that couldn't take time to shine his shoes wasn't trying hard enough. So I guess this was a good sign.

If the Chief didn't cuss too much, anyhow.

I opened the door, and said, "Welcome in, Chief. May I introduce you to my Mother? Mom, this is Chief Michael Carmichel. Chief, this is Mom."

Chief just grinned. "Will Mrs. Taylor do fer ya, ma'am, or should I call ya Mom?" His eyes twinkled, and I could tell he was kidding me. I really should have introduced her as Mrs. Taylor. I gave myself a mental kick about that slip. A faux pas, as Miss Millefleur would say.

Mom gave a grin back in spite of herself. I could tell she was trying hard not to like him, and coming up short. "Mrs. Taylor'll do fine, Mr. Carmichel." She was eying him carefully to see if her deep and gravelly voice was going to take him off-guard and make him recoil. It sometimes had that effect on men.

"Mr. Carmichel don't work fer me a bit, ma'am. Chief Carmichel, maybe. Or just Chief. Mike's better yet." He extended his old pug's hand to shake.

Mom took his hand a little astounded. She hadn't ever been around a man who had refused to wear the Mr. moniker before, and it took her a little out of her comfort zone. "Chief Carmichel, then."

"You've a fine lad there, Mrs. Taylor. He's quick on his feet an' gettin' quicker with practice. His hand speed's pretty go-- . . . gosh-darn good, too. Think he'll be as good as I ever was, an' that ain't light praise, iffen I do say so myself." He shook her hand gently, and released it.

"Well, then, I'm glad of it. I've always been proud a' my Bobby. Cain't say I approve much a' this whole boxin' thing, though. Bobby's got too fine a' head on his shoulders ta go lettin' people punch at it fer no good reason." Her eyes were hard, and she was letting him know this wasn't an idle complaint.

"Well, ma'am, I can sure see how ya'd feel thataway. Most a' what I'm showin' him is how to not get his da-- . . . darned head punched, though. Ya see, boxin' ain't about beatin' on other people near so much as it is about not lettin' 'em beat on you." Chief smiled, and I could tell that Mom's complaint cut no ice with him, but he wasn't going to oppose her viewpoint, either. I breathed a gentle sigh of relief.

We went in to the dinner table, which Mom had laid out in grand Sunday-go-to-meeting style. Her linen tablecloth and company china were accompanied by her silver gravy boat, which I had often seen, but never seen in use. The roast beef steamed from its platter, and the bowl of mashed potatoes had a small lake of butter in the crater centered in the bowl. The green beans were mixed in with bits of bacon, and the corn had those funny red things that Mom put in for decoration. She had "done me up proud", as she'd promised.

Calvin had begged off, saying something about wanting to see his girlfriend. I knew the truth. He was intimidated by the Chief, and didn't really want to eat dinner with him, especially in his mother's house. Too much like being emasculated on your own home turf.

The three of us sat down to dinner, and conversation was a little uncomfortable. For me, at least. The only thing Mom and Chief had in common was me, of course. I hadn't foreseen the fact that I would be the focus of most of their interaction.

"Chief Carmichel, did Bobby tell ya he was number one in his class at school?"

"No'm. Did 'e tell ya he was finishin' up on the knife I designed fer him ta make?"

"No sir, he didn't. Bobby, why come ya din't tell yer mama you's almost done with that knife? Ya tole me that Chief Carmichel thowed the first 'un inta th' river, though. Why come ya ta do that, sir?" Her face was showing her 'invisible smile'. I hoped the Chief would take it as a joke instead of an attack.

"I done it 'cause he can do better, an' I expect it outta 'im. Iffen he don't work ta my standards, he can live with the results of it." Chief's jaw jutted a little, and I could see he was ready to fight about this point.

No need though. "That I can understand, sir. Iffen he's ta do somethin' a'tall, he oughtta be doin' it right." Her eyes had actually laughed, not just smiled. I didn't know if the Chief could see that, though.

He grinned himself, though. "I figgered that'd be a thing ya'd understand, ma'am. Ya don't strike me as the type a' woman that'd be satisfied with yer boy doin' things half-a-- . . . halfway."

"Yer too right, sir. Iffen he ain't givin' it hunderd percent, ya be as tough on 'im as ya think ya need ta be. Hard work ain't gonna be no stranger to 'im, an' the sooner he gets on good speakin' terms with it, the better it's gonna be fer him." They shared a grin and a nod, and the Chief even winked at my mother!

Of all possible outcomes, this was not one I could have fathomed. I wasn't sure I even liked the way this conversation was going, especially the part about talking about me like I wasn't even there. I had pictured the two of them not getting along very well at all. Instead, it was almost like I was a ball they were taking turns kicking. I decided to do something about it.

"Mom, did you know that Chief was a hero in The Second World War?" See how he liked being on the hot seat.

"Think that might be paintin' things a bit thick, ma'am. Heroes are somethin' fer serial movies an' dime store novels. 'Bout all I can say is I was there, an' I tried doin' my part." He said, self-effacingly. I couldn't believe it. It seemed so out of character for him to act modest.

"Chief Carmichel, I'd bet m' boy's got the truth of it, but iffen it makes ya uncomfortable, th'ain't no need ta tell me 'bout it. There's really only two types a' people been in a war. The ones wanna not talk about it, an' the ones don't never wanna talk 'bout nothin' else. I'm glad ta see y'ain't in the latter groupin'. An' I ain't approved a' the Navy ever since I heard tell a' them Sullivan boys. That weren't right. An' it weren't smart. Those poor boys' mama. Cain't help but think a' her, an' how she musta felt."

"War ain't never pretty, ma'am. An' it don't always make fer the best judgment nor decisions. Iffen I'd been asked, I'd 'a split them boys up, no damn matter what they whined about it. 'Cause yer right. Ain't smart puttin' all a' yer eggs in one basket, 'specially iffen yer pa's dead, an' four boys is all that woman's got left in the world." The Chief just nodded his head. "Yer dead right about them makin' poor calls on that score, ma'am."

That didn't work at all. The two of them refocused on me all over again, talking about how well I was doing at knifemaking. I resigned myself to being in the spotlight, and tucked away as much of the roast beef as I could.

Chapter Twenty-Five

For the next week, I heard more about what the Chief had said about me from my mother than I cared to. And the two times I headed over to the Chief's homestead, I heard entirely too much about what my mother said. I began to think that getting the two of them together was a truly wretched idea, at least from my viewpoint. Mom had liked Chief despite herself, and I couldn't believe that the Chief actually liked Mom, especially with the kind of baggage he was toting around about women.

It was a busy and confused week, with finals coming up, and Christmas just around the corner. I'd been working quietly on several projects to give as Christmas presents. So maybe it was a little understandable that I hadn't seen Jeannie in several days.

It was Tuesday before I realized that I hadn't seen her at school. Wednesday rolled around, and I decided to check up on her. Then Thursday came, and I followed through on my resolve.

I could see from the treeline that Mr. Riley was home. His jalopy was parked askew right in front of the kitchen door. I decided to try the pebble trick, since Jeannie's shutters were closed.

The shutters didn't fly open, and I began to wonder if Jeannie was in her room at all. But then the front door flew open, and her father bounded across the threshold, shotgun in hand. He cut loose with one barrel in the general vicinity of the treeline. I was scared, but decided I'd be safer sitting still like a rabbit than trying to outrun a shotshell. From the sound of the pellets against the leaves, I figured he'd loaded up birdshot, anyway. At that range, it would barely break the skin. Unless he hit my eyes. I shuddered a little, but stuck tight.

He squinted and peered hard into the woods surrounding his house, and was muttering under his breath. I had no idea what he might have been saying, but it didn't sound like an invitation in for high tea. Whatever he was sitting around the house for, I knew he'd leave fairly soon. He had whiskey to tend in the woods, not to mention a limited supply of drinking spirits. He'd need to reload. Himself, not his shotgun.

I waited a good two hours, well after dark, but he never stirred out of the house again. I still had no sign of my best friend. I needed to get home and study. I told myself that tomorrow night, he'd be out to the still, since it was Friday. He always spent Fridays at the still, drinking what he couldn't sell.

I wish I could say that I worried about her all day long, but the truth be told, I was concentrating on my French final. Miss Millefleur had put together a difficult test, with fill-in-the-blanks, matching, multiple guess, and even a few short essay questions. In French, yet. "En francais, et en francais seulement, s'il vous plait, etudients!"

So I didn't spare her a thought until after school. And wasn't in any hurry to get over to her house, since Mr. Riley wouldn't be out to the still until after dark. So I visited the Chief again, to pass time after dinner.

He looked over my hunting knife. It had barely changed a bit in the last half dozen hours of grinding. We were down to the subtleties, and it was pretty frustrating. I could see the slight amount of work that still needed to be done, but the grip was perfect already. The octagonal hammerhead pommel and rosewood handle were buffed smooth as glass. Even the spots in the wood where the brass bolsters held them together were so smooth as to feel seamless. Only the blade required more work, and all the shaping was done, really. All it lacked was the final hollow-grind on the edge.

I looked at it carefully. I calculated and estimated . . . about two hours more, then final sharpening—another three hours. I was really almost finished with it! I was very proud of my work. The metal wasn't polished to a high luster like a fancy-knife. There wasn't anything fancy about it. This was a knife meant for work, and designed and built to perform it. I knew whatever the task; my arms would give out long before the knife would.

"You done good, boy. There's a knife ya can be proud of, son. I ain't touched it oncet. It's all yer work. An' if I was tougher on ya than ya'd have liked, it's jest 'cause I think yer a person it's worth tryin' ta teach." The Chief patted my shoulder awkwardly, and continued. "Ya can wear it around now, iffen ya'd like. Maybe show it off ta yer womens. An' yer ma, iffen ya want."

I looked up at him and grinned. "I don't have a sheath for it, Chief.

But I appreciate you letting me take it out of the shop."

He coughed and looked away. "Maybe I've got somethin' that'll work fer it. Lemme look a minute, Bobby." He opened a drawer on the desk, and pulled out a sheath. It had been right on top. He said, "See iffen that ol' thing fits it. Ain't got no use fer it, so iffen ya want it, it's yours."

I looked at it closely. It was not an 'ol' thing.' It was new. And handcrafted. He'd made it from the tail of a West Virginia whitetail deer, and it looked wonderfully barbarous. I slid the blade into it. The sheath fit snugly and precisely. Exactly how he must have measured it. "Thanks, Chief. I appreciate it. Who made it?" As if I didn't know.

"I cain't even 'member, boy. But I guess it'll do fer ya. In a pinch, that is." He looked away again.

"Thanks, Chief. It's a good mate to the knife. Its lots better than just 'doing in a pinch,' too. It's better than anything I'd have imagined for it." I patted his shoulder only a little less awkward about it than he was.

"Well, good, boy. Now woncha get ya on outta here. Show it to yer womens, or yer ma, or somethin'. I got work ta do here, ya know. Cain't be playin' wif ya alla the time." He grinned just a little, but I could tell, he did want me to go. I wasn't sure why, but 'why' wasn't an issue for me then any more than now. Knowing he was done for the moment was enough. So I left, my almost-done knife on my belt.

I played with it all the way to the Riley place. I practiced pulling it out of the sheath in a quick-draw motion. I practiced drawing it with my left hand. I even threw it at a tree once. It stuck, too. Once I had the edge ground on it, I'd be a lot more careful with such things, but until then, I knew I couldn't hurt the knife much. It was too solidly put together.

I was really looking forward to showing Jeannie what I'd been working on all these months. Her 'purdy little knife' I made for her was something that she treasured, and I must admit, it wasn't half-bad. At least for a first serious attempt. But it wasn't anywhere near in the league of the masterpiece I was carrying now.

When I came to the Riley's, the jalopy was still parked askew in the backyard. I didn't like that a bit, since it was well past dark. Mr. Riley should have been out at his still, either drunk or well on his way. I crept silently to Jeannie's window, and listened carefully.

There was no noise from within, and I risked slipping my new knife blade between the shutters to flip the latch hook open. It made a slight click, but I didn't think that anyone outside the range of five feet could have heard it. I pulled the shutters open very quietly and gently, and stuck my head in the window.

Jeannie was lying on her stomach on the bed, on top of the covers. Her face was buried in the pillow, and her arms were crossed over her head. I whispered, "Psst. Psst. Jeannie!"

She never looked up. "G'way, Rob. Ya don't wanna talk to me right now, boy. I'll come see ya when I can."

I reeled back a little. She'd never refused to see me before. I thought,

"Bullshit, too!" I hopped into her room, never mind her gun-toting daddy. I could tell she was upset, and I thought maybe, just maybe, she needed me.

When she heard my feet touch the floor, she did sit up and turn around. She was absolutely amazed. "Dincha hear me, Rob? Doncha know Daddy's home? Ya tryin' ta get yerself shot, or what?"

"You look like you could use a friend right now, Jeannie. How come you haven't been to school all week?" I looked her over surreptitiously, but there were no obvious bruises, nor any indications that things were any worse than normal. I paused a moment to ponder just how remarkable the human spirit is—the things that it can adapt to and accept as 'normal.'

"Ain't felt like it, Rob. I just ain't felt like leavin'. I just wanna lay here and . . . well; just lay here, for right now. I've been sleepy. I've slept a lot, last week or so. Reckon I know why, too." Her face clouded over, and I could tell she'd been crying, and crying hard. Not long ago, either. She didn't look like the next time was going to be far off, for that matter.

Why, Jeannie?" I couldn't imagine what could make someone so tough, so resilient, act so devastated. The life that this frail-looking girl endured would kill about anybody else I knew. What could have made it so much worse, and so suddenly?

She looked at me bitterly. "You wanna know why? I'll tell ya then, Rob. An' then you'll leave and hate me, too. Yer gonna be the only one ta know. I'm late, Rob."

"Late for what? What did you miss that would make you lay up in here all week?" It wasn't anything to do with school, and I was lost as to what appointment she missed.

"Late for my courses, Rob. I'm gonna have a baby." And she looked at me, fell into my arms, and cried bitterly.

I felt like someone had plunged my new knife into my stomach all the way up to the hilt. This was maybe the worst news in the entire world. She was going to have a baby. And she wasn't married. And she was still living at home, under her daddy's roof. Maybe it won't be as clear to those who weren't raised back then, but having a baby when you weren't married was a big deal. Especially in rural West Virginia. Maybe even more because it was McClellan County.

I felt a fist in the pit of my stomach. Not like a punch, but like something cold was knotting its fingers in my vitals. It was grabbing tight, and I felt like I'd taken a hard shot to the crotch. In a manner of speaking, that is right where her words hit me, though.

Chapter Twenty-Six

I went over to the Chief's the next day. I tried to figure out a way to handle things, a way to make things right for Jeannie. I was just heartsick for her. I decided that if I drove myself hard enough, maybe the answer would come to me. Therefore, not just a workout or knifesmithing, but both.

I didn't come up with any answers, but I did manage to finish the grinding on the knife. My mind was so filled with worry that I didn't have enough focus left over to be bored. I looked at it. It was a thing with a peculiar beauty. Heavy in the hand, more weight in the blade than the hilt. It was tool enough for any job I would ever want a knife to do. And weapon enough, for that matter. The blade ended up being a smidgen over six inches long, and once I did the final honing, it would be as sharp as a straight razor, and hold the edge through not just use, but absolute abuse.

I sighed. I'd love to talk this over with the Chief, but something inside me warned against it. Like I'd be betraying Jeannie's trust. It was my story to hear, but not to tell. I shrugged.

The Chief didn't say much, but looked somewhat surprised when I sheathed the knife and stripped down to 'workout' clothes. I pulled on a pair of shorts and a cut-off sweatshirt, worn over my old sneakers. I went through the relaxing routine of speedbag, double-speedbag, and heavy bag. As the sweat started to trickle off me, I could feel the tension leaving. I still had no answers, but sometimes there's respite in simple exhaustion.

He sensed I was troubled, and tried his best to ease it, I think. He asked if I'd decided which one of my 'womens' to give the robe to. I just shrugged, which was no answer at all. Not that I had one.

The Chief backed off, not wanting to press. We jumped rope and did handjive speed-drills. He could still beat me, but only barely. The absurdity of the two of us making the ludicrous hand-movements never failed to lighten my mood, and it even helped some today. I went so far as to crack a smile. I sighed, and thanked the Chief. I needed to see Jeannie. There wasn't any way around it. For the first time since the night she'd entered my tent, I wasn't looking forward to talking to her.

I felt guilty about that. Just because she was hurting, and really needing me, something in me wanted to run away from her. Because she was bringing my mood down. A part of me really was angry with her for making me feel this way.

It was a small part, though. I logically knew that it wasn't her fault. That she would have given anything to not be going through all this. That she was suffering through this much worse than I was. I berated myself silently on my way to her house. I despised that part of me that would even be thinking such selfish thoughts.

Mr. Riley was gone this time, so I just marched on up to the door and knocked. Jeannie came to the door, looking a little more composed than yesterday, at least. I could tell she'd been crying, but I didn't think she'd been out of control the way she'd been last night. I'd never seen her like that before. I'd never seen anybody in that state before, to be honest. I hadn't known how to react to it other than on an instinctive level—I'd held her.

Today, I petted her hair softly, and made soft-sounding meaningless phrases that comforted through familiarity and good intent, rather than logically consoling. I looked her over carefully. No new bruises. No more cuts. Eyes slightly less puffy than yesterday. She still looked like she needed not just a hug, but a platoon of hugs. A whole boxcar of hugs. I did the best I could.

"Jeannie, baby? Are you okay?" Of course I already knew she wasn't, but I had no idea what else to say.

"I'm so lost, Rob. I ain't got no idear what I'm gonna do. I just don't got no idears. I mean, I do, but none a' my options is any damned good." Tears welled in her eyes, then gave up and spilled down her cheeks. There was no sobbing, no noise whatsoever. Somehow that made it worse, more visible. Her agony was thick and palpable in the air between us.

I still had no better plan or idea than to hold her. Maybe ask her what some of her options were. "Jeannie, what ideas have you come up with?"

Her eyes dried a little, and she pulled back from me enough to talk with her hands, as she did when she was excited.

"First off, I could find me a yarb-woman. Someone ta help me slip the baby. Or I could have the baby and hope it ain't deformed er dead. Or I could kill myself. That'd solve the whole stinkin' mess." I looked at her, stunned. The idea that she might be even considering suicide as an option had never occurred to me.

"Hey, Jeannie. Don't even talk like that!" My voice seemed to come from somewhere else. No power behind it. My shock robbed my voice of all potency. It sounded more like a whisper than a command.

"Like what, Rob? Does one of 'em really sound any worse than the others?" Her voice was bitter and hard, not at all the soothing gentle timbre I was used to.

"Jeannie, you can't kill yourself, honey." That was a start, but I had no idea how to follow up. "I'd miss you too much. I'd never forgive myself for not protecting you better." I felt like a heel to use my feelings for her as a weapon against her, but if that's the only weapon at hand, I knew I could be ruthless. "I couldn't stand to lose my best friend, Jeannie."

"But couldja look in your best friend's face an' know she murdered her baby? Or that she had a monster growin' inside a' her?" Her eyes were strangely dry, and the questions almost seemed rhetorical, as if she wouldn't or couldn't hear the answer anyway.

"Jeannie, honey, it's not like you carry the responsibility for all this stuff. But if you kill yourself, Jeannie, that would be something that you did. I couldn't stand that." That was a little better, I guess. Logical and rational. Right?

"Killing my baby and living myself would be something I did too." Her eyes, normally so soft and tender, were hard and cold. She was scaring me. I wasn't used to being afraid of anyone or anything. Not even Calvin, anymore. "Birthin' a baby to suffer an' die er live a horrible disfigured sufferin' life would be something else I did. All a' my options are bad, and they're all somethin' I'd be doin', Rob."

Damn. She didn't speak perfect English, and I guess I'd never gotten over my intellectual snobbery. Hillbilly talk was for stupid people. But she was so far from stupid that she'd shredded the first thing I'd thought of as at least a reasonable argument without even trying hard. "Jeannie . . . " How could I argue with her? Her options were all wretched things to pick from. But some were worse than others, I guess.

"Jeannie, Mom's an herb-woman." She's helped women have babies before, I know. And her herb garden was even better tended than the vegetable garden. But would she help Jeannie lose her baby on purpose? Did she know how, even? And was that something that I wanted to encourage her to do?

"She'd be the onliest one I'd talk to 'bout it, too. She ain't spooky like Widder Thompson, an' she ain't all creepy-touchie like Miss Wilcomb in town, neither." The look on her face let me know that she knew Mom was an herb-woman long before I'd said so.

"You could talk to her about it, anyhow. Not after you'd made up your mind, but to help, maybe." I thought that perhaps Jeannie would be able to get some comfort from talking to another woman. I sure didn't have any answers. Was it just because of my gender, I wondered? Would Mom know what to say, what to do?

"Maybe I could, Rob. Couldja ask her for me, maybe? Iffen she don't wanna, I understand. But . . . I just don't know what I'm gonna do. Or iffen I'll be wantin' the guilt of slippin' the babe on purpose. Or iffen any of my options is the right thing." Her chin quivered a bit. All of a sudden, I could see that the stony exterior of my best friend was just a front. She was just as broken as she'd been last night. She was just learning to deal with being shattered. That wasn't the same as mending.

Chapter Twenty-Seven

It was three days before I worked up the nerve to ask Mom about it. I watched her beating hell out of some seemingly innocent dough and wondered how to bring any of this up. She always made bread when she was upset . . . of course, she made bread when she wasn't upset too, but I sometimes could tell the subtle difference in the way she punished the dough while kneading it.

"Mom?" I started out, but she seemed so intent on the dough that I stopped. She looked up at me and glared, seething with anger. I recoiled a bit at this display. She seemed like she was angry with me, and I hadn't even started yet.

"Air it Cal's?" She demanded, as if this were plenty enough of an explanation.

"Is what Cal's, Mom?" I was genuinely confused on this one, and maybe enough of it showed for her to notice. She calmed a bit, and dropped the dough. She slowly went through her motions of making coffee.

"Air Jeannie's baby Calvin's. That's what I'm a-askin' ya, son." Her back was to me, and I couldn't see the expression on her face, but her shoulders were slumped and she looked almost defeated. This was impossible. My Mama couldn't be defeated, not at anything.

Maybe her posture made me skip the obvious question about how she knew. "No, Mama. It isn't Calvin's at all. Calvin doesn't even know about it, and he hasn't been with her in almost a year."

Her shoulders somehow slumped even lower, but it looked like relief, at least from my vantage point. "Thank ya, son. That's the onliest good news I've got all damned day." For my Mama to swear, her day must have been pretty bad indeed.

"Mama, why did you think it was Calvin's? You know he's been seeing Donna. And I know that he's not seeing Jeannie at all anymore. He couldn't hide that from me, Mama. We share a room. We hang out whenever I'm not at the Chief's." Or with Jeannie. Or Donna, when I could. Not to mention that Jeannie would tell me the truth if I had even needed to ask, which I didn't. She'd put all her bad habits aside, ironically enough. But that wasn't what we were talking about, really.

"I knew that they's up to monkeyshines a coupla years back. When I saw 'er down t' the grocery, I knowed she was with child. An' I jest wanted ta make sure it weren't Cal's." The grief mixed with relief on her face made my heartstrings quiver.

"So you knew she was with child?" I thought this might go easier than I'd thought. "Mom, she'd like to talk to you about it."

"An' say what?" Mom had her suspicious face on now.

"Just talk to you. She doesn't have a mother, and I thought that maybe you could talk to her about it or something." Hearing it said aloud, it sounded pretty stupid. "Because you're a woman, Mom. And you know about herbs and stuff."

She just looked at me. I knew I'd better come up with something pretty quick.

"She asked me if it would be alright. She doesn't have anyone else to talk to!" Sheer ignorance and bravado might be enough to pull me through. Ignorance, because I didn't have any idea what I was doing. Bravado, because if I just plowed ahead and showed Mama my ignorance, then maybe she'd do this for Jeannie just because she could see I didn't know what else to do.

"I reckon th'ain't no harm in it, son. But th'ain't much good of it, neither. Cain't do much, y'ken? I can talk to 'er as a woman, but they's only so much a yarb-woman can do for 'er." She gazed at me with impenetrable eyes, and I had no idea what message she was trying to send.

"She just wants to talk to you, Mom. She's got no one to turn to besides me, and there's not a thing I can do for her at all, Mom. I need your help." I turned my eyes down, because I didn't want my mother to see the tears in them.

"Reckon it cain't hurt, son. Don't know iffen I kin do no good t'all, but I'll chin with 'er, anyrate." She had a soft look in her eyes, and laid her hand on my shoulder gently. "Sometimes not doin' no harm is the best y' can do, boy. That's mankind's lot there fer ya in a nutshell. Bein' a hero is often just makin' the best of a dirty deal, doin' the best y'kin, an' not makin' it no worser." She saw my expression and laughed her deep, heavy laugh. "Oh, yer mama knows, child. I've known a few heroes, y'ken?"

I wanted to ask her who she meant, and what being a hero had to do with anything. Who was the hero in her eyes? Jeannie? Herself? Me? Calvin? I didn't get it at all. Not at the time.

On a loose piece of paper stuffed between these two pages:

It was some years before I realized that my mother was proud of me at that dinner-table conversation. I hadn't imagined it at the time. Granted, there were other things on my mind: Other cats to whip, as the French say. But when I did grasp that my mother was calling my actions heroic, I was so proud and so humbled simultaneously that I cried. She actually saw something of the heroic in a frightened boy looking to his mother for help. She probably never realized that from my point of view, she was the hero. Or heroine, I suppose. She's always been one of my heroes, though. Maybe someday I'll find the words to tell her so.

I sat at the workbench at the Chief's, honing away at my blade. I had already taken it to a wicked keen edge, and was trying to get the blade to maximum sharpness. The Chief watched me over my shoulder, and finally snarled, "Leave the goddamned thing be, boy. You're done. It's sharp, already. Sharper than it needs to be, you damn fool. Didja keep it at 28 degrees the whole time?"

I grinned and nodded. He took the knife from me, and said, "Now watch ya this, pup." He grabbed up a piece of pine lumber laying around, about the size of a two by four. Then, to my horror, he hacked away at the board, using my knife as a hatchet!

"Hey! Chief! Damn! I just sharpened that!" I wanted to grab him, but his frantic flailing with my blade against the lumber made me fear for my safety. And I had to admit, it was whacking away quite a chunk of the board.

He severed the plank, and then grabbed my wrist. "Lookie here, boy." He slowly drew the blade over the hair of my arm, and despite rough use and abuse, well beyond what the knife was designed for; it still popped hairs and left a bare patch.

He handed the knife back, and said quietly, "Ya done good, Bobby. Not as good as I'd've made it, maybe . . . but I'd hate ta live on the difference. Now, whaddaya wanna do wif it?"

I hadn't ever given this any consideration. Wear it, of course. Use it. What was the Chief getting at? I looked at him for some clue as to what he might be talking about.

"Do ya want me ta teach ya knife-fightin'? I done my fair share and then some, I reckon. I could show ya a few pointers, an' ya could work out the rest on yer own. A knife's a potent weapon in skilled hands. Iffen you's ta try usin' it without knowin' how, ya'd probably do alright, so long as the feller yer fightin' ain't a knifesman hisself. But I wouldn't mind showin' ya the bits I knows." He looked down, and actually scuffed his boot, looking for all the world like a little boy.

"That would be great, Chief! Is it a lot different than boxing?" I hadn't ever thought that the Chief might be a skilled knife-fighter. I suppose it shouldn't have surprised me. Spending all those years in the service, stopping in the godawful-est ports in the Far East, and then looking for the worst spots you could find while you were there . . . It would behoove a man to be able to fight with a weapon as well as with his fists.

"Okay, Bobby. Ain't much like boxin', not a'tall. More like dancin', er playin' the handjive drills fer real." He took the knife, and to my surprise, didn't take it and tuck it up under his wrist in a reverse grip.

"Chief, I thought that real knife-fighters held the knife under their wrist, along their forearm, not sticking out like they were going to whittle or something!" I was shocked. Calvin had shown me the way that the hoods from Jefferson held their knives, and had seemed impressed with their skill.

"Nah. That's a bunch of hokum, son. Tucking yer knife under yer wrist is good if yer tryin' ta hide it from somebody, but unless yer goin' ta use it ta assassinate somebody, ya don't need ta worry 'bout all that bullshit. Other than hidin' it, can ya tell me one advantage of havin' it tucked up under yer wrist?"

I thought about it. "Maybe keep it from being kicked out of your hand?"

He snorted, and said, "That'd put the edge into somebody's foot pretty easy. But my way a' dealin' with that'd be ta point the tip into their foot.

Rather have yer foot cut, or the goddamned thing impaled?" He demonstrated how to angle the blade right into a rising kick. I shuddered a bit. That would be godawful nasty effective.

"If yer outta questions, son, I guess we can get ta the lesson?" So we did.

Chapter Twenty-Eight

"Calvin, how are you and Donna getting along?" I hadn't talked to Calvin about her in weeks. The tentative detente also held with Donna. I hadn't asked her about Calvin, either. And fortunately, she'd finally started talking to me as a person in my own right, not just an adjunct of Calvin.

"Reckon we do all right, Bobby-boy. Ya wanna go campin' this weekend, maybe? Down ta rivercamp, just like we used ta?" Calvin seemingly was in the mood to talk, and treat with me as an equal. Or as close to it as he ever did.

I thought about it. "Donna coming?"

He grinned and shrugged. "Depends on you, I s'pose. Iffen yer gonna agree to it, then you could prob'ly get her outta th' house."

"I suppose it might be okay, Calvin. You bringing the meat, or do I need to provide it and cook it too?"

"I'll bring the meat. You bring the pans and Donna." He tipped me a wink. "You up for some checkers?"

We played for a few matches, with Calvin being just the way I liked him to be. And it didn't seem to be due to the favor he'd asked. He was in a genuine good humor, and I ate it up. When I beat him three straight, he tackled me to the floor and started tousling my hair, holding me in a headlock. I countered with a reversal that left his arm twisted behind his back, and tousled his hair right back with my free hand.

We were whooping and laughing, and ended up kicking the checkerboard and checkers everywhere. About the time we were really going at it hammer and tongs, there was a sudden hailstorm. We split apart, rolling for cover.

Mom stood over us, flailing madly with a wooden spoon in one hand, and a serving ladle in the other. "Godless heathens, the both of yas!" She aimed a hard swat at my head with the ladle, and missed. But she did catch Calvin with a no-lookie backhand with the spoon, right across his eye. He hollered and scrambled for the door. I wasn't far behind, and the spoon cracked across my rear end anyway.

"She's quick, ain't she?" Calvin rubbed his eye ruefully.

"And stronger than she looks, too. I'll have a welt from that spoon." I rubbed my sore rear.

"Yer damned lucky she missed ya with the ladle. That shit ain't funny, ya know? I caught a good crack across the head before I knew she was there!" He laughed.

We laughed together, since it wouldn't have done much good to cry about it. We had a great afternoon, preparing the camp for the weekend. We chopped wood for the fire, and made minor repairs to my 'cabin'. I worked on a framework for a windbreak. This would hopefully make sitting around the fire as a group more pleasant. Calvin even used his greater strength to uproot some larger stones near the river to use as seats around the campfire. I helped him roll/drag them into place, and we kept collapsing, laughing over the strain of it all. We knew it was ridiculous to be hauling huge stones to use as seats, but didn't care. It was part of the fun of the day.

Later that evening, I walked into town to see Donna. Her father greeted me warmly, clapping me on the back and welcoming me in. "How's Donna's math goin', son? Any hope for 'them fractious ratios'?" he asked, eyes twinkling.

"Well sir, I know she could do it. She's smart enough, but she's decided that she isn't. And I suppose that you'd know better than anyone what it's like to try and convince her she's wrong about something." I grinned back.

He laughed uproariously, and clapped my back again. "Yer too right about that son. Too right by half. Come on in and let's have a cuppa coffee or cocoa, iffen ya like."

"That sounds wonderful, sir. It's fairly chilly out. Better weather than we could expect in December, but chilly all the same." And it was fairly cold. But not too cold for camping.

"What're you and my girl up to now, Bobby? It's been a while since I seen ya. I know yer always doing somethin' different, though. I liked that 'French party' ya put together for 'er. She's tole me all 'bout it, ya know. I 'preciate it, Bobby. Broke 'er a' always wantin' somethin' fancy. She was plumb discouraged 'bout that caviar." He laughed, and I couldn't help but join him. He served out a cup of coffee for himself, and made a quick cup of cocoa for me. I'd never had instant cocoa before . . . and I was glad that we didn't have the money for such things. It wasn't anywhere near as good as Mama's was.

"It was pretty awful, Mr. Duquesne. I can't imagine why anyone would want it. I think it's as the Chief said. When they figured out that it tasted horrible, they just charged more money for it and called it a delicacy." I grinned at him. He was a thoroughly likeable man.

"Reckon ya didn't come all the way inta town ta just chin with an ol' man, didja, son?" Raising his voice a little, he called over his shoulder, "Donna? C'mon down here, girl. Yer boyfriend's here!" He looked at me to see how I reacted.

Predictably enough, I guess, I blushed furiously. I wasn't really her boyfriend, but I sure would have been in a heartbeat, if she'd have me. He grinned at me, only half-right about why I was blushing.

Donna came downstairs in a black skirt, pink blouse, and a snowy-white cardigan. Her hair was up in a pink ribbony-type thing that looked like lace. She was smiling and doing a little blushing of her own, from all appearances. She looked like an angel, descending the stairs in her own glow.

"Daddy, doncha go embarrassin' me n' Bobby, now! Ya got better manners 'n that, I know!" She spoke harshly and roughly to him, but it her affection was evident. She really didn't even mind being embarrassed. Of course, she and I both knew that I wasn't really her boyfriend, and that probably had a good bit to do with her lack of true venom.

"Doncha go bossin' me girlie! Y'ain't too big fer a spankin' yet, Donna Nell! Doncha fergit it, neither!" His rejoinder was as hollow as her scolding, and I was glad. I didn't want to think about another one of my 'womens', as the Chief jokingly called them, in that sort of life. Home was a sanctuary to Donna, at least. For Jeannie it was more like a concentration camp.

Donna finished up her little pouting stomp act next to me. While looking at her, it was difficult to get my voice to work. "Donna, would you like to camp out Friday night? We've made some improvements to the rivercamp. It should be warmer and more comfortable than ever." I swallowed hard, because my mouth suddenly seemed too full of spit.

"Sounds like fun to me, Bobby. Would that be alright, Poppa? Iffen I go campin' Friday night?" She turned her eyes on him with a pleading expression, and I knew he was a goner. Once she turned her gazed on me, I knew I'd move heaven and earth for her if that's what she wanted. Her father would be just about as susceptible to her magic as I was.

I was right. "Reckon it'd be alright, honey. Iffen yer gonna be home before eleven on Saturday mornin'. There's a new movie playin' over ta Jefferson. I was gonna surprise ya with it, but reckon y' oughtta know why yer trip has ta get over by eleven. I'll be finishin' up with the paper fer the day 'bout ten, and I'll get cleaned up an' we'll go fer lunch an' a picture show." He stopped an' looked at the wall for a moment, then turned his eyes towards me. "How 'bout you, Bobby? Gotcha any plans fer Saturday afternoon?"

He caught me flatfooted with that one. "Uh, no sir. I don't think so, anyhow," I blurted, looking at Donna to try gauging her reaction. She seemed pleased. What did that mean?

"Hows about ya see iffen yer Ma's got any objection ta ya goin' with us over Jefferson way. My treat, too. Like ta tag along on yer date with my daughter, so ta speak." He gave me a wink.

"Well, sir, I'll ask Mama. I don't know if she'll have any plans for me that afternoon." My palms were sweaty and I was nervous. I didn't know where that was coming from, or what it meant for Donna and me, if anything. She was still smiling, though.

"Iffen ya can come, just get cleaned up an' stick around after ya walk Donna home Saturday mornin'. Be glad ta have ya, son." He clapped my shoulder and tipped his coffee back. "Reckon I'll go tune in the news an' let you young 'uns jaw ta yerselves."

I stood there with Donna, uncertain what I was supposed to be doing, and she leaned over and kissed me gently, her mouth slightly open, as soon as her father's back was turned. "Drink your cocoa, silly. It's getting cold."

It didn't matter how cold it got. I'd dropped it in astonishment. My heart stopped in my chest, I'm fairly certain. She'd kissed me! I'd thought about kissing her for two years, and it happened so fast that I wasn't aware of it until it was over! All the things about kissing that Jeannie taught me, all the dreaming I'd done about the moment, and I'd frozen up like a deer in the headlights!

She grinned at my dazzled look. "Let's get that cocoa cleaned up, Bobby." She winked, and I wondered exactly what it was she was up to. As she wiped it up, she looked up at me and grinned. I stood there, feeling stupid and useless. I hadn't been in their kitchen before. I didn't know where anything that I'd need to clean it with might be kept.

"Why'd ya go an' thow the cocoa on th' floor fer?" she demanded, mock-angry. She finished wiping up the mess with a moistened towel. It hadn't been under the sink, where I would have looked first. It was in a drawer over by the oven. I shook my head to try and clear the stars. I hadn't been rocked this badly even in the final round of the Golden Gloves. I was physically dizzy!

Donna rolled the dishtowel into a rattail and snapped my butt with it. I yelped in surprise. What the hell had come over her? I shook my head with an absolute lack of comprehension.

She grinned. "What's wrong, Bobby? Yer lookin' a bit pale 'round the gills, boy. Dincha like it?" She put one hand on her cocked hip and looked at me saucily.

I couldn't think of any diplomatic or suave way to even try to come across with this one. "Donna, what's with this sudden change? The last time I tried to kiss you . . . well, it didn't work out so well. Now you're kissing me? I like it. I've dreamed about it for years. But I can't help feeling like there's some sort of trick or mistake here."

She smiled. "I ain't makin' no mistake, Bobby Taylor. An' I ain't tryin' ta trick ya, neither. Jest been doin' some thinkin', that's all. Calvin's still seein' them gals from Jefferson, an' doncha bother tellin' me he ain't. An' iffen he ain't gonna be true ta me, then I ain't obligated ta be true ta him. An', Bobby, jest because I'm in love with Calvin an' I'm gonna marry 'im, that don't mean that I don't love ya too. 'Cause I do, ya know. Yer a special kinda fella. Always been real good ta me. An' yer awful cute, jest standin' there wif yer gob hangin' open. Think ya might have a kiss in that thing fer me? Better use fer yer mouth than catchin' flies, there." She glided into my arms like she was on skates.

It's a good thing that Jeannie had taught me all she knew about kissing, and that I'd had plenty of practice sessions, because if it hadn't been for the fact that kissing was second-nature to me by now, I'd have just stood there fishmouthed. Instead, I was able to kiss Donna. Deeply. Openmouthed. Tongues and all. She nipped my lower lip lightly, and for a moment, it felt all wrong. Then I realized what it was. Donna's teeth were perfect, straight, white, and sharp. I was used to kissing Jeannie's broken-toothed mouth, and it felt different.

When I could breathe again, (notice I didn't say normally), I said, "Donna, what's this mean to us? And you and Calvin? What am I supposed to be to you? Friend? Boyfriend? A minor affaire d'couer?"

She wrinkled her nose like I'd asked a really stupid question. "We're friends, ain't we? An' yer brother's seein' me, an' yer seein' me. Jest like the ol' southern belles did it. Lots of suitors, an' they was ta act gentleman ta one another. Jest ya look at it like that, Bobby, an' quit makin' things hard."

Was I making things hard? Was I deluding myself? Was she using me? And did I care?

Chapter Twenty-Nine

I walked by Jeannie's on the way home, and saw that Mr. Riley wasn't in. I knocked on the window of her room to see if she was home. Occasionally, she'd be out to get groceries or to visit her aunt, but tonight she was there. She didn't look any worse, but she didn't look any better, either. She did have a weak grin for me as she opened the window.

"Hey there, Rob. Lemme see that there knife ya finally finished up with, boy." She looked pale and there were circles under her eyes. In her face, I could tell that she'd lost weight. Could it have only been two weeks since I found out about her pregnancy? And weren't women supposed to gain weight while this was going on?

Without a word, but a big smile, I handed the knife on over. She tested the edge with her finger, and gave a low whistle of admiration. She held it to the light and stroked her fingers lightly over the glossy wood and the hammerhead on the hilt. She said, "Too heavy fer my hand, but not so heavy as you'd think from the look of 'er. She's awful pretty, Rob. You got every reason to be proud of this 'un." She opened her drawer by her bed and showed me the little knife I crafted for her. It wasn't nearly as well made as the one I'd just finished.

"I'll make you a better one, Jeannie. I—" She cut me off promptly.

"I like this 'un just fine, Robert Taylor. This is the first one ya ever made all by yourself, and it's mine. It means more to me than just the knife. That's the first time anybody's ever give me anything without wantin' somethin' in return. So you just leave my purdy li'l knife be, and we'll both be happier for it." She stomped her foot a little bit, and got a little more serious. "So is there anything new with you, Rob?"

I figured I would get to the important business before telling her about the other news. "Jeannie, honey, I talked to Mom. She said it'd be alright to talk to her about it any old time. Stop by any afternoon, and she says stay for supper, if you like." I had to bite off the impulse to ask how she'd been. How the hell did I think she'd been? It's funny how stupid most of the niceties of human interaction are when exposed to more than surface scrutiny. The hell of it is she'd have probably have told me she'd been fine just as reflexively.

"That's good, Rob. Did she seem—"

I knew what she was going to ask, and didn't even want the words coming out. "No. She's not real happy with the situation, and isn't thinking of you as a saint, Jeannie, but she isn't going to look at you like a criminal, either."

"You didn't tell her anything about . . . who the baby's father is, did you?" She looked despondently at me, as if sure I'd done that very thing.

"It's not my story to tell, Jeannie. To hear, and to help you live, but not mine to tell. That's the way I look at it, anyway." I hugged her tight.

"You tell Mama whatever you want to, though, and she'll surprise you with how smart she is. If anyone can help, Jeannie, it's her." I started rocking her slowly as we stood there in each other's arms.

I wanted to tell her about Donna, and what had happened at the Duquesne house tonight, but didn't know exactly how. It seemed tacky, on the one hand. On the other, Jeannie was my very best friend in the entire world. I was supposed to share things with her, right? She felt the tension in my body as I wrestled with the question.

"What is it, Rob? I been pretty selfish, reckon. Jest 'cause we got this goin' on don't mean your life's standin' still. You gotcha some news?" She looked up at me with her eyes still wet, but so attentive! What had I done to deserve such a friend?

"Well, it's an odd situation, Jeannie. Donna kissed me tonight when I went to ask her to come camping this weekend. Calvin had sent me over to find out, and she was just . . . very open, I guess. She said that since Calvin wasn't being faithful to her yet, she didn't see any impediment to her kissing me."

"She said 'yet'?" Jeannie stood very still, still close to me; close enough to hug each other without moving our feet. But we weren't.

"I think she's really in love with him, Jeannie. But she said that she had feelings for me too. I don't know what that really means in the long run, but God! I've dreamed and wanted her to kiss me for so long . . . It doesn't seem real!" I got caught up in my memory of the moment, and the smile that came to my face was involuntary. I was confused and not able to really understand what was going on, but loving every minute of it.

"So iffen I'm gettin' all this right, she's still plannin' on linkin' up with Calvin in the long haul. Yer just gonna be her boy-toy in the meantime?" Jeannie's eyes were hard now. Harder than I'd ever seen them. No trace of tear remained.

"That makes it sound so . . . " I knew what it made it sound like, and I didn't want to say the words. Suddenly the idea of it raked over me with jagged claws. But then I had a moment of epiphany: I knew how to explain it so that it wouldn't be as cheap and dirty as it sounded.

"Jeannie, other than the fact that you're not in love with me, it's not much different from what you and I are doing, is it? Would that be so wrong?"

An indecipherable expression flickered over her face. "Rob, I ain't sayin' it's wrong. I ain't even saying that she's bad. But how will Calvin take it iffen he found out? Can Donna cope with that? And can you stand to be discarded like trash iffen she does ever get her hooks into Calvin the way she thinks she can? I ain't worried 'bout her, Rob. Don't care 'bout what she wants, nor what happens to 'er. But what about you, an' yer feelin's? That's all I'm worryin' about." She turned her head aside and looked down.

"I can't worry about that, Jeannie, honey. It's like that old saying: Love like you can't be hurt. I can't help it, and if this is what I can have, I'm happy to have it."

She actually smiled then, a peculiar twisted little grin, and said, "I guess I understand that, Rob. Reckon I see where you're comin' from." She straightened up and looked me in the eye, "But just remember that you've always got a friend here to come to iffen ya need me." Suddenly, I thought there was a patina of tears over her eyes again, but she ducked her head away before I could tell for certain.

I repeated, "Why don't you plan on coming over for supper one of these nights? After dinner, you, Mom, and I could talk, or I could go chase my tail for a while if you'd rather. You look like you haven't been eating too well. Mom may or may not be able to help with your problem, but I guarantee that she can get a good meal inside you."

She grinned wryly. "Ain't felt a whole lot like cookin', an' even when I did, ain't felt much like eatin'. Guess supper over ta yer house sounds pretty good."

I looked her over carefully, and smiled a little bit, even if it was only on the inside. She looked a little bit better already. I kissed her deeply, gently but with passion. She seemed to drink it in like wine. When I straightened up, she looked even better than before. I made my goodbyes, and started walking home.

As I walked, I realized why she'd looked so much better after I came by. There was an element there when I left that wasn't there when I had arrived. Hope.

Chapter Thirty

When Calvin and I had all the wood chopped that we'd need, we finished up minor repairs to our minor repairs. He grinned and told me to fetch Donna, and he was going to get dinner. I started the hike into town.

All the way there, I wondered exactly how the fact that Donna and I had kissed and touched would affect our camp dynamic. Usually, Donna sat beside Calvin and simpered quietly about him and to him. I was generally across the fire from them, and grumbled and grunted occasionally. Calvin would hold forth about his favorite subject, or a variation thereof: how wonderful he was and the great things he'd done and was going to do.

Somehow, I got the idea that things might not be the same any more. It would be interesting, at a minimum. I knew I should be anxious and worried, and wondering if Donna could keep her mouth shut. Instead, I found myself thinking that it would certainly get cute around that campfire if she couldn't. I wasn't afraid of Calvin any longer. I didn't like the idea of hurting his feelings at all. The idea of hurting him, on the other hand, did not bother me one little bit. If it rednecked him to lose a girl to his little brother, then he'd just have to be mad. I felt as though I had a prior claim.

The image of me dusting Calvin's chin for him as he scrambled across the fire towards Donna and I was a potent and thrilling one. It wasn't that I wanted to beat up on Calvin, exactly. But the idea of a little bit of payback for all the times he'd thrashed me as we were growing up wasn't a bitter pill to swallow. I could admit that, too.

I daydreamed and fantasized about how tonight was going to unwind the entire trip into Folsom Hollow. I probably could have hitched into town with one of the trucks that passed me, but I was entirely too excited about the upcoming night.

When I knocked on the door, Donna almost pulled me into the house with the draft of the door opening. She laughed and giggled, bounding out the door with a very fetching exuberance. "Hey there, Bobby Taylor! Ya gonna tote my pack fer me?" When I nodded, smiling, she flung herself into my arms. "I'll have ta give ya somethin' special fer that, later on tonight," she whispered in a sultry voice. I was instantly aroused and my breathing speeded up. She tossed me her pack, laughing.

The whole way back, I walked hand-in-hand with her. We talked of many things, about things we loved, about her dream of visiting Paris, and about her dream home. She wanted a two-story house out in the country, with running water and flush toilets. Not just one, but two. She wanted a bathroom just for the master bedroom. And it had to be white, with a front and back porch. It had to be at least four bedroom, too. She wanted a little boy and a little girl, and a bedroom just for company, if she ever had any. She wanted a room just for her washer and she wanted a clothes-drying machine. She also thought a white picket fence around the yard would be the perfect touch. Of course, she'd plant a rose garden of her very own, and have a small vegetable patch to keep her busy.

I laughed. A lot of these things sounded like crazy dreams at the time. But I promised myself, even as I laughed at her and teased her about her wild fancies, that if I were ever the man in her life, I'd try to make them happen.

We talked of many different things on the way to our rivercamp, but one thing we didn't discuss was Calvin. Nor did we discuss our relationship or the change in its nature. It was obvious that it had changed, though. She would lean close to me and give me a kind of hug as we walked, or give me the kind of smiles from her that I'd wanted all this time. The entire time that we spent walking back, even as I was talking with her, I was still fantasizing about how things would go tonight.

We walked into camp and found Calvin sitting with a quart jar on his lap. A pint jar was already lying empty nearby. He'd gone back to the house and returned with the backstraps of a deer, and a couple of pounds of bacon. He'd also brought a dozen eggs, a block of cheese, and a quart of milk.

"What's all this stuff for, Calvin? You just hungry for a breakfast at dinnertime?" I was perplexed. The venison made sense. The other stuff did not.

"Got me an idear, Bobby-boy. Read 'bout it the other day." He grinned at my skeptical look. "It's true, ol' boy. Jest 'cause yer a better reader'n me don't make ya the onliest one in the goddamned world that can do it." He laughed. "Yer gonna hafta help me, but I'm gonna do the cookin' tonight, as a s'prise."

I was dumbstruck. Calvin? Cooking? What was this all about? Either he was up to something dirty, or he was trying harder to impress Donna than he'd ever tried with another girl before. "What are you going to cook, Cal?"

"Ya'll are gonna like it, but I ain't gonna tell ya what I'm up to. Bobby-boy, you just whip them eggs like yer gonna scramble 'em."

"All of them?" I asked, incredulous.

"Yep. Fork 'em good. An' Donna, you jest sit over thar on that thar rock an' look pretty." While I whipped the eggs with a fork, he started grating the cheese into shreds. The whole block of it. I shook my head. What in the world was my brother up to?

Calvin preheated his skillet, and spitted the tenderloin on a long skewer, then wrapped it with the bacon, as if he was gift-wrapping it. He set up a primitive rotisserie, and placed the bacon-wrapped venison over the fire. Then he grabbed my bowl of well-whipped eggs, and dumped a good dollop of milk in it. "Whip that in there good, boy." He turned to the tent and pulled out a small sack. He had diced peppers and onions in a small jar. Mom had canned several jars of onion/pepper mix with vinegar, and a couple without. This was without, I hoped. He also pulled out the camp salt-and-pepper shakers.

I had no idea what he was up to, but I watched in amazement as he poured a skillet-full of my egg/milk mix. Instead of forking them around, as if he was scrambling them, he let it sizzle and sear. Then he took a handful of the pepper/onion mix and threw it in the pan, spreading it throughout the pan. Then he added a handful of the shredded cheese.

I had no idea what he was cooking. I'd never seen Mama do anything similar. And I wasn't familiar enough with cooking myself to even have a guess. I could cook, but I showed next-to-no imagination. He looked up at me and grinned, enjoying having the edge on me in his surprise.

He said, "Now's when I need yer help, Bobby-boy. You can flip eggs better'n I ever could. I always bust the yolks, Donna. Bobby's got a smoother hand fer it. Jest flip it inta three parts. Left side to the middle, right side ta meet it."

I slid the spatula under it and did as he instructed. "Now, flip the whole thang over."

"Calvin, I'll need another spatula, or it'll break." I didn't know if he'd planned this all the way through. I was hoping that he had something else, because I really wanted his surprise to work out the way he planned. I was too curious to see about this thing he was making.

Donna leapt to the rescue. She slid a plate up under the part of the thing I was holding up with a spatula. "This do?" she winked.

Together, we flipped the thing over onto the skillet, and Calvin grinned cheerfully. "Now, it's jest gonna take another minute or so, an' that un 'll be ready." He turned the meat on the spit so that the other side of the bacon-wrapped backstrap would get done evenly.

After we'd made two more of these odd breakfast things, Calvin pronounced the meat done. He pulled the bacon off of it and flung it into the fire. I squawked in indignation. "Why are you wasting the bacon?"

"Ain't wasted, boy. All the flavor got soaked up inta this here deer meat." He sliced it open, and it was pinker than either Donna or I was used to. "Perfect!" Calvin exclaimed. "It said ta get 'er out after the red was gone an' afore the pink was."

He dished out the plates, and served us all some of his meal. Donna tried her egg-thing first, and said, "Wow! Calvin, that's just great! What's it called?"

"It's an omelet. French stuff!" He laughed delightedly and slapped his knee. "Snuck one over on you two, din't I? French food ya ain't know all about 'fore I did!"

I had to laugh. If I'd thought about it, I'd have known what it was. An omelet just seemed like too much of a stretch towards the high-class way of life for Calvin. I tasted a bite, and nodded approvingly. It was delicious.

And the venison that had been wrapped in bacon was another surprise. It didn't taste like regular venison, nor more than a hint of bacon. It was easily the best deer meat that I'd ever eaten. What had gotten into my brother to even try cooking? Whatever it was, I encouraged it thoroughly.

He had excellent ideas.

Chapter Thirty-One

It was well after dinner before Donna or I stopped raving about his culinary skills. He'd grown tired of it, though, and told us to 'jest hush, now.' I think it embarrassed him to succeed so well at 'woman's work'. Even though it was meant as a one-time surprise, he felt a little emasculated by the whole project.

After we'd gotten finished praising him, we played a few hands of rummy. I beat Calvin by a wide margin, and I got the impression that Donna was paying more attention to Calvin than to her cards. She made silly discards that she'd have to know I was collecting. After drubbing them both soundly, I tossed in my cards.

I was frustrated. I knew that the two of us had something special to share. That things were different now. But Donna was still acting as besotted with my brother as ever. Didn't the things that we shared mean anything to her? I threw my cards in the middle of the stone and stretched, preparing to go to my cabin.

"Doncha go runnin' off, Bobby Taylor," Donna said, with a wicked grin. "Ya wouldn't wanna miss the best card game in the world, wouldja?"

I was really in no mood for another card game in which I was the only interested party. The two of them were too busy making eyes at each other. Ordinarily Calvin's competitive streak would come out, and he'd pay better attention. But not tonight. "What game would that be, Donna?"

"Strip poker, Bobby. Whether I win or lose, I think it'll get interestin' 'round here in a hurry."

Calvin laughed, a harsh and grating sound. "Donna, you ain't serious, air ya? Strippin' down in front of my li'l brother? I reckon the sight'd just about kill 'im. Don't think 'is heart could take it."

I would have added something myself, but for some reason, my throat seemed to have a stone or something in it, and no words would emerge.

"Serious as a sawed-off shotgun, Calvin Taylor. Think it might liven things up 'round this here camp." She looked at him with a devilish grin.

All of a sudden, I understood. This was a ploy to make Calvin jealous and more attentive. And it sure seemed to be working. I knew I should get up and leave. I knew that I was just a pawn in her game with Calvin. I still had my pride!

And I still had an erection. The idea of it seemed so erotic and thrilling that I simply couldn't leave. The image of Donna slowly peeling out of her clothes was a siren-song that I couldn't resist, despite my realizations.

"I'm game," I squeaked.

"Are ya then?" Calvin's face got calm all of a sudden. "I don't reckon that ya are, really. Let's make it winners-keepers, just ta make it intrestin'." This would up the stakes a good bit. If Calvin won Donna's clothes, or mine, I could well imagine him refusing to give them back, in order to stymie our trip into Jefferson tomorrow. How would I explain either of us being less than fully clothed?

I decided that if Donna was willing to risk it, then I definitely had no qualms. But I wasn't going to take the dare without her saying so. "What do you think of that rule, Donna?"

"Keepers 'til mornin', Calvin Taylor. Y'ain't gonna keep anything I might lose. But I'll give ya custody 'til the mornin' light." She stuck out her chin with a defiant snap to her eyes and I knew she had him.

"Good enough. Do the two of y'uns good ta be shiverin' under blankets in the altogether tonight. Jest ta learn ya ta have such stupid idears." Calvin was grinning again, but it was a malicious grin.

We sat down to pitch cards, everyone paying much closer attention this time. The first hand, Calvin lost his hat, and Donna lost . . . her earring. The left one. With a sour look, Calvin and I seemed to have at least one thing in common: disgust with the greater pool of discards that Donna had. We both felt rather cheated, even if we were both out to win.

But we were clever fellows, and quick to follow the lead. If earrings were clothing, then so were all the gimgaws in our pockets, and a belt, knife and sheath were three separate items. Even shoelaces. The

Taylor brothers might not have been the brightest fellows to ever come from McClellan County, but we were fairly sharp when the wind was right, all the same.

Twenty hands or so later, we were down to <u>real</u> clothes. We were glad it was unseasonably warm for mid-December, only about fifty degrees that night. Even so, when I laid down my full house, I saw a good bit of gooseflesh on Calvin's chest . . . and Donna's.

My concentration went to hell in a hurry. Her small upright breasts in her bra there . . . I couldn't seem to think right. By the time I got my head right, I'd lost my shirt and last sock. I didn't know how Calvin was doing, but I was pretty much down to pants and drawers. Tearing my eyes away from Donna's beautiful torso, I checked him. He was in the same boat. We had two apiece. Donna would have . . . I checked her thoroughly. Just her bra, skirt, and underthings. Hmm. How many underthings did she have on? Girdle? Panties? Corset? Slip? I wasn't sure what all those things were, and whether they went under a skirt or not. For all I knew, she could still have forty articles of clothing left.

But evidently, she didn't. When Calvin won the next hand, I stripped to my boxers, and she stood, and with a little wiggle, dropped a pair of panties to the ground. I was pretty sure that the other stuff went over panties, not under, so she was down to two. Just like Calvin. And I was down to one.

The next hand was a squeaker. My pair of threes took the day over Calvin's deuces and Donna's Ace-high. I was really worried about that. I knew that despite the cold, it was obvious that seeing Donna there in her brassiere and knowing that there were no panties under her skirt was affecting more than my card-game. When she released the catch on her bra and slid it across the stone towards me, I nearly did pass out. From lack of blood flow. I couldn't believe that it could have gotten any harder than it already was. But it did. Calvin's face was red and angry, and he tossed his jeans at my face. I caught them, and folded them and added them to my pile of clothes.

So there we sat with one article of clothing apiece. "Guess this is gonna be everybody's last hand," Calvin growled.

Donna just smiled. "We'll see here in a minute."

She dealt out the cards, and I was almost positive that she palmed a couple, as well as dealing off of the bottom of the deck. She was good at it, but not that good. If Calvin hadn't been hitting the moonshine, I know he'd have caught her. And called her on it, too. But he had, claiming that it helped keep him warm. I knew better, having studied the phenomenon in Biology class, but didn't bother trying to argue with him.

We looked at our cards, and I knew I had a winner. Three Kings. I had it whipped! And I'd get treated to the entire vision of Donna's gorgeous body! My breath started coming faster.

Calvin looked at me angrily from across the stone. "Think ya gotcha somethin', Bobby-boy? Ya gots ta work on them tells, baby brother.

As if yer dong don't tell enough, the way yer about ta split yer drawers!" He was furious, and I knew that I was antagonizing him needlessly, but I couldn't have refused the opportunity to see Donna like this for all the gold in Fort Knox. I just grinned at him. He grinned back, still a furious grin. I could tell he thought he had something in his hand, too.

Donna was serene and smiling gently at both of us. She leaned back, exposing her lovely breasts to their best advantage. "Let's see, boys."

I dropped my kings with glee, knowing that she'd set this up this way on purpose. She'd palmed cards and bottom-dealt to get me my kings! Calvin snorted.

I looked over at him with a triumphant expression that I couldn't keep inside. He was more irate yet when he saw it. "Good hand, Bobby. But you still cain't beat Aces over Eights!" He threw his full house at my face. Three eights . . . and a pair of aces. "Gimme them fuckin' drawers, you little shit!"

Donna held out a restraining hand. "Sorry, Calvin."

"Sorry what?" he demanded.

"Sorry, but I think this takes you." She dropped down a royal flush, and looked away, tipping me a wink.

Calvin and I both gaped, stunned. There could have been a violent reaction very easily. Calvin hates to lose once he's committed himself to a game. But when I burst out laughing, it seemed to defuse the time bomb. He started grinning, and we stood up in unison. We stripped down bareass simultaneously, laughing the whole time.

"I guess you win, girly!" Calvin laughed.

"Not yet, Cal," she said demurely.

"How ya figger?" he demanded.

"I want a chance to win some a' my clothes back before mornin'! You got my shirt, and Bobby's got my sweater!" She tipped me a wink, and I suddenly knew that whatever game she was playing, it didn't have anything to do with winning her clothes back.

"Alrighty, then, one more hand is all ya got the ante for, though. I'll toss in yer hose, too, fer all the warmer they'll help." Cal tipped me a wink. For some reason, this was funnier to him than I would have believed.

Calvin dealt this time, and I watched him carefully. No bottom-dealing or palmed cards there. He saw me watching him and grinned. "Straight game, Bobby-boy. Too late ta try cheatin' my way outta a hole now, anyway!"

I had a handful of nothing. Looked like I wasn't going to get the skirt after all. High card was a jack.

Calvin flipped his hand over, showing a pair of sixes. Donna scowled, and threw her hand down, face-down. "Takes me, boys." She stood, and with what I'm sure was deliberate provocative intent, wriggled out of her skirt. She turned slowly around, letting me appreciate her beauty. And I could tell she was cold indeed.

Calvin shook his head in amusement. "Ain't we three a set?

Dumber'n sled-tracks. December finds us playin' strip-poker outta doors. I guess that's last hand, anyhow."

"Not yet," Donna said.

"What now, girl?" Calvin was starting to look annoyed again.

"I got one more thing ta wager. Ya both want it, an' I already got it. So this is jest between you two, reckon." She grinned impudently, but was serious, as far as I could tell.

"Yer fuckin' kiddin'! Ya cain't be serious!" Calvin yelled. I couldn't make myself believe that she was saying what I thought she was saying.

"Iffen you ain't gonna keep that thing," she pointed at his crotch, "outta them girls from Jefferson, I don't see why I should keep this," she pointed at her own, "reserved for yer personal use."

Calvin's mouth opened and shut ferociously, but no sound came out. Evidently, he hadn't known that she knew about his indiscretions.

"And I think Bobby's a cute 'un. So let's see iffen I spend the night in your tent, or his shack." She tossed one hip out, with her hand perched on it sassily.

While this was going on, I picked up the cards that she'd flung down face-first. A seven, a six, a nine, a five, and an eight. Straight. But I just shrugged. Whatever game she was playing wasn't poker.

She grabbed up the deck from me and shuffled, then dealt. I wasn't going to watch and see if she cheated. I didn't want to know. I looked at my hand. Three nines.

Calvin looked over his cards at me. He was dumbfounded and furious. He didn't know whether to shit or go blind, and his thinking had been pretty sluggish since he finished off the quart. I looked at his face, and could tell his feelings were hurt. I was hurting them, and so was Donna. I didn't want to hurt his feelings. I wanted her more than I wanted his feelings unhurt, though. So I said, "Can you beat three of a kind?"

He looked at his cards stupidly. He just shook his head, and showed two pairs, jacks and sevens.

What he did next amazes me to this day. It was the very last thing I would have predicted. With a pained attempt at a 'tough-guy-and-I-don't-care' look on his face, he stood up. Instead of yelling, or trying to pick a fight, he simply bent, took the pile of clothing in front of him, and silently made his way to his tent.

I couldn't believe it. He was just walking away, and I saw heartbreak in his slumped shoulders. For the first time, I saw that my big tough older brother was just a man after all, not the deified entity that I'd always believed. He did have feelings, and they could be hurt. The shock of seeing this rendered me incapable of motion.

Until I felt a small chilly hand on my shoulder. Donna asked me quietly, "Would you rather look at him, or at me?"

Chapter Thirty-Two

When she reminded me that she was standing right behind me, completely devoid of clothing, I stopped thinking about Calvin and his heartache instantly. I whirled to look at her, eying her hungrily. I probably should have tried to play it cool, and act as though this sort of thing happened to me every day of my life, but I'd burned and hungered for her for so long! Not just a woman, any woman, but this specific one! And for some bizarre and twisted reason, she was here. For me.

"You hurt him, Donna." Somehow, that wasn't what I had meant to say at all.

"I know. But I think it might do 'im some good. Let 'im know what I been goin' through, hearin' 'bout them Jefferson city girls through the grapevine." She stepped closer to me and slid one hand to the back of my neck. "But is that what you want to spend the night talkin' 'bout, or is there somethin' else ya'd rather?" She craned her neck to reach my mouth, and I slouched down to her helplessly.

We kissed, slowly, passionately, and thoroughly. Her hand touched my chest, and one fingertip slowly traced from my left nipple to my breastbone, then down to my navel. I drew my breath in with an audible gasp, then she gave a little laughing whimper into my mouth, and her hand was on me, gripping me. Gripping hard and tight almost to the point of pain. She bit my lower lip and trapped it between her teeth, nipped in almost hard enough to draw blood, and jerked roughly with her hand. She moaned in excitement from using me so brutally, and that was all I could take. I shot what must have been quarts, all over her stomach. She laughed happily without releasing my lip, and sighed contentedly.

She bit in a little harder then, and suddenly released me with her mouth and hand simultaneously. She whispered, "I thought that you might need that the first go 'round. I've been watchin' it all night. Ya been hard since we started playin' the real game."

My knees couldn't take it. I collapsed in a heap, right on my heap of everyone's clothes.

"Pick all them up, Bobby. Let's go ta yer shack." I looked up, bleary-eyed and dizzy, and was treated to the view of her luscious body walking seductively toward my cabin. I couldn't stand up properly, but I staggered, all the clothes in my arms.

When I got there, she had found the lit candle and was suitably impressed. "Lots warmer in here, ain't it?" She looked down and saw that I was still as hard as ever, and said, "Let's see what we can do about that there."

When she dropped to her knees in front of me, I just about died. This was more than I had ever dared to dream of. And when she engulfed me with her mouth, never breaking eye contact, I almost fell over. I had to hold myself up against the wall. She was relentless, fiercely diving as deep as she could. From the sounds she was making, she was having almost as good a time as I was. Suddenly, she gasped around my shaft, and shuddered, closing her eyes for the first time. She locked her hand around the base of me, and lowered her head for a moment, panting and moaning.

After a moment, she straightened her neck back up, and with a devilish grin, said, "You'll be needin' another one before we get any further, I reckon," and bent her mouth back to my service. Looking into her hungry eyes while watching myself disappear into her little mouth was too much. I started shaking, and she got really excited by the impending rush. She was nodding and making noises of affirmation, and I lost all control. She sighed contentedly again, and swallowed up every drop.

I collapsed to the blankets beside her, legs shaking due to what Jeannie had called, 'aftershocks', and my head shaking in disbelief. I wouldn't have dared dream of such decadence out of angelic Donna.

"Like it, Bobby?" She was grinning, well pleased with herself.

"Oh my God." I still couldn't think straight enough to come up with anything more coherent. She was curled up around my kneeling posture, her thighs pressing against the outer length of my thigh. "Donna . . . I'd have never dreamed—"

"Oh, Bobby, you'll find I'm full a' surprises." She winked and stretched languorously, arching her back to show off her breasts to their very best advantage.

"Maybe I've got a few for you, too," I whispered, dipping my head to caress her breasts with my tongue, hand mirroring the motions on her opposite breast. She groaned in delight, and dug her nails into my shoulders.

"I thought I'd hafta show ya everythin', Bobby. Calvin said ya was a virgin." This came out in a breathless gasping voice.

"I guess I am. Never been swimming, but I've waded around a good bit, so to speak." I laughed a little, and then scooted down her flat tummy to put my mouth to better use.

I held her prisoner there, returning the favor she'd shown me. Just the way Jeannie had taught me. Listening carefully to her noises to discover what she liked best, and how to do it. Repeatedly, I brought her off, feeling her quivering contractions inside her tight wetness with my finger.

Finally, she cried out, "Please, Bobby! Now!" But I wasn't done with my feast just yet. I'd dreamed of this too long. I slowed my tongue down and teased every fold of her one more time, drinking her in like ambrosia.

When she was whimpering and seemingly about to weep with frustration, I allowed her to pull me up by my hair, and let her kiss me, tasting herself on my mouth. She got into the side of her camping pack and pulled out a small object. Slowly, she stroked me from between our bodies, and before I realized what was going on, she'd unrolled a prophylactic down my length. She reached down to guide me into her, and I tried hard to help.

It just wouldn't go, though. From my explorations down there, I wasn't sure I'd fit. But I was about the same size as Calvin, I'd seen. He had. Was I doing something wrong?

She grabbed me around the shoulders and tossed me over onto my back, and quickly straddled me. Evidently, this angle was much better—she slid down and slowly impaled herself on me, not stopping until she had taken all of it in.

She opened her eyes and looked down at me from her erotic perch. "That where ya been wantin' ta be, Bobby?" She wriggled her hips in a small hard circle, punctuating her question.

I groaned in response, and tried to arch against her. She dug her nails into my chest, hard enough to hurt. "Yer gonna wait on me this time. Let me drive this bus, boy."

She started rolling her hips slowly, changing the angle a lot, but not the depth of penetration. She started moaning, and I moved my hands to her breasts. When I thought it would be too much, and my breathing started faster again, she slowed, and stopped.

When I was back under control, she began changing depth, having apparently found the angle that she wanted for the moment. When she started gasping and her eyes got wide, she dug her nails into me again. "Now, Bobby! Pound it in there good!" She gripped me with her thighs and pulled me over on top of her, wrapping her legs around my waist. I was too close to do anything other than what she asked, and when she gave a short scream and sunk her sharp, white, perfect teeth into my already bleeding shoulder, I unloaded into her so hard I passed out.

Chapter Thirty-Three

When I woke up, Donna was in my arms, and it seemed to be a little bit before dawn. I looked down, and in my sleep, she must have removed the condom and cleaned me up. I felt sore around the shoulders and chest where she'd bitten and clawed, and sore around the groin from our exertions. I'd have never believed that pain would feel good, but I felt absolutely wonderful, despite the aching. Maybe even because of, I mused.

While I lay there soaking in the events of the evening before, I groaned a little. Had I really 'stolen' Cal's girl away from him? I had liked her first. I wanted her before he did, and he took her knowing that. Did that make what he did wrong? Was it wrong to take her back like this? I pondered it idly, but not really caring about the rectitude of the situation. Right or wrong, I got her back, and that was worth any amount of bad marks against my karma.

Donna slowly stretched in my arms, rubbing her delicious body the full length of mine. In a trice, soreness notwithstanding, I felt myself becoming aroused all over again. I lightly traced the outline of her breast and her nipple with my fingertip. It hardened to my touch immediately and her breath slowed to a happy sigh in her sleep.

A few moments of that, and her eyes came open sleepily.

"Mornin', Bobby. Ya sure know how ta make a woman feel good, boy."

I smiled. I was glad that Jeannie had taken the time to show me. I didn't know how to respond to her statement, though. 'Thank you' sounded condescending. 'Yes,' sounded conceited. And telling her how good she'd made me feel in return sort of made it sound like she was a wanton. So instead of tripping over my tongue, I kissed her instead. The kiss slowly turned from a salutation to something hotter, and our hands started roving over one another's bodies.

I felt her move against me, and whimper. "I'm sore, Bobby. Be gentle this mornin'." That was very stimulating to me for some reason. She'd clawed and bitten at me and left me sore. I'd made her sore without meaning to, and she loved it enough to want more. I slid into her more easily this morning, and we made love in a slow tempo.

We moved together slowly and deeply, and instead of cries, she uttered gasps. She was tender with me this morning too, not tearing into me and devouring me. I loved it when she'd done that last night, but it was so beautiful this way too; I didn't know what I liked better. I did know that I loved both. Finally, I managed to bring her to climax at this slower, gentler pace. Her soft muffled cries were too much for me to take, and I spilled into her as she shuddered.

I probably should have been worried about her getting pregnant. But that concept held no fear for me. If she got pregnant, we'd 'have' to get married. So what? I couldn't imagine a better outcome for anything if I'd tried. Donna pregnant with my baby? Don't throw me in that brier patch!

She sighed, fulfilled, and cradled my head to her chest. "Oh, Bobby. I'm gonna have to show Calvin some a' the things you do, boy."

I froze. What did she mean? "Donna, I guess I thought after . . . "

She laughed. Not cruelly, but very surprised. "Bobby honey, I still want Calvin. Don't lose sight a' that. I need ta spur him toward me some, though. Iffen he's gonna take his pleasure where he finds it, I figger it's only fair ta show 'im I'll do the same. This oughta be a good wake-up call, I think. And I wanted it ta be with you, because I am awful fond a' you, Bobby Taylor. An' I wanted you ta have somethin' ya wanted so much."

I couldn't quite wrap my mind around the words that I was hearing.

"It was wonderful wif ya, too. I don't know who's been showin' ya 'round a woman's body, but you've got a way of showin' a girl that you care how she feels." She made a contented sound that was almost a purr, and squeezed me tight.

I stayed quiet. If this was what she was offering, why complain? I had gotten to make love to the woman that I loved, and had dreamed of for years. What in the world did I have to complain about? I shrugged and squeezed her to me.

I started to fondle her again, playfully, but she stopped me. "Ain't you had enough ta last ya awhiles? 'Sides, we gotta get ready an' head back ta town. We're goin' to a movie with Daddy today!" She hopped up and started plundering through the pile of clothing. Between us, we had most of the clothes she needed. I left to go to Cal's tent to get the rest.

He was gone. All of our clothes were in his tent, along with his blankets, but he was nowhere to be seen. There wasn't any frost on the inside of his tent, either. It was almost as if he hadn't slept there tonight. Suddenly I felt like a thief. Regardless of how I felt about it, Calvin had looked at Donna as his girl. He didn't behave towards her the same way that I would have, but that didn't mean his feelings weren't the same.

But that guilty feeling didn't last very long in the overwhelming joyful atmosphere that I swam in. I was where I had dreamed of being, or at least a close facsimile thereof. I wasn't Donna's dream man, but I'd been promoted to one of her inner circle, anyway. She had to love me—otherwise, how could we have shared the wonderful experience we'd just had? I knew I'd win her in the end. Coldly and clinically, I analyzed my decision. I'd chosen Donna over my brother. And I wouldn't change it for the world.

We got dressed in a smiling, knowing silence. I helped her on with her things, and was surprised to find that dressing a woman was nearly as erotic and stimulating as undressing her. Donna seemed to find it arousing as well, and finally slapped me away, laughing. "We ain't never gonna see no pitcher show iffen ya don't leave go!"

We walked back into town, laughing and toying with one

another the whole time. We were drunk on what we'd discovered our bodies could do to and for one another. And, with the misplaced confidence of youth, I just knew that the wonderful sensations that we could generate together would be the very thing to win her over to me forever.

Chapter Thirty-Four

Mr. Duquesne was geared up and ready to talk with me while Donna got herself ready. He scanned me surreptitiously in the manner of a drill instructor inspecting a troop. I could tell I was getting decent marks for my shave, since he couldn't tell that I wasn't like Calvin: Calvin could shave before school, and upon returning home, if he wanted to look respectable instead of like some white-trash hobo, he had to shave again. I wasn't naturally hirsute, nor did my facial hair grow at the lycanthropic rate that my brother's did.

He nodded, apparently approving of my appearance, with the unspoken codicil that I was getting leeway because we'd been camping the night before. If he'd had any notion of what had gone on in the rivercamp last night, he'd have shot me on the spot. Instead, he was nodding, approving of my courtship of his lovely daughter. Life never ceases to amaze me with its oddities.

"Iffen ya wants ta, ya can warsh up in th' powder room, Bobby. They's towels under th' sink." He clapped me on the back, fortunately not noticing the wince that followed his hand slapping across the claw marks that his lovely daughter had raked across my back.

I availed myself of the opportunity he had offered, and washed the minute traces of road dust and sleep from my eyes. I contemplated a more thorough wash, but thought the better of it. The last thing I wanted to explain was the slightest sniff of sex—not with his daughter spending the night in my camp the very night before. I had a strong notion that washing my groin area would swiftly permeate the house with the smells of spent passion. I shuddered to think what might happen if we were caught.

When I returned from the powder room, Donna had come downstairs again, wearing a pink cardigan, white turtleneck, and a sleek white skirt. For some reason, she had also adorned herself with blush, or rouge, or some kind of teenage girl warpaint. I didn't see that she had enhanced her appearance any, and couldn't imagine why she'd want to cover up that beautiful skin. She didn't need make-up. Her complexion was perfect, and the idea of covering up her skin with any ridiculous cosmetic was asinine. A complete waste of time.

It seemed that her father agreed. "Donna Nell, you get your hind end back up them stairs and wash that trash off your face! You ain't need no make-up! An' even iffen ya did, ya ain't wearin' it to an' from my house, by God! You're a young lady, young lady! Y'ain't some street-walkin' tramp!" I looked at his face, and he seemed livid. Well beyond the response that a little gunk on her cheeks would seem to merit, from my point of view.

Donna blushed severely enough that it was visible through the stuff, whatever it was called. She looked on the verge of tears, and turned and rushed back upstairs. Being bellowed at in front of her (lover?) boyfriend seemed to have made her feel about eight years old again. Mr. Duquesne turned to me with a sheepish grin.

"Don't really care, ya know. Jest hafta let her know that I'm a'keepin' the ol' eyeball on what she's up to. She din't really have enough a' that stuff on 'er ta show, but she gets this funny little look on 'er face whenever she thinks she's gettin' by with 'er didoes. It's tough ta see it, but believe it or not, Bobby, Donna wants to be caught. She's pushin'. Seein' what she can get by with. Iffen yer smart as I think y'are, you'll be payin' attention to that look, son. Iffen y'all end up hitched, you'll be seein' it too, I reckon." He grinned his awkward grin again, and said, "Might be gettin' the cart afore the horse, there, but it sure don't make it bad advice, Bobby." He looked at his shoes and scuffed his feet against the carpet ineffectually. "Let's wait for 'er in th' car."

I didn't know why he might want to do that, but I presumed that he was a little embarrassed as well. So I eased his tension a little, when he noticed me shuffle-stepping and doing a reasonable facsimile of the hand-jive drill, wondering whether to ride up front with Mr. Duquesne, or in the back seat. I didn't really know what the proper protocol would be, and was kicking myself for not finding out before now.

With a big laugh, he said, "Jest suit yerself, son. Iffen ya wanna ride up front with an ugly ol' man, go ahead. I know at yer age, it wouldn't a' been no tough call fer me!" He grinned and it seemed that his normal jovial mood had returned.

Other than that, I don't remember too much about the trip. Donna sat very close to me in the back seat, and made it very tough for me to answer her father's questions. She was holding her jacket in her lap, and underneath it, her hand was stroking my thigh. I was shocked, but I had a limited capability of expressing my dismay. Donna liked playing this dangerous game. Easy for her, I grumbled behind my attentive expression. She wasn't the one that her father would throw out of the car and make walk clean back from Jefferson!

We saw a movie of some sort, and ate at the McDonald's in Jefferson. I persistently tried to pay my way as well as Donna's, but Mr. Duquesne wouldn't have a bit of it. "Ya might be seein' my daughter, but yer my guest! So it's my treat!" He laughed as if he'd told a fine joke. If he had, I'd missed it, somehow.

I passed the day in a sort of haze, wondering how everything was going to shake out now that Donna had changed all the rules in our relationship, as well as all the dynamics between the three of us: Calvin, Donna and me. I carried off my confusion as weariness from not sleeping all that well in the camp, and I think that Mr. Duquesne believed it. Donna just wore a knowing smile, and didn't seem to be any worse for wear, despite not having gotten a bit more sleep than I had.

Chapter Thirty-Five

During our school's Christmas break, I saw Donna a few times, and Jeannie a couple. I still hadn't managed to tell Jeannie about the way things had changed between Donna and me. For some reason, despite wanting to share the feelings with my best friend in the world, I instinctively knew that it would hurt her more than it would make her happy for me.

I worked out with the Chief a few more times, and he expanded on my knife-fighting lessons. It was amazing how the knife felt in my hand, almost like a part of my body that I didn't know wasn't there until now. When I moved my weapon hand, it was as easy and fluid as swinging a hook, or snapping a jab. The Chief never praised my work in this, but nodded silently as he watched my footwork and the weaving of the blade in a guard pattern.

For Christmas, I'd decided to give Donna a carving I'd made with my knife. It was a surprisingly intricate work for the kind of blade I used, if I do say so myself. I'd used a chunk of Japanese Red Maple that the Chief had given me. He enjoyed watching me carve when I was visiting. I'd carve, and he'd sit, watching, drinking his liquor. He was always amazed at the things I could do that he hadn't taught me. And for some reason, was inordinately proud of my schoolwork.

The carving was of a rosebud, captured in the act of opening.

I'd gone so far in detail to leave enough wood to illustrate the veins of the leaves. It was easily the finest thing I'd ever carved. She loved it, and was simply in awe that I could carve it at all. When she heard that I'd done every cut with my knife, she was stupefied. She shook her head in wonderment and kissed me slowly, eyes open, looking puzzled and hungry at the same time.

For Jeannie, I had pondered long, and decided to make her a scarf-y shawl-y cloak-type thing. I'd tanned the hide of the deer I'd gotten this fall, and used an awl to punch the holes for sewing in the lining. The lining I crocheted myself from yarn Mom had given me. The cape was a lot of work, really. More than I'd thought it would be. But I knew Jeannie would love it. It was unusual, and despite all my hard work, was pretty obviously not done by a professional. It should be warm, though. The leather would keep out the wind, and the crocheted lining had air pockets for good insulating quality. That was why I'd gone to the trouble to do it: I knew it would be warmer than the flannel I'd originally planned on. The hood would keep rain off her hair, and there were internal buttons if she wanted to close it to her waist. It would be loose enough to not bind her arms even then. In addition to the cape, I wrote a poem for her, telling her that I hoped that my gift would keep her as warm as her friendship made me inside. When I'd given it to her, she'd cried, and kissed me almost savagely. I knew I'd done well.

Calvin was hard this year. I didn't have time to make him a

knife. At least not a knife as fine as I wore, and I didn't want to send the message that he wasn't worth the trouble to make him a good one. So I figured I'd cross him up. I got him a book of Yeats, and inscribed it to him. I mentioned that it was romantic poetry, and that he could read that to girls. They'd eat it up, I said. I even kept a straight face while I said it. And it's not my fault that I knew Donna didn't like Yeats. I wished my brother all the luck in the world with all the women in the world. Except one. Calvin didn't know that, and he looked appreciative, albeit a trifle suspicious.

For Mama, I'd whittled and carved her five new crochet hooks, a set of knitting needles, and made a chopping block with matching knife stand in wood shop class. She loved it. Anything that I'd made, she was going to love. Anything that was for doing housework, she was going to love. I knew I couldn't go wrong with these things, combining the two assets.

The Chief was hardest of all. Especially because if he had wanted for anything, he could have bought it. Not that he was so rich, but his desires were easily obtainable from his budget with plenty of cash left over. For him, I wrote a nice letter, and got Mama's permission to invite him to Christmas dinner with us. She also said to let him know that he was welcome at her table 'any ol' time he happens ta be in the neighborhood'. I knew that this was more important to the Chief than anything I could buy or make for him. A chance to interact with, if not belong to, a family. He really enjoyed Mama's turkey and dressing, and loved beating Mom at checkers afterward.

Jeannie had somehow found time to make me two belts. One was beaded and very intricate, and the other was plain leather, with a geometric pattern burned into it. Upon looking closer, I could see 'Rob' hidden in the pattern over one hip, and 'Jeannie' on the other. Where my friend had found enough solace and serenity to accomplish anything at all was amazing. That she'd found time to bead a belt and burn such a complicated pattern into another one was miraculous. She'd smiled, and said that she wanted to see me wear my belts to carry my pretty knife with.

Mama had sewed me four new shirts, and two new pairs of jeans. She also saved enough money to buy me a book—it was a biography of Napoleon. She had known I loved to read, and knew that Napoleon was French, and I loved my French class, therefore a book about something French was ideal! I loved it.

Calvin got me an inkpen, along with several bottles of ink. I'd never owned one before, because they were messy and expensive. We'd always written with pencils. Calvin shuffled his feet and looked away as he told me, "Figger ya'll end up bein' some kinda guy that wears a suit er somethin'. Ya'll be needin' ta know how ta use one a' them." It was almost enough to make me regret getting him the book of Yeats.

Donna had bought me a small bottle of aftershave stuff. I didn't know if that was a subtle way of telling me that I stink, or a comment that she viewed me as a man. I didn't mind the smell of it very much, and splashed some on my neck so she could tell I liked it. She laughed delightedly and leaned in close to me to smell it. The sensation of her hot breath where my neck met my shoulder was intoxicating. I kissed her hard, and squeezed her tight to me. She gave a little gasp, and I let her go. I wasn't sure if it was a surprised noise, a hurt noise, or a noise of pleasure. But I wasn't sure I dared push things too far.

The Chief gave me a beret. At first, I thought it was more of the French class idea, but the story was far more detailed than that. He'd taken it from a sailor in the French navy after beating him out of all his money at cards and dice, then beating his head in when he tried to fight him to get it back. He told me that the Frenchman was tall and lean like me, and too drunk to see straight. Then he boxed me over one ear gently and said, "Booze ain't th' onliest thing a man can get drunk on, Bobby-boy. Women's just as bad in they own way." Then he shook his head and started over. "Anyhow, son, that's a genuine piece of history, an' iffen ya don't wanna wear it; it's still a pretty nifty lookin' thing ta hang on a bedpost." He shrugged his shoulders, and gave me a grin. "Ever figger which a yer womens ta give that damned ol' robe to?"

I just had to shake my head. I couldn't really tell him how I felt about it. It was more complex than just deciding which one of the two I liked best. This wasn't a decision I wanted taken lightly.

I had pondered hard about whether or not to give Donna or Jeannie the wondrous kimono that the Chief had lost to me. I wanted them both to have it. I wanted to give my beloved friend Jeannie the robe in order that she might have something of beauty of her very own. The poor girl hadn't had much beauty in her life, and I felt like offering her the robe as a token of love, a tangible reminder that she meant so much to me. Yet I wanted to give it to Donna, too. I dreamed of seeing her in the sheer silk material, and wanted to demonstrate my love for her with such a wondrous gift as well. My only problem was that I wanted them both to have it, and the robe was without duplicate, unique in its beauty. I could only give it once, and I didn't want to have regrets over my choice, so for now, I opted not to opt.

Chapter Thirty-Six

Jeannie was composed as she came over to talk to Mama. She was well-scrubbed and wearing her nicest clothes. I met her at the door, and escorted her to the kitchen, where Mama was starting on her afternoon pot of coffee.

I had just seated Jeannie at the table when Mama looked at me pointedly and gave the rumbling grunt that passed as throat clearing for her. I immediately stopped pulling out my chair, and smartly about-faced. I went to my room to try reading again.

I was currently working on Melville's "Billy Budd". This was conceivably the hardest book to follow I'd ever essayed to read. It was less than a hundred pages, but it was taking me over ten times as long to read as I would have imagined. I had finally found someone's writing that I hated worse than Steinbeck's.

They were in the kitchen for about two hours, talking. I didn't dare interrupt them even for a snack or drink. The look on my mother's face was too sharp for me to try crossing. I'd be informed when I was welcome back. Until then, I was going to find something to do anywhere else but there. I was anxious, but pretty eager to stay away. Finally, Mama hollered out to me to come on in and walk Jeannie-girl home.

I came down and their mood was serious, but not unfriendly. It was as if they were two old friends called together as a team. I couldn't help it. I smiled to feel the atmosphere the two of them had created. Jeannie looked at my expression quizzically, and Mama seemed to bridle at my apparent mirth. I shrugged it all off: there was plenty of time later to discuss it with each of them individually. I held out my arm to Jeannie, and started to escort her back home. We had an ample sufficiency to talk about as we walked together.

Jeannie had talked things over with Mama, and Mom went over all her options as she saw them. Jeannie told me that Mama had some herbal concoctions that might help her 'slip' the baby. She said too, that they were more likely to take affect if the child was improperly formed. That would be some balm to her conscience, I thought.

Mama had also told her that these were sometimes dangerous, and could cost her her life. The side effects were not to be taken lightly. In addition to being potentially fatal, the medications could render her sterile, or cause long-term 'female problems'. I didn't know what that might mean, but the generalization seemed ominous to me.

Another option was to have the baby and offer the child up for adoption. Mom was clear on this subject, though. If the baby wasn't perfectly healthy, most prospective adoptive families would not be interested, and Jeannie might be unable to find a home for her child other than the state home for the mentally disabled.

She could also keep the baby, but that was one potentiality that Jeannie never seriously considered. She couldn't allow herself to shoulder such a burden at such a young age. The baby wasn't something that she'd asked for, nor even bore the responsibility for, in my eyes. To me, at least, that was a mitigating circumstance.

As I walked her home, Jeannie and I discussed all her options, and she seemed pretty committed to trying the herbal remedy for the entire pregnancy. She didn't like the idea of being directly responsible for the death of the child, but neither did she want the possibility of having to try to raise a baby with a high chance of birth defects. She didn't feel as though she could handle the strain of seeing the evidence of what she viewed as her sin every hour of every day, for the rest of her life. It wasn't a good option, but she felt that it was her only choice.

"She wasn't cold to me, Rob. She was as good to me as she could be, really." Jeannie seemed near tears as she recounted their conversation. "She ain't paintin' it out to be prettier than it is, nor actin' like there's a good way out. She's a straight shooter, Rob. I like 'er."

"I knew my Mama would be able to help, Jeannie. Sometimes she's a hard one, and no mistake. But she's always fair, and always kind." I smiled. I couldn't help but feel like everything was going to be all right now. Mama was helping. For all that I was a man, albeit a young one, I still had a little boy's faith: Mama could always make things right.

"I think I'm gonna have her help me slip the baby, Rob. I hate ta think a' havin' a monster 'cause a' my Pa. An' bein' stuck with it fer life. It ain't my fault. I shouldn't have ta carry this all alone, but th'ain't no help fer it, 'cept what yer ma's talkin' 'bout." Her eyes were dry, but I could tell from her face that this was all the way 'round the world from all right. She wasn't happy with this, but she did have a solution that she could live with.

"Jeannie, honey, it's going to be okay. It isn't ideal, but at least there's a way out. Mom's on the job, and I'll be right beside you. You may be on hard times, girl, but you've got friends." I held her to me as gently and firmly as I could.

"That's the onliest thing that's keepin' me sane, Rob. Ain't never had friends afore. It's scarier'n hell, but y'all do make me feel safe fer the first time I can remember." She crushed herself to me with a fierce need, and I saw tears well in her eyes. She grabbed a handful of my hair in back, dragged my mouth to hers, and kissed me with an almost frightening fury. As suddenly as she had seized me, she let go, and stepped back, looking away. "Sorry, Rob. Din't mean ta scare ya or nothin'."

I was taken somewhat aback by her intensity, but we'd kissed plenty of times before. "You didn't scare me, Jeannie. I've kind of missed kissing you, really. We hadn't since . . . " Since the night she had told me about her pregnancy, I didn't dare say.

"Don't I just know it, Robert Taylor." Her eyes were soft and liquid-looking, and I wasn't sure exactly what it was that she meant. "I've missed kissin' you too, boy. Kiss me again."

So I did. When our lips parted, she sighed and nestled her head into my chest. She said, "Reckon we'd better get me on home, Rob. Gonna hafta get Pa's clothes washed." She smiled her real smile for the first time in a very long time. It was good to see. Suddenly it struck me anew how much I loved this girl. She was my only friend. And that was worth more than I knew how to express.

"You tell yer mama that I should be comin' over round 'bout three days from now, iffen I don't change m' mind. Don't reckon I'm gonna, but she said that I might. An' that I oughtta wait at least that long. But I ain't waitin' no longer'n that. Soonest begun, an' all that. Now get you on outta here, Rob."

"I'd better let you walk the rest of the way in by yourself, then. Don't want your father getting all hostile with you." I hugged her to me lightly again, then let her go. Her smile didn't fade as I watched her slowly turn and head up the path towards her house. I was glad to see it back. Crooked-toothed or not, that smile brought me a warmer, purer, happier feeling than about anybody else's on this earth.

On a much newer scrap of paper wedged into the notebook:

It occurs to me at this point that I haven't been forthright. At least not forthright enough. For starters, here's a little newsflash from the front lines: I wasn't the father of Jeannie's baby. In fact, by strict definition, we'd never had intercourse. Maybe we were just being coy about it, but we'd done 'everything but'. And somehow, it would have made things different if we'd 'gone all the way'. Now that it's been established who _wasn't_, I guess I need to open up and tell who _was_. It's a shameful secret only four people on the planet ever knew: Jeannie, my mother, me (of course), and Jeannie's father, Patrick Riley.

Jeannie's home life was pretty terrible: I've made that adequately clear. Yes, her father was beating her on a fairly regular basis. Yes, her mother had left her there with the hateful bastard years before. Yes, she was expected to not only go to school and maintain good grades, but also be the woman of the house. In every aspect, so to speak.

Not to put too fine a point on it, her father was raping her several times a week. And there was no one for her to go to about it. In those days, a man's home was his castle. And if he was a shitty king, then that was nobody's business but his serfs. Yes, there were laws on the books about it. They were on the books, but unenforced, for the most part. You know what I call a law that isn't enforced and carries no penalty? Advice.

Chapter Thirty-Seven

As the three days went by, Mama began to prepare. She had been skulking around her herb shed, brewing, concocting, and generally acting mysterious and supernatural. I had to grin. Mama would never admit it, but the brewing of her herbal medicines was a lot like a little girl playing witch, with the bonus of generally making useful 'potions'. She didn't take nearly the joy in this one that she usually did, though. I imagine it had a lot to do with the purpose of the brew. Stated baldly, if this concoction worked properly, it would result in loss of life. Hopefully only one. It was a sobering thought, and a harsh critique on our world. Jeannie's only escape route was wading through the blood of an unborn child.

As the day Jeannie was supposed to come over neared, Mama grew more and more nervous. Once, I thought I caught her crying over her coffee. But she kept turning away from me, and I couldn't see her eyes. I wanted to know, but the idea of Mama crying was terrifying. It would mean that she was as upset as I was. And my Mama wasn't any mere mortal, was she?

On the appointed day, suppertime came and went with no sign of Jeannie. Mom was prickly and waspish over dinner. As I washed up the dishes and Calvin prepared to go see Donna or one of his Jefferson girls,

Mom snapped, "I've got a crawly feelin' 'bout that girl, boy. Ya leave them plates ta me, an' go see 'bout 'er. Iffen she wants the brew, tell 'er she's ready fer drinkin'." Mama nearly snatched the dishtowel out of my hands and did actually shove me towards the door.

It was a welcome respite. I didn't like washing dishes, and I was getting to go visit my friend. With good news of a sort, even. Much better duty than dishwashing. I jogged most of the way there, snapping jabs with my left hand.

When I got to the Riley place, all my exuberance ran out of me as if someone had tapped a spigot into my spine. Mr. Riley was lying dead drunk in the yard, a half-carved ax-handle in his hand. The end of it was darkened and spattered, and something cold sprouted in the pit of my stomach. I didn't know true terror until that moment. True terror can't be experienced other than on another's behalf.

I stepped over Mr. Riley's reeking body, and snatched up the ax-handle. I didn't want it in his hands if he awoke. Walking to the partly opened front door, I entered the house without the courtesy of a knock or a yell. If I was right, then they weren't necessary. If I was wrong, there was plenty of time to apologize to Jeannie later.

Jeannie wasn't in the front room, a combination living/dining room. Things were strewn everywhere, and there was a broken ewer in a puddle of water in the corner. I didn't even break stride. I moved into the kitchen, and saw a pair of boots protruding from around the edge of the table.

I ran to Jeannie, and saw the blood. It was puddled underneath her head, and soaking through the front of her dress. I knew that I wasn't supposed to move injured people, but I never even thought about it. What choice did I really have? She was lying there bleeding, and I had no idea how much time I had to fetch help.

When I turned her over into my arms, I saw that the blood had covered her face, but didn't seem to originate there. Her hair was soaked entirely into a tangled mat of gore. I carried her out to Mr. Riley's pickup, and didn't even think of the consequences of stealing it. I needed to get her to Mama, and I needed to move faster than I could carry her walking. I was in great shape, but I couldn't carry her three miles quickly and gently enough. I laid Jeannie gently onto the bed of the truck, fortunately full of haybales instead of wood for the still. I was able to put together a makeshift couch with many of the bales, and threw any that might fall over onto her in transit over the side.

I cranked up the old truck in a cloud of foul-smelling smoke, and Mr. Riley stirred a little in his stupor, but didn't ever really offer to get up. I didn't care. Mashing the clutch to the floor, I worked the shifter into first, and eased us out to the road as tenderly as I could. I worked us up into second gear, and almost ran off the road craning around to check to see if Jeannie was doing okay.

It was a short trip in the truck, but it seemed to take hours. I didn't help anything trying to turn into the drive too sharply. We stalled out, jerking the truck back and forth. I was worried that I'd hear Jeannie scream in pain. As I started the truck up again, I started to get anxious because I hadn't.

I didn't even stop in the yard, but drove right up to the back door and whipped the truck abruptly so that the tailgate was pretty close to the entry. I yelled out to Mama as I put the parking brake on, and switched the truck off. I was sure hoping that Mama was in the kitchen, and she didn't disappoint. She jumped up into the bed of the truck, and looked things over before nodding briskly. "Ya done good, boy. Get 'er inta the kitchen, an' I'll see what we can do for 'er."

When I carried Jeannie through the doorway, she gave a nearly inaudible moan. I hated that she was hurt and in such pain, but I was so grateful for the sign that she was alive I almost cried. Mama had swept everything off of the table into the floor in the corner, wooden salt and peppershakers, cream pitcher and all. I took the hint and laid my friend on the table.

"Now you getcha self on outta here, Robert Taylor. I'll holler iffen I need ya. Fetch me some water, and my blue dress, too. And fetch my willow bark and a pouch of tobacco, too. Get on with ya!" She swatted me across the shoulders with her hand as though I was the one who had hurt her.

I gathered up the things she had asked for without a word. Ordinarily, Mama would tell me what these things would be used for; but evidently, she didn't have time right now. After she had assured me roughly that I was strictly in her way from this point on, I knew where I was going. I felt the comforting weight of my knife at my belt, hanging from the beaded belt that Jeannie had made, and a wave of rage crashed over me like a waterfall. I wiped ineffectually at the bloody spots on my shirt, and idly considered that everything I'd ever read about real killing fury was wrong in almost every regard. It wasn't a bloody, hot red blanket. It was cold, and beneath the icy blanket that was cocooning me, I was scared. Of myself, and what I might do. Because at that moment, I had no idea exactly what I intended to do, or even what I was capable of.

I only knew that I needed to take Mr. Riley's truck back to him. And I thought that I might stay long enough to talk to him a little bit while I was there.

Chapter Thirty-Eight

I drove right into their yard with a disregard of Mr. Riley's shotgun that would later awe me. I was in the grip of battle-rage, and for now, didn't feel that exogenous variables like shotgun pellets or bleeding to death even applied to me.

I didn't even take the truck out of gear, just killed the engine. I slowed enough to jump out, and let it slowly travel into the side of the cabin. I was at the door an instant after the truck hit.

Mr. Riley helped me a great deal. His timing couldn't have been better for me. When he flung the door open and started out, preceded by his shotgun barrel, I didn't even need to adapt my pace. I grabbed the barrel with my left hand, and stabbed it upward toward the sky.

As I heard the cry of surprise get drowned out by the roar of the gun, I drew my knife with my right hand. It felt like an extension of my arm, not at all like a tool in my hand. Everything seemed like I had all the time in the world to finish what needed done. Like Mr. Riley was moving underwater, and I wasn't.

I placed the edge of the knife across his throat, and pinned him against the wall just inside the door. His hands went limp around the gun, and I pulled it from his unresisting hands. I looked at his petrified expression and smiled mirthlessly. It even felt eerie on my face.

It occurred to me that I didn't know whether he had touched off both barrels when I grabbed the gun or not. I kept smiling and slid my hand down the gun until I found the break for it. I opened it, and realized that I didn't want to take my eyes off of him long enough to check. So I snapped it shut again, and stabbed it into his groin. He made a pathetic gurgle, but didn't lean forward into my knife. A piece of me felt profound disappointment.

"Is there a round left in the gun, or did you touch off both barrels, you son of a bitch?" I demanded. His eyes narrowed, and a sneer crossed his face.

"Piss off, boy. Either cut m' goddam throat er run away, but I ain't tryin' ta talk to ya, ya little fairyboy." He thought he could get the upper hand here, I marveled.

"Let's see if you fired them both, then." I thumbed both hammers back, and watched his contemptuous expression waver a bit.

"You ain't got the balls, boy. Don't try skeerin' me. I looked down the barrels of Kraut rifles in Normandy, you little shit. I know killer's eyes from up close, kid. You ain't got the eyes, an' y'ain't got the sauce ta do it."

I pulled both triggers simultaneously. Dry clicks. Again, I felt thwarted in that dark, bloody corner of my soul. Some part of me was afraid. Afraid of myself. What was I capable of? What did I intend to do?

Did I really mean to kill him?

Mr. Riley was much more impressed with the results, evidently. A high gobbling sound passed his lips, and I smelled the acrid smell of urine. I was disgusted. Even his urine smelled like alcohol. Evidently, he hadn't known whether he had fired one barrel or two, either.

"Still think this is a joke, Mr. Riley? Are you sure you'll be alive when I leave tonight?" I didn't even recognize the voice as my own. "Let's get something straight right here and now. If you ever touch Jeannie again, I will see you dead. I'll take this gun from you again, and carve you from neck to nuts with this knife." As I spoke, I slid the blade on a slight draw cut right above his Adam's apple. A small rivulet of blood, too heavy to be a trickle, I must admit, ran down the blade and into the front of his shirt.

His arms were quivering, and he was making a high, whining sound. I wasn't sure that the noises he was making were meant to be words, but regardless, they weren't. Surprisingly, actually seeing the blood cooled me off a little bit. Simultaneously, I was more tempted to slash him across his throat, but I restrained myself. Instead, I slowly dragged it down his chest and stomach, just about a quarter inch under the skin. The knife slid through his flesh like I was running it through water. He screamed, and tears actually started coming out of his eyes.

"You want to remember this, Mr. Riley. I will kill you. I mean it. If you hit her, touch her, kiss her, or even think about her wrong, you can believe that I will field dress you like a deer. And I may not kill you first. Think about it. I'll know, old man. You'd never hear me coming for you. And if I come for you, only way even God can save you is to give you a heart attack before I send you to hell." I pulled the knife out of his stomach and snapped the blood from the blade into his face.

"I mean it, mister. All I need is half a reason to come cut your fucking heart out and make you eat it before you die. If I were you, I'd spend the rest of my life working hard on not giving me that half a reason." I threw his gun on the floor, and then I hit him with the double-jab with my left hand. His head snapped back against the wall, and I felt his teeth cave in under the punches. Part of me ate his pain up like dessert, savoring the feeling of destruction my hand had caused. It felt too good to punch him, to repay him for all he'd done to my Jeannie.

I followed through with my right hand, not bothering to drop the knife. If he got in the way of the blade, then so be it. And, that dark corner of me *wanted* him to catch the blade across his face, across his arms, across his throat. If there was ever a man that 'wanted killin', Mr. Riley was that man. My weighted knuckles crushed his nose into an overripe tomato.

He fell to the floor, and I think that my boxing training was the only thing that saved his life that night. I immediately took two steps back, looking for the neutral corner. If he hadn't fallen, I'm confident that I'd have beaten the man to death with my bare hands, or he'd have slipped into the path of the knife. He rolled over onto his back, and I observed my handiwork clinically.

His nose was broken, and I heard him sobbing breath through his ruined mouth. There was a thin line of blood running from the light slice I'd made in his neck and a much thicker sluice of gore weeping from the long slash from collarbone to belt buckle. His urine stained his pants. A harsh sound finally penetrated my reverie. The ragged, hungry sound of my own breath.

I had to leave before I lost control of myself again. Not for his sake. For Jeannie's and mine. There was too much pleasure in punishing this man. And it just felt too good to release all the tension in me on anything. I couldn't trust myself anymore. Once I had let go of my control, it was too hard to cage my barbaric temper again.

I backed to the door, not taking my eyes off the weeping shell I'd left on the floor. His eyes were open, and they watched me move away with undisguised relief and amazement. It was plain that he thought I was going to kill him that very night, no matter what I'd told him. And but for the break in my unchained rage that the boxing training gave me, he would have been right.

I kicked the door shut behind me. I waited outside the door for a minute or two, half-hoping he'd run through it with his shotgun. When he didn't, I made my way to the road, not knowing where I was headed yet. Part of me felt satisfied that he'd never think of touching my friend again. And the darker part howled its wrath at being denied unchecked vengeance.

I couldn't go home like this. I was shaking with unspent passion and a veritable maelstrom of conflicting emotions. There was only one place I could go that might help.

Chapter Thirty-Nine

I ran the entire way to the Chief's homestead. I was out of breath and somewhere along the way, my eyes began to stream tears. I wasn't sad, and I wasn't hurt. There was just too much emotional turmoil within me to hold there. When there's no other release for it, tears or laughter will erupt. And despite my foray into a madman's world, I didn't feel much like laughing at the moment.

The Chief was sitting on his porch, watching me reel up the drive. He didn't call out across the yard, but waited for me to get to the stairs. "Let's hear the story, son." He stood and held his door open for me. I staggered inside, panting for air.

We went into the kitchen, where the Chief's eyes flickered astonishment at the way I was liberally painted with blood. He took in the bloody knife that I still hadn't put away, and the expression on my face. Shaking his head, he took the knife and put it on the counter by the sink. "Here, Bobby. Drink up. Looks like ya needs it," he said, handing me a generous two fingers of bourbon.

Ordinarily, I didn't accept his liquor when he offered it. Celebratory times were the only times that I had shared a drink with him. But for some reason, this bracer seemed not only fitting, but necessary. I knocked it back at one draught, and sagged into one of the two chairs at his tiny kitchen table.

More softly than I'd ever heard him speak to me, he said, "Talk when you're ready, son." He turned back toward the sink and started washing my knife off. A piece of me felt as though he was taking something from me by doing that. It was my knife and my mess. I should clean it myself. But for the most part, I just felt relief. And the spreading warmth of the medicinal shot the Chief had poured.

"Chief . . . I—" I started, but couldn't continue. "I don't know what . . . "

Impatient with the stammering, he refilled my glass with a slightly heftier libation. Waving aside my look of protest, he said, "It ain't helpin' ya none ta be all knotted up an' eatin' yer own guts, wonderin' what ta say. Tip 'er back, an' let's get the story out."

I nodded, and coughed a little as the sour mash rasped against my throat. "Uh, Chief, I don't know,"

I tried again. "I went to Jeannie's house tonight." He nodded, encouraged that I'd started. "I'd gone there after her dad." I stopped again, unsure of how to carry on the story.

"Goddammit, boy, did you kill the man?" he demanded, oddly without any surprise or condemnation in his voice.

"No! Not that I didn't want to, Chief. But when I beat him down, I took my two steps toward the neutral corner. It kind of broke the rhythm. And that let me leave before I did kill him." I explained earnestly.

"That's a fuckin' shame, too. How bad ya cut 'im, then?" He waved the knife, as if to demonstrate that there wasn't any point in trying to deny it.

"Not too bad. A little slice on the neck to scare him, and that felt so good I cut him from collarbone to crotch, no deeper than a half inch or so." For some reason, I felt apologetic for using the knife he'd shown me how to make. Like I'd tainted my knife somehow.

"An' how bad didja beat 'im?"

"Broke his nose, broke his teeth out, and jammed a shotgun in his balls."

The Chief's reaction was the last thing I would have anticipated. He started laughing and roared until tears rolled down his face. He slapped his knees with both hands, and whooped laughter like a lunatic. When he calmed down a little bit, he said, "Shoved Riley's own shotgun in his balls, didja?" Then he went off into further gales of laughter. "Didja ever think that 'e might be wantin' ta kill ya fer that?"

"As a matter of fact, I don't think he'd even dare to do anything that might make us cross paths again. He'd rather stab himself in the face with an ice pick." I felt a little better just from the laughter that had boiled forth from my coach's heart.

"Well, boy, what finally snapped the lid off of that box ya keeps yer temper in?" The mirth left his face. He knew that whatever it was, it had to be serious.

"He hurt Jeannie, Chief. Hurt her bad. And I wanted to make sure he knew that he'd never do it again and live through it." That was really what I started out to do. Halfway through, though, I wanted to kill him so bad I could taste it. And only partly for what he'd done to my Jeannie.

"Think he'll learn from it, son? Only you can tell, because you're the one was lookin' in his face after."

"I know that he'd never dare cross me again. And that means not crossing Jeannie. Or I'll go see him again."

"Sayin' it an' meanin' it's two differnt things, Bobby. Do you mean it, or do ya just think ya do?" Chief asked in a cautioning tone.

"Oh, I mean it, Chief. I mean it like I've never meant anything before in my life. It was all I could do to let him go tonight, even after stepping back broke my trance."

"Good, then, son. As long as ya don't regret it, then ya done good. Sometimes what most folks'd say was the moral thing and the legal thing ain't always the right thing. An' iffen yer glad ya done it, then I am. Ain't never had a lot a' use fer women, but ain't got no use fer a man what lays his hands on one rough, neither." With that, he clapped me on the back, and said, "Let's get ya cleaned up, son."

He handed me soap and a towel, and ushered me toward the shower. "Gimme them clothes, an' I'll get 'em washed up. Wear a set a' yer workout togs home. Lemme have them shoes, an' I'll scrub 'em down while ya shower."

As I pulled off my shoes, I asked, "Chief, what if I had killed him?" Would you still be so calm and helpful, I wanted to ask.

"He'd be fuckin' dead, then, wouldn't 'e? An' good riddance to one a' the plumb rottenest sons-a-bitches I ever did meet." He locked his gaze with mine, and I knew that he was aware of what I was asking. And I knew why he wasn't answering. He didn't want to seem to be encouraging me. But he'd have let me in regardless.

"Ever done anything like this yourself, Chief?" I got the feeling he had.

"Beggin' yer pardon, son, but that ain't none a' yer fuckin' business. Go get cleaned up, and let me drive ya home. Yer mama's prob'ly worried sick by now." He shook his head, and went out to warm the car up, and then clean my shoes.

I showered in silence, not thinking of anything. I just watched the blood slowly dilute to pink and wash down the drain. But when I looked at my hands with the scuffed knuckles under the water, it seemed that they were still bloody. I thought that they might be stained forever. But I didn't care very much.

Chapter Forty

The Chief had driven me home in silence, only gripping my shoulder in a gesture of support as I opened the passenger door. He handed me my cleaned and polished knife, and shook his head. "Good luck to ya, Bobby-boy. Dunno iffen yer ma's up ta hearin' this story er not. It's yer call. But if ya want my advice, if she don't ask, ain't no need ta tell 'er. Iffen she does, I wouldn't lie, son. That mama of yers'd sniff that out in a heartbeat." He shook his head again, and said, "Get outta my car, boy. Go get some sleep."

I nodded and gave him a grin. The Chief always knew what to say to me. I shut his door carefully, and waved as he backed out of the drive. Then it was time to go see what was going on in the house.

When I swung the back door open, Mama was on her feet in a flash. "Where you been, Robert Taylor? I know I tole ya ta get out from underfoot, but ya done run off an' left' that girl here bleedin' on my table!"

"Sorry Mama. How's Jeannie doing? Is she gonna be okay?" I asked Mama gently. When she nodded and smiled a little, I dared to ask about the other. "How about the baby?"

Mama just shook her head. "No. An' it's more than likely a blessin'. From the way things looked, the babe wasn't comin' together right.

She'd a' likely lost it anyhow."

For the first time in my life, I snapped at my mother. "So? Do you think that's going to make Jeannie feel any better?"

Surprisingly, she didn't slap my head clear off my shoulders. She shook her head sadly, and said, "Prob'ly not, son. But I ain't talkin' ta her right now, am I? Talkin' ta you. So th'ain't no point in talkin' hateful at me. Iffen ya do it again, I'll switch ya good, grown man though you think ya are."

"I'm sorry, Mama. I didn't mean to snarl at you. I'm just upset. I'll try not to get like that any more." I lowered my head, genuinely abashed.

"You see that ya don't, son. Yer near grown, but ya ain't there yet. Woncha duck yer head inta yer room an' see iffen yer girl's doin' okay. You an' Cal'll be sleepin' in the barn fer the next couple days, reckon. Don't need ta tell ya that th'ain't ta be no monkeyshines with that girl jest 'cause she's in yer room, right?" Mom looked at me with one eyebrow raised.

"Mama, I know she isn't going to be up to anything for some time, after a miscarriage." I can't believe that my mother felt the need to ask me that question.

"Ain't matter what she's up to. Iffen she was perfect healthy an' sleepin' in yer room, still wouldn't be no monkeyshines. This is still my house, son. An' my rules are still in effect." She laid her hand on my forearm gently. "You'll be grown soon, an' can do as ya will. But until then, Bobby, I will be minded."

"Okay, Mama. I understand." I hugged her to me, and grinned to myself at her discomfort when being shown affection. Enough baiting my mother, though. Time to check on my Jeannie.

I opened the door to my room with trepidation, not knowing what I might see. Would she be pallid and bloodless, looking like she had when I carried her to the truck? Or would she be peaches-and-cream again, restored to health by my mother's witchcraft? Somewhere in between?

Jeannie was reclined on my bed, braced up with four pillows. She was reading a copy of "The Old Man and the Sea" that I had bought at a yard sale. "Hi, Rob!" her voice sounded every bit as chipper as always, just lacking volume. Her color wasn't perfect, but a lot closer to normal than I would have expected.

"Hi, Jeannie, honey. You doing okay?" Mama hadn't even given me a status report on her. Was that to remind me that it was her house and her rules? Or was it her version of the patient/doctor confidentiality code?

"As well as can be expected, I reckon. Yer Mama says I lost the baby, though." There was a shade of grief that fell over her face momentarily as she talked.

"I guess so. That's what she said to me, anyway." I was suddenly ill at ease. I wanted to ask her what had happened, but didn't know if it would be too personal to pry into. I wanted to tell her that this was the last time it would ever happen. But what if she asked why I hadn't done it a week ago? Six weeks ago? A year ago? Did I have a good answer? Or any answer at all?

"I wanna thank you, Rob. For comin' ta check on me. Yer mama says I prob'ly wouldn't have made it if you hadn't gotten me here when you did. Didja really steal Daddy's truck?" Her eyes were wide, and her expression made me yet more uncomfortable. She was looking at me like a hero or a savior or something in the same vein.

"I took it back, but yes, I swiped the truck. I didn't figure there was time for me to carry you. And even as little as you are, I wasn't sure I could carry you here in time and gently enough." I felt my face flush. And it was embarrassing. Here I could've stopped this at any point in time, but I hadn't done it until it was too late. I had failed her miserably, and she was looking at me as if I'd hung the moon.

"Betcha he was mad about the truck. How'd ya get it back without him shootin' at ya?"

"Guess I didn't. He didn't hit me, though. And we had a talk, Jeannie. He's decided that he isn't ever going to touch you again. Not gently, not roughly, not at all. He's going to leave you alone from now on." I had been wrong. Before I said that and saw her reaction to it, I had just *thought* I was blushing.

"Oh, Rob! How'd you get him to even say it? You shouldn't

take chances talkin' ta Daddy 'bout anything, let alone me!" Her face held a muddle of emotions. Relief, skepticism, worry, gratitude, and concern. I felt like a heel.

"He and I worked it out between us that we both thought it'd be damned unhealthy of him to bother you again in any way." And no matter how much she asked, that was all I intended to say.

"You did, huh?" She looked skeptical, but hopeful. And that hero-adoration expression started creeping back.

"That's the story, Jeannie. You look awful pretty there, with your hair spread out over the pillow." Maybe she could be distracted with compliments. And it was true, too. Her hair fanned out in a curtain of glimmering coppery brown around her slim shoulders. It looked almost like a flower of some sort.

"Thank ya, Rob. Yer the onliest one ever said that 'thout wantin' somethin' from me. Yer too good to ol' Jeannie. I dunno how I ever got a friend like you, but I'm sure glad I ever done it. You've taken better care of me since we got to be friends than anybody in my own family cared to." Her eyes misted, and she spread her arms wide. "Come hug ol' Jeannie, Rob. Hug me and lemme see if you remember anything at all 'bout kissin', boy."

I didn't know if Mama's definition of 'monkeyshines' permitted hugging and kissing her while she was in my bed. But I knew that Mama was better at understanding real healing than most doctors. Maybe it wouldn't ever be written down at a pharmacy, but loving and being loved has saved at least as many lives as penicillin. I kissed and cuddled my Jeannie without a single conscience pang.

Chapter Forty-One

I was still cradling my Jeannie in my arms when Calvin swung the door open and sauntered in. He had been contemptuous and harsh since the night Donna had come to my shack at the rivercamp. I knew he'd been hurt deeply, but I couldn't have turned her away any more than I could've jumped over the moon.

"How cute, Bobby-boy. Got Mama's permission to snuggle with yer side-hump right in our room," he sneered.

I bounced to my feet with my fists doubled. I'd had about enough out of Calvin. And I definitely wasn't going to sit idly by while he assaulted my Jeannie. Jeannie gave a low cry of dismay.

"Wassa matter, boy? Don't like the truth?" Calvin taunted, circling away from the left hook, his own hands up. "You tell her you been pourin' the coal ta Donna ever' chance ya get?"

I wanted to look at Jeannie's face to see how she was taking the news, but I knew that as soon as I did, I'd have one of Calvin's fists in my mouth. The room suddenly seemed darker, as if the malignance of the secret had poisoned the light around us.

"Calvin, to want to hurt me is one thing. I guess in a way you might even owe me one. But to hurt Jeannie as a conduit to hurt me is pretty low-rent, even for you." I stared at him, not hiding my willingness to hurt him.

"Hurt her? Who cares if she gets hurt? She's just the town pump, Bobby-boy. You got your turn on the handle a little later than the rest of us, but—" He couldn't finish, because I was pushing that double-jab out there again. He slipped the first one, but was too slow for the second. I caught him high on the cheekbone, feeling good contact under my already-sore knuckles.

He sped up his circling, trying to keep away from what he remembered as my dangerous shot. The left hook had him edgy. So it took him by complete surprise when I snapped my feet in a reversal and started boxing him left-handed. Now the right hand was out in front, and his revolution was taking him right into the arc of the hook I was throwing from that side.

He tried to slip the punch too late, and my fist crashed into his temple. Calvin hit the floor with his eyes showing nothing but whites. There was none of the temptation to keep pounding this time. This was my brother. My out-of-line brother. My rude brother. My needing-a-lesson-very-badly brother. But my brother nonetheless.

I turned to look at Jeannie. She was very pale again, keeping her mouth in a tight line. She looked like she was trying to fight back tears. I didn't know if it was because I hadn't shared the news with her, or because of the cruel things Calvin said to her. Because we'd had a fistfight in front of her. Or because of some other unrelated reason. After all, the girl had other things on her mind besides me and my stupid brother.

"Jeannie, honey, are you alright?" I didn't know what else to say. I knew damned well she wasn't all right. But I didn't know why, and I thought that asking might help her to open up to me.

"Rob, is it true? Did you and Donna . . . " The look in her eyes was piercing. That was the only time throughout our relationship that I wanted to lie to her. I wanted to tell her that Calvin was just being nasty and hurtful. I wanted to proclaim my innocence. But ironically enough, I loved her too much to spare her feelings.

"Yes, Jeannie. The other night at the rivercamp . . . " I filled her in on all the details. "And she loved the things that you showed me. All the lessons on how to please a woman were spot-on, honey."

She said softly, almost to herself, "Well, they would be." A little louder, she said, "I'm so happy for you, Rob." And I could look into her eyes and see that it was so. But there was something else there as well. I looked for a way to ask her what it was.

"You do seem happy for me, Jeannie. But what else is it that you're thinking? I can see it lurking around behind your soft brown eyes. Talk to me, honey. What good is a best friend that you won't talk to?" I knew I sounded plaintive, and I knew it was dirty pool. But I was after results, not a cleanly fought match.

Jeannie was never a stupid girl, however. It was too easy for me to forget that, despite the fact that I knew better. "That's a good question, Rob. When were you going to tell me about all this? What good *is* a best friend that you won't talk to?" She smiled sardonically.

Ouch. I guess she didn't have a lot of interest in playing fair either. "I did want to tell you, Jeannie, but you had so much on your plate already . . . "

"That dog don't hunt, boy. I knew you had a platterful yourself when I tole you what was goin' on with me, Rob. Iffen disclosure ain't two-way traffic, it's kinda hurtful. Makes me feel like you don't trust me." I could tell that there was more to what she was thinking than what she was saying, but couldn't grip what it was. What it even could be.

"I'm sorry, honey. It just didn't seem right at the time. I know that you'd want to share the joy, but I guess I just didn't have my head on straight." And I thought that was the truth of the matter.

"Head's righter than the heart, Rob." She looked at me with her liquid brown eyes and for once, I felt like I was getting the whole story. Unfortunately, I had no idea what that meant.

"How do you figure, Jeannie?" I wanted her to elaborate on that last statement, but she wasn't having any part of it.

"Yer a smart young lad, Rob. Maybe you'll puzzle it out. Even if you don't, tryin'll keep you honest an' offa the streets." She laughed, and I got the sense that all was right between us again.

I didn't know the rules to the game I was playing, but I had enough grip on the basics to at least be glad that things were good between us. I needed that right then.

I looked down at the floor, and scooped Calvin up to a sitting position. I shook him gently, trying to wake him. "Calvin? Wake up, ol' boy."

He groggily opened his eyes. "Bobby?"

I grinned. "Got it in one." I never wanted him to talk to or about Jeannie like that again, but I couldn't help but love him. He's my brother.

"Helluva trick, that. Footswap and then boxing lefty. Won't catch me with that trick again, shithead." He slowly shook his head, trying to clear out the cobwebs.

"That's okay, Calvin. I've got plenty of others." With that, I helped him all the way to his feet, and we both bid Jeannie a pleasant night. We had some making up to do before either of us would feel comfortable sleeping in the presence of the other one.

As Calvin and I headed out to the barn, he asked me, "So what'd I do ta make ya hit me, Bobby-boy? Makin' fun a' Jeannie?"

"That's about the size of it, Cal. I didn't appreciate you making fun of her. And I didn't like the fact that you came in and told her about me and Donna just to hurt her, either." I had my 'away' hand folded into a fist already. I didn't know if he was going to try jumping me; preparing a surprise for him if he was going to try it was just good tactics.

"Ya know, it ain't like she's some blushin' virgin, Bobby. Me n' a couple other fellas—"

"I don't care, Calvin. And I don't want to hear about it. It's not my business. And if you had any aspirations to be a gentleman, you wouldn't spread such things." My words sounded high-handed and haughty even to my ears. "Mostly, Cal, I don't want to hear you running her down anymore. She's trying to get back up from all the years of being walked on. Don't keep knocking her down. I don't like it."

"It's your party, Bobby-boy. Do what you want." We kept walking to the barn. We already had our blankets stashed out there. His was the one he'd swiped to make out with Donna on. Mine was the one that Jeannie had made for her and me.

When we had the fire lit in the old stove, and our blankets spread out on opposite sides of it, he spoke up again. "So what'd Mom say to you about knockin' 'er up?"

It took me a moment to try and decipher what he was talking about. Almost a long enough moment to blow the cover story for Jeannie. "She wasn't a bit happy when I told her." True enough. "She said she was proud that I came to her about it, though." Also true.

"Iffen it'd been me, she'd a' been beatin' at me yet! I don't mind so much that she likes ya better, Bobby, but the way she lets you get by with ever'thing's enough to make me spit!" He turned his face away, but not before I saw his bitter expression.

"You honestly believe that?" I was incredulous. "She's always liked you better, Mr. Sports Hero! 'Why don't you play basketball like Calvin? Football like Calvin? Baseball like Calvin?'" I shook my head. "I'm forever getting asked why I'm not more like you!"

Calvin laughed, and for the first time since the night that Donna came to my shack, it was a healthy and happy laugh. "I'm always getting the same thing, boy! 'Why ain't yore grades better? Why cain't you take them big math classes like Bobby's doin'? Why you signin' up for gym class, study hall, glee club, an' shop class?' I get asked that instead!"

We looked at each other and laughed a little bit. There was tension between us, and there was no denying it. Both of us wanted the other to drop their relationship with Donna. And both of us knew that it wasn't going to happen. But it helped to know that the other person had some of the same problems that we had ourselves. Some others in the bargain, but the fact that there was common ground made us both feel better.

I slept with both eyes closed that night. I hope that Calvin did, too.

Chapter Forty-Two

The next day I awoke alone in the pile of haybales. Calvin's makeshift bunk had been refolded and his blankets hung up. I was surprised—Calvin wasn't much of an early riser, and it was Sunday morning. No need for us to be up all that early. I had expected to be the first one up, because I wanted to check on my Jeannie. But curiously enough, there was his empty bunk.

I made up my rack as well, and headed into the kitchen. I wasn't stunned at all to see that Mama was up already. She wasn't ready to make breakfast yet, but she was already on her second pot of coffee. The grounds for the first one were in her compost pail, for spreading on the garden.

"Mornin', Bobby-boy. How'd ya sleep out there, son?" she asked with a grin. She knew perfectly well that I slept as well in my shack at the river as I did in my bed, and the barn as easily as either.

"Made a few mistakes, Mama, but I figure it'll work out alright in the end." Since she was teasing, I knew I wouldn't get in trouble for 'sassing back'. I punctuated my silly spiel with an impudent grin.

Mama grinned back. "Bobby-boy, I wanna tell ya I'm awful proud a' the way you took care of yer little gal there. Iffen ya hadn't got her ta me when ya did, don't know iffen she'd be doin' okay right now. Taught ya yer whole life not ta take what ain't your'n, but ya done right. I'm awful proud, son." For Mama, this was an incredibly long speech. Especially a speech of praise.

"I just did what I thought I had to, Mama. There was so much blood, I panicked."

"Scairt an' panickin's all the way 'round the world from each other, son. You may a' been skeered, but ya sure din't panic. She's gonna be fine, boy. 'Cause a' you." She pulled me to her, and hugged me. I was astonished. Mama doing that just wasn't the done thing around our household.

"She's going to be okay, then? Even with all that blood?" I couldn't quite believe that so much blood could come out of someone so little and not cause lasting damage.

"Blood's cheap, son. Ya make more just about overnight. 'Specially when it's woman-blood." She nodded sagely, and I decided to leave it go. When she started talking about 'female' stuff, I already knew what I needed to know: Mama knew. Good enough for me.

After she finished her coffee, she got up to make breakfast. Without me even asking for them, she made waffles. This was a treat that just wasn't often granted. Waffles, sausage, bacon, eggs over easy, hashbrowns, and milk. She really must have been pleased with me. All my favorite breakfast foods.

When I'd eaten, before she made herself a plate, she made me up a plate to take up to Jeannie. "Mind you get her ta eat at least the meats, boy. She'll be needin' the strength it'll give 'er."

With a good bit of misgiving, I pushed the door to the room open quietly. Wasn't I supposed to let sick people rest? What was the deal with this waking her up to eat stuff? I'd always found it very easy to eat, and difficult to sleep. Didn't make a lot of sense to me to interrupt someone from doing the hard thing to do the easy thing, but Mom was the expert.

I gently set the tray beside the bed and sat down on the quilt beside my Jeannie. I stroked her cheek gently and whispered, "Jeannie honey?"

I couldn't have gotten a harsher reaction from her if I'd seared her face with a branding iron. Her eyes flew open in an expression of abject terror, and she bunched her arms over her chest vehemently, balling the quilt over her breasts. Her mouth was locked open in a silent scream, and she bunched her legs up sideways.

As she slowly realized that it was just me, her face relaxed into a faltering sheepish smile, and her arms slowly eased back against the mattress. "Hey there, Rob. Didn't mean ta scare ya. Thought you was . . . somebody else . . . there fer a minute."

My heart broke a little for her. "Nobody but me, sugar. It isn't your dad, Jeannie. And it won't ever be him again." The steel in my voice surprised her. Hell, it even surprised me. I wasn't used to feeling like I was made of blue steel and whip-leather.

Jeannie smiled at me, showing her broken teeth in a rare wide-and-natural grin. "Looky here! Sounds like my Rob growed into a man while I wasn't lookin'!" She laughed delightedly. "I ain't makin' fun, Rob. I mean it. You're really aimin' ta pertect ol' Jeannie?" She had a queer look on her face, like she was in front of the president, or somebody important.

"I swear to you, Jeannie Riley, if he ever hurts you again, in any way at all, I'll make it the last time. I'm not bragging, honey. And I won't be proud of it. But I'll tell you like I told him: I'll see him dead before I see you hurt again." I kept my eyes locked to hers, willing her to see that I spoke the truth.

She shook her head in incredulity. "You really mean it, don't you? You went ta th' house an' told Dad that?"

"Told him and showed him, too." I couldn't keep the slight swagger out of my voice. I was still pretty new to this role of being a man, after all. I felt like Superman, Tarzan, and G.I. Joe all rolled up into one.

"Showed 'im how?" she demanded, eager for the story as a six-year old girl at bedtime. "How'd you show 'im?"

I didn't feel much like bragging and swaggering anymore. I was proud that I was protecting her, even if I did start way too late. I wasn't proud about the way that I'd gone about it, though. Busting through a man's front door and offering him violence in his living room wasn't the way that

I'd always intended to solve problems as an adult. It seemed positively medieval, in hindsight. "I put my knife to him, and let him know I'd use it for real next time I had to see him."

Her eyes grew wide and she laughed delightedly, and even clapped her hands together. "No! You didn't!"

"Did too. And took his gun from him." I couldn't help but grin back at her. To see the melancholy purged from her face was more contagious than gossip. She was happier than I'd ever seen her.

"God, Rob! It's like somebody belled the cat in that old story! Or finding out that yer a hero just like Beowulf!" Her eyes gleamed with tears, and I didn't know if I could take this.

"Nothing so grand, Jeannie. Too little, and too late. I should have done something a year gone by, when you first told me. And I should have guessed before that, with all the things you said and didn't say when we talked. Your dad isn't any Grendel, Jeannie, and I'm sure no Beowulf. I'm a pale shadow of the hero you should have had, Jeannie."

She shook her head and grabbed me to her, hugging me fiercely and with a zealous gratitude that was downright embarrassing. I hadn't done it to be a hero. It was just something that needed done. And there wasn't anybody else to do it.

And I'll never forget the tear-filled look of appreciation on her face as she looked up at me from hugging my chest. "Iffen you're just a sham hero, Robert Taylor, God help me if I should ever need a real one!"

Chapter Forty-Three

The rest of the school year passed in a blur. Calvin and Jeannie were graduated that spring. She graduated with honors, and he didn't. He did have numerous athletic achievements lauded at the commencement, however. He had become the leading scorer in our basketball history, and was the league MVP at baseball. He was also in the top five quarterbacks we'd ever had at the high school, as well as tying for most sacks in a single season. All in all, I'd have to say that the administration made a far bigger fuss over Calvin's athletics than they did Jeannie's academics. Curious way to run an educational institution, isn't it?

I was leading my class in GPA by a comfortable margin. With two years of high school left to go, there were several of us with a 4.0 average. When it was broken by percentage points, I was four points ahead of my nearest competitor, Jimmy McFarlane. That was a soothing barricade. Barring unforeseen complications, I was going to be the valedictorian.

Jeannie got a job right after graduation at Johnson's store. Ever since the night I'd talked to her father about her, he hadn't touched her at all. Not so much as a pat on the back, or a fingertip contact over the saltshaker. Of course, Jeannie had moved all her things out of his cabin two weeks after that night. She'd been living with the Widow Jenkins just a mile up the road.

Mrs. Jenkins was more than willing to room and board her for company and chores; mostly company, I suspected.

Donna was working at the Folsom Hollow Chronicle. Her job description wasn't all that well defined, but it seemed to consist mostly of looking pretty and answering the phone. Not that too many people were calling the newspaper. Mainly people with local news, like Bessie Lou's cousin was in from Wheeling this week, or Jack Wilson bowled a 250 game last week in the Black Gold Bowling League. The sort of thing that makes a small-town paper invaluable to residents of a small town, and laughable to those just passing through. But it let her father keep an eye on her, and pay her money that she had ostensibly earned.

Calvin started working for Black Gold Mining the day after graduation. They made sure that they took plenty of pictures of him wearing his hardhat covered with Black Gold emblems to send to the Chronicle. Good publicity to hire the sports hero and show the locals how much you like and admire the things that are important to their little hick minds. He started working second shift underground. Of course, there were only two shifts, and that meant he was working from seven in the evening to seven in the morning. And that was generally seven days a week, too. Literally overnight, the household was flush with cash, comparatively speaking.

Just as an added bonus, there was less time for Calvin to be sparking Donna. Not being a believer in net-zero-sum economics, I was forced to believe in net-zero-sum relationships. Donna had much more time to spend with me because of Calvin's horrid work schedule. Conversely, I had less time to spend with Jeannie.

Over the summer, Donna and I met at least three times a week. Often at the rivercamp, and occasionally in the barn. We made love with a frequency and enthusiasm that would have made a rabbit blush. Most of the time we used a prophylactic as birth control. She would get Calvin to buy them for her, and the poor devil rarely got to use them. Calvin wasn't great at math, but I'm sure he had to be able to put two and two together in a figurative sense. As I looked back on it across years of harsh experience later, that struck me as tacky. In that summer, I didn't care one single bit.

Again, later in life, I would ponder how the way the relationship between Calvin and Donna shaped his psychology, and affected his behavior. Would he have been a different person if I hadn't, if not stolen outright, started using his girlfriend as a timeshare? All this is hindsight, since the Donna half of their relationship was the only part I cared about during that summer.

Jeannie and I still got together to kiss and cuddle, but even long after that horrible week she laid in our bedroom recovering from her miscarriage, we never made love. She never said no, but I never asked. I didn't want to remind her of all the boys that had used her before. And I felt that it wouldn't be fair or honorable, unless she was the one to initiate. We were still playing all around the edges of it, I admit, but 'everything but' still isn't making love.

Why didn't I get a job? Mom wouldn't hear of it. "Got plenty ta be doin' 'round here, boy. Ain't no call a'tall fer ya ta go gallivantin' around workin' fer others when I can use ya here." Good as her word, she had a solid eight hour day planned for me each morning except for Sundays. Of course, being young, hale and hearty, I was up early and finished that eight hours work in a little over six hours. So from one in the afternoon on, I was a free man.

Calvin subcontracted chores to me, as well. Instead of slopping the hogs and feeding the chickens before he went to bed in the mornings, he paid me five dollars a week to take care of that for him. That was a good bit of change back then. A lot of it was for his own convenience, but he was also being generous with his little brother. I appreciated it for what it was even back then, and never begrudged him a little extra work. If Mom asked him to get the trash on his way to work, I'd hop up and do it first.

At the end of July, Calvin bought a used pick-up truck. It was the first vehicle in the Taylor household that wasn't an agricultural implement. It ran very well, but that wasn't good enough for Calvin. He was tinkering under the hood and tweaking spark plugs and distributors and whatnot any time he had a day off. He let me practice driving it, as long as he was with me. He tried to teach Mama, but she'd have no part of it. "Ain't never needed to drive afore. Don't reckon I need ta drive now. Jest 'cause ya gots ya a truck don't mean I gots me one. Sure as I start a'drivin' I'll decide I need somethin' a m' own ta drive."

Funnily enough, Calvin and I were getting along better than we had in years. It was almost as if by competing for Donna's attentions, he'd been forced to acknowledge me as an equal. Perhaps an equal with different strengths, and different tactics, but an equal nonetheless. He didn't like it, I'm sure, but I think that when I'd cracked his head for him over what he'd said about Jeannie, it had finished the process that competing for Donna had begun: Calvin respected me.

September of 1965 found me starting my junior year of high school desperately looking for classes to take. I had signed up for the trigonometry/precalculus class, which was pretty much terminal. There were no further math classes offered in high school anywhere in the state at that time. And I had already finished the two-year French program that MCHS offered. I doubled up in Language Arts, taking Junior and Senior English/Literature, but knew that would leave a gap in my Senior Schedule. This problem was further compounded by taking Economics and Modern History this year as well. I also took my final required Physical Education class, and opted for the advanced biology class offered.

I was abstractly worried about what there was left to take in my senior year. The guidance counselor called me into his office and excitedly told me that I wouldn't have to worry about that if I didn't want to. I could graduate this year! In addition, he mentioned that I qualified for the military academies, if I could get the paperwork in on time.

The idea of the military academies appealed to me. Not only a free education, but also actually being paid to get my degree! A degree that was second-to-none, at that, along with real world experience. Becoming an officer and a gentleman in one fell swoop. I knew just who to talk to about the military in any aspect.

Chapter Forty-Four

The Chief wasn't happy about my questions. He didn't seem to think that the military in general, much less the Navy, was any place for someone like me. "Ain't fit fer ya, Bobby. Got too much common sense ta spend yer time in the peacetime Navy. Y'ain't set up fer the asskissin' that goes on."

I complained, "But most of the time you were in the Navy it was peacetime, Chief. You did pretty well for yourself, didn't you?"

"Sure. But I wasn't a fuckin' officer, Bobby. Their games is differnt. They gotta play them games. A division officer ain't nothin' but a secretary for the chief. A department head ain't nothin' but an intermediary for the skipper. An' a skipper's just a group commodore's bitch. By the time ya advance ta the point that real decisions are made, ya been away from the deckplates so long ya cain't remember what it's like." Chief shook his head.

"But how would I go about it if I wanted it anyway, Chief? I mean, I know the education is first-rate, and it's free! They even pay you to get your degree!" I knew that this had to be a big selling point. Getting the Navy to pay for something good was always a plus, right?

Wrong. "Bobby, ya ever heard the expression 'tanstawful'?"

The Chief looked amused.

"No. What's it mean? Is it a Navy acronym? I know that the military loves their acronyms." That, at least, I'd gotten from the stories he'd told me already.

"Not Navy. It's Heinlein. Shorthand for 'There Ain't No Such Thing As A Free Lunch.' Tanstaafl." He grinned. "The Nav won't take your money. They'll bleed it out of you, or sweat it out of you, or break your heart or spirit and suck it out that way. It won't cost you a cent, it's true. But that's a far cry from being free, son." His grin faded into a sorrowful look, and all of a sudden, he seemed very far away.

"All you need is a letter of endorsement from a congressman or senator, and a good set of grades and stuff from school. Yer grades'll be fine." He shook his head sadly.

"But what about that letter? How would me wanting to be in the Academy be important enough to bother a congressman or senator?" I was distressed. There was no way that writing a letter for me would merit even one minute of a congressman's time!

"Aw, bullshit. Most of their day's spent writin' anyway. Ain't got no real work to do. Jest babykissin', gladhandin', speechmakin', an' backslappin'. One more letter won't overtax 'em a bit. An' if you make it all the way through it's good publicity for the state." He pursed his lips like a disapproving Sunday school teacher. If I hadn't been so wound up, I'd have laughed.

"Get ya on outta here, son. Got things to do, an' jawin' with you ain't gettin' 'em done no quicker." He swatted my behind and scooted me out his door.

I jogged all the way into town. I wanted to share the news with Donna. See how she reacted to the idea of me being an officer in the United States Navy. I knew she'd be in the Chronicle offices at this time of day, looking pretty at her father's desk.

Donna was a little more enthusiastic than the Chief, but only a little bit. "Who's gonna be around for me, then? Iffen yer off ta Annapolis, an' Calvin's workin' all the time out ta Black Gold, then what am I gonna do?"

"I'll get to come home for holidays and sometimes during the year, I think. And you and I can be together then. And I'll get to wear my uniform! Imagine going to Jefferson on the arm of a midshipman in full dress uniform! That'd catch some eyes at the movie theater, wouldn't it?" Somehow, she didn't understand what an opportunity this was. "And, Donna, they give you one of the best educations in the country, Donna! And I'll be getting it a year early!"

"Yeah. And here I'll be, stuck in stupid high school another year. Who'll help me with math? And English? I'm glad yer excited over it, but to me, this sure ain't much 'count. Plum rotten, iffen ya ask me."

I hugged her in a daze, and gave her an absent-minded kiss as my mind reeled. This kind of reaction was not at all what I had expected. I was devastated. Chief hadn't liked it, after I'd been sure he'd have been proud as could be about the idea. And Donna wasn't really any happier about it than Chief. I shook my head and walked out of the office. Was there anyplace I could go and get the response that I so needed to hear right then? I knew there was.

I headed for the Widow Jenkins place, hoping that Jeannie would be in. I needed my Jeannie that day worse than I could ever remember needing her before. Nobody else was happy for my news, and I knew that she would be. She'd have to be. She would love it for me even if she weren't happy about it for her. That was just the way she was.

Jeannie was washing up dishes from the supper she'd made. She was a pretty good cook, when she was given decent ingredients. Mr. Riley could have eaten lots better through the years if he'd just spent more on groceries and less on the components of his moonshine. Served him right, though.

She gave me a big smile and welcomed me into the kitchen. "Hey there, Rob. How's school goin' for ya so far this year?" She hugged me tightly, and I was aware of how good it felt to have my Jeannie in my arms again.

"Not so bad, really. I think I'll be able to graduate this year, with the senior class. I think I'll be able to be valedictorian of this class, if Joann Carmichael doesn't rally her grades. She's not done as well this year, since she started seeing that Jefferson guy on the weekends." I grinned and spun her around like a clumsy version of Fred Astaire.

"That's great, Rob! What are you plannin' on doin', then?" Her eyes were sharp and inquisitive, and I could tell that she genuinely wanted to share this with me.

"I'm going to try to get into the Naval Academy, Jeannie." I waited for a moment, to see if she'd react as poorly as the first two people I talked to about it. When she smiled and hugged me tighter, I exhaled, realizing that I had really been holding my breath. "I think I'd like to try to get into the All-Navy Boxing Team, just like Chief did."

Jeannie let one of her musical laughs go freely. "That's wonderful, Rob! I think you'd be a wonderful officer! Yer so smart and you'd look so sharp in the uniform!" She made a show of ogling my lanky frame with approval. I had to laugh with her.

"How do you like the way things are working out, with you at Johnson's?" I knew that she had aspirations beyond being a corner grocery clerk, but she needed the capital that the menial work provided.

"It's not too bad, really. Mr. Johnson is always so good to the girls that stock and run the register! He gives us time off a lot of the time, and pays us for it anyway. And he gives us an employee discount on groceries! It's really helping me save up for my school." She looked apprehensive. "What kind of school do you think I'd be good at, Rob? I don't have any real plans at all. I don't think I'd like being a nurse, and I know they have to study lots of science and math. I'm better at English and stuff like that. I don't want to be a teacher, either. Maybe secretary school? Do they even have those?"

"I'm sure that you'd be good at any of those things, Jeannie honey. And I think there's a business college in Charleston. Maybe the Chief would know." Most of his knowledge of Charleston was of the seedier side of town, I knew, but maybe he'd know at least a little bit about the respectable side, too.

"You think I could do that?" Her eyes were wide. "I've never lived anyplace but Folsom Hollow. Where would I live? And what would I do when I wasn't in school? And would I be able to get a job there, while I went to school?" It was as if the catalog of potential choices before her was more fearsome than the awful past she had left in many respects. She'd never had any options before. Now, the freedom was almost stifling in its ubiquity.

"Sugar, I know you could do anything that you wanted to. You never had a problem with your smarts, Jeannie. Just your belief in yourself. And I've got enough faith in you for both of us. If you wanted to be a nurse, or a doctor, or a research chemist for that matter, I know you could. If you wanted it." I squeezed her tightly, rested my chin on her little head, relishing her soft hair against my throat.

"Really, Rob? You think I could go be somebody someday?" Her voice sounded so tiny and frail that it could have been issuing from my shirt pocket instead of from the pretty young woman in my arms.

"You're somebody now, Jeannie Riley. And you can be anything you want to be, darlin'. If you're willing to work at it, there's no door that you can't open."

When she leaned back and looked up into my eyes, I saw the tears glistening in them. She started to speak two or three times, and found that the words wouldn't come. She finally shook her head and tucked her face into my chest again, trusting in the feeling to communicate more than she did her words. I think I understood that better anyway.

Chapter Forty-Five

I'd told Mom about my plans, and while she still didn't approve of the Navy, and she wasn't all that keen on my being in the military at all, she was supportive of my dream. She smiled at the thought of me coming home in uniform.

I knew I had to take the standardized tests that were standard fare for seniors in my junior/senior hybrid year. I wasn't sure whether the SAT or ACT would give me a better shot at acceptance into the Academy. The counselor, Mr. Mackey, said that the SAT would be fine, and would accentuate my strengths more. I scheduled it for December since that would give me time to retake the test if I didn't do well enough to suit.

Mr. Mackey was excited by the prospect of me going to one of the military academies. He was also elated with the idea that I would get out of high school a year earlier than scheduled. I'm not sure why he felt such a sense of accomplishment about it, however. I had scheduled all my own classes, and hadn't even spoken to the man before this fall. But if it was something that enlisted his enthusiastic aid in my endeavor, I was more than willing to let him feel like he'd given outstanding counsel. It didn't cost me a thing, after all.

Calvin puffed a little bit and seemed proud of the idea, while simultaneously sneering at me. He seemed to feel that it was his influence that swayed me towards the military. "Wants to be a sojer-hero, since he ain't a sports hero like his brother!" He clapped my shoulder in a manly gesture of affection to a subordinate. Since he started working at Black Gold, he had reasserted himself as a 'real man' in his own eyes, and therefore relegated me to the little brother status he was more comfortable with.

I was studying for the SAT for at least an hour a night. It was not a tough study load with the lack of difficult classes left for me to take at MCHS. It seemed like a fairly silly sort of test, with all the analogy questions, and the simple vocabulary. I knew the math portion of the battery wouldn't be all that taxing, since the majority of the problems were basic and advanced algebra, with only a smattering of trigonometrical problems.

I was visiting Jeannie at the Widow Jenkins' house a few nights a week, letting her know about my progress with the paperwork. We never cuddled and kissed at the widow's house. When we wanted to do that, we'd abscond back to the barn, and the blankets we still had stashed in the loft.

I was working on another small knife for Jeannie at the Chief's, this one a hideaway type defensive blade. It wasn't long, but it was double-edged and wide-bladed. The cutting edge was nearly triangular and about two inches wide at the base. The octagonal handle was polished rosewood with brass bolsters, with a flush-shaped hammerhead at the end of the full tang. I hoped to talk her into a few self-defense lessons with the knife as the centerpiece. I didn't know where my Jeannie was going after she saved up a nest egg, and I wanted her as safe as I could make her wherever it was.

Donna and I weren't able to meet as often as we used to, but we still got together five or six times a month to talk and make love. She was still enjoying the things that Jeannie had taught me, and still loved Calvin and pined for his attention as badly as she ever had. They were meeting about as often, and probably for the same purposes. The major difference was that I loved her, and Calvin had completely cut her out of his heart, root and branch. Seeing her disappear into my shack that night had changed everything for him, and not in the way that Donna had hoped.

Occasionally I got the silken kimono out of the lovely cedar box and looked at it. I still didn't know who I wanted to have it. Both of the women in my life would look marvelous in it. And I wanted them both to have it for their own reasons. I kicked myself occasionally for not deciding, but I knew that the decision was irrevocable, and there was only the one kimono. I still wasn't sure, and until I was, I'd get it out every couple of weeks, ponder the outcome, and put it away again with a sad sigh.

When I finally took the test, I was so nervous that I couldn't eat the night before, and all I could stand to eat that morning was a glass of milk and a little oatmeal. There were only four of us in the cafeteria that Saturday. I wasn't either the fastest or the slowest. All I knew was that I finished both sections of the test with time to spare, and beyond that, I had no clue how I'd done. I just hoped that I'd make the nine hundred combined that was the minimum acceptance score to the Academy.

Soon after the SAT, it was Christmas break again. I gave Jeannie her new knife, and she got me a book of Edgar Allan Poe's poems. I loved "The Raven", "Annabelle Lee", and "The Bells". Jeannie remembered how I'd read them aloud to her. I was deeply moved by her infallible memory when it came to things I'd shared with her. She tended and protected the experiences we had tasted together. When I opened up the book and read the inscription, my eyes teared up and I felt like I physically had been punched in the chest: "To Rob Taylor, who opened my soul to all the poetry I have yet to write."

For Mama, I made a kitchen knife with a glass handle and stainless bolsters. It was a good-sized knife; long enough for anything she might want to carve up or dice. She made me five new shirts, three pairs of pants, and a new coat. It was a mid-thigh brown oilskin jacket with a belt. Wearing it made me feel like a WWI doughboy in my trenchcoat, epaulets and all.

I found time to make Calvin a knife too. It was a stainless blade, with a full tang inside the leather wrapped hilt. I had made it a clip point about five inches long, with a larger handle than usual to accommodate Calvin's larger hand. There was plenty of belly on the blade to use as a skinning knife, plenty of weight to make it balance well. I felt like I had given a wonderful gift to him, but he trumped me again.   Cal had bought me a deer rifle, complete with sling, scope, and case. A Remington 700 bolt-action, chambered in 30.06. It had the most beautiful stock I'd ever seen, and Calvin puffed up with pride as I opened it. "Only been shot enough to sight it in, Bobby-boy. Shoots a one-inch group at four hundred feet, boy. If you can shoot as good as the rifle can, you'll be doin' well." He clapped me on the shoulder, and looked like a king granting boons in his court.

For Mama, Calvin had bought a real diamond ring. She was flustered and embarrassed, I think. But she also loved it. It was plain that Calvin was enjoying having the job with Black Gold. Having the money to bestow these gifts on us made him feel like he was big and important, just like being the sports hero in high school. I was glad for him, really. He needed the boost that the external affirmation gave him. If acting the benevolent giver was a role he needed, then the fact that he had it made me glad.

For Donna, I spent a long time working on a poem. It was difficult to write, and I erased it a hundred times, working on the meter and the rhyming pattern for hours. When it was finally finished, I put it in a frame I'd made in woodshop the year before. Working on the handwriting was agonizing—I made fourteen copies before I made one that satisfied me. The text was something that I was very proud of–

The Chant of the Lorelei

Weave an enchantment, my Lorelei.

Sing a tale of valour and love.

Sing the way we exist, my Lorelei.

Tell the story of our gifts from above.

There was a young man, quoth the Loreleim

Much stronger than others in ways.

He'd always been young; young would he die

Though he live for two lifespans of days.

He hid his might well, sang the Lorelei.

He became more than what he would seem.

But sometimes within those dark eyes

The sparkle would grow to a gleam.

And there was a girl, quoth the Lorelei

Who grew from the heart of desire.

Her mystery burned and she never knew why

But no one could quench her white fire.

She clove to her powers and never did hide

All the odd strengths locked within

The beauty and blaze flaming inside

Shattered the hearts of many young men

The two of them met and they were so amazed
To find another with skills like their own
For quite a long while they just sat and gazed
For they were accustomed to being alone.

Dancing an odd dance and threading between
All of the people who stepped in their path
Such intricate artistry had never been seen
Nor would be when their time had passed.

I've spun you a tale, my fine sailing man
Now of me do you ask yet more?
Only this, Lorelei. Give me your hand
And swear my bones will not litter your shore.

She'd bought me a package of Galouise cigarettes, a bottle of Dom Perignon champagne, and a 'coffee table' book of the art in The Louvre. Donna knew I loved the French language classes, and their culture, and this was her way of bringing it home to me. I even tried one of the cigarettes while wearing the beret the Chief gave me, eying myself in the mirror the whole time. I liked the way I looked, but I sure didn't like the way they tasted. Smoking wasn't for me, and I knew it. I did like the fact that she'd given that much thought to the gift she'd gotten me, though.

Chapter Forty-Six

When the SAT results came back in, I was dumbfounded. I had scored a 1320—seven hundred on the verbal, and six twenty math. That was enough to get me into any college in the country when coupled with my transcript of straight A's. My package went to the congressmen the very next week.

Calvin and I sometimes went over to Jefferson to see movies on the weekends. We were adapting well to the new dynamic of our relationship, I think. We had finally gotten to the point where we could enjoy each other's company as at least quasi-adults. Just the two of us most times, but sometimes, Mama would deign to come along. She didn't like most of the new movies: thought they were too racy by half. Mama always came along when they showed "Gone With The Wind", which I found ironic. Prostitutes and something that bordered on rape right there on the big screen, and Mama wouldn't have missed it for the world. Silly beach movies where everyone was in swimsuits but nobody was actually doing anything sexual at all, though, were vulgar and repulsive to her. I loved my Mama very much, but I didn't understand her a lot of the time.

It seemed after we got our first semester grades back that I was a shoo-in for valedictorian. Joann Carmichael had gotten a C in Senior

Biology, since she only did her frog lab half-heartedly. She would still graduate with a 3.96 GPA, but that was .04 away from mine. It wouldn't even have to come down to percentage points! I suddenly realized that I was going to have to give a speech at commencement, though. This wasn't good news. I wasn't scared of speaking publicly, understand. I just hadn't ever done it. And I didn't know what to talk about.

I contemplated talking about many things, having heard the speeches of the previous two valedictorians. One had spoken on our responsibility to the colored people, which I found fairly stupid. There weren't any in McClellan County, so even if we bore some responsibility to them, there wasn't any avenue to carry out this duty. The other had spoken on the evils of drink, and cautioned the graduates about celebrating too vigorously. I wanted to do better than that . . . but I didn't know what I wanted to speak on.

In early April, the return letter came from the US Naval Academy. Report to the Academy in Annapolis no later than 28 July for remedial preparatory classes. There was a long list of things I wasn't permitted to bring, and a much shorter list of things I was expected to bring. Jeannie and I celebrated the good news. Donna looked miserable. The Chief shook his head, but couldn't hold back his proud grin. Mama was similarly torn. Calvin, curiously enough, was happiest of all for me. He seemed proud of me, and for once, was willing to show it.

"Ya allus said takin' them classes on the maths and stuff was gonna help ya. I reckon ya was right, boy. Iffen ya do as good at their school as ya done here, you'll be a general in no time, Bobby-boy!" I was so pleased at this rare positive feedback from my elder brother that I didn't even point out that there were no generals in the Navy.

I spent several weeks working on the speech I was to give at commencement. I chose to address the class and other attendees on the subject of philosophy. Not philosophy by connotation, but by direct translation from the Greek: love of knowledge. I wrote of the paths that knowledge would open up for my classmates. I wrote of the benefits of a continuing education, formal or otherwise. I sighed as I completed it. I knew it was all true. And I knew that it was strictly pearls before swine: my classmates wouldn't care if they ever read another book after graduation. They'd get jobs at Black Gold, or join the military, or go to work on a farm somewhere. Not one in ten would go on to college. My speech was an impassioned plea to deaf ears . . . but I was going to speak my piece anyway.

Chapter Forty-Seven

I had everything packed and ready for my trip to the Academy. It was a bit depressing, looking at my meager pile of possessions. All the items I was permitted to take to Annapolis fit in a medium duffel bag, with room to spare for all my clothing. It didn't seem like much to anchor me to my home, the trifling amount of personal objects allowed.

I was leaving in a week. I opened up my wardrobe and looked at the cedar chest with the kimono in it. Something in me knew that I had to decide whom to give it to in that week or I'd be sorry. It would be an albatross around my neck in much the same way it had wyrded the Chief. It was a beautiful garment, but part of me wondered if there wasn't a gender-specific curse on it. It hadn't brought the Chief anything but grief. And it hadn't done me any good at all. It was something that had forced me to spend tortuous hours changing my mind, unmaking and remaking it. Maybe if it belonged to a woman, it would stop hurting males. I laughed at my silly sentimentality. Anthropomorphism at its sappiest . . . I think.

I decided to give it to Donna, so that she'd have something to remind her that I loved her while I was away at school. Jeannie knew I loved her, and didn't need the reminder as much. I had made up my mind for good . . . or so I thought.

Donna was coming to the rivercamp that night. We were camping all on our own, without Calvin's presence whatsoever. He had plans to go into Jefferson and whoop it up with the boys on his crew. Just as one of life's peculiarities, compared to the other fellows on his crew, he was a gentle voice of reason. He didn't cause near the trouble drinking that he did in high school. While he had been among the rowdiest in high school, he couldn't begin to raise hell like a veteran coal miner out on the town.

I got to the camp early, straightening up my shack, airing it out, and running any uninvited guests out. Mainly spiders and other bugs, but the memory of grabbing a copperhead out of the woodpile reared its head every time I grabbed for more firewood. Cleaning was my excuse, but I think I intended to imbed my rivercamp in my memory.

I looked around this magical place, wondering when I'd ever see it again. My little shed. The rocks Calvin and I had dragged over by the permanently black spot where our campfire always burned. The quiet murmuring of the river as it made its slow way past. The squirrels barking defiantly from the trees. (Did they have squirrels in Maryland?) I knew I'd miss this particular place. But I wasn't sure about Folsom Hollow in general. I was finally escaping. But what about Jeannie? And Donna? And Momma? Maybe they'd come visit after I got established out there doing . . . whatever it is that Academy alumni did after they did their obligatory tours, I guess. Whatever they did and wherever they did it.

A small tug of melancholy gripped me lightly. I was going to miss more than my camp. All the people that knew my name lived in this little pocket in the hills. And while part of me hated living here, it was still home. An oppressive yoke to shoulder, sometimes, but awkwardly comforting in its familiarity nonetheless.

I shook my head and grinned at my own self-important musings. I had to admit to being introverted and introspective by nature, but this trend of thought seemed overly theatrical, even to me. Just because I was moving away didn't mean I couldn't ever visit this place again, after all. I wasn't being exiled; I was leaving of my own free will, to follow an opportunity. Life was about to be the grand adventure I'd always dreamed of.

So I was grinning when I heard the footsteps moving up the trail. I caught a glimpse of Donna as she slowly moved towards the camp. Something in her step made me apprehensive. Usually, her head was up and looking sassily at the entire world, as if it were just a matter of time before she conquered it all. The top of her head was visible, and her face was hidden behind a veil of her hair. She wasn't bouncing down the trail in her customary cheerleader's perky gait, either. She was moving like a dog doing something it knew wasn't allowed, skulking along with a foredoomed air.

Instead of running to her, as part of me insisted, or running away from her, as another part demanded, I split the difference. I waited for her, feeling the anxiety she transmitted across the glade as she crept up, almost trembling. As she came near, I stood. She slid her arms around my neck and burst into tears.

"Donna honey, what is it? What's got you so upset?" I didn't know what else to say. I'd never seen her act so . . . defeated.

"Oh, Bobby! Oh, God," was all she'd mutter, over and over, tears starting in earnest as she tried to bury her face into my chest and shoulder.

I strove to swallow the stone in my throat. "Donna, what's got you in a knot, girl?" I cradled her to me tightly and rocked gently. I couldn't imagine that anything, other than my brother, could have caused this turmoil.

"Oh, Bobby. It jest cain't be happenin', can it?" she sobbed. "He cain't really mean it, right?"

I was lost, now. "Who can't mean what, Donna?"

"Calvin! He says he ain't gonna marry me!" She burst into a fresh gale of sobbing. "He-he-he-says it prob'ly ain't even his'n!"

"Calvin says what isn't his?" I must admit to being a bit baffled at this point. After all, Calvin had a fine sense of ownership. If he was claiming something *wasn't* his, odds were that it was true. God knows, he'd have fought God himself over ownership of a single thing that was!

"The baby, Bobby! You payin' any attention ta me a'tall, or are ya just plumb ignert?" Her voice went from weepy to harsh in a godawful hurry, and I didn't care much for being talked to in that tone. Especially from her.

I have to admit, though, the words drew a shiver down my spine that had little to do with her tone. We'd had intercourse every bit as often as she and Calvin had. Maybe even more often. Maybe it wasn't Calvin's. But we'd been careful! I hesitated to ask the next question, but I had to know. "Donna . . . do you think it could be mine? Instead of Calvin's?" I knew it couldn't be anyone else's. Calvin and I were the only two she was ever with.

Her eyes snapped with fury instead of terror and sorrow. "A' course it's Calvin's ya stupid git! Always used rubbers wif ya, dint I? I like ya fine, Bobby, but I dint want yer baby. Wanted Calvin's! So he'd hafta marry me!"

The words hit me like a sledgehammer. She'd done it on purpose.

Chapter Forty-Eight

(Scribbled in a furious hand with tear-blotches on the paper)

    I can't believe she's so stupid! Calvin's been pretty plain about how he felt about her ever since that night at the rivercamp. Can't she see that I'm the one who loves her? Has always loved her? And Calvin might have . . . but that's all done with now. Maybe I shouldn't have followed Donna's lead that night. But maybe Calvin shouldn't have started with her if he knew how I felt about her, which he did. So if what he wanted and Donna wanted and I wanted couldn't coexist, then I suppose the fault lies equally with each of us. Donna doesn't have what she wants—Calvin. I don't really have what I want—Donna, all by myself, in her heart. And Calvin doesn't have what he really wants, either. He can't have Donna all to himself, the damage to his self-image undone. So be it, I guess. I'd rather have half the loaf than none.

    What to do about this, though? Calvin won't marry her. Talking to him didn't produce much more than a sneer. Asked me why I was so sure it was his. And even if it was, why it was any of my business.

    Donna's in a tough place. And the fact that she made it herself doesn't change the fact that I hate seeing her there.

    I will be leaving Folsom Hollow in a few days, for at least the next eight years or so. Hopefully forever. The door to the town that has felt like a cage for all my life is finally open. And Donna will be trapped here forever. Navy midshipmen aren't allowed to leave campus without permission, never mind have wives, or I'd have gladly taken her with me. Taking care of her in her time of need might finally win her heart over to me.

What if I were to stay, though? Stay in Folsom Hollow . . . ask Donna to marry me . . . But I'll never be able to escape, if I miss this opportunity. The only way I'll ever get a college education is to get into the Academy. Without the full scholarship offered by the military, I'll never afford the education I want. And if not now, then never. I'm only going to have one chance to grab the brass ring on this one.

Of course, I'm probably never going to have the chance to get married to the girl I've dreamed about for years again either. Two things I want so desperately . . . but which do I want more?

I knew that Donna needed someone. Without me, she would be so alone, with her baby! Desperate, and ostracized. The town would collectively turn its back on her, and whisper behind her back about her. She'd never be anything but the town whore, no matter if she stayed untouched by another male hand for the rest of her life. And her father! Such a prominent public figure, maligned and scorned by the very community he was a pillar of. For something he had no control over.

Donna's happiness and security is important to me, make no mistake. But what of my own? As long as I could remember, I've aimed at being the valedictorian. Not because being valedictorian means anything in its own right, but because that's the ticket out. The lighthouse that will illuminate the safe way out of Folsom Hollow--to the rest of the world. To places where people didn't have to work in a filthy and perilous cramped hole in the ground in order to make more than mere subsistence. To places where everyone can read. Where if the streets aren't paved with gold, then they are at least paved!

What to do . . . stay here with Donna, and help her in her hour of need, swinging in like Tarzan to the rescue? Or off to college, out to sea, and reach for my own dreams? There is no clear-cut answer—I have to choose one or the other. The two desires are simply incompatible. So I have a decision to make. A decision that no one can help me with. Not really.

             *   *   *   *   *

*

I mulled it over for three days, but I'd quietly made my decision. I couldn't leave Donna here to face the music on her own. And I wanted to marry this girl. I'd wanted her for my own for as long as I'd been old enough to understand about wanting a girl. The idea of having her forever was a lot like a dream. It wasn't an easy choice, mind you. I'd wanted to escape Folsom Hollow for as long as I could remember. I'd wanted to live the life of a big-city man, wearing a suit to work, not just for Sundays. In the final analysis, it was a lot like the old question about whether it was better to serve in heaven or rule in hell. I could break free of rural West Virginia, kick the cowshit off my boots forever, and go to live in a world that was what I'd always wanted. Or I could stay in my prison . . . with the girl I loved at my side.

I walked into town the next day, and visited Donna at the desk of the Chronicle. When I asked Donna to marry me, she looked at me with relief on her face. Not joy, not happiness . . . not even surprise. Just relief. And I hated her a little bit for that. "Reckon so, Bobby-boy. Yer a good fella, an' I know I'm lucky ta have ya. 'Specially now I'm in the family way an' all. I'll try bein' a good wife to ya."

Maybe it was the anger at her diminished reaction boiling over. Maybe it was that all I'd just given up for her she took for granted, like it was just a chance to go to Jefferson for a beer. Maybe it was jealousy that she'd been so sure it was Calvin's baby. Maybe it was because I was pretty sure it was Calvin's baby myself. But for the first time, I took a harsh tone with her. "One thing, Donna. That 'Bobby' shit is going to stop. You call me Robert from now on." I'd meant to say 'Rob', but it stuck in my throat. That was my Jeannie's name for me. To put it in Donna's mouth would have felt like a betrayal.

She smiled almost shyly, took my hand, and said, "Robert." I didn't get the feeling of a hawk riding a rising air column from hearing it the way I thought I would, but it felt pretty good. Like getting my manhood acknowledged, or something.

I hugged her to me, and told her, "Things are going to be alright, Donna. You'll see. I'll take better care of you than . . . anybody else ever could." I couldn't believe that I had almost brought Calvin's shade between us myself. Not at this moment. "You'll see, Donna girl. Things are going to be just fine."

I kissed her chastely on the mouth and left, not daring to look back at her. Part of me was elated with circumstances, but there was a part of me screaming primal rage. If the part of me that wanted to go to the

Academy could have gotten to the part that loved Donna, I don't think that there'd been enough of me left to even bother burying.

I walked the pike past Jeannie's old house, and paused. I hadn't even told her that I wasn't going yet. That should make her happy, I thought. We'd still be able to be friends. Once I was married, we couldn't cuddle and kiss and . . . do the other stuff we did sometimes. But we'd still be friends. I had a funny knot in my stomach as I turned around to go see Jeannie at the Widow Jenkins' house. I pondered it bemusedly . . . why in the world would I have a ball in my gut before I talked to my only real friend in the world?

Chapter Forty-Nine

I headed up the widow's walk, grinning to myself over the pun. Jeannie was sitting on the front porch swing, reading. As I got closer, I saw that it was a tattered copy of "Gone With the Wind". I stifled the ironic laugh over that: My chances for the education I'd wanted, and the escape from the boondocks were just that. Of course, I knew even then that nothing in life was free—I'd made my choice, and while I was satisfied with the decision I'd made, it didn't mean that I wasn't regretful over the way things might have been.

Jeannie saw me coming, and dropped her book to the floor of the porch with a delighted squeal. She bounded off the widow's veranda with the exuberance of a puppy. She flung her arms around my neck, and her inertia swung her all around. I couldn't help but swing her further and faster, caught up in her joyful mood. After a few revolutions, she snuggled into me instead of extending herself out and enjoying the ride. I took this to mean that she was done swinging, and slowed our rotation to a stop, laughing right along with her.

I hadn't seen her for almost a week, since I'd been packing for the Academy and saying my goodbyes to Donna. She didn't know that all that was changed, and I was eager to share my news flash with her. But I could tell that she had something on her mind, too.

She had the demeanor of a well-shaken bottle of soda pop, visibly straining not to just blurt out her story. I'd never seen her like this before, and wondered what information could be so weighty. She said, "Rob, there's somethin' important I want ta tell you before you go runnin' off ta Maryland. Maybe make your time away from home so long easier ta take." Her eyes weren't just laughing, they were actually giggling. The merriment and exhilaration she emitted were as rich as Mama's Texas brownies. "It's something I been meaning ta tell ya for a long time, too. I wasn't sure I was ready to say it, before. And I'm not sure that you're ready to hear it, either. But God hates a coward, ya know? It's just something I need you to know before you go. Come on up on the swing with ol' Jeannie, an' let me bend your ear a bit."

I took her extended hand and followed her up to the swing, eager to hear what this might be . . . but there was something I had to tell her, first. "Jeannie, I don't think I'm going to Maryland, after all." I sat back on the swing, and started us rocking gently. For some reason, she remained perching stiffly on the edge of the swing, teetering precariously every time the swing reached the end of its pendulum motion.

"Why, Rob? You been so excited 'bout the Academy ever since you started talkin' about it! They didn't change their mind, did they? You got the best grades and the letters from the politicians and all, right? How can they tell ya that ya cain't go?" She turned to look at me over her shoulder, fear and anger replacing her earlier elation. "Ain't right, Rob. You was all packed an' ever'thin'!" Her speech degenerated with her agitation, until she was speaking as she did before she and I ever started talking.

"It's not them, Jeannie, honey. It's me. There's something else I need to do instead." I couldn't stifle my grin. This really was great news, even if I didn't get to escape Folsom Hollow. She would be so happy for me!

"There ain't nothin' on God's green earth that you been wantin' as bad as ta get outta here an' get yer schoolin'! What in hell d'ya need ta do instead a' that?" In under a minute, she'd gone from elated to terrified and furious to absolutely bumfuzzled. "Rob, you gotta help ol' Jeannie out on this 'un."

"Donna's pregnant, Jeannie. She caught back about a month ago, I think. I asked her to marry me, and she said yes." I smiled and waited for her response.

She deflated like a punctured balloon. "Oh," she said, in a quiet voice. Then, I guess the impact of what I'd told her caught up with her. She smiled back, as broad as she ever did, and said, "You must be so happy, Rob! You been wantin' her forever, ain't ya? Got 'er now. That's . . . that's wonderful, Rob Taylor. You got the one thing ya been wantin' more'n yer schoolin' an' gettin' outta Folsom Hollow. That's just . . . glorious, Rob." She turned her face away sharply, overcome with emotion.

I hugged her gently from behind, and she turned into my arms, squeezing me surprisingly tightly. The vehemence of her grasp took me off guard, and she actually knocked a good bit of the wind out of me. She buried her head into my shoulder, and we rocked like that for a while, not saying anything.

I waited, a little uncomfortable with the stillness. It wasn't the soft silence we'd often shared before, but a hard-edged not-speaking. There's a big difference in the way it feels, if not how it sounds. I finally shuffled around a little on the seat, and tucked my Jeannie into my arms more tenderly. "So what's this thing you wanted me to know before I left for Annapolis, anyhow?" I thought that talking about that might ease the tension a little.

She shook her head, face downturned and hidden by the soft cascade of her hair. "Just wanted to tell ya . . . that . . . I was thinkin' a' movin' outta Folsom Hollow too. Maybe goin' ta th' big city an' gettin' a job typin' an' filin' an' all. I got me some money saved up, see? I ain't gotta stay t' Johnson's no more. I can get a job any ol' where, now. I was gonna get yer address an' all, so's I could write ya letters when I got where I might stay a while." She still was looking at our feet.

"That's all, Rob. It's a little enough thing, reckon," she said, and I thought I heard a catch in her voice. A moment later, I knew it. I saw a water droplet fall to splatter on the floorboards from behind the buttress of her hair.

"Leaving's tough, isn't it, Jeannie-girl? I know exactly how you feel. It isn't long ago I thought I was going to be leaving myself." I hugged her to me tightly. I knew I'd miss her, but I understood the motivation to leave. To go somewhere where nobody knew she was that drunk Patrick Reilly's daughter. Where she wasn't always going to be remembered as the girl that the boys of MCHS passed around like a hat at a tent revival. Someplace new, where she could be someone new. "I'd like to come visit you sometime, if that'd be okay."

"'Course, Rob. Still gonna be yer friend, ain't I?" She looked up at me, and her eyes were dry. "Why doncha meet me at the rivercamp tonight? There's somethin' that wants doin' afore I leave town an' you go gettin' yerself hitched up." Her hand softly traced my skin from right behind my ear down the nape of my neck, and circled lightly around the collar of my shirt.

"Sure," I said, looking for a suave tone. It probably would have worked out better if my voice hadn't cracked mid-word. I wasn't positive what she had in mind, but I had some speculations.

"Reckon it'll have ta be another case of last time payin' fer all." Her voice cracked a little too, as she stood up off the swing, squeezed my shoulder, and went inside the house without a backward look.

Chapter Fifty

I sat there a moment, stunned. She'd never walked away from me before, and I wasn't sure exactly how to react. I got up, and started to knock on the screen door, but thought the better of it. She was heading to the rivercamp tonight, right?

I walked back towards the house. I knew I had to tell Mama, and I wasn't looking forward to it. She wouldn't voice disapproval, but not voicing and not communicating were a far cry apart. She'd be disappointed that I wouldn't be going, but glad I'd be staying. Not that saying either one of those things would be easy for her—she was more than just tough, she was old-time tough, mountain-tough. Talking about the way she felt about her kids, especially to her kids, just wasn't a natural act. She'd had to be too strong for too long, and being tender felt a lot like being weak to her.

Pondering these things while I was walking the pike back home was a lot like wearing seven-league boots. Before I knew it, my steps had gobbled up the road, and I was turning into the drive to our house. I figured Mama would be out back of the house, either hanging up some of the endless laundry or coddling her already-weedless vegetable garden. I remember her telling me once that when she was caught up on housework, cooking, and cleaning, she'd go out and pamper her garden. Not because it needed doing, but because if she wasn't working on something during daylight hours, she got an uncomfortable feeling, like she was stealing or something.

As I walked around the house, I heard the sound of thudding fists. Far from being alarmed, I smiled. Mama was making bread again. She kneaded dough as if she hated it. I always thought she took out her frustrations of the moment out on the bread ingredients. Very healthy, I ruminated. Both for her mental well-being and my constitution.

I pulled open the back door, and stepped into Mama's kitchen. If her home was her castle, then the kitchen was her throne-room. She ruled the entire place without question, but the kitchen was the seat of power. She was thumping the dough with gleeful malice, pounding it flat and resurrecting it to a different, but likewise doomed form.

There was a placid expression on her face. Making bread was this mountain woman's meditation. She was completely at mental peace, even as her body went through its exaggeratedly violent motions, maiming the dough. Something about the scene was bait to a fit of caprice—leaping across the room, I hollered, "I'll take care of that for you, Mama!" and bumped my mother out of the way. I then proceeded to throw a series of jabs and crosses into the lump of dough until it was smashed into several smaller lumps across the counter.

"That should do it, shouldn't it?" I grinned at her.

She looked at me for a moment, trying to keep a vexed look on her face, but finally returned the grin. "Still, Bobby Taylor, that ain't no way ta treat your mama. Runnin' in here an' wallerin' me all over the place, yellin' an' skeerin' me outta ten years a' m' life, an' then doin' all yer boxin' foolishness on my poor ol' bread! It's funny once, boy, but I hope I don't hafta tell ya that twice wouldn't be near so funny." She picked up her spatula beside the stove and waggled it at me in a threatening manner.

"So what's got your sap runnin' so high today, Bobby?" Mama looked at me curiously. "Ya look like th' cat what done eat two canaries an' got a third un hid!"

"You know how you've been worrying about me going off to the Naval Academy? Always worried about me being in the Navy? You don't have to worry about that anymore, Mama. I've changed my mind. I'm not going." I waited apprehensively for her response. I didn't know whether to expect relief, or confusion, or anger.

Looked like confusion was the first response, anyway. "Why, Bobby? I thought you was all geared up for this thing. What changed yer mind, son?" She walked a few hesitant steps closer to me, and lifted her hand as if to place it on my shoulder before changing her mind.

"I guess you could say that I got a better offer. Donna and I are getting married, Mama." I gulped. Again, I couldn't tell what her reaction to this was going to be.

"Gettin' married? Ain't you a little bit young fer all that? An' why Donna? Iffen it's gotta be somebody, why not that Jeannie? She's awful sweet ta ya, son, an' she's an awful purdy gal, too." Her eyes searched me for a response.

Something about the line of questioning took me off-guard. I said, "Jeannie's just a friend, Mama." I ignored her grunt and continued, "Besides, Jeannie's not with child."

"An' I guess that means that this Donna is?" Mama's eyes were hard and suspicious. "That what yer sayin', Bobby?"

"Yes. She is." I didn't know what else to say. It was the only answer I could give.

"So why is it you're skipping the Academy thing, though? Why cain't you take her with ya?" Mama didn't know about the rules at the Academy. They didn't accept married cadets.

"It's not allowed, Mama."

"Well, how'd this Donna get ta be more important than yer schoolin'? Why you feel like you gotta marry 'er?"

"I've got to face up to my responsibilities, Mama." She'd raised me to do that very thing. Why was this coming as such a shock?

"How ya figger? I mean, how's it yer problem, son?" She still was shaking her head from the shock of it all.

"Because, Mama, we've . . . been intimate. It's my baby." I couldn't meet her eyes as I told her. How disappointed she must be in me!

She slowly lifted my chin up with her hand until I had to look her in the face. "No, Bobby, it ain't."

Chapter Fifty-One

I gaped at her. What could she mean? "Yes it is, Mama."

"No, son. It ain't. I never told ya, but there ain't no way. When you was still a wee little tot, the doctor . . . well, he made a bad mistake. Ain't good at rememberin' what he called it, but yer balls wasn't down in yer bag. The doctor wanted to wait fer a bit, and check up on it later. Well, later come, an' they still wasn't down. He said that iffen they din't come down, that you'd lose 'em. So I tole em he could try gettin' 'em down. While he was doin' it, he broke the tubes that carry yer sperms. An' they's no way that you can be a daddy, son. Not with that Donna, nor nobody else." She wouldn't look me in the eye, but looked at her cold cup of coffee.

"Mama . . . how come you never told me? Were you going to tell me? Ever?" I couldn't believe that my mother would keep such a secret from me. Then I paused. How exactly would you bring such a thing up? Just say, 'oh, by the way, you're sterile. Pass the peas?'

"I didn't think I'd need to be tellin' you 'til you was thinkin' a' gettin' married. 'Til then it wouldn't a' mattered. An' still don't, I reckon." She looked at me full-faced again. "So I reckon ya ain't gettin' married no more, then? Still goin' ta Annapolis now?"

"No, Mama. I made my choice, and I'll still be marrying Donna. I love her, you know. It doesn't matter whether or not the baby's mine. And . . . I guess this might be the only child I'll ever have, too." I looked down. This was a pretty hard shot to grasp. I reached for it, but even then, I knew it would take a while for all of the ramifications to strike home.

"Love 'er, do ya? How's Calvin feel about all that? Ain't he seein' this Donna?" Mama's piercing eyes were boring holes in me now, and I fought the urge to squirm under her gaze.

"Yes, he is. But he doesn't want to marry her, Mama. If he doesn't want her and the baby, then I do." I thrust my jaw out without really even meaning to.

"So this time the baby's his'n, then? Don't s'prise me none. But I gotta admit, I'd a' thought he'd a' been man enough ta face his mistakes himself, 'stead a' havin' 'is little brother do it fer 'im." She got an exploratory look in her eyes, and said, "Unless there's more ta this story that yer tellin' me. Ya wasn't lyin' 'bout bein' intimate wif 'er, was ya son? Y'ain't meant fer lyin', ya know. Not at least ta yer ma. Naw, you've been wif the girl, an' I know that's the truth. But why're you 'n' Calvin both ruttin' after the same gal? Ain't like she's th' onliest pretty gal in the county. You'd a' thought that you'd a' had better sense, even iffen he din't."

"I don't know, Mama. All I can tell you is that I've wanted her as long as I've known what wanting a woman was. And if staying here is the price I've got to pay to be with her, then I'll pay the shot. Because she's worth it to me." I felt that she needed to know that this wasn't just some passing whimsy. And that I hadn't been with Donna out of some competitiveness, or spite towards Calvin. I thought about what she meant about 'this time'.

Yes, she'd asked me if Calvin had been the father of Jeannie's baby . . . but she'd never asked me. Despite that being the more logical place to look. I guess I was too full of myself to accord my mama the proper respect. I hadn't ever thought to wonder why it was she'd asked about Calvin, but not me.

"Why, son? You're meant for bigger things than this li'l ol' town." She grunted at my look of surprise. "You think your mama didn't know you had wings you're achin' ta use? This place ain't fer you, son. Your brain is a gift. Touched by God's own finger. You ain't fer diggin' coal, nor no other job they got 'round here. You got a mind like them folks tryin' to get a man on the moon. You should be out there helpin' them, son. Or somethin' else like that. But not here, boy." She shook her head, and smiled at my expression.

"Son, this is a good place. For some, it's the only place. I b'long here. Don't make me bad or worse'n you, or nothin'. Just differnt. An' it's a good place fer Calvin. He needs somethin' straightforward and simple. Diggin' coal's a good thing fer him. He uses his body, his strength, ta earn his bread. An' that's what he was put together for. You, Bobby, need ta get out there an' find what your work's s'posed ta be. 'Cause 'round here, we prob'ly ain't even heard a' the things you ought ta be doin'."

I shook my head. Not in denial, but just to clear the muddled feeling. "Mama, it is a good place. And maybe I could be one of those guys, if I wasn't here. But I'm needed here. Folsom Hollow isn't brimming with opportunities to expand the intellect, I'll grant you. But there are other things that might be just as important in life. Like love. And keeping faith."

"Bobby, I cain't stop you. Yer old enough to make yer own mistakes, and I guess that makes you a man. That's what I raised ya ta be, any rate. I don't think it's a good idea. An' I dunno if any good'll come of it. But as much as I dislike the idear of ya bein' on one a' them battleships, it's a whale of a chance yer turnin' aside. Fer a girl that ain't true ta ya, an' ya know it's so already." She shook her head. "It ain't what I'd a' had fer ya, son. But if ya made up yer mind, there ain't no swervin' ya from it. Iffen ya was any other way, ya wouldn't be the son I raised. I jest wish that yer first hardheaded stance as a man had been on somethin' I agreed wif ya on." She did pull me to her, and cradled my head against her shoulder. I had to bend low to accommodate the pose, but I was more than willing. Mama's affection was too rare to eschew over something as trivial as discomfort.

And, looking back on it, at that moment, I needed my mama.

Chapter Fifty-Two

It was a jagged pill to swallow, and I was awful glad that Jeannie was coming to the camp tonight. So many times, she healed me just by being herself. I tried hard to imagine what life was going to be like with her off to another town, living (at least in part) the life that I'd dreamed of. No more snuggling, no more 'lessons' about what pleases a woman, no more long talks about books we read together. We could write, of course, and probably would. But that's not the same as being able to bask in that comfortable glow that feels like a homecoming no matter where you're spending time together.

I sat on the floor and looked underneath the cot. Forgotten in the burst of Donna's revelation, the cedar box with the enchanted kimono still waited. I had resolved to give it to Donna to remember me by, when I was planning on going to Annapolis. In a gunslinger's fingersnap, I changed my mind. It would be my Jeannie's robe now. It wasn't a decision I'd made lightly, nor without consideration. But I knew that I wanted Jeannie to own it. Both of 'my womens' would look lovely in it, but Jeannie was going away sometime soon, and I wanted her to have a keepsake. After all, Donna would have me around forever.

I opened the box and gazed at the lovely robe. It was still as beautiful as the day the Chief showed it to me, and still struck me as haunted. I thought to myself that the curse would be broken when it graced female shoulders. It had to be so—I couldn't bear the thought of giving Jeannie something that might cause her pain in any way. I heard footsteps moving up the path, and hurriedly stashed the box back under the cot.

I knew the footsteps had to belong to Jeannie. Neither Calvin nor Donna, despite their athletic prowess, moved that silently. Donna was easily the most agile of the four of us, but Jeannie had a kind of grace that can't be trained into a person. It was simply innate, attributable only to nature.

I was rising to my feet when Jeannie poked her head in the door of the cabin. "Hey there, Rob! Got a s'prise fer ya! Hope ya can cook a steak over the fire you still need ta build, boy!"

I goggled. "Steak? Jeannie, who's butchered lately? I didn't know any of the farmers were planning on slaughtering a beef!" Usually, the good cuts of meat were eaten fresh, the majority of the rest either smoked or salted for preservation. And the last family to butcher a cow had been mine. Months ago.

"Johnson's store, employee discount! An' I got some roastin' ears, butter, some bakin' tata's, sour cream, an' a big ol' can a' peaches fer dessert!" She laughed gleefully, and I was delighted to see her smile. Her real smile, too. The one that showed her teeth, broken though they were.

"What's the occasion, Jeannie-girl? You just find out you were related to the Rockefellers?" I knew she had been saving her money for her move to the city.

"I'm leavin' tomorrow, Rob. Mr. Johnson's brother needs another girl for the secretary pool in Charleston. When he heard I could type sixty-four words a minute, he said I'd do! It all happened so quick, but the opening come up, an' you're gettin' married soon, so I decided I'd go ahead and grab for it!"

I couldn't believe this. "Tomorrow? But Jeannie . . . " It didn't seem fair. First, my dreams of Annapolis drifting away, then my very best friend in all the world was leaving. Tomorrow.

"That's part a' yer goodbye present from me. But yer gonna hafta cook it by yerself. I got somethin' else I'm workin' on." She gave a jolly laugh, and picked up the other sack she'd brought. "Mind you, doncha come creepin' down by the riverside fer a while. I'll be back in a few shakes."

I gaped as she strode purposefully toward the bend in the river. "Mind ya don't burn that steak, Rob Taylor! You keep a good eye on yer cookin' an' don't you dare try sneakin' an' ruin my surprise! An' you get them ol' cracked plates outta yer shed an' let us eat proper tonight. I brunged some silverware in that there sack!" I shook my head in bewilderment, and started on the fire.

I tossed the potatoes into the embers as soon as I had some, and then the corn soon after. Finally, I started on the steaks. T-bones. I couldn't imagine what my Jeannie had paid for this feast, but I was touched. I didn't know quite how to react to it, though. I shrugged, and tried to get Jeannie's steak as close to medium as I could, while trying to keep mine just a touch past blood-rare. About the time I got her steak slid onto her plate, she came walking back from the river. I looked up at her and just gaped.

Jeannie had put her hair up in a style I'd never seen her wear before. It fell gracefully back from her face in a gentle wash of auburn, exposing her high cheekbones. She had adorned herself with lipstick, mascara, and a light brushing of blush, I think. Her outfit flattered every curve of her body, a grey skirt and business jacket worn over a red blouse. She was dressed for the office, and was nothing short of stunning. As she approached, (wearing dress shoes!) she gave a shy smile.

"Jeannie . . . what's all this? You look gorgeous! That's just . . . gorgeous! You've always been pretty . . . but you look gorgeous!" I was completely flabbergasted. Where had my friend gone, and who was this stunning creature sent in her place?

"I wanted you to see how I'm gonna . . . going to look at the office. I've been workin' on talking proper . . . properly. And I've been practicing with the widow's old Remington manual typewriter. It's been a lot of work, but I want to be successful at the office. And I wanted you to see and hear me before I go. I want you to be proud of me, Rob." She looked at the ground, and then shyly up at me just from the tops of her eyes. "Do you like it?"

"God, Jeannie! You look just ravishing! I mean, it's entirely appropriate for the office and all, you don't look cheap or anything like that, but you just look beautiful!" I stared at her, noticing absently that my jaw was hanging open, but not caring.

"Rob, you wouldn't have ol' Jeannie on, would you? You really do like it?" She looked at me full-faced, with so much fear! I wanted to rend and tear the people to bloody gobbets who had made this lovely girl doubt herself so much.

"Oh, Jeannie. There's no teasing going on at all. Look at me! I'm stunned! 'Cause you're stunning! It's what happens, see?" I tried to laugh it off, but the manly laugh I'd meant to issue stuck in my throat. "I can't even talk, honey! You're looking great!"

"Oh, Rob. I've been so hopin' . . . hoping that you'd like it. I've been wondering if you'd be proud of me. I think part a' . . . of me really needed to hear that. Let's eat this lovely dinner you've cooked, and then I want to show you the other part of your surprise."

"I can't imagine much that could top this part, Jeannie. I mean . . . wow!" I gazed at her just awestruck.

"Oh, there's more yet, Rob Taylor. You just think you're surprised right now," she said with a wink and a mischievous grin.

Chapter Fifty-Three

I sat mesmerized, and probably googly-eyed, watching this gorgeous creature my friend had turned into. I'd seen butterflies come from caterpillars before, but there was always at least a period of transformation, a time in a chrysalis! She'd gone around the bend of the grove just my Jeannie and come back looking like she'd just stepped out of a big-city office building!

She sat on one of the rocks around our fire, somehow not looking incongruous, knees carefully together, and reached out her hand for her plate. "Rob Taylor, are you just going to sit there starin' at me like I'd grown another head, or do you plan to dine tonight?" Her eyes twinkled merrily both at the strain she'd put on me and the game of speaking correctly and playing the lady.

"Sh-sh-sure!" I stammered, and extended her plate to her with a shaking hand. She leaned forward, never parting her knees, and speared a potato out of the fire.

"Could you pass me the sour cream, Rob?" She grinned.

And that was just the beginning. She ate with table manners that were simply impeccable, despite balancing her plate on her knees. She smiled and positively reveled in the effect her surprise had wrought in me.

We laughed and talked all through the dinner, which is still the image conjured when I think of a really good meal. She offered the same type of conversation that we always had, but somehow it seemed wittier, more urbane, cosmopolitan, even. Watching this vision across the fire from me, discussing philosophy and literature, I couldn't believe that it was the same woman.

I felt myself scrambling to get back on my mental feet. She'd whirled my world into an insane orbit, like a playground ball booted off-center in a game of kickball. There was only one thing I could think of that might send her reeling a bit herself.

"Jeannie, love, I've got a present for you." I said, feeling foolishly triumphant over the fact that I didn't stammer or stutter at all when I forced the sentence out.

"Why, Rob, you didn't have to do that! I wanted to make tonight special for you, not steal the stage for me!" She looked astonished, then. Her face looked like the naive country girl she was again, just for an instant. It was enough.

I trotted over to the cabin and brought out the cedar chest. "I've been wanting to give this to you for a long time, Jeannie, but the time wasn't ever right. I don't know if it's really right now, either, but I'm out of chances to wait on that right time, I guess." I couldn't meet her eyes directly as I laid my offering at her feet, but I couldn't help but look sidelong at her through the shield of my lashes.

She sat looking at the chest a moment, expressionless. I feared I had really stepped on my crank somehow, but then I saw her chest spasm in a gasping breath, fighting off a sob. Her shoulders hitched suddenly, and her right hand extended to the box, forefinger extended, tracing the ideograms on the lid. The first tear fell free, disdaining her cheek altogether, plunging directly from her eye to the hard-packed earth. She looked up at me with such a torrent of emotion that I couldn't even tell what she was feeling; only that it was powerful and deep.

"This is gorgeous, Rob. I . . . dunno what ta say . . . What do the pictures mean? They're writing, aren't they? "

I knew now what the Chief had felt at my worship of the chest when he really had wanted me to open the box. I was tempted to tell her the same way, with the same words, but somehow the moment had gotten too solemn for such frivolity.

"They mean beauty and love, my Jeannie. But you really need to open it up. The box isn't the whole gift, honey." I wanted her to be agog at the kimono. I wanted to know that I'd given her something that was as priceless to her as it was to me. I wanted to see her expression of delight, and know that I'd put it there.

She opened the box with an air of almost religious awe, and struggled for breath when she saw the back of the neatly folded robe. She looked almost afraid to touch it, extending her hand twice before daring to trace the embroidered bonsai on the back. "So soft and smooth, Robert! It's too pretty, too much! Why aren't you giving this to your . . . to Donna?" Her face looked almost broken in her turmoil.

I'd wanted to rock her back on her heels a little bit, just to let me catch my breath. I hadn't meant for this to hit her so hard, though. If I'd known . . . I might still have done it. Even knowing then what I know now. "Jeannie, honey, I want you to have it. To help you think of me. To remind you that I'm still your Rob, still here for you if you should ever need me." I moved closer, to sit beside her. I started to hug her to me, but hesitated. I didn't know if I should pull her to me when she was wearing her new clothes. It almost seemed like she was a different person, wearing them.

She helped me out of my moment of confusion. She always had. She put her hands around my neck and laid her head on my shoulder, crying softly. "Oh, Rob, I never dreamed of owning anything so beautiful. Thank you, Robert. Thank you so much!" She accentuated each 'thank you' with a fierce hug. This was more the reaction that I'd hoped for.

And she surprised me again. She stood, and gathered the box to her. Then she smiled shyly at me, and walked into the cabin, shutting the door behind her. Just a brief moment later, she called out to me.

"Come in here, Rob Taylor. Or don't you want to see what it looks like?"

Chapter Fifty-Four

I vacillated there on my rock for a moment. Of course I wanted to see what the kimono looked like on a woman's body, not just in the box, or held up to the light to appreciate the watermarks. But could I take the sight of it? Would it be better to imagine it forever, or to have seen it, at least this once? Would Jeannie understand, if I decided not to come look?

I still hadn't made up my mind, but I guess I made up my feet instead, because they carried me to the door in four running steps. I opened the door, and as the door gradually exposed more of the cabin to view, I saw my Jeannie, her back to me, hair held off her neck by bobby pins, hairspray, or just pure fucking magic, for all I knew. The robe was across her shoulders, and she was belting the obi, her head down. She was absolutely gorgeous from behind, the way the silk clung to her curves and seemingly caressed her.

She had to have heard me come in, but she stayed focused on her task. Some vestigial shyness must have remained in my heart, because instead of looking at her with the passion that seeing her in the robe inspired, I gazed away. And saw her new lacy underthings on top of her new clothes. She was wearing the robe right next to her skin!

It would have taken a stronger man than I am to have kept his eyes averted with such knowledge caroming off the walls of his skull. I raked her from shoulder to knee with my gaze, nearly groaning at the waves of ardor pounding through me at the uninterrupted line of sheer, sexy silk. I wanted to feel her through the kimono, to run my hands over the territory that my eyes had traveled, and my mind wouldn't leave.

She slowly turned, one hand behind her head, one hand on her hip, striking a pose like a fashion model. I thought of telling her that she didn't need to assume unnatural positions in order to enhance her appeal, but words failed me. Instead, I pulled her to me as gently as I was able, and kissed her deeply, passionately, hungrily, hands caressing her back and her supple bottom.

When I paused for breath, I held her out at arm's length to see how the gown looked from the front. It crossed her chest low enough to see her cleavage in a sexy angle, but high enough to not seem deliberately titillating. It was lovely on her, embracing her every curve and angle, leaving nothing to the imagination, but even so, revealing nothing. The image was far more erotic than anything I'd ever experienced.

She smiled up at me, caressing my wrists where they hung quivering, just in front of her shoulders. "I wish I had a mirror, but I guess from your reaction that I don't really need one, at that."

I kissed her again, stroking and squeezing. Slow, thorough, and passionate. And when my mouth moved from her mouth to her neck, nibbling and flicking my tongue against her creamy skin, I heard her whisper, "The second part of the surprise is that tonight, there's no more dancing 'round it, boy. I want you to make love to me at least this once."

I was almost staggered enough by this to pause in my adoration . . . almost. I kept kissing and touching her gently, but my mind was wobbling harshly, gears grinding instead of meshing. We hadn't ever discussed the whole question. We just never had actually had sex together. It was an unspoken talisman of some sort. But all that was going to change tonight.

She kissed me back with matching fervor, slowly working my shirt over my head. As she tossed it aside, she locked her lips to mine and pinched my nipple with her nails, just enough to hurt a smidgen. As I gasped in . . . pleasure? she laughed quietly. "Ol' Jeannie may have showed you everything you know, Rob Taylor, but that ain't the same as showing you everything that *I* know."

Then we were on the bed, and the kimono was open, revealing her body to me draped in the finery. She was kissing my chest, undressing me. She was dominant and submissive by turns, teasing and satisfying. She straddled my legs, working her mouth on me until I was quivering and on the edge of release, then stopping, and enticing me to do the same to her. When I couldn't stand it any longer, I sat up and eased her back to the mattress gently, taking control for a while.

I licked her nipples, nipping lightly with my teeth as she encouraged me. I dipped between her thighs, tasting her hunger and need. I pinned her there with my hands squeezing her buttocks, holding her hips up to my mouth as I feasted. Then she spun away from me, and lowered herself over my mouth. I flicked my tongue against her eagerly, and nearly lost my mind when I felt her lean forward and put her mouth on me even as I had my mouth on her.

After she'd brought me off once, I set out to do the same for her, first gently moving her to her back on the cot, then nibbling and licking faster, harder, more focused on her center of pleasure. She fought against it, but I finally pushed her over the edge, nails digging into my scalp, fingers knotted in my hair, legs locked around my cheekbones, rocking me like a carnival ride.

Seeing her panting in passion, robe still flung around her shoulders, and hearing her cries of fulfillment had brought me back to full arousal all over again. She guided me to her; one hand on my shoulder; one gripping me and helping me find the angle. As I entered her, there was a simultaneous sigh from each of us, one that said, "Finally!" without either of us saying one word.

Again and again, we rocked against one another in loving passion, trying to make up not only for lost time in the past, but for the times in the future when we would be separated. I was getting married, and she was leaving town. This night may well have been the last time we saw each other for years, and we made the most of it. It was nearly dawn when we collapsed, panting and sweaty into one another's arms to find what dregs of sleep that were left in the night.

Chapter Fifty-Five

I awoke the next morning to a shed that was cool in the early-morning summer dew. The door was slightly ajar, and Jeannie's things were all gone. Even the cedar box. I felt an odd pang at its passing from my life—it was a burden that I was glad to be free of, but there was still a small part of me that felt bereft without it. I had taken a perverse pleasure in the torture it gave me, and with the decision made, irrevocably, I would never again know the anticipation and indecision of having *not* decided.

Beside me on the bed lay a plain white envelope with just one word on the flap: Rob. I had a sickening feeling within me as I stared at it. A piece of paper shouldn't be able to look ominous and fear-inspiring, but the cheap envelope with my Jeannie's flowing script embossed across the flap tucked inside managed it.

I noticed my hand was actually trembling as I reached for the letter and pulled it to me. I laughed a little at myself, with myself. I tried to convince myself I was being silly and melodramatic about the foreboding feeling welling within me, but being aware of your attempt to sneer at your fear tends to negate the effectiveness. I nervously pulled the flap open to retrieve the contents, and biting my lower lip, began to read.

Dear Rob,

I'm not really sure how to begin. I'm not sure how to stop, either, I guess. Begin the letter, or stop loving you the way I've come to.

Because I'm pretty sure that is what needs to happen. It isn't right for me to love a man who's married (or at least, the next thing to it) this way. It isn't the way a young lady should behave. And despite what anyone may say about Jeannie Riley, I am trying very hard to become a lady. That's different from a woman or a girl, you know. I know you understand what I'm trying to say, Rob. You always did listen and understand better than anybody.

Which is what makes things so difficult for me. I know you're in love with Donna. And I know you're not in love with me. Me wishing it was so doesn't make it that way. I'd give anything for you to look at me, to think of me, to want me . . . any and all of it, really, anywhere near as much as you feel these things for her. That was what I was wanting to tell you about the day you came to the widow's to tell me about you and Donna. That I loved you. More than just as my best friend.

Not that I don't value your friendship, you understand. You've been the best (and only) friend I ever had. I don't want that overshadowed by this confession. I treasure and cherish your friendship . . . but I confess to snapping up any scrap of affection in excess of that that you ever gave me. I relished teaching you how to please a woman in bed for the joy it gave you, and for the joy that it hopefully will give your wife . . . but I loved every minute of it for myself and for the sake of being loving with you.

It may be in poor taste to tell you this on the day I leave, and poorer yet to tell you in a letter, but I honestly don't think I've got the courage to see you again after the night we spent together. This was the best night of my life, Rob Taylor, and you gave that to me, from start to finish.

Each moment is etched into my memory: your confusion over the dinner supplies, your reaction to me showing off my office clothes, your wonderful WONDERFUL gift of the komomo? kimono? (however you spell it!), your reaction to seeing me wearing it, and best of all, the long slow lovemaking we shared afterward. I lay in your arms and couldn't sleep at all. Not because I was uncomfortable—quite the opposite. I just didn't want to have missed even a little bit of our last night together. I watched you sleep and even loved the funny little snoring noise you make sometimes when you're about to turn over. I cradled you in my arms and loved you until I had to go. I hope that some part of you knew that already, and didn't need to be told.

You've given me more than I ever gave you, Rob Taylor. It's not for want of wishing on my part—there's nothing I have that I wouldn't, that I haven't given you. But some of us just don't have as much to give as others, I guess.

I'll write when I get established in Charleston. If this letter makes you uncomfortable, then we don't have to talk about it. Please write me back, though, Rob. You're the only friend I've ever had, and I'd feel the fool if I lost that by telling you how I really felt about you. You're a good man, Rob. I hope in some small part, I may have had a little bit to do with that. I'll miss you, Rob. Take good care of yourself, and I'll try to do the same for me. Don't come to say goodbye to me at the bus stop. I can't stand the idea of crying all the way to the city.

Love,

Your Jeannie

I half-reclined in the bed reading the letter, shaking my head in disbelief, and rereading it. How had I missed all this? Where had this thunderbolt come from? And what should I do about it? Should I do anything at all about it? What did this mean for our friendship? And should I go see her at the bus stop? Shouldn't I be trying to stop her from going? But then, what about Donna?

I lay back and stared at the ceiling, eying the imperfections in the roof. Granted, I'd put it together out of scrap lumber, but I could have maybe gotten this corner a little tighter . . . I kicked myself mentally for fleeing the important questions with trivia.

I gritted my teeth. Jeannie was leaving, going off to seek her fortune in the big city. She was escaping Folsom Hollow, living part of my dream for me, in a way. I needed to let her go. And I needed to write her back. But if she had felt like this, could I have been feeling the same way without knowing it?

Of course not. She was the best and only friend I ever had. I knew that for a fact. She and I had shared a great deal over the past few years. But Donna was the woman I loved. And it was a damned good thing, I grinned mirthlessly. Because I was going to marry her, just as soon as I asked her father.

Chapter Fifty-Six

I went back home to get the water ready for my bath. I was going to ensure that everything I was wearing was beyond reproach, that everything I said was proper and correct, and everything that could be done to lessen the blow to her father was done. I knew also that none of these things would help my cause at all, but that I owed the man the respect embodied by these actions.

Mama had pressed and starched my Sunday shirt for me without being asked. She hadn't said a word about it, but soon after I told her about my plans, she had hung the shirt up on the back of my door. Mama wasn't much on hugs and kisses, but she always had her way of letting me know that she loved me.

It was a tough walk into town, trying to avoid the road dust and the occasional mud puddle. I don't think it helped anything that I was anxious about Mr. Duquesne's reaction. He'd asked me if my intentions were honorable. I had promised him that they were. And from my point of view, it was the truth. He probably wasn't going to be seeing things from my viewpoint, I glumly acknowledged.

Finally, I stood on the sidewalk in front of their home. I took a deep breath and kept standing there for a moment, steeling myself for the terrifying unknown lying before me. Even this respite wasn't going to be granted me very long, though, because Mr. Duquesne came out the screen door carrying a tray with a pitcher of iced tea, a couple of glasses, and a magazine on it. He saw me and made a nodding gesture, an apologetic grin on his face for being unable to wave. "C'mon up here, boy! Fancy a glass a' tea? Mighty hot work, this readin'!"

I took another deep breath, wondering why I bothered. All these deep breaths didn't seem to be helping in the slightest. I smiled my best smile, and headed up the walk to the porch.

As I climbed the stairs, his face knotted in confusion. "Son, wasn't ya s'posed ta be gone off ta Annapolis by now? Thought Donna said that you'd be leavin' some time back."

I fought off the urge for another deep breath, and sat down on the cast-iron glider rocker across the table from him. "Well, I've decided not to go to the Academy, sir."

He stifled his questions for a moment, and poured me a glass of tea. "Why, Bobby? I thought you were pretty excited 'bout the idea of bein' in the Navy, an' bein' an officer an' all." He shook his head. "There a better offer someplace else?"

"In a manner of speaking, sir. It's what I've come to talk to you about." I struggled to hide my wince at his questions. Without all the information, it must seem inexplicable that I wouldn't be going to the Academy. With all the information, the man might well scramble for his shotgun and put daylight in me.

"Well, son, talk away. I'm not sure how I might be fittin' inta yer plans, though. Paper's not big enough ta need any help, an' the law practice requires education." Seeing the expression on my face, his own hardened a bit. "But you're not talking about a job, are you, Bobby." His inflection made it pretty clear that he wasn't asking a question.

"No, sir. I've come to ask for your daughter's hand in marriage." Not smooth. Not suave. Just blurting things out. I mentally kicked myself.

"Well, son, I don't understand. What's the hurry? If you and Donna have something good going between you, a little time apart wouldn't hurt you, would it? You didn't need to turn down the Academy. Love would have seen you through, you know. If it was meant to be, you'd have been able to meet up afterwards." He shook his head in bewilderment. "And, son, I've got to admit, I'd have looked more favorably on this marriage if you'd had some means of support. What are you planning on doing? Working at Black Gold like your brother?"

"I'll do whatever it takes to support Donna, sir." Time enough later to talk about grandchildren, I figured.

"You still didn't say why the rush, son. Have the two of you . . . gotten into trouble?" His face was harsh and fearful.

"I guess you might say that, sir." Trouble! It seemed like trouble at the time, but it was a minor difficulty compared to what came later.

"God damn it, boy!" He shook his head, and I saw that his small hands were shaking with rage. "God damn it! How could you, how could she . . . God damn it!" He shook his head again, and the fury drained from his face as though he'd pulled a plug. His hot rage seemed to be spent. Now he got cold, and this was even more frightening, really.

"So you want to marry my daughter, then. What does she have to say about this?" His brows knitted into a single fierce line above his glasses.

"I've asked her, sir, and she agreed." I didn't know how else to phrase it. To say that she pledged me her undying love would have been a lie. Saying that she was overjoyed would have been worse. It really was something that I wanted more than she did, I guess.

"She'll never be able to finish high school in the family way, you understand. You'll be taking care of her for the rest of your life. I'm just glad you had enough honor to fulfill your obligation. I can't tell you I'm not disappointed, Bobby. In you and Donna both. But you're going to do the right thing. By God, you are."

I got a little miffed, but swallowed my pride and anger. After all, he had every right to be angry. "Yes sir, that's my intention, anyway. So you'll grant me your daughter's hand in marriage?"

"Grudgingly, boy. Very grudgingly. But you're not working in the goddamned mines, either. If you're marrying my little girl, you're not going to come home broken-up or dead from that damned place and leave her all on her own."

"All right, sir. I'll find another way to support us, then." I didn't particularly want to work the mines, but if I didn't, what else was there? Working at Johnson's like Jeannie? That would pay just enough to starve to death for a family man. Anyplace else . . . ?

Seeing my consternation, he said, "I've got thirty acres outside of town, boy. You'll set up a farm out there, I guess. It's good enough ground, I guess. You'll need to get a house put up, though. You can look at it as your wedding present," he sneered at this, "or you can look at it as a father's last act of charity. Because the two of you aren't going to get anything else out of me."

"We'll be grateful for your wedding present, sir." My fists were aching to pound him for his derision, but I kept in mind what it must seem like I had done . . . was doing to him.

"I'll give you fifteen hundred dollars to get your house built. Anything you need beyond that, you'd better make. Maybe your side of the family will be able to throw a bone your way for anything else you'll need. And I see no point in a public wedding, either. I wanted better for Donna than this. I wanted better for Donna than you, to be perfectly blunt about it. And I had your word on it, as well. So seeing the justice of the peace is plenty good enough for the likes of you."

"I agree, sir. That would be fine. And I appreciate all that you're doing for us. I'd like to find Donna and tell her of your generosity, if that's all right with you." I was struggling to control my temper, and knew I'd better put some space between the two of us before his sneering contempt blew through the thin wall of my restraint.

"She's in there somewhere. May as well go on in. Nothing you can do to hurt any more than you've already done." He shook his head and waved me in dismissively, turning his head not quite quickly enough to conceal the tears forming in his eyes.

I made it inside the screen door without snarling a reply, which was as good a victory as I could have garnered, under the circumstances.

Chapter Fifty-Seven

Donna was in the kitchen, looking at a bowl of vanilla ice cream and a few pickles and onion slices in a small dish beside it. She didn't seem to notice me coming in, so I watched for a moment, wondering what she was doing.

Finally, I couldn't take it any more. "Donna girl, what are you doing?" She had just continued to look at the small dishes as if they were going to start a vaudeville show or something.

She looked up with a start, and then laughed nervously. "Oh! Hi, B- . . . Robert. It's kinda silly, reckon. I always heard that women wanted weird stuff ta eat when they was with child an' all. Sally Jo said her sister wanted ta eat chalk an' laundry soap. An' Esther tol' me that she wanted ta eat pickles, onions, an' ice cream. So I figgered I'd rather eat the ice cream with stuff. Least that's food, right? Not like wantin' that other stuff. I was kinda waitin' ta see if I'd wanna eat this mess, mostly." She looked away, feeling foolish.

I sat next to her, and tried not to laugh. "I don't think it works quite like that, Donna. The cravings will come to you, not the other way around." I hugged her to me. "I asked your dad if it'd be okay if we got married."

"What did he say?" Not particularly worried about it, she had an air of idle curiosity.

I swallowed my irritation at her lackadaisical attitude. "He offered us the property outside of town as a wedding present, and enough money to build a house with. He wasn't really happy about it, but he seemed to think this was the only way out, really."

"Sounds pretty good. Why come we gotta live all the way outta town, though? It's gonna be just us out there fer miles an' miles. Won't hardly be any company." She complained casually, not even griping with feeling.

I got tired of swallowing my vexation, first with her father, then with her. "I suppose that might be part of his plan, Donna. Keeping us out of the public eye, so to speak. It's hardly a badge of honor to 'have to' get married because of the trouble. He probably doesn't want tongues wagging any harder than they already will. Keeping us out of sight will keep the gossip to a minimum." I didn't let my temper go full force, but I didn't try keeping all the nasty out of my tone either.

She wrinkled her nose at me, and looked at me as if I'd just then walked in the room. "Maybe so, Robert. I guess that'd be okay, though. What are we gonna do fer money, though?"

"I guess I'll be farming that land, Donna. It's good soil out there, you know. I could raise a couple head of beef, a couple head of dairy cows, and maybe a pig or two. You could keep the chickens, an' we'd have enough to eat, anyhow." It wasn't very different from how we got by my whole life, really.

"That sounds awful!" Donna made a horrible moue, and even an artificial shudder. "All the time eatin' on animals we'd been feedin' an' pettin' an' stuff! I never really did get used ta the idear a' that, even after you an' Cal fed me that bacon offa that poor pig."

"Donna, I didn't make you eat that. That was Calvin, if you'll remember. I don't think there's going to be a whole lot of choice about it, anyhow. Your father seems pretty intent on keeping us out there, since he forbade me to work in the mines. Other than Black Gold, there's no money to be made in this town, and we both know it. So does he. He wants us out of town, and he wants us to be too busy to be making all kinds of trips into town. And right now, we don't have much choice in the matter. We don't have the resources of our own, so we're pretty much obligated to take what he chooses to give. And he chooses for us to be out of town on the farm there." I kept my voice even, but again, some of the underlying aggravation leaked through.

Donna ignored it as if it were of no real consequence. "I s'pose yer right, Bob—Robert. We can do it, though, right? You know how, right? Growed up that way, din't ya? I reckon I can do it too. Just so long as I got city water an' 'lectric light, ya understand. Cain't go livin' like a caveman or somethin', country life or not. So when you build that house, you best be makin' sure it's got them things, Robert. Cain't go actin' like we's pioneers or nothin'."

       I stifled the urge to laugh. I'd try, but that would make things a little bit tougher. Having electricity out to the house meant another bill, which needed cash money to pay it. Electric companies weren't real good at accepting eggs and meat as payment. But I'd see what I could do.

       "So when you wanna do this, Robert? Get married, I mean?" She looked at me curiously. "I guess we prob'ly oughtta get it done before I'm too far along, right?"

       "Why don't you talk that over with your father, Donna? You and he could come up with a date, and whenever's good for you all, I guess is fine with me. I just need time to get the house put up out there, I guess." I felt a little daunted. I was a fair-to-middlin' carpenter, but I'd never built anything on the scale of a house before. I hadn't even built all that much on my own. I'd always had Calvin with me to show me things, to point out tricks and shortcuts. I sure couldn't afford to have it built for us, not on start-up money of fifteen hundred dollars. With that, we'd also need to buy the stuff for farming, and the basic necessities for starting a household, as well.

       "Reckon so. How long'll it take ya ta build a house, anyhow?"

       "I don't know, Donna. Guess I'll talk to Calvin about it, though. He's worked on stuff like that before, especially since he started working up at Black Gold." I internally snickered at the irony. I was consulting my brother, who had made part of this mess, to help us adapt it to the way we wanted to live. Of course, I was grateful to him in a lot of ways . . . but at the same time, I felt a little resentment. He wasn't giving up anything at all . . . and it was his baby.

At the mention of Calvin's name, Donna's eyes lit up. "Think he'd help us build it?"

I snorted condescendingly. Now that Calvin was going to be involved, it wasn't just a 'me' project, it was a 'we' project. Some things didn't change, I guess.

Chapter Fifty-Eight

Mr. Duquesne had gone so far as to mail the promised check to Mama's house instead of a more personal method. The only thing resembling a note was the line on the memo portion of the check—Wedding Gift, he'd written. So be it.

Calvin drove me down to the lumberyard the day after I'd cashed the check. He'd already worked eight hours on the midnight shift, and was hopped up on coffee with too much sugar. He and I had worked out a list of all the things we'd need. Over all of Calvin's objections, it had materials for wiring and plumbing the house on it. I wanted the house to be everything that Donna wanted from it. It was her house, after all.

"It makes it a whole whale of a lot tougher to build, you know. We gotta get the framing up, then the plumbing, then the wiring. All that before we start puttin' insulation in, an' the panelin'." Calvin protested. "We'd have this house up a whole lot quicker iffen ya'd just let go this here idear a' 'lectric an' plumbin'."

I thought of another late addition to the list. "Gas line, too. We'll need that for the oven an' the furnace I'll be puttin' in someday."

Calvin put his hand on my shoulder. "Why doncha just pick up enough fer the oven fer just now, Bobby. Ain't no need in spendin' today's money on someday."

I knew he had a point, but also thought of another requirement. "Hey, Calvin, I'll be needing enough for the water heater!"

Calvin sighed. "Okay, Bobby. But let's us get the damn place up 'fore you go buyin' the appliances, that a'right wif ya?"

We finished up our initial purchases, and headed out for the building site. It was on the far side of town from the state road that the Riley place and Mom's house were. The farm was a lot nearer the Chief's than the area that I considered my 'stompin' grounds'. The Chief's was only four miles away, and Mom's was nearly ten.

Calvin and I started by laying out forms for the foundation. We'd need to pour concrete in, let it set, then start framing the house. Calvin measured his lumber carefully, and made the marks for me. After I'd checked four or five of his marks, I gave it up as unnecessary, and started taking the saw to them as soon as I found his next blue line.

We had the forms finished and laid aside that first day, then started working on leveling the ground. It's a tough job with nothing other than shovels, rakes, and a three foot level. We moved more earth around for less motion on that little bubble than I'd have believed. But by the time the sun was moving deep into the west, the ground was level enough for our purposes. We had worked hard all day long, and Calvin was headed into the mine tonight. He needed to get his rest.

I was eager to continue, but until we had the concrete poured and dried, there wasn't much else to do. I could have started framing up the walls, but there wasn't much lumber, and there wasn't much point. The sun was getting lower in the sky, and the light wouldn't last too much longer. Calvin tossed me the keys to the truck, and said, "Why don't you drive us on home, Bobby-boy? I'm awful tired, fella. An' you could use the practice, anyhow." He punched me in the arm playfully, but a little harder than I would have liked.

I was tired too, but not too tired to let that kind of thing pass lightly. I snapped two jabs into his arm, and waggled my power hand threateningly, grinning all the while. "I could use the practice driving, Calvin Taylor, but you need to get back into fighting shape 'fore you go 'round thumping on your betters!"

He laughed, and tousled my hair. At that moment, I knew that my brother and I were going to have a great summer working on this house. It was going to bring us together the way that I'd always wished we could. As equals. As men.

Chapter Fifty-Nine

We worked hard until noon, and Donna came out to bring us a lunch. Hell, who was I kidding? She came out to bring Calvin lunch, and since I was there, she brought enough for me as well. She was still moon-eyed over him . . . but I had to admit, I was pretty moon-eyed over her. Maybe that was enough. Either way, maybe it was going to have to be.

With the concrete poured, the framing started. And the plumbing and wiring. Nothing fancy with the wiring, but at least one receptacle in every room, and an overhead light. Calvin was, by my good fortune, mechanically gifted, and I trusted his plumbing much better than mine. In fact, I even trusted him enough to let him run the gas lines.

Donna helped us make the frames, and there was a good humor about the whole project that I really loved. I was getting along with Donna well; I was getting along marvelously with my brother. Both of them were getting along and having fun with me as well as one another. I think in many ways, the time we spent building that house was the last and best moment of my youth.

We tin-roofed it. It made the best roof, for one thing. It was inexpensive, light and easy, reflected heat off better, and was less flammable. I knew I'd want to insulate underneath it pretty thoroughly--they weren't great at keeping heat in without good insulation. But they were loads cooler in the summer.

After the house was put together, Calvin and I started on the barn. I'd built it big. I needed lots of space, for things I knew I hadn't even thought of yet. I knew I'd need a place to keep the livestock warm in the winter, and keep the weather off of the tractor, and put a workshop together. Maybe even a spot to have a small gymnasium? We'd just gotten the roof put on it when the Chief rolled up in his old beat-up truck.

"You there, worthless!" he growled at Calvin. "Grab these stoves out of the back here."

And there were two stoves, freshly blacked, straight out of the Chief's shop.

"Thanks, Chief! I appreciate it!" I started helping Calvin lug the big iron stoves out of the bed of the truck. One was for the house, of course. The other, I knew, Chief wanted me to have for my gymnasium. Or barn. Both, for me, I guess.

"Figure out where you'll have them, and I'll measure for chimney-pipe." Chief waved off my appreciation. "You'll need to keep warm of a winter, and I'm glad to give you a wedding present, boy."

His stoves lasted me all my life. They're in the barn and house yet. Some of the piping had to be replaced a couple of times over the years, of course. But the stoves, with sanding and painting every two or three years, have kept right on.

So at the beginning of September, 1965, the property was ready. The second week of September, Donna became my wife. It was a brief ceremony at the courthouse, with Mama crying, and Calvin as my best man, and both of them called to witness.

That first winter was lean. No, that doesn't cover it, really. That first winter was hungry. Cabbage and apples, applesauce and coleslaw, dried apples and sauerkraut . . . venison and goat, usually in a slumgullion with cabbage of some sort, root vegetables, and applesauce to thicken the broth. Calvin would drop off loads of sawmill slabs to help us keep warm. We'd have run out of food if we hadn't been so damned sick of everything we had to pick from. September is a damned poor month to begin farming, if anybody ever asks you.

Spring was better. Chickens laying, a good garden patch laid in along with five acres of corn. several Indian gardens--Three Sisters, or succotash beds, The food wasn't ready yet, but we could see the menu of our summer growing around us. Calvin brought a handful of shoats to root acorns and fatten in the woods as they would. I'd drop what slops I could manage and afford, and they'd root out what they could. Hopefully there'd be three to slaughter come fall time. He might have bought them, or just grabbed them from some other farmer. Either was as likely, and asking him wouldn't have gotten me any closer to the truth. He generally dropped us off sawmill slabs still, and seldom showed up to visit without some sort of present or improvement to the property. He and I worked up a woodshed to season the wood I cut and hauled, and a smokehouse we planned to cure the hams from the shoats.

Donna and I took to married life pretty well. I worked the farm, she helped as she could, and learned to cook with what we had. I was as besotted with her as I ever was--and she tried hard to be a good wife to me, a helpmeet, and a partner.

My . . . our son was born in April. He was beautiful, and strong, and so angry! Mama helped as Donna's midwife, and Calvin and I waited on the porch. He sometimes brought Mason jars of O'Reilly's with him, and kept a jar in the cupboard until he finished it off. He sipped his 'shine and smoked a cigar, and we rocked in our chairs and didn't look at each other, and pretended we didn't hear Donna screaming in pain. I don't know what he was thinking about. I was contemplating the irony of both of us listening to our son being born. The child of his body, but my heart. From my wife, but his girlfriend. I loved her, and he didn't. She loved me, maybe a little, but she adored my brother. If that's not irony enough to suit you, I don't know what would do it.

Mama came to tell us when he was born, and that we could come congratulate Donna and look at the baby. When we went upstairs to see, Mama grunted in disapproval when we both went in while she was breastfeeding, but it wasn't the first time for either of us . . . and it wasn't Mama's house. She was allowed to disapprove, but I think that may have been the first time I discounted that as a man.

Donna wanted Calvin to hold the baby, but he wouldn't have it. I cradled Ritchie's head carefully, and marveled at him. He had a full head of hair, and was still damp from the bath Mama gave him. He smelled of baby oil, and baby. My son had his eyes open, and was looking around as best he could. Donna was looking at Calvin and holding his hand, but she was looking over at me and Ritchie almost as often. I rocked the boy in my arms, and watched his mother.

Calvin didn't visit us as a family near as often after Ritchie was born. He still dropped off loads of sawmill rounds and stubs for firewood, and cases of canning goods, or shooed some shoats into the woods, but he visited Donna more often when I wasn't around. When I 'd run up the road and visit the Chief, or Mama, or I'd be felling trees in the far pasture, or be slaughtering the chickens for freezing, that's when Cal would come to visit Donna. He'd visit me in the barn or the fields, and visit Donna in the house. Sometimes, they'd take off together in his truck.

No, Calvin and Donna didn't quit sleeping together when we got married. And Donna and I were pretty typical newlyweds in our own right, as well. We didn't talk about it. It was just tacitly understood, I guess. These had always been the rules, since Donna had made them the rules, and we didn't want to disrupt the balance we'd found. Everyone was happy, right?

Chapter Sixty(Fall 1966)

Jeanie's letter had come in October, and Calvin dropped it by the house on one of his visits. I made sure to have the new address on the letter I sent her back. I told her of the house, and the property. And my new wife.

She told me of Charleston, and the secretary pool. Jeanie was still reading and studying in her time off. She thrilled at the difference in the libraries there in the state capital. So many more books to read! Magazines she'd never even heard of, and newspapers from across the whole country! Jeanie was in love with the library.

She roomed with a widow and her daughter, and was able to walk or take the street car to work most days. She was able to save much of her paychecks, since she had simple tastes and low expenses. She was succeeding. She was on her way to becoming a lady. And she loved me and wished me well.

To write her back of how things were going on our farm seemed awkward. She was mine . . . not in a way that I owned her or had a claim on her . . . but more that she had a claim on me. I felt like I had to live up to her approval, in some way. And I knew that Jeannie wouldn't approve of how the three of us were set up in an unspoken menage a trois. So I wrote her about the books I was reading. The way that I'd shadowbox, work the speed-bag, or do some combination work on the heavy bag in the evenings if I had any gas left in my tank. About how the crops were going. And how cunning little Ritchie was. How I'd take him with me to go plow and bushhog the ground on the old tractor I got second-hand. Anything but Donna and me . . . and Calvin. Somehow that felt right. Like I was keeping my heart and attention separately partitioned . . . safely encapsulated, each love to its own partition.

I'd try to get out to see the Chief at least every month or so. Often it was just a cup of coffee in the morning on my way into town, or sometimes he'd stop by and check out my evening work in my far humbler gymnasium. He didn't talk much about my not going to the Academy. He didn't approve of officers . . . but I think he approved of Donna Duquesne and the choices I made even less. He was a good friend to me, and never said those words.

If you've been singing along with Mitch, you know that we're talking about the late fall and early winter of 1966. '66 was the year of the heaviest conscription of the Vietnam War. Calvin left for Army bootcamp in mid-November, and Mama was choking back tears at Thanksgiving and Christmas that year.

He wrote me a couple letters from bootcamp. Mainly griping about the chow and being bossed around. Calvin wouldn't have been my first choice as a soldier, but he seemed to take to it pretty well. Which, in hindsight, makes pretty good sense. He was always a big participant in team sports, and took direction well. He was aggressive and competitive, and practically glowed with team spirit, given the opportunity. This team was a little bit bigger than the football squad, but the same factors that made him excel in one helped him thrive in the other.

Calvin sent Donna a couple of postcards, but couldn't be bothered to write her anything even as detailed as he sent me. I know he sent Mama a couple postcards, sending his love, but that was about all that we heard from him until he got leave after boot camp.

When he hit town with his green-bean suit and fresh-cut whitewalls, he was all grins. Donna and I brought Ritchie to meet him in his pickup truck at the bus station in town, and drove him out to Momma's house for supper. He was in high spirits, and seemed to be liberally sipping from a pint flask (of high spirits) from his jacket pocket. Donna sipped with him when he offered, but I declined. I said something about driving, and he said he understood.

Dinner was a treat--Mama made fried chicken, green beans from the summer canning, baked potatoes, with fried cabbage to fill in the cracks. Apple pie with whipped cream for dessert. Mama always was the best cook. I remember the way everything that night tasted with a sharp clarity that seems out of place, really. It was a meal not terribly unlike any other Mama had made on any number of occasions before or since. But in some ways, that was the last supper, for me. My last meal as a boy, in a lot of ways. Because later that night, I tasted something bitter that I haven't gotten the taste out of my mouth since, I reckon.

Chapter Sixty-One

After dinner, I was set to drive Donna and Ritchie back home. It was Calvin's truck, of course. I figured he'd want to take it out and strut around his old hometown in his army greens, showing off his PFC ranking he'd gotten in boot camp. I was right. At least, part right.

When I pulled up to the drive, he got out with me and Donna. "Hey, Bobby-boy? You don't mind watching the baby for a little bit, do ya? I wanted to drive around with Donna a little bit."

The fact was, for the first time, I did mind. I minded a lot. The past couple of months out of Calvin's shadow, being on my own, providing for my wife and son on my own, enjoying their company . . . well, they'd made me pretty possessive. I needed to explore these thoughts before I was comfortable talking about them, though. So I gave a shrug, and took Ritchie from Donna, and walked into the house.

Feelings are never as simple as folks would have you think. I loved my brother. I reckon a part of me always will. And a part of me will always be yearning for his approval, that 'attaboy' that he sometimes actually did give me. He was the closest thing to a father figure or male role model I'd had, until I got to know the Chief.

Hated him too. Hated him with a pure and glowing passion like I've never felt for another soul on this green earth. And he deserved it. Because of things like this. Like driving off with my wife--mine! in his army greens and his pint bottle in his pocket, leaving me with a hungry baby. That was my child in spirit, but his in body. Oh, yeah, Calvin deserved my hate.

It wasn't fair of me to suddenly feel this jealousy, though. This had been how things were from the giddy-up, after all. My feelings didn't trump the understanding we'd operated under all this time. Especially when I'm the only one who knew I felt this way.

And a cold ugly part of me was calculating and thinking rational, mathematical, actuary-type tables. Calvin was a few weeks from shipping out to a strange land that we only just suddenly heard of. That land was full of things that were sending our boys home in their aluminum coffins, youth and fire extinguished. This was a real thing. A real possibility. Frightening in some regards . . . and so promising in others. I'd never feel this way again, if he came home like that. But I'd never share a glass of lemonade and a laugh after we put up hay together, either. What kind of man was I that I could even think like this?

Ambivalence is often misunderstood. It's got a connotation of being a synonym for apathy, or 'just don't care'. That's not so. Ambivalence is caring a lot. Both pro and con, for and against, good and evil, even. You're invested in both sides of the coin flip, so it's tough to cheer for one or the other to come down. Ambivalence is not the lackadaisical whimsy of not caring. Ambivalence is caring too deeply for both horns of a dilemma.

I didn't know the answer then, and I don't know it now, either. I'm a man. Flawed, imperfect, and real. Should I have felt that way? Don't know. But I did.

Chapter Sixty-Two

I swallowed my jealousy. I swallowed my anger. I swallowed my hate. I knew it didn't have to be for long--Calvin's leave was only fifteen days from beginning to end, and it'd taken him a day and a half to hitchhike back home from Fort Polk, in Louisiana. He'd need to give himself a little leeway on the other end . . . eleven days in between, the first one was already done . . . a little less than ten more to put up with, then.

Donna didn't come home at all that night. I took Ritchie with me to do morning chores on the farm. It wasn't too taxing, really. He was a serious little guy, slow to laugh, and slow to cry. Just took everything around him in so calmly, with his big baby's eyes. She came in about midmorning, still staggered from her drinking with Calvin the night before. I just sent her to bed.

When I woke her up around suppertime, Ritchie and I were pretty good and hungry. I could have shifted to toss some lunch together for myself, but I wasn't equipped to feed the baby. He'd made do with fresh cow's milk in the morning, but it wasn't his preference, and I had no other options to offer. So after she fed the baby, she fried up some breakfast for dinner . . . which was always one of my favorites anyway. Simple fare, fast and easy . . . fried egg sandwiches and a little sausage on the side.

I wanted to ask, but I didn't know how. She seemed cheerful and unaware that I was struggling with anything. Was this going to be how things were from now on? At least when Calvin was in town?

Turns out, that yeah, it was. I never asked, and she never answered, but things never changed. Calvin went to AIT in Louisiana, and found himself in Vietnam shortly thereafter. The Army classified him as 11B, or Eleven Bravo, as they put it. Calvin said Eleven Bang Bang . . . regardless, to the rest of us, he was an infantryman. The basic unit of the modern army, a footsoldier with a rifle. Fundamentally unchanged from the eighteenth century--and only the weapon changed from the time of Philip of Macedon. Swap the rifle for a pike or spear, and the tradition fades into the mists of history.

He went through his tour of duty without being wounded. He stopped writing letters altogether. Occasionally he'd send a package home, and we could usually guess what he intended us to do with the contents. He sent a beautiful bamboo picture frame that we figured he wanted Mama to have. He sent a switchblade knife with mother-of-pearl inlaid handles that we figured was for me. And a leather flight jacket that could only have been for Donna--it was way too small for me or Mama. It was Navy issue, not Army or Air Force. Anything we couldn't tell what he intended to do with, we gave to Mama to hang onto. Like the four or five ceramic Buddhas he sent. And the model Saturn rocket.

When Calvin came back to Folsom Hollow in the early winter of 1969, he was a different fellow than the young man who built the house with me. He spoke less, he was thinner, and there was a harder edge to everything he did. Calvin was never much of a people person, maybe . . . the Army hadn't changed that, exactly. But he didn't bother to hide it near as much after he got back.

He was a little upset that we hadn't figured out that the Saturn rocket model had been for Ritchie. "Ain't all the kids crazy for space stuff and astronauts now? All the guys said that was all the rage for their kids." He seemed a little hurt that we hadn't intuited his intentions. We hung the rocket in Ritchie's room, of course. He was a little short of three years old. He seemed happy enough with it, thanked his uncle gravely, and then asked a few questions.

"This will fly? Rocket flies like a bird?" he asked.

Calvin looked a little surprised. "Well, not like a bird. See, fire shoots out of the bottom end and makes it fly."

Ritchie looked skeptical. I didn't blame him. He hadn't ever seen anything but birds fly, and they weren't on fire. And the rocket didn't have wings, either. I'm not sure he really ever believed in that rocket.

Calvin was in town for a couple of weeks again, visited Mama, came to dinner at our house a couple of times, and took Donna out overnight twice, and just for the evening once. When he left, he made a point to take the Buddhas he'd sent. I must have looked confused, because he laughed and shook his head.

"These were for me. I shipped them here to pick up when I got back stateside."

When I still didn't get it, he shook his head again. "There's plenty of ways to make a buck or two overseas. It's like the stock market. You buy low, and sell high. Well, there are things you can buy real low in Vietnam, that sell plenty high here in the states. Like heroin."

I was a little discomfited. I wasn't really comfortable with the idea of heroin . . . but I didn't really know a lot about it, either. Just that it was some kind of thing that junkies in the big city used. On the other hand, West Virginia had a proud heritage of not giving much of a damn what the federal government thought of what we did. Moonshining, growing marijuana . . . was heroin really any different? Either way . . . it wasn't a choice I was making. It was on Calvin, regardless. Especially if he was getting the stuff out of Mama's house, anyway.

"Why don't you hang onto that old truck? I won't want it in the city--sticks out too much. And the wrong way. I'll pick myself out something when I get there if I want it. You don't mind giving me a lift to the bus station, do you?" I was glad to help Calvin get out of town . . . for all kinds of reasons. I loved my brother . . . but I was very tired of my brother, too. I'd found that it was far easier for me to love him from afar than when he was at home . . . and in my face.

So I was set up for farming . . . and marriage . . . and my family prospects were looking up with Calvin leaving town again. It wasn't the future I'd dreamed of, but I had a plan, and possibilities.

Chapter Sixty-Three (Spring, 1970)

That spring, the gas company prospected our ground, and dropped a well or two, and ran the pipeline under some of our woods higher on the property than I was farming. That eliminated our gas bill, and even gained us a small quarterly income from them. I had learned that subsistence farming tasted better when I kept a wider variety of vegetables in the garden. Keeping a breeding sow and a few shoats every year kept us in pork easily enough, and a place to cycle garden scraps as well. A chicken coop is small effort, handled properly. It's not hard to accumulate enough eggs to sell extras with a reasonable effort at assembling the coop.

Keeping a field or two fallow and using it as pasture for a couple beeves and goats was not only good crop rotation practice, but kept us in beef and brought in a chunk of cash as well. Goats are handy as companion animals for cattle, and are pretty good eating in their own right. They can be shorn and their hair can be spun into yarn, too. Lots of trouble for what you get out of it, though.

I'd set up eight different fields, each about an acre. I was playing with winter crops, different rotations, and different fallow schedules. Between the pigs, chickens and the time the cattle and goats got to spend time in the barn, I was moving their free fertilizer around and aging some in compost piles as well. Turns out, I was an organic farmer before that was anything special. 'Round here, we just called it 'living poor'.

Ritchie and Donna were helping out too. Ritchie loved feeding the chickens, and Donna kept her herb and spice garden, gathered the eggs, slopped the hogs, and ran the house. Evenings, we listened to the radio, and played gin rummy or cribbage while Ritchie played around at our feet. We didn't stay up too late, though. I'd managed to catch a deal on a few head of dairy cattle. Donna would wake up early for the morning milking, and I'd finish my day in the barn catching the evening shift.

Life was sweet. Sweaty, but sweet. Some days when I was sort of caught up in the fields, we'd take the wagon and ride the edges of the fields, gathering deadfalls for cutting into firewood in slack times, or even go felling some trash trees just for firewood if the pile got low. Ritchie loved working a limbing saw on downed trees--it made him feel like such a big boy!

I'd just about gotten all the summer crops in the fields when

Calvin roared back into town in a red convertible Cadillac Deville. The drop-top was white, and the whitewalls and wire wheels on that thing glittered like diamonds. It was far and away the showiest car in McClellan county. There were other Cadillacs, and even other convertibles. But no other convertible Cadillacs . . . and especially not red.

I knew he was home when he came slewing up the drive, revving the engine and flogging the horn. "Whoo-ee, Bobby-boy! Damned good to see ya! Let's go for a ride, son!" I shrugged and looked at my fields. I had just finished preparing the last field for planting squash, corn and beans--Three Sisters hillocks. I could delay the planting until tomorrow, and I hadn't seen Calvin in several months.

"Let me get cleaned up, and the tractor in the barn, and I'll be ready to go!" Why not? It was a pretty rare thing to get to see Calvin all on his own anymore.

We grabbed a couple of cold beers for the road, and Calvin proceeded to show me what his new Caddy could do. Which wasn't a whole lot, given the terrain. An engine like that, and handling like that was better suited to straightaways . . . which were in short supply around Folsom Hollow. He enjoyed driving it anyway, and I had to admit, it was a beautiful car.

"So where'd you get this monstrocity, Calvin?" He'd left his truck with me for the farm, but I had a tough time believing that my brother had spent the kind of money this car would cost, even if he'd made a small fortune selling off his smuggled Buddha heroin.

"I picked it up in Philly. I'd gone up there to sell off that stuff I sent back. I could've gone to Charleston, but the market was going to be way better in Philadelphia. I didn't want to nickle and dime it out, and that's the first place big enough to have someone interested in buying the kind of volume I had, especially as a one-time run." Calvin seemed to have picked up on a lot of intricacies since he left town. I had never thought about the mechanism or pipeline that heroin or any drug really traveled in. It was illegal. People bought it. People sold it. How'd it get there? Well . . . like most people, I knew it didn't magically appear, but for all the thought I'd put into it, it may as well have.

"Finding where to sell it wasn't too tough, though. Just had to find where people were buying it," Calvin explained. "Not to sell to them, though. They just had enough money to buy a few hits at a time. And not to their dealers, because they were interested in prepackaged doses, not bulk product."

Fair enough, I conceded. "So how'd you go from the easy first step to finding out where the dealers got supplied?"

"Honestly, Bobby, it isn't really a fun story. I chased their backtrail for awhile, and finally got to this mid-level distributor with a '67 Continental with the suicide doors? He was stalling me and playing tough guy. After I'd already put his driver down with a tire tool, ya know? That really made me mad. So after I busted his hand and twisted it around to get the directions I needed, I put the tire tool over his ear a couple of times and took that Lincoln with me." I wasn't all that surprised, really. Calvin never did have a lot of regard for his fellow man.

"I was able to make a pretty good chunk of cash offloading the junk to the upper-tier distributor. He got a bargain, I got a good wad of cash, and it was time to get out of Philly. So on the way out of town, I sold the Lincoln to a dealership, and caught a bus to a dealership across town and bought this beauty for cash."

He was beaming, pleased with his own cleverness and success. I smiled back. It was good to see my brother happy, even if I didn't really understand why he was that happy about acting so dangerously. He pulled into the drive and stopped just off the road.

"I'm going to take Mama for a ride, if she'll go. Might pop over and see you guys later tonight, too. Take good care, Bobby-boy. I'll talk atcha later." And off he wheeled in his Cadillac, planning on enticing Mama to go for a ride.

He did swing by later that night, but it was just to pick Donna up. He didn't come in and visit. Donna didn't come home the next morning, but the morning after that. When she came back, she was redolent of whiskey and cigarettes. I cleaned her up with a washrag a little, and just put her to bed. I drove Ritchie out to the fields with me, and we had a firewood gathering day, for lack of a better reaction plan.

It was getting harder and harder on me, this unspoken arrangement. I couldn't say anything, because I hadn't objected last time. Or the time before. And now it felt like I'd given tacit permission. Which I had. Kinda. And it wasn't anyone's fault but my own. If I needed things to be different, it was incumbent upon me to pipe up and say so. Everyone else was playing their previously understood roles.

But I watched Ritchie work his little sawblade on the limbs, working so hard, looking so serious . . . and I couldn't regret it, either. Donna was my prize, my beloved, and my treasure. But I couldn't imagine a life without Ritchie in it. Without this arrangement, there would be no child.

And without the child, there would have been no marriage. I married her out of love, but Donna married me out of necessity. There was that to think on, before I grew too bitter about things.

I watched my boy work diligently at limbing the trees, and worked alongside him. I wasn't at perfect ease with all that lay in my life, but I was beginning to find serenity and joy in it, imperfect as it may be. I tousled his hair, and drove back to the house for lunch with my son in my lap.

Chapter Sixty-Four (Late summer/Fall 1970)

Donna and I worked together all that summer, canning the vegetables, potting the meat, and tending the garden. She was a hard worker, and sweated right through the fall with me, until I noticed her swelling belly. I recognized the signs from her being pregnant for Ritchie. When I would grab the tractor and head out to the further fields, that's when she'd either clean the house, see to the garden, or mow the grass around the house. There was no shortage of work to be done on the farm. It was hard work, but we were working together. We were sweaty, and happy.

Calvin had bought a two-piece pool cue and a fancy case for it. He'd always liked shooting pool, but he'd bought himself the leisure to really practice and read up on it with his bankroll from Philly. In August, he absented himself to go on a tour of the southern states with his fancy Cadillac and his pool cue.

Donna and Ritchie and I made time to go fetch firewood whenever we could. That boy would saw until blisters came and popped, and saw right through it. There wasn't a drop of quit in my son. He was a little more than four, that summer, I guess. He grabbed for my belt, and demanded to use my knife. Well, I knew what I needed to do for Christmas, then.

The Chief rolled his eyes when I told him about my Christmas project. "He'll just lose it, you know." But he didn't mind me using his smithy and forge. He even worked a little on Ritchie's knife while I wasn't there--filing the edges a bit, removing burrs around the tang. I made it a scale model of my knife, sized for an almost 5 year old's hand. Scaling the octagonal hammerhead hilt was a challenge; I suspect the Chief's hand was at play there, as well. I'd spent a couple hours fighting the scaling and shaping on a couple of evenings, and didn't think I was much closer to having it right . . . then it was perfect the next time I'd come over to tinker with it.

I think I finished it up in late October. It was a beautiful little thing, and every bit the tool that my own was, only smaller. True to his pattern, the Chief had made a sheath for it from the tail of a whitetail deer . . . he'd scaled his pattern back to use less of the tail for the blade, and trimmed more from the base. It was a beautifully crafted sheath that he claimed to have just 'sitting around' again. Not that either of us found that remotely credible, but it let him pretend to the distance he needed.

Thanksgiving that year was a little peculiar. Calvin hadn't written, and Mama was missing him. She was tickled to have us all around, especially little Ritchie. But it was different from when he'd been away in the Army. He was off gallivanting, and not under orders. Mama was hurt, and it showed. Not in her cooking, of course. That was as copious and as delicious as ever. Her demeanor, though, showed her sorrow. At least to someone who could interpret her silences and grunts as well as I could.

I gave Ritchie his knife for Christmas. He cut himself promptly, of course. But he started learning respect for the tool right away. I don't think I saw him without his belt knife ever again, except when he was in his pajamas. Donna was mad at me for a week about him cutting himself. "He's just a baby. He didn't need a knife!"

"He's not going to stay a baby forever, woman. Bound to have cut himself with his first knife anyway. He just got it out of the way early." Maybe it was a little callous. But it's true, for all of that. And he learned early, and respected the tool early. And he felt ten feet tall, wearing that knife. He was daddy's little man before that Christmas, but that knife set the stamp on it for good.

A few days after Christmas, I'd gone out to milk the cows after supper, and Ritchie was belaboring a stovelength on the chopping block near the front porch. He was sure trying to split it with the hatchet, but it was just more job than a five year old could handle. Before he saw me, I headed back to the barn. I grabbed a chisel and a splitting wedge, and found an engineer's hammer.

When I got there, Ritchie had stood the firewood up again, and was about to whop it with the hatchet. He knocked it from hell to Harvard, and looked like he was heartbroken.

"Son, hold on a minute. Why don't you try this way instead?" He looked up at me hopefully. I held out the chisel and the hammer.

"You don't split kindling with this." Simple statement of fact. I didn't. He was right.

"Well, I'm a bit taller than you, and I can swing down on top of them easier. When you get taller, you can split with a hatchet too. Meantime, you can get good work done with these."

I set it up and showed him how to get started. Hammer the chisel in until you get a crack started, then job the wedge into the crack. Drive it through the split until it pops and you've got a piece of kindling. Slower, but possible. And doable even for a five year old. Ritchie nodded gravely, and took the tools.

Ritchie caught on quickly, all right. I had to be careful how much firewood I stacked on the front porch. If I was gone in the far fields all day, he'd split wood for hours on end. I noticed that he'd split more kindling than we'd need for the next year. If I kept giving him stovelengths, he'd have turned our whole store of firewood into kindling, bless his heart. He had callused hands at five. He'd have done any job we set him to, and if we didn't give him one, he'd assign himself work.

I'm glad he was such a helpful little tyke. Donna needed help more and more as she swelled up. He helped his mother get out of her chair when she asked, or helped her to the outhouse. He washed the dishes in the kitchen sink so it'd be easier on her back. He'd fetch her drinks for her, and help her cook dinner. Having a solemn five-year old with a zealous work ethic is about the most earnest help a person can have.

I don't mean to give the impression of a mopey, surly child. Ritchie was joyful and happy. He was just a fiercely focused child, with a hardworking streak in him that most adults would envy. He was mature and workmanlike, not flighty or bouncy. It was his nature to be happy, but seem sober and serious. Much of his joy just seemed to come from the satisfaction of a job well done.

Chapter Sixty-Five (Spring '71)

Spring found me thoroughly busy. With Donna so swollen and awkward, I tried to cover more of the planting myself. I think getting the garden out around the house by hand took more out of me than the tractor work, really. My back was sore, and my ankles were swollen. I wondered if this was some kind of karma . . . Donna was pregnant, with a sore back and swollen ankles. We could share our misery.

Mama was coming over and visiting with Donna a couple times a week. With Ritchie's help, and Mama visiting and cleaning as she talked, things were getting done around the house. With me working for two out in the fields, things were getting done around the farm. March was muddy, but I'm glad the frost let go early. I needed the extra time to get the crops in, working alone.

April brought Ritchie's birthday--I'd wanted to make him a hatchet to go with his knife, but I hadn't been able to spare the time since Christmas. The Chief would have been tickled with the company, and I would have loved the break, but there was just a little too much to do to make those 'fun trips' possible. Instead, we brought balloons from town, and Mama brought over the ice cream maker, and Ritchie did the lion's share of the cranking on the old hand crank, swapping arms when he got tired. Only when it got really stiff did he yield the handle to me. I gave it another couple of minutes, but he'd about gotten it finished. Six years old, and for fun, on his birthday, he worked like a bank mule. There he sat, sweaty and smiling, eating his ice cream and cake with his flushed little face and his haystack of blond hair . . . we didn't have a color camera back then. But I can still see that picture just fine.

Mama was really growing to appreciate Donna. She liked visiting and helping her out, seeing her grandson, and listening to their stories on the radio together. I couldn't believe it, hearing my mother's deep laugh come from the house. Ritchie would climb into my mother's lap the moment she sat down, and regardless of what she was doing, shelling peas, shucking corn, stringing beans, knitting, crocheting, darning socks, or mending the laundry, she'd find a spot on her lap for him where she could both cuddle the boy and keep right on working.

She helped Donna birth the baby at the beginning of July. Donna was so proud of her daughter! She named her Bobbie, after me. I couldn't contain my pride. I could feel my chest swelling, and laughed at myself. My daughter, named after me. I thought I was terminally full of pride with my son . . . . but with Bobbie's birth, I discovered I was wrong. She was so tiny . . . holding her in my hands, she looked like a little doll.

Ritchie wanted to hold her right away. I was hesitant at first, but Gran just chuffed at me. "You think the boy's big enough to carry that cutlass you made for him, and to chop kindling, and limb the trees with ya, but too little ta hold a baby?" Given that logic, I had to grin and shrug. Ritchie cradled Bobbie carefully with his arms, and started whispering to her. I couldn't hear exactly what he said to her, but I heard 'keep you safe' and 'you're my baby sister forever' for sure.

From then on, a couple of times every day, Ritchie would want to hold his sister. And he rocked her, and he liked to sing to her in his little boy's soprano. When he was done, he'd often run outside and ride his bicycle around the yard, or split some more kindling, if I'd provided him some stovelengths. Sitting still was such a struggle for the little guy, but it was so important to him to hold his sister that he was willing to suffer it for awhile.

Donna was more and more mobile that summer, as she got her legs back under her, and just carried Bobbie with her wherever she went. She'd wrap a shawl across her shoulder and kind of make a little sling with it that cradled the baby girl if she needed both hands for something. By

September, she was in full swing again, even mowing the grass around the house, just like she always did. Mama still came to visit her, but there was less for her to do around the house, because Donna typically had it all done. She kept a clean and happy house. She and Mama traded recipes, and she'd turned out to be a pretty good cook, once she got a little practice.

That fall, Donna brought the kids on our wood-fetching trips. It was kinda like a hayride, with the wagon being dragged behind the tractor, and a couple haybales to make it comfortable. Piling the logs onto the wagon was a good bit of work, but we all enjoyed the time together. Bobbie was just a baby, but she seemed to enjoy the time outside in the fresh air.

Donna and I would snuggle on the couch and listen to the radio together at night. Sometimes we'd read together, and talk about the books. We were tender and gentle with each other. Being married to her was so much different than I had dreamed of as a young teen. Yes, there was lovemaking and passion, but we knew how to do that. We were learning how to really be in love, and that was pretty intense and beautiful.

"So you think that Scout Finch ever grew into a lady the way her aunt wanted her to?" Donna was interested in following characters after the story arc left them, for some reason.

"I guess I never thought about it. I mean, I reckon she probably did, growing up in that era. Sure, she was a tomboy and all as a young'un, but when she grows up, there isn't much demand for tomboys on the marriage market. There was a good bit of pressure on girls to get married, before they got to be old maids." I shrugged, and she squeezed me tight.

"I'm glad you didn't make me be an ol' maid, Robert Taylor. You're my hero, you know. Better'n Boo Radley." She snuggled her face deep into my shoulder, suddenly shy.

I felt myself flush . . . I didn't know how to react. I squeezed her tighter and just told her I loved her.

Ritchie started school that fall. He was headed off to first grade on the bus. He woke up early enough to feed the chickens, grab the eggs, help his mama milk the cows, and eat a quick breakfast with us before he ran out to the end of the driveway to meet the bus. Donna could cook about anything from her recipe book and notes, but she got really good at the breakfast skillet. Her squeamishness about meat she'd known personally was a thing of the past.

Ritchie wasn't studious about his classes at school. He directed his razor-sharp focus full strength at school, and utterly ignored it until he had to return. He got straight A's, and enjoyed reading, at least at school. While he was at home, he had no time for anything so sedentary. He was running full tilt from the moment the bus doors opened until he stopped for supper. He'd hold his sister a little bit after supper, but then he firewalled the throttle again until bedtime. That boy had a whole day's worth of energy to burn off, and they'd corralled him for the first half of it. He pestered me and his momma to let him run a paper route. I think he was less interested in the money than in the work.

Jeannie's letters had been coming in about every other month, keeping me updated on how things were going for her in Charleston. She'd bought a small apartment building downtown, and was living in one of the units, giving half-rent to a retired construction worker in exchange for him handling the maintenance, and renting the others out to cover the mortgage and restock her bank account. She was office manager at the place she'd started as a secretary in the pool, and had bought a nice second-hand car for the trips the bus wouldn't take her to.

Donna asked how she was doing when her letter came in this time. I passed on the news almost absent-mindedly. "Doesn't she have a fella, Robert? It's been a few years. She's bound to have met a nice guy in Charleston by now, if they have any."

"Well, it always kinda felt like prying to ask her, Donna. She lets me keep my secrets, and I let her keep hers. If there's a guy, she hasn't told me about him. And it's her story to give, not mine to take, y'ken?"

Donna wrote Jeannie a letter the very next day. Evidently, she wasn't bound by the propriety I was. And it turns out that there wasn't a man in Jeannie's life. By design. She told Donna, "I know what men are like. And I know what Rob Taylor is like. If I can't have the one, I'll be damned if I settle for the other." Maybe a little waspish in tone, but civil. Donna stewed over it a week, and then showed me the letter Jeannie had written her.

"It ain't right, Robert. That woman's in love with you. And she's pining. You ought not let her pine like that." Donna looked like she was in distress, but determined to see it through.

"Well, Donna, I don't see how I can stop her. She's always been a friend, and always been someone I loved dearly, but I'm married to you. I love you." Wasn't all this as plain as day?

"Robert Taylor, you're the very smartest man I know. The smartest man I've ever even heard of. And you'd think it'd do a heart good to know that even the smartest people can be pretty boneheaded stupid sometimes. But it don't." She glared at me. "You know we ain't like other people. You know I ain't give Calvin up. Don't mean I don't love you. Don't mean you don't love me. But you lettin' that Jeannie wither on the vine because we got married is ugly. And beneath you."

It hadn't ever occurred to me that there was any option.

"I want you to take my next letter to Charleston yourself." I looked up at Donna, confused.

"There's the crop in the field, and the farm to look after, and wood to be brought in--"

"Think I don't know what needs done, nor how to do it? You'll leave Friday night. I'll expect you back Sat'day sometime. I'll have fried chicken for supper. You can eat it hot if you're early, and cold iffen you're late. Tastes good anyrate." With that, Donna was done talking about it. Her mouth made a hard line when I tried, but that was all she intended to say about it.

Charleston was the better part of a two hour drive. I'd come in from the fields a little early, and Donna had packed me a couple of sandwiches and a jar of lemonade for the road. She'd laid out clothes for me. Not work clothes, but not my suit, either. I hadn't had much occasion to wear khakis and oxfords for awhile. "Get you gone, Robert. I love you. Mind you, put my letter in her hand and tell her to read it right then." She kissed me softly, and turned away quickly. I stepped towards her, but she waved me on. "Shoo."

I ate the sandwiches as I drove. Meatloaf and cheese, one of my favorites. The lemonade was delicious. Why did Donna want me to take this letter myself? Why was she writing to Jeannie anyway? What the hell was I doing?

Chapter Sixty-Six (Late Fall 71)

It wasn't hard to find the apartment building. Once I stopped for gas and got directions to the street, the apartment building was just a question of counting. It was a well-maintained brick building, with a small parking lot next to it. I pulled in and parked, hoping I wasn't disrupting some taboo I wasn't aware of.

Jeannie's apartment was 1B, and I knocked on the door. She answered the door, and her jaw dropped. She'd had her teeth straightened. I saw that straightaway. I smiled to see her, dressed in the skirt and button-down blouse from work that day, but her hair taken down for the evening. Her hand raised and lowered, reaching out and pulling back . . . she was totally taken aback.

"Can I come in a minute? You look great, Jeannie! I've missed you, girl." She sighed a little, and stepped aside almost sadly. She reached up and hugged me as I stepped inside, just a little squeeze, careful to angle her face away from my shirt.

"Rob, I cain't . . . can't believe you're here. You're in my home." She blinked rapidly and looked away. "I've missed you too, boy. You're looking good yourself."

I handed her the letter. Jeannie looked confused, but took it. "What's all this?"

"Donna wanted I should bring that to you personally. Wouldn't take no for an answer, nor discuss it further. I got marching orders." I shrugged helplessly. I had no better explanation than that.

"Well, if it's important enough to hand deliver, I reckon I oughtta read it, aye? Didn't figger t'see the day Rob Taylor turned postman." She smiled gently to show she was teasing.

She opened the letter, and unfolded it. Almost instantly, her face crumpled and it looked like she was in pain. She looked at me, looked at the letter, extended it towards me, and whipped away like she'd been shocked or branded. She almost ran into the next room in, the kitchen. I saw her TV dinner on the table as she grabbed up a dishtowel and held it to her eyes.

She was leaned against the sink, turned away from me, her

shoulders shuddering and heaving with sobs. I glanced down at the letter. It only had two lines on it. "If I was the woman you thought I was, I wouldn't have sent him. If you're the woman I think you are, you'll send him back." No salutation, no signature. Just statements.

I gathered my Jeannie up in my arms, and held her to me as she cried. It seemed like forever before she cried herself out, but it probably wasn't more than ten minutes. We slowly made our way to the sofa and sat down.

"I've missed you, Rob Taylor. I'm happy to have you here. I'm happy enough to bust. Burst. But I'm fearful ashamed, too, of how I thought of Donna. Wasn't fair to that woman, I wasn't." She buried her head into my shoulder, afraid to look at me.

"What do you mean, Jeannie?" Ashamed? What?

"Rob, I didn't think she appreciated you. I thought she looked at you like a backstop for your brother. And I know she and I never really got on, and she's got no reason to care about me one way or t'other." She looked up at me with eyes brimming with tears. "She sent you to me, knowing damned well that you're all she really has. Do you have any idea how brave she has to be?"

I got a little choked up at that point. I hadn't realized, fully. I knew I loved Donna and would do anything for her. It was humbling, really, to see for a brief moment how much she loved me back. She gave me my Jeannie back. She didn't have to. She did it just because she felt it was right. To me. And to Jeannie. Jeannie was right. Donna had the courage of a gladiator.

Jeannie whispered, "I know she didn't give you to me, not really. But she did send you on loan. Come to me, Rob Taylor. Take me to bed."

And I did.

The bedroom window faced west, but the rising sun reflected off the windshields in the parking lot to throw glare through the curtains. I stretched languorously, and looked to Jeannie. She was already awake, laying on her side just looking at me.

"I never thought to see you here, in my home, in my life again. I savored your letters. I reread them over and over. I just don't know what this means for me, for you, for us. You're mine, but not mine to keep. I'm yours, but I'll not be going back to McClellan county in this lifetime. Donna gave us the stamp of approval . . . but is it just this once? Will I see you again? Will she loan me her husband now and again? What's to come?"

She shook her head. "Sorry, Rob. I don't mean to drown you in questions. Especially not questions there may not be answers to. I don't want to sound ungrateful. I've already gotten more of you than I had any hope of. But I can't help feeling greedy and wanting more."

"I don't see this being a one-time thing. She compared you and me to her and Calvin, and she seems pretty adamant about that continuing. We hadn't talked about it, really. Until she sent me with her letter." Not that there was much discussion. Donna had made her mind up what she thought was right.

"I'll be plain, Rob-boy. I told Donna that I'd not settle for other men after I saw what you were, and what could be. I mean it, you know. I've had enough other men for a lifetime. I don't want them. I'll be waiting for you to come and visit me, not because you're all there is for me, but because I don't want what else is on offer. Whatever time you can spare me is better than anybody else's best effort."

Evidently a sad look crossed my face, because she pounced fiercely at me. "Don't you look sorrowful on my account, Rob Taylor. Don't you dare! You taught me I had the right to choose, and that I didn't have to put up with shabby treatment. Don't pity me that I don't choose it now that I know better!"

I looked up at her, "Jeannie, honey, it's not pity for that. It's just regret that nobody else showed you that they could be good and giving."

"They had the chance. I don't think it's in most of them. And the rest don't bother to let it out to stretch its legs." She sniffed. "Well, Rob, I'll need to send you back to Folsom Hollow soon. Love me up good, and I'll fix you a good breakfast." She bent her head down to kiss me, and we loved each other up good.

She did make a good breakfast. And I was home to eat hot fried chicken a little after noon.

Chapter Sixty-Seven (Early Spring 72)

Nobody had heard a peep from Calvin since last August, but he roared into town in his red Cadillac a little after Groundhog Day that February. He rolled right up to the farmhouse, and started honking the horn to gather everybody out to the driveway.

He was grinning like a possum, waving to me and Donna, and laughed as we looked puzzled and waved back.

He yelled, "Bobby, help me get this damned thing out of my car!" and walked around the trunk end. I saw that the trunk was wide open, and tied down against a mover's quilt-covered mass.

We untied it, and opened the trunk wide, and moved the blanket aside. It was a console Zenith, with a beautiful cherry cabinet. "Calvin, what the hell?"

"Won it in Memphis. Playing 9-ball. I din't have nowhere else to keep it, so I figgered I'd park it here, iffen you want it." If he grinned any wider, the top of his head would fall right off.

"Guess that'd be okay, Calvin. You sure you don't want to sell it, or have someplace else to put it?"

"Mama will come watch her stories with Donna if I bring it here. You guys would have to pack up the kids to go see her. Easier for her to drive over here. And selling it is more trouble than it's worth. Let's see how it works!" It was a helluva load, but he and I got it onto the porch without breaking our backs. From there, thank God, it had casters under it.

"You'll need to make an antenna, but you can read up on that at the library. Might get Charleston or maybe even Huntington, if the clouds are right." We wheeled it into the parlor, next to the radio. Nothing but static, of course--and that'd be the state of things for another few months, until I had time to design and build the antenna. After that, he was right--I could pick up Charleston all the time, and Huntington when the clouds were right.

"I've got a few errands to run, and a few calls to make, but I'll try and stop by in the next day or so. Enjoy, y'all!" And with that, he roared back down the driveway.

Ritchie kinda shook his head. "Uncle Calvin is a pretty noisy guy."

I laughed. "Yeah, I reckon so. By our lights, he's pretty loud indeed."

He and Donna were only out overnight that visit once. The baby was too little to be away from her that long. And she was too full of milk to suffer that at length. Whether that was a factor or not, Calvin blew back out of town not even a week later, intending to visit the Grand Canyon and to check the veracity of some of the Chief's wilder stories about Tijuana.

Time flew by, in the quiet happy way it does. You don't always recognize the good old days when they're passing. Donna was nursing the baby, and Ritchie was trying his best to emulate me, and I was keeping crops in the ground and trying to keep food on the table. Every couple-three weeks, I'd make time to visit Jeannie in Charleston. Mom would come over and she and Donna would listen at their stories, either on the television or the radio, and fold clothes together. Sometimes momma would run out of chores for them to do and she'd have to just either help Donna or sit idle. Donna would giggle when she'd tell me about those times. Seeing my mother look discomfited at being idle would have been quite a sight

Ritchie and I would take Donna and Bobbie on our wood-chopping hayrides now. Donna would have to sit under the baby most of the time, but Ritchie and I worked well together. He'd use the back of his knife to pop the small branches off the trunk just like he'd seen me do. Even used the hammer-pommel to drive a nail all the way in a couple of times. Donna would just watch and smile as she saw the amount of me that was in our son . . . We had plenty of wood for the winter that fall.

Ritchie was banking all his money from his paper route--he'd seldom treat himself to even a nickle's worth of candy or a soda. He wasn't sure what he was saving up for, but he said, "Whatever it is, I want to be able to afford a good one!"

Bobbie was toddling around the house and yard on her own steam now. She wasn't able to keep up with Ritchie's pace, so when he'd let her come with him, he'd just piggyback her around with him. Seeing the scrawny little thing toting his sister around never failed to make me smile.

Calvin rolled back into town around the end of May. He hadn't scored any big wins or made lots of money playing pool or poker this time--the very lack of a victory story was a telling factor. His eyes were bloodshot, and he had dark circles under them. For the first three days, about all he did was rest up out at Mama's, and get fed up on some home cooking. Despite not feeling wonderful herself, when he came to pick her up, Donna went.

The first night, she came in about daybreak, stumbling and mumbling. The reek of the corn squeezin's was strong, and she plainly was feeling poorly, even if she wasn't hurting of her usual aches and pains. I held her hair while she sicked up the worst of it, and cleaned up after her. I got her put to bed, and sent the boy off to school with a baloney sandwich, an apple, and some leftover cookies in his pail.

The next night, Calvin came by again, and I expected Donna not to go. She had just been awake for a couple of hours, and was still badly under the weather from last night's bender. Her eyes were as bloodshot as Calvin's, but she went. I tuned into the radio, instead of the TV, since it got local news out quicker.

She didn't come home at all that night, and I sent Ritchie off to school with another baloney sandwich, some hickory nuts, and a hammer. Bobbie and I got some of the close-to-the-house work done, and surprisingly, Donna wasn't home by the time I started looking for Ritchie to come home from school. The next car up the drive wasn't Calvin's Caddy, but a deputy's cruiser.

"Mr. Taylor?" If Deputy "Big John" Franklin was calling me "Mister", things were very ugly indeed. I waited to hear what he had to tell me. "I think you'd better come with me. There's been an accident just over the rise."

"Is Donna okay?"

He looked confused. "I can't help you there, Mr. Taylor. It's about your boy."

* * * * *

I rode in the front of the cruiser. I had Bobbie in the back. Nowhere else to put her, and I needed him to take me there, right quickly. When we got up to the curve just over the rise, I could see the guardrail was banged up pretty good, and there was broken glass along the shoulder. About twenty yards back, there was a set of skidmarks, and a pile of rags in the road. The ambulance/hearse was there, but the lights were off. The men were in no real hurry, and it looked like they were waiting on us.

Big John said, "Can you come take a look with me, Mr. Taylor? We need to be sure that we've got the right boy. The right family."

I didn't know what I was feeling. Felt almost like I was floating beside myself, observing my behavior and emotions without being a part of them, or affected by them. Hmmm, is it a sign of wickedness or evil tendencies that I'm hoping that some other child, any other child is the actual victim? That I'd sacrifice all of the children in town for my own right now? We walked to the pile of rags.

Under the old army blanket, there was a little boy, too small to be Ritchie. Ritchie was so much bigger, so much more vibrant and bouncing . . . so much more alive. This couldn't be right. He was wearing Ritchie's clothes, and Ritchie's haircut . . . and that was Ritchie's lunchpail over by the busted-up guardrail. From that odd space floating about eight feet off to the side, I heard my voice say, "Cover 'im up. That's my boy."

I turned away. I couldn't look at this small broken copy of my boy anymore. I looked at the guardrail. And the long slash of cherry-red paint left on it.

Big John waved the EMTs over, and they brought the stretcher. "Let's get you back home, Mr. Taylor." I let him lead me back to the car, not looking at the pile of rags that was really what was left of my boy. Just that slash of paint.

When we got home, I thanked the deputy. How's that for a dose of irony? I thanked him for bringing me the news that had broken my heart. But I did. I thanked the man, and carried little Bobbie inside. I mashed up a baby portion of green beans and carrots, crushing them with the tines of a fork. I fed her like an automaton . . . but I fed her. I couldn't think yet. I couldn't feel yet. So I had to take care of my daughter on autopilot. So I did.

Much later that night, long after I'd put Bobbie to bed and laid myself down in a grief-stupor, Donna came home. She was mumbling and stumbling around the living room, evidently still feeling the effects of her long day out with Calvin. I went to fetch her to bed.

"Donna, you need to lay down. Come on, honey." I tried to lead her gently by the arm, but she snatched her arm away and snarled at me.

"Don't you be sweet to me. Don't you act thataway. Robble garble humpher!" Her eyes rolled back into her head and she collapsed into my arms. Whatever that was about, I just shrugged it off and carried her to bed. She reeked of whiskey and cigarettes, cheap fry grease stained her dress, and her knees were bloody and scabbed. I sighed and undressed her for bed, knowing that I'd have to tell her about Ritchie in the morning.

In the night, she started crying in her sleep, and saying something incoherent . . . there were a lot of no's in there, and my brother's name. I remember thinking that if this wasn't the low point of my life, that I'd surely prefer to die rather than suffer a worse night. My son lay dead, and my wife lay drunk beside me, mumbling to the brother who killed him with his shiny fast car.

*　　　　*　　　　*　　　　*　　　　*

*

When she woke up, I was bleary-eyed, unable to cry for my boy yet. The loss was too fast, too raw, too surreal. I'd just made his lunchpail and sent him off to school with it yesterday. I'd boiled a pot of coffee for us, and fried up some breakfast. Bacon, eggs and toast. All things I could do without any real thought involved, thank God. Coherent thought wasn't high on the list of things within my grasp that morning.

She came downstairs, looking weary and unrested as well. She'd brushed her hair, and used the pitcher and ewer to rub the crust out of her eyes and around the corners of her mouth. I waited until she sat down at the table, and poured her a cup of coffee.

"Donna, honey, I need you to look at me. There's been an accident." I reached out to steady her, but she ducked under my hand.

She said nothing, but looked at me almost defeated already. "What happened?"

"Ritchie was hit by a car just up road. They took his body into town to ready him for the funeral." I was prepared to catch her in my arms if she collapsed, but she just slumped further into the chair, and silently started weeping.

I didn't know if she was going to scream or fall to the floor . . . but I hadn't expected this show of utter defeat and desolation. She just sat there, shaking in time with her sobs, and silent. I'd never seen her so bereft. I moved to gather her into my arms, but she shrugged me away, shaking her head.

"Not now. I just can't right now. I can't let you, I can't accept this!" She stood clumsily and staggered to the porch, where she collapsed in a ball on her rocking chair. She looked so little, so solitary, and so broken. I didn't know what to do. So I sat in the rocker across the end table, and just remembered my son, how he'd work and play so hard . . . how proud I was of him, and what a hole in my heart he'd left.

*　　　*　　　*　　　*　　　*

*

We buried him in the city cemetery. We got through the funeral, somehow. Things were so hazy and dreamlike. That surreal feeling hasn't ever really gone away since that day, just lessened over time. Time really did stop for a while. It was one of those milestones that ever after you measured your life in relationship to. Before the car wreck, or after. Donna wasn't ever really the same after that. Of course, neither was I. Bobbie was so little . . . I don't know how big a sway it held over her and how she developed, but that's the kind of thing that you never really get to know, even in the life you're living, never mind someone else's.

Once he was buried, it was time to get back to work. I didn't feel like doing it very much, but the work was there to be done, and there wasn't anyone else to do it. Running a subsistence farm takes manpower, and it's not much on holidays. I had work to keep my body and hands busy, while my mind and heart were still trying to process everything. He wasn't there to help with the firewood any longer, but it still needed cut and stacked. I was far faster and more efficient working alone, but it was mechanical. There was no joy in it. Donna had taken to drinking a tot of whiskey in her coffee, and probably in her afternoon tea as well. She still kept the house up, but I could see the mechanical muscle memory taking over for her as well.

Her mind and heart were just as busy as mine. We were grieving simultaneously, but somehow not together. My work was taking me from the house, and hers was keeping her close to it. When we were together, sometimes we would take comfort in each other's arms. Other times, she couldn't bear to.

Everyone grieves differently, and I didn't and don't pretend to understand why sometimes she had to turn from me and keep her sorrow to herself. I could see that it was so, and let her be her. I didn't even know what I needed to help me through, so I had to take on faith that she was healing the best way she knew how.

The summer went as summers do--we worked together on the big jobs, canning, preserving, drying the food for the winter. We worked, though, because there wasn't time for leisure in the good weather. Even my visits to Jeannie had to slow down and taper off to once a month or so. Anytime the actual farm work wasn't making demands on me, gathering wood for the winter is a chore that never really gets done. There's no such thing as 'enough'.

All that time my body was busy, my mind was churning things over and over. I kept seeing that broken bundle of rags in the road, and that swipe of candy-apple paint on the guardrail. My missing brother, who left town without saying where he was going this time. My beautiful boy, who I buried with the knife I made for him. My wife, who was grieving our son in her own way. Which was involving a couple-three quarts of corn whiskey every week.

Summer gave way to fall, and the fall squashes were coming in. We prepared and we canned. We canned the parts of the deer that I didn't smoke or freeze. Got a handful of hams curing in the smoking shed, and several slabs of bacon. The fall was coming on chilly, and Donna was just starting to come a little further out of the shadow of her grief, when I saw a drastic change in her.

She looked like she was smiling and crying at the same time, sometimes. Happy and bereft. If you could picture the perfect image of ambivalence--torn between two conflicting emotions--that was her. On the second day after she started smiling through her tears, she disappeared overnight. I knew my brother was back in town.

He wasn't staying with Mama. I found that out by a discreet visit, taking over a few cans of tomato-pepper-oil. By stopping in the county co-op, the dog that didn't bark told me that he hadn't driven through Fulsom Hollow proper in his fancy car. Calvin had only ever had admirers or enemies, never really any friends. There were only a few places left he could possibly be staying in the county.

            *   *   *   *   *

*

I slid behind the wheel of the old pickup, and drove across town. I went right past Mama's drive, and went across the bottomland instead. I saw what I thought I'd see at the rivercamp. Calvin's Caddy, backed deep up under the overhanging branches, looking just the same as it always had. And there was Calvin, sitting by the campfire, poking at it with a stick. He saw me coming, and stood up.

His posture told me everything. His shoulders were slumped and registered defeat and shame. He didn't look me in the face. He wasn't looking at me at all. But when I buried my knife under his sternum on the upward angle, his head flew up and his eyes flew wide. I'd missed his heart, but I'd neatly bifurcated his right lung, and pierced his diaphragm on the way to do it. He gave a little cough and a groan, and collapsed backwards off of the knife that I was holding rigidly.

He gasped twice, and reached out to me, with a pleading look in his eyes. He couldn't talk, not with that wound. But there's only one thing he could have been asking for at that point. I gave it to him. I bladed him gently, but deeply, under the jawline on both sides. Carotid and jugular both. With that kind of opening, there wasn't long to wait. His eyes fluttered in seconds, and closed forever in just a couple more. That deep chest quit struggling to rise, and instead of my dying brother, all that lay by the fire was a carcass.

I threw the body in the backseat of the Caddy. I lowered the roof, and rolled down the windows. I looked carefully around the campsite, and gathered anything of Calvin's that I saw, stashing it in the trunk. In the trunk, I found my missing hammer. From Ritchie's last lunchpail. I fired up the Caddy's engine, still runs with barely concealed aggression, I thought. I engaged first and just stepped out of the driver's door as it slowly accelerated through its idle towards the water.

The water's twenty, twenty-five feet deep here at the bend . . . That car won't be seen again. Won't have to explain to Momma or Donna . . . or anyone else. That's settled, then. Then I sat down beside my brother's last fire, and let myself weep. I wept for my lost son. My boy. My lost brother. My hero. And most of all for myself. Because I let my brother take my son, and then I took his life. I cried for probably twenty minutes there at that fire, and I built it up as big as I could before I left with the wood we'd stacked for our convenience. I doubted I'd be back to visit my brother's resting place very often, and if I did, I'd just have to cut some firewood.

I dried my eyes, and drove to see the Chief. I'd done what I must. But it was a terrible thing. And the two people besides me who might mourn my brother could never know.

*　　　　*　　　　*　　　　*　　　　*

(on a scrap of paper stuffed between pages) I went to see the Chief because I had nowhere else to go. My wife, my mother, my daughter . . . not only could they not be a part of my grief, they couldn't be privy to it. The justice I'd visited on my brother wasn't legal, but it was right. The right thing isn't always easy. It doesn't always help you sleep at night, either. I couldn't confide in the Chief, but I could sit with him. I could talk with him about unrelated things and take comfort in that he didn't sense I was a monster, a fratricide. I don't think we ever spoke about it openly. But I'm sure the Chief knew.

That night, I got home and Donna was already in bed, lightly marinated in whiskey, comparatively speaking. I spooned into her gently, and she settled back into me with a satisfied murmur. I couldn't talk to her about the feelings that were washing over me, but I could hold her and let her give me the warmth and comfort that brought. It's not perfect, but thank God that it's plenty. And it did me fine.

Donna seemed to be a little out of sorts, probably wondering if

Calvin ran off without telling her again, but she seemed to settle back into a groove of complacent sorrow, I guess. Our Ritchie was gone, and that little boy took up such a large, warm space . . . Donna didn't slow her drinking down much, but she'd found a comfortable spot where she could function through her day without feeling too much pain. That's often as much as can be expected, through grief.

She started showing me another pregnancy. We had gotten used to the changes and how she'd sometimes be sick in the mornings. By Christmas, she'd started to show to the outside world as well. Mama was acting a little hurt that Calvin hadn't stopped by or called or written through either Thanksgiving or Christmas, but she put a brave face on it, and wouldn't speak of it.

Donna and I discussed baby names again . . . We decided that Donald Calvin would be a good family name for a boy. The girl's names were far more contentious. "I'd like to name our daughter after you, Donna. And maybe mom?"

"Oh, yeah. Donna Belle. Twouldn't be no time before she was Dinna Bell instead. She'd never shake that off once she started school. No thanks. That's almost as bad as Hannah." I blinked at that. "There's never been nobody a'tall named Hannah in McClellan County. Check the county clerk's office. I did. Dad set me to it when I was little. There is not now, nor ever has been a single person with the name of Hannah in the county, first, last, or middle. Folks around here just don't think nothin' a that name."

We finally settled on Belle Donna instead--I privately wondered about the toxic flower, but shrugged it off--not many in the county would know of it, or connect the two. Not like a dinner bell, by a long chalk.

Winter passed, and spring started showing signs of arrival. This pregnancy was taking more out of Donna than Ritchie and Bobbie had. She was short and cranky with everyone, and she didn't lighten up much on her drinking. Momma and Donna would watch their stories in the afternoons and fold laundry, or knit or crochet, sometimes quilting. I'd see them through the parlor window sometimes, seldom talking much. They were grieving together . . . for Ritchie, that they knew about. For Calvin, that they didn't. But I was glad they could take comfort from any source. I was doing my own grieving, and my only grief-mate was the farm. It wouldn't let me get too distracted by sorrow.

When Easter came and went with no word from Calvin, Donna spoke waspishly about it to me. "You'd think he could at least call or write his mother on holidays, even if he won't come back to town."

I just shrugged. "Maybe he figured he'd done enough damage here in McClellan county for a lifetime." I could see the shock and hurt in her face, but I couldn't bear to absolve my son's killer of the wounds he'd caused. I wasn't sorry. I didn't need to write my brother a pass for killing my boy. I went back to work getting the fields ready for the summer.

Donna seemed to sink a little further into her grief . . . and whiskey . . . after that. She had less patience for Bobbie, and talked less in general. If it kept her from talking to me about Calvin, I was willing to make that tradeoff. As near as I could tell, she seemed healthy enough . . .

Until she delivered the stillborn baby. It wasn't time for him, yet. And he was born blue. I couldn't tell much else about him, because Mama whisked him away and covered him up. Donna wept silently, wordlessly, and wrung her hands. Pain, sorrow, grief . . . she was suffering in silence and would not be comforted. She didn't shrug away my arms, as much as ignore them. She would permit herself to be cradled and held, but it was plain she was deriving no comfort of her own. God help me, I cradled and held her anyway.

After some hours, her tears subsided, and her sobs settled to smooth breathing. She would and could look at me when I spoke, but she wouldn't respond. If I insisted on talking for too long, she'd turn away and make it plain that she wasn't paying me any mind. She slept through the pain. She'd nap upright in her rocker, never ceasing her rocking.

On the second day after the stillbirth, I had to get out to the fields. Sorrow was a fact of life, but so was work, and so was food. There was work to be done so there would be food on the table. Simple syllogism. Whether you laughed or cried, there needed to be food there either way.

I came home for lunch to find my baby girl beaten into a pudding. She had bruises on her face, and was slumped over on the porch swing, finding it tough to breathe from some sprung ribs. I cradled her to me gently as I could, and rocked her to sleep. I called Mama right away. I hoped that she'd have some way to cure this sickness in Donna, or at least to protect my girl from it. The last baby I had left, and I was heartbroken at my inability to protect her. She was so little and so strong already . .. but I didn't want her to have to be.

Bobbie closed the journal there. She knew this part of the story already. But her head was spinning. Her father's hands, her father's knife, her father's history . . . all these things she'd never known about the man. From here, it wasn't her father's story anymore, but her own.

Made in United States
Orlando, FL
01 April 2024

45338438R00232